Patricia Scanlan lives in Dublin. Her books, all number one bestsellers, have sold worldwide and been translated into many languages. *With All My Love* was a top five *Sunday Times* bestseller in both hardback and paperback, and reached number one in Ireland. Patricia is also the series editor and a contributing author to the Open Door series which promotes adult literacy.

Find out more about Patricia on Facebook:
www.facebook.com/patriciascanlanauthor

Also by Patricia Scanlan

Apartment 3B
Finishing Touches
Foreign Affairs
Promises, Promises
Mirror Mirror
Francesca's Party
Two for Joy
Double Wedding
Divided Loyalties
Coming Home

Trilogies

City Girl
City Lives
City Woman

Forgive and Forget
Happy Ever After
Love and Marriage
With All My Love

Patricia SCANLAN

A Time for Friends

SIMON &
SCHUSTER

London · New York · Sydney · Toronto · New Delhi

A CBS COMPANY

First published in Great Britain by Simon & Schuster UK Ltd, 2015
A CBS COMPANY

This paperback published 2016

1 3 5 7 9 10 8 6 4 2

Simon & Schuster UK Ltd
1st Floor
222 Gray's Inn Road
London WC1X 8HB

www.simonandschuster.co.uk

Simon & Schuster Australia, Sydney
Simon & Schuster India, New Delhi

A CIP catalogue record for this book
is available from the British Library

Paperback ISBN: 978-1-4711-1082-5
eBook ISBN: 978-1-4711-4956-6

Typeset by M Rules
Printed and bound by CPI Group (UK) Ltd, Croydon, CR0 4YY

MIX
Paper from
responsible sources
FSC® C020471

Simon & Schuster UK Ltd are committed to sourcing paper
that is made from wood grown in sustainable forests and supports the Forest
Stewardship Council, the leading international forest certification organisation.
Our books displaying the FSC logo are printed on FSC certified paper.

I dedicate this book with much love to the dearest of friends:

My sister Mary, who is also the perfect friend, and who kept the show on the road while I took some time out to finish this book.

Aidan Storey and Murtagh Corrigan – my stalwarts, who gave me their guest room, fed and watered me, and made me laugh when I needed it most.

Pam and Simon Young and Mary Helen Hensley, who are with me every step of the way and beyond.

And to the memory of Anita Notaro: a true, loyal and steadfast friend. Our great loss is heaven's gain.

Don't put the key to your happiness in someone else's pocket!

Anon

PROLOGUE

The sun is shining through the window on the landing. Rays of diffused light streaming onto the red-gold-patterned carpet that covers the stairs. This will be one of the many things to remember on this life-changing day that will be buried deep in the recesses of the mind in the years that follow.

The sounds will never be forgotten either. The groaning and grunting getting louder at the top of the stairs. The absolute terror of feeling something is wrong. That a loved one is ill.

The bedroom door is open. The sickening tableau is revealed. A gasp of shock escapes as innocence is lost, and life alters its course forever in that instant.

The man and woman turn at the sound. Horror crosses the man's face as the woman untangles her legs from him. Both of them are naked. The woman's hair is mussed, cascading like a blonde waterfall over her rounded creamy breasts. The man grabs his trousers to hide his pale-skinned, hairy nudity.

'Wait!' he calls frantically. 'Wait!'

But it's too late.

A burden is added to the hurt and sadness already borne.

July 1965

'Do I *have* to ask her to my party, Mammy? She just is so mean to my friends. She says horrible things and she tells Aileen that she's *fat!*' Hilary Kinsella gives a sigh of exasperation as she studies her mother's face to try and gauge what Sally's response will be. Surreptitiously she crosses the fingers of both hands behind her back as she gazes expectantly at her mother who is rubbing the collar of her elderly father's white shirt with Sunlight soap, before putting it in the washing machine.

'Colette shouldn't say things like that, but I think she's a little bit jealous of you and Aileen being friends. She doesn't really mean it,' Sally says kindly. 'And it would be a bit cruel not to invite her to your birthday party. Wouldn't it now?'

Hilary's heart sinks. She has been hoping against hope that just this once she can have fun with her friends and not have to listen to Colette O'Mahony boasting and bragging about her huge birthday party which will be two weeks after Hilary's own.

'But, Mammy, she says that we can't afford to go on holidays to Paris on a plane like she does, an' she says her mammy and daddy have more money than we do,' Hilary exclaims indignantly, seeing that she is getting nowhere.

'Well we can't afford to go abroad and the O'Mahonys *do* have more money than we do,' Sally says equably, twisting another shirt to get rid of the excess water before dropping it into the twin tub. 'But do you not think you have much more fun in our caravan, going to the beach every day and playing with your cousins on our holidays, than walking around a hot, stuffy city, visiting art galleries and museums with adults, and having no children to play with? Do you not think it must be very lonely not to have any brothers and sisters?' Sally remarks, a smile crinkling her eyes.

'I suppose so,' sighs Hilary, knowing what is coming next.

'Poor Colette with no sisters or brothers, and not many friends either. And no mammy to have her dinner ready after school like I do for you, pet. You're so lucky with the family and friends you have. You always have someone to play with when you come home from school, so wouldn't it be a *kindness* to invite Colette to your party? Because I know that you are a *very* kind little girl. Now go and play with her and I'll bring some lemonade and banana sandwiches out into the garden for the two of you, and you can have a picnic for tea,' her mother says briskly.

But I don't *want* to be a very kind little girl, Hilary wants to shout at her mother. But she knows she can't. Sally has high expectations of her children. Kindness to others is mandatory in the Kinsella household. Whether she likes it or not, Hilary has to be kind to Colette O'Mahony and, yet again, endure her unwanted presence at her much anticipated birthday party.

Tears smart Colette O'Mahony's eyes as she scurries away from the door where she has been listening to Hilary and Mrs Kinsella discussing whether or not she should be invited to Hilary's crummy birthday party. Colette's heart feels as though a thousand, no a *million* nettles have stung it. Mrs Kinsella has said 'poor Colette' in a pitying sort of voice. She is *not* poor. She has her own bedroom and doesn't have to

3

share with an older sister. She has loads of good dresses and other clothes. Hilary Kinsella only has *one* good dress for Sundays. *And* most important of all, Colette has a *servant* at home to make her dinner when she comes home from school.

Mummy calls her 'the housekeeper', but Colette tells all the girls in her class that Mrs Boyle is her 'servant'.

Mrs Boyle will make jelly and ice cream and many delicious fairy cakes and chocolate Rice Krispie buns and a *huge* chocolate birthday cake for her birthday. Hilary will only have a cream sponge and Toytown biscuits and lemonade and crisps. This thought comforts Colette. It is only through her supreme sense of superiority that she is able to process the enormous envy she has for all that Hilary has. She hates that her mother works four days a week and Mrs Boyle – who is quite strict for a servant – looks after her three days, and Mrs Kinsella minds her on Thursdays.

How she longs to spend a summer in a caravan and play on the beach all day. How she longs to join the Secret Six Gang that Hilary and her sister and cousins are part of every summer in Bettystown. It sounds even more exciting than the Five Find-Outers stories that Mrs Boyle sometimes reads to her. Well she is going to start her own secret gang and Hilary is not going to be allowed to be part of it, Colette vows.

The nettle stings in her heart are soothed somewhat at this promise to herself as she observes Hilary marching out of the kitchen with a cross look on her face. 'We have to go and play outside and then we're having our tea in the garden,' she announces with a deep sigh.

'*My* servant gives me a push on *my* swing before *my* picnic in *my* garden,' Colette declares, eyeballing her best friend. 'It's a pity *you* don't have a servant or a swing,' she adds haughtily before sashaying out into Hilary's back garden.

'Get me twenty Player's, and ten Carrolls for your ma and get yourself a few sweets.' Gus Higgins hands Jonathan a pound note and pats him on the shoulder. 'Don't be long, now,' says Gus. 'I'm gaspin' for a fag!'

'OK, Mr Higgins,' Jonathan says, looking forward to the Trigger Bar he's going to buy as his treat. The fastest way to the shop is through the lane, halfway down his road, but he decides against it. The lane is a gathering place for some of the boys in his class to play marbles or football. It is no place for him. 'Nancy boy' and 'poofter' they call him, and while he does not know what 'poofter' means, he knows it's a nasty and spiteful taunt. He takes the longer route, and crosses the small village green to Nolan's Supermarket. 'Hi, Jon,' he hears Alice Walsh call, and smiles as his best friend catches up with him.

'Guess what? My daddy gave me six empty shoeboxes from his shop so we can make a three-storey doll's house with them. Can you come over tomorrow?'

'Deadly.' Jonathan feels a great buzz of excitement. 'Mam has some material from curtains she is making for Mrs Doyle; we can use it for our windows. And we'll make some ice-pop-stick chairs and tables. But I have to clean out the fire and set it and do some other jobs for Mam first and then I'll come over. See ya.'

'See ya!' she echoes cheerfully before he opens the door to the shop and hears the bell give its distinctive ping. Mr

Nolan is stacking shelves and he takes his time before serving Jonathan. 'Don't smoke all those at the one go,' he says, giving him a wink as he hands over the change. All the big boys buy Woodbines after school. Jonathan tried smoking once and it made him sick and dizzy, so Mr Higgins's and his mam's cigarettes are quite safe.

'Did you buy something for yourself?' Mr Higgins asks when Jonathan hands his neighbour his change and the brown paper bag with the cigarettes in it.

'I bought a bar,' he says when Mr Higgins takes the Carrolls out of the bag and hands them to him.

'Gude wee laddie. Nie here's the cigarettes for your mother. It can't be easy for her being a poor widda woman. I have three daughters of ma own to support but at least I bring home a good wage. Tell her it's a wee gift.' His neighbour is not from around Rosslara. He and his family moved into the house next door to Jonathan's two years ago when Mrs Foley died and sometimes Jonathan finds it hard to understand him if he talks fast. He says 'nie' instead of 'now' and 'wee' instead of 'small'. The first time Jonathan heard him say 'wee' he was shocked because he thought he was talking about wee wees. Until his mammy explained it to him, saying that people from different parts of the country had different accents.

Jonathan's mammy has to work very hard doing sewing and alterations, as well as working every morning in the doctor's surgery answering the phone and making appointments for patients. Jonathan's daddy died when he was three and his mammy has to pay a lot of bills and take care of him and his two older sisters.

Mr Higgins says his mammy is a grand wee woman. He's kind to her and buys her cigarettes, because she can't afford them herself. Jonathan thinks this is a great thing to do and so he never minds running errands for his neighbour.

'Tell your wee mammy, ma missus will be wanting her to make a communion dress for ma wee girlie. She's away into town to get new shoes for them all and I'm having a grand bit of peace.' Mr Higgins gives a little laugh and pulls the sitting-room curtains closed.

'I'll tell her, Mr Higgins,' Jonathan says politely, wondering why his neighbour is opening the button at the top of his dirty blue faded jeans. Perhaps he's going to lie on the sofa and have a nap, he thinks.

'Before ye go, I want you to do me another wee favour. It's just between you and me now. Our little secret. And there'll be another packet of ciggies for your ma and a treat for yourself next week if ye do as I ask,' Mr Higgins says. His breathing is raspy and his face is very red and Jonathan is suddenly apprehensive. Something isn't right. Something has changed but he's not sure what. And then it's as though everything is happening in slow motion, even the very particles of dust that dance along a stray sunbeam that has slipped through a gap in the closed curtains, and even the pounding of his heart thudding against his ribcage, as Mr Higgins advances towards him.

PART ONE

1990

Upwardly Mobile

CHAPTER ONE

'See you tonight,' Niall Hammond said, planting a kiss on his drowsy wife's cheek.

'What time is it?' Hilary groaned, pulling the duvet over her shoulders and burying her head in the pillow.

'6.35,' he murmured and then he was gone, his footsteps fading on the stairs. She heard the sound of the alarm being turned off, heard the front door open, then close, and the sound of the car reversing out of the drive.

Hilary yawned and stretched and her eyes closed. I'll just snooze for ten minutes, she promised herself, before drifting back to sleep.

'Mam, wake up, we're going to be late for school.' Hilary opened her eyes to see Sophie, her youngest daughter, standing beside the bed poking her in the ribs.

'Oh crikey, what time is it?' She struggled into a sitting position.

'8.12,' her daughter intoned solemnly, reading the digital clock.

'Holy Divinity, why didn't you call me earlier? Where's Millie? Is she up?' she asked, flinging back the duvet and scrambling out of bed.

'She's not up yet.'

'Oh for God's sake! Millie, Millie, get up.' Hilary raced into her eldest daughter's bedroom and hauled the duvet off her sleeping form.

'Awww, Mam!' Millie yelled indignantly, curling up like a little hedgehog, spiky hair sticking up from her head.

'Get up, we're late. Go and wash your face.' Hilary was like a whirling dervish, pulling open the blinds, before racing into the shower, jamming a shower cap onto her head so her hair wouldn't get wet. Ten minutes later, wrapped in a towel, she was slathering butter onto wholegrain bread slices onto which she laid cuts of breast from the remains of the chicken she'd cooked for the previous day's dinner. An apple and a clementine in each lunch box and the school lunches were done. Hilary eyed the full wash-load in the machine and wished she'd got up twenty minutes earlier so she could have hung it out on the line seeing as Niall hadn't bothered.

She felt a flash of irritation at her husband. It wouldn't dawn on him to hang out the clothes unless she had them in the wash basket on the kitchen table where he could see them. Sometimes she felt she was living with *three* children, she thought in exasperation. Typical that it was a fine day with a good breeze blowing and her clothes were stuck in the machine and would have to stay there until she got home.

Millie was shovelling Shreddies into her mouth while Sophie calmly sprinkled raisins into her porridge. Sophie was dressed in her school uniform, blonde hair neatly plaited, and yet again Hilary marvelled at the dissimilarity of her children. Millie, hair unbrushed, tie askew, lost in a world of her own, oblivious to Hilary's hassled demeanour. At least they'd had showers, and hair washed after swimming yesterday, she thought, taking a brush from the drawer to put manners on her oldest daughter's tresses.

Twenty minutes later Hilary watched the lollipop lady escort them across the road, and smiled as Sophie turned to give her a wave and a kiss. It was hard to believe she had two children of school-going age. Where had the years gone? she wondered as she crawled along in the school-run traffic.

It shocked her sometimes that she was a wife and mother to two little girls and settled into the routine of family life that didn't seem to vary much when the girls were at school. At least she'd spent a year au pairing in France after leaving school, and she'd spent six weeks on the Greek Islands with Colette O'Mahony, her oldest friend, having an absolute blast the following summer! That had been fun. Hilary grinned at the memory, turning onto the Malahide Road, and groaning at the traffic stuck on the Artane roundabout.

Colette would never in a million years be stuck in school-run traffic, she thought ruefully. Colette had a nanny to bring Jasmine to school in London. No doubt her friend was sipping Earl Grey tea in bed, perusing the papers before going to have her nails manicured or going shopping in Knightsbridge. Their lives couldn't be more different. But then, even from a very young age, they always had been.

Colette, the only daughter of two successful barristers, had had a privileged, affluent childhood. Her parents fulfilling her every wish, but handing her over to the care of a succession of housekeepers, as they devoted themselves to careers and a hectic social life, before packing Colette off to a posh and extremely expensive boarding school.

In contrast, Hilary's mother Sally had been a stay-at-home mother, although she did work a few hours on Saturdays in the family lighting business. Hilary's dad, Mick, owned a lighting store and electrical business and Hilary had worked there every summer holiday, either in the large showrooms, that stocked lights and lamps and shades of every description, or in the office working on invoices and orders and deliveries.

Her parents, unlike Colette's, were extremely family orientated. Hilary and her older sister Dee had grown up secure in the knowledge that they were much loved. Sally and Mick enjoyed their two girls and had bought a second-hand caravan so they could all spend weekends and holidays together. Hilary's abiding memory of her childhood was of her mother making scrumptious picnics in the little caravan kitchen, and her dad lugging chairs and windbreaks and cooler bags down to the beach and setting up their 'spot'. And then the games of rounders, or O'Grady Says, with their parents and aunts, uncles and cousins joining in, a whole tribe of Kinsellas, screeching and laughing. And then the sand-gritted picnic with tea out of flasks, or home-made lemonade, and more often than not, a gale whipping the sand outside their windbreak as clouds rolled in over the Irish Sea, the threat of rain somehow adding to the excitement. And when it did fall, all hands would gallop back up the bank to the caravans, and Mick would laugh and say, 'That was a close one,' when they'd make it inside before the heavens opened.

Sally enjoyed the company of her girls and, when time and work permitted, they would head over to Thomas Street, and ramble around the Liberty Market, browsing the stalls, especially the jewellery ones, oohing and aahing over rings and bracelets. Kind-hearted as ever, Sally would fork out a few quid for a gift for Hilary and Dee. Their mother had steered them through the ups and downs of their teen years and had urged her daughters to spread their wings and see the world and follow their dreams. She had been fully behind Hilary's decision to go to France after her Leaving Cert and be an au pair and become fluent in French.

After her year of au pairing and her six weeks roaming the Greek Islands with Colette, Hilary had planned to do an arts degree with a view to teaching languages but Mick had suffered a heart attack the August before she was to start university, and she had felt it incumbent on her to put aside her own plans for her future, especially as she'd been abroad for more than a year, enjoying the freedom to be carefree and unfettered. She had stepped up to the plate to help her parents in their hour of need. Her older sister Dee was in the middle of a science degree and there was no question of her dropping out of university.

Hilary was desperately disappointed at having to postpone her degree course; she had been so looking forward to going to university and enjoying the social side of life. Dee might study hard, but she partied hard too and lived on campus, free of all parental constraints.

Hilary had been looking forward to moving out of the family home. Having spread her wings in France, she was keen to have the freedom to live her own life but her father's illness put paid to that. She buried her regrets deep and put her shoulder to the wheel to keep the showrooms ticking over, while Bill O'Callaghan, Mick's senior electrician, looked after that side of the business.

Hilary had taken a bookkeeping and accounts course at night school soon after, and it was at a trad session one sweltering bank holiday weekend, in the college grounds, that she had met brown-eyed, bodhrán-playing Niall Hammond. She had tripped over someone's handbag and tipped her Black Velvet Guinness drink down his back.

He'd given a yelp of dismay and jumped to his feet and then started to laugh when he'd turned round and seen her standing, hand to her mouth in horror, her glass almost empty.

'I ... I'm terribly sorry,' she stuttered; dabbing ineffectually at his shirt with a tissue, while his friends guffawed.

'Don't worry about it,' he said easily. 'I was getting too hot anyway.' He pulled the soaking shirt over his head, exposing a tanned torso with just the right amount of dark chest hair to make her think: *Sexy!*

Students were in various states of undress because of the sultry heat, so being shirtless wasn't a big deal, she thought with relief, trying not to gaze at her victim's impressive pecs while he wrung out his shirt and slung it over his shoulder.

'You are such a *clutterbuck*, Hilary.' Colette materialized behind her and gave a light-hearted giggle. She rolled her eyes heavenwards and held out her dainty hand to the hunk in front of them. 'Hi, I'm Colette O'Mahony, and this' – she made a little moue – 'is Hilary Kinsella who has two left feet as you've just found out.'

'Well, hi there, ladies. Niall Hammond is my moniker and I guess we should have a round of fresh drinks to get us back on track.' He waved politely at a waitress and she nodded and headed in their direction. 'Guinness for you, Hilary? Did you have anything in it?'

'Um . . . it was a Black Velvet,' Hilary managed, mortified, and raging with Colette for saying she had two left feet. Her friend could be so artless sometimes.

'Brandy and ginger,' Colette purred gaily, fluttering her eyelashes at him.

Hilary saw Niall's eyes widen slightly. Typical of Colette to go for an expensive short when someone else was paying.

'Er . . . mine's with cider, not champagne,' she added hastily in case he thought they were way OTT.

Niall winked at her and gave the order and added, 'A pint of Harp for me, please. So, ladies, are you students here?' he asked, smiling down at Colette. Hilary's heart sank. It was always the way. Once men saw blonde, petite, dainty, effervescent Colette, she was forgotten about.

'Hilary is. She's doing a boring bookkeeping course; I'm just here for the craic! I'm studying Fine Arts in London. I'm home for the weekend.'

'Interesting! Fine Arts. How did that come about?' Niall leaned against a pillar, thumbs hooking into his jeans, and Hilary thought how typical of her luck to encounter a hunky guy when Colette was home from London on one of her rare jaunts across the Irish Sea. Since she had moved to London to live with her father's widowed sister, her friend rarely came home, and wasn't great at keeping in touch either. She was having a ball going to polo matches, and weekend parties in the country, and drinking in glamorous pubs in Kensington and Knightsbridge and shopping in Harvey Nicks and Harrods.

'My parents wanted me to study law. They're both barristers,' Colette added, always keen to slip that bit of information into any conversation. 'I couldn't bear the idea,' she trilled, throwing back her head so that her blonde hair fell in a tumbling mane over her shoulders, and giving a gay laugh. 'My dad's sister has a big flat in Holland Park, and her husband died and they have no children so I went to stay with her for a while and she knew someone in Dickon and Austen's Fine Art and I worked there and did my degree and that's where I've fetched up.'

Fetched up, thought Hilary irritably. Colette was becoming more English than the English themselves.

'And yourself?' Niall's heavy-lidded brown eyes were focused on Hilary. But there was a twinkle in them that she liked and she found herself responding with an answering smile.

'I work in my dad's lighting and electrical business—'

'She's a shop manager,' interjected Colette brightly. 'Oh look, here's our drinks.'

'Let me pay,' Hilary urged. 'After all I've ruined your shirt.'

'Another time,' Niall said firmly, taking his wallet out of the back pocket of his jeans and extracting a twenty.

'And what do *you* do apart from playing the bodhrán fabulously?' Colette arched a perfectly manicured, wing-tipped eyebrow at him, before taking a ladylike sip of her brandy and ginger.

'I work in Aer Rianta International, in travel retail. And in my spare time I play gigs with these hoodlums.' He indicated his three band buddies in the background.

'Really? An interesting job, I'd say?' Colette was impressed. 'Do you travel much?'

'I do indeed.'

'I *love* to travel,' Colette commented gaily.

'What's your band called?' Hilary interjected, knowing that unless she steered her off track, Colette would launch into a description of her travels and Hilary would end up feeling like a real gooseberry. She was beginning to feel like one already!

'We're called Solas, which I'm sure you know is the Gaelic for "light". Somewhat of a synchronicity, Hilary, wouldn't you think? Both of us work with light!'

'Umm.' Hilary was caught mid-gulp of her Black Velvet and was afraid she had a creamy moustache. 'I guess so.'

'Well, I should get back and play another set, or Solas won't get paid tonight. It was nice meeting you both.'

'Are you playing anywhere else over the weekend?' Colette asked casually.

'We are. Are you into trad? I wouldn't have thought that would be your scene,' Niall remarked.

'Oh I *LOVE* it,' Colette fibbed. 'I adore The Dubliners and . . . er . . . um . . . eh . . .The Clancy Brothers.'

'And yourself, Hilary?' Niall turned to look at her.

'I like trad.' She nodded. 'I like the liveliness of it, the buzz of a good session.'

'And who do you like?' he probed.

'I like The Bothy Band, Planxty, De Dannan, and The Chieftains are amazing.' She shrugged.

'A woman after my own heart. They're all unbelievable musicians, aren't they?' he said enthusiastically.

'The best,' Hilary agreed.

'So where are you playing tomorrow?' Colette persisted, annoyed that she hadn't thought of naming any of those bands, although she only vaguely knew of them. She was more into The Rolling Stones and The Eagles.

'O'Donohue's. Why, are you going to come?'

'Well, who knows?' Colette flashed her baby blues at him. 'But if you don't see me there you can always ring Dickon and Austen's and catch me there. Thanks for the drink,' she drawled before sauntering back to where they had been sitting.

'Do you think they would take a collect call?' Niall grinned and Hilary laughed.

'Not sure about that.'

'So will you both be coming to O'Donohue's tomorrow night?' he queried.

'Not sure about that either. We're doing a big stock take in the shop, and I have to be there. And it's much easier to get it done after closing time.'

'Sure, if I see you I see you,' he said easily. 'Enjoy the rest of the evening.'

'You too and sorry about your shirt and thanks for the drink,' she murmured, heart sinking when she saw him glance over to where Colette was now chatting animatedly to a tall bearded guy, looking like a dainty little doll beside him.

'Another brandy and ginger coming up soon, I'd say,'

Niall said wryly, amusement causing his eyes to crinkle in a most attractive way.

'What?' She was caught off guard.

'Your little friend has expensive tastes.'

'Er . . . she doesn't like beer, or Guinness,' Hilary said loyally, taken aback by his directness.

'She's lucky to have you for a friend; you have a very steadfast quality, Hilary. Would you come out for a drink with me sometime, when your stock taking is over?'

'*Me!* . . . Oh! . . . I thought it would be Colette you would ask out if you were asking either of us,' Hilary blurted.

'Did you now? Well, ladies who pour their Black Velvets all over me to get my attention are much more interesting than flirty brandy and ginger drinkers.'

'I didn't pour my drink over you to get your attention. It was an *accident*. I *tripped*!' Hilary protested indignantly.

'Well, it worked, didn't it? I'm asking you out for a drink,' he pointed out.

'Is that right?' Hilary said hotly. 'How very arrogant that you would think I'd *want* to go for a drink with you. I'm not *that* desperate to get a man that I'd waste a Black Velvet on him.'

Niall guffawed. 'Sorry, Hilary, I couldn't resist it. Just wanted to see if you'd rise to the bait. I was only teasing, honest. I know you tripped. Come on, give me your number and let me make amends,' he smiled.

'You'll get me at Kinsella Illuminations, Kirwan's Industrial Estate; it's in the phone book. Don't call collect,' Hilary retorted, but she was smiling as she made her way back to the table.

Colette and Beardy were at the bar, Colette making sure she was posed just where Niall could see her as he rapped out a toe-tapping tattoo on his bodhrán. She could pose all she liked, Hilary smiled to herself. For once in her life, her friend had come in second. Niall Hammond had asked Hilary out for a drink, and out for a drink she would go.

'He asked you *out*?' Colette couldn't believe her ears later that night as they tucked into a kebab on the way home. Colette was staying the night at Hilary's, before heading back to her parents' detached, palatial pad in Sutton the following morning.

'Yeah, I told him we were stock taking tomorrow and I wouldn't be in O'Donohue's, so he's asked me out. He's going to ring me.' Hilary licked the creamy sauce off her fingers and took a slug of Coke to wash it down.

'Ah ha! It will be interesting to see *if* he rings. You know what they're like,' Colette said dismissively. 'How many times have you sat waiting for a phone call from some bloke? Don't hold your breath, now,' she advised, nibbling neatly on a portion of their shared kebab. She never dribbled sauce or got it on her fingers. Hilary would have had no problem polishing off a whole kebab and she was always irritated that Colette would refuse to have one, and then tuck into hers.

'You make it sound as though I'm permanently sitting by the phone waiting for a fella to ring,' Hilary said crossly, coming down from her high. Perhaps Colette was right: Niall might not bother to ring her. She had waited on a few occasions for a guy to ring after he had taken her number, and had waited in vain. Colette rarely had such problems. Men were drawn to her like bees to honey. And just this once, Hilary had thought *she* might be the one to get the boy! Now she was beginning to have serious doubts.

'I'm just not wanting you to get hurt, that's all,' Colette said kindly. 'Men can be the pits. Remember what I went through with Rod Killeen?' Her pretty face darkened into a thunderous scowl at the memory of the rat Killeen who had dumped her for a tubby little tart with a raucous laugh and a penchant for sci-fi that Rod was into as well. 'That guy broke my heart in smithereens,' Colette reminded Hilary. 'Used and abused me! And behind my back was having it off with lardy Lynda. Little fat slut!'

Hilary sighed as Colette went into her usual rant about her ex-boyfriend. Colette had fallen hard for the good-looking, laid-back rugby player who was in his fourth year of medical school. Hilary had been dragged to rugby matches, in howling gales and on rain-spattered afternoons, for the duration of the short-lived romance. Rod had initially been very taken with his 'little blonde bombshell' as he'd nicknamed a delighted Colette and they had enjoyed a lusty couple of months in the early stages of their romance. But Colette's demanding ways had proved too much for the muscular medic and he had wilted under her need for constant emotional reassurance, and the tantrums and traumas that ensued when he had had to knuckle down to study for his exams. Rod had taken comfort in the arms of a cuddly, good-humoured student nurse from Cavan who couldn't have been more different from Colette in personality and appearance. The fact that Lynda was a stone overweight seemed to incense Colette more than anything. How could Rod find that *fatso* more attractive than her? she raged to Hilary, completely oblivious to the fact that because Hilary herself carried a few extra pounds she too could be considered a fatso, in Colette's eyes.

Personally Hilary could see why Rod would like Lynda's curves, as well as the rest of her. Hilary had bumped into them one night in O'Donohue's after Colette had taken flight to London, and Rod had introduced her to Lynda. She was a down to earth, warm, friendly type with sparkling green eyes, and a mop of auburn curls that cascaded onto smooth creamy shoulders, and a full and ripe bosom, and was far from the 'carrot-haired, fat bogger' Colette had so disparagingly described. Natural and voluptuous, Lynda certainly did not share Colette's clothes hanger sophistication.

Rod's rejection of Colette had been too devastating to bear and, when her mother had suggested that she go to London to get over her broken heart, Colette had agreed.

An angry honking of a car's horn at the Artane roundabout brought Hilary back to earth and real life. Thank God it wasn't directed at her, she thought guiltily. She had been driving on auto pilot, her thoughts way back, what was it, ten or more years since the days of their giddy early twenties? And now both of them were married, she to Niall who had indeed phoned her to arrange a date, and Colette to Des, a London-based financier whom she had married in a fairy-tale wedding in Rome.

Both of them married, both of them mothers, she to Sophie and Millie, Colette to Jasmine. And both of them with very, very different lives, Hilary reflected as she stop-

started her way to work. Colette was such a complex character, it was a wonder their friendship had lasted as long as
it had. She was one of the most competitive people Hilary
knew. She *had* to be the centre of attention. Had to have a
bigger car, better job, sexier boyfriend than any of their circle
of friends. But Hilary knew that behind the confident, smug,
superior façade lay a young woman who was plagued by
insecurity. Hilary was one of the few who knew the real
Colette. The Colette who was generous to a fault, the Colette
who would cry buckets because of a broken heart, the
Colette who had longed to be 'ordinary', just like Hilary
and her sister Dee, and have a mother who was waiting at
home when she came in from school, who would be interested in hearing about her day, and who would have a
yummy dinner waiting for her. Even though her friend
could drive her mad with her selfish, thoughtless behaviour, Hilary could never stay annoyed with her for long,
because she was a big softie and she knew Colette's vulner-
abilities and she knew that Colette thought of her as the
sister she'd never had.

Colette wouldn't be stuck in traffic, doing the school run
and the bumper-to-bumper commute to work though.
Hilary couldn't help the pang of envy, knowing that her
friend had a nanny and housekeeper in her luxurious
London flat. She wouldn't come home to breakfast dishes on
the draining board and a hastily swept kitchen, or a moun-
tain of clothes in the linen basket that had to be washed,
ironed and put away, like Hilary would. Their lives had
always been dissimilar, even when they were little girls, but
their friendship, imperfect as it was, had lasted this long.

That in itself was an achievement, Hilary thought, amused, remembering some of their humdinger rows as she swung into the car park of Kinsella Illuminations, the showrooms of the family's lighting and electrical business.

CHAPTER TWO

Colette O'Mahony stretched luxuriously between her Frette Egyptian cotton sheets and watched the sun dapple the apple-green leaves of the trees that lined the street on which her white-painted, stucco-pillared Holland Park mansion of luxurious flats stood.

She was tired and a hint of a headache lingered around her temples. She was sorry now that she'd told her husband that she'd accompany him on a business trip to Dublin. They were booked to fly from Heathrow later that evening, after meeting a Japanese client for afternoon tea in Cliveden House, and the thought of traipsing around that grey, grim tunnel they had the nerve to call an airport terminal made her head ache even more. What was it about Heathrow that always left you feeling wilted, hot and sweaty, no matter what terminal you went to? She'd stay in bed for another twenty minutes and then pack. Colette yawned and turned over, snuggling into the pillows, dimly aware of the sound of the vacuum down the hall. At least *she* didn't have to get up and set the flat to rights. That would have been the pits, she thought groggily.

They had hosted a dinner party the previous evening for

some of her husband's Wall Street colleagues who were in London for myriad meetings with their UK counterparts, and while it had all gone very well – as all of her dinner parties did, thanks primarily to her housekeeper, Mrs Zielinski, her caterers, and, of course, her own organizational skills – it was still wearing. Des always amped up the psychological pressure in the days coming up to an impress-the-hell-out-of-the-colleagues dinner party.

'Have you scheduled the mini-maids and the window cleaners? Have you ordered the lobsters? Should we have venison instead of steak? Have you ordered the flowers? How about orchids only? Are you using the Crown Derby and the Lalique?'

'Yes, yes, yes and yes, Lalique for the champagne, pre-dinner drinks, Waterford crystal for the meal and the brandy. STOP WORRYING, for God's sake!' she had exclaimed in exasperation.

'This is important, Colette. There's a big promotion coming up, and it's between me and Jerry Olsen and you know how competitive he is. He's taking them to Gordon Ramsay's but I want to entertain at home, so they can see the whole package. Let them see class! And talk to them about your work in Dickon and Austen's. Tell them about our pieces. Impress the hell out of them – some of them wouldn't know a Monet from a Manet.'

Neither did you until I got my hands on you, Colette thought sourly.

Des paced up and down, agitatedly firing off instructions. The trouble with her husband, Colette had realized shortly after meeting him, was that he was nouveau riche and it showed. He had made his impressive wealth in a relatively short but successful banking career, accumulating a substantial portfolio of stocks, shares and properties. Image to Des was everything! And she, always impeccably coiffed, groomed and dressed, was his greatest asset. He knew it and she knew it, Colette reflected. It was her finesse, her nous and her taste that kept them on the straight and narrow of the perilous path of who was 'in' and who was 'out' in the society circles they mixed in.

Des Williams had come from an affluent, solid, middle-class background in the north-east of England. His father was a dentist; his mother ran a travel agency. They had two foreign holidays a year and a summer house in Cornwall. But Des, an only child, had wanted to escape his boring, insular life and his boring, insular girlfriend. The bright lights of London beckoned and as soon as he had finished his finance degree at Manchester University he had moved south and, now, rarely went home.

Ambitious, competitive, acquisitive, he had worked tirelessly to climb the career and social ladders. He had lost his northern twang, he dressed in sharp designer suits, he ate in expensive restaurants and he mixed in seriously wealthy circles.

By the time, Colette had met him at the debut launch of an up-and-coming abstract artist called Devone, Des was very much the sophisticated, successful, well-heeled young financier. He had been more than impressed by her confident discourse on Devone's striking colourful brushwork, which to his eyes looked like something a five-year-old in a crèche might paint for playtime. And he'd been more than taken with her petite, trim figure, which had looked extremely fetching in the pale pink Chanel shift dress she was wearing.

Colette, still suffering from the devastation of Rod's rejection of her, was very taken with the good-looking, blue-eyed, tawny-haired man who had made a beeline for her. She was even more impressed when he had suggested they go for a drink afterwards, and had driven her in his top-of-the-range, sporty Merc to a pub on the banks of the Thames where they had quaffed champagne in long elegant flutes, raspberries floating on top of the sparkling bubbles. When Des brought her home to her aunt's ground-floor-over-basement Holland Park flat, he had given a low whistle as he pulled up outside. 'Nice pad.'

'It needs a complete revamp. Since my uncle died ten years ago it's gone downhill. My aunt has no enthusiasm for anything now. She's a bit of a recluse. I'd love to get my hands on it and get the builders and decorators in to update it. My big fear is that she will leave it to a dog charity or something,' Colette confessed.

'Are you serious? How horrendous would that be?' Des frowned. 'Is there a mortgage on it?'

'No. It was her husband's family home, bought yonks ago, and it was signed over to him before his mother died.'

'Very valuable now. Worth a mill or two. In a prime location, so close to Kensington. You should work hard on your aunt to make sure it goes to the right person. You know what I'm saying?'

'I do,' Colette agreed, liking his frankness and the fact that his thoughts mirrored hers.

'Maybe I could take you and your aunt down to the river

for Pimm's and a picnic some day? Might she enjoy that?' Des suggested casually.

'She might,' Colette shrugged. 'And then again she might not. Thanks for a lovely evening.' She blew him a kiss and was out of the car before he realized her intention.

'I'll call you, what's your number?' he asked, looking somewhat startled at her abrupt departure. He took out a business card and loosened the top of his fountain pen. She looked at him, with the evening breeze ruffling his hair as he leaned back in the leather seat of his sports car, pen poised.

'Ring me at Dickon and Austen's. Byeee!' And then she was clattering up the marble steps, keys jangling in her hand. 'I'm not that easy, Desmond Williams,' she murmured as she closed the heavy red door behind her.

She had kept him at arm's length, meeting him when it suited her, dating other men in between, letting him know that he wasn't the only one. No one was going to break her heart ever again. She was *always* going to be in charge of any relationship she was in and that was that.

Later that year, at the end of the summer, Colette had gone home for a long weekend to celebrate her mother's birthday, starting with a lavish barbecue at their house on the beach in Sutton. The O'Mahonys had invited the Kinsella family, and Colette was looking forward to catching up with Hilary and telling her all the news about her exciting new life in London.

Poor Hilary, she lived such a boring life in comparison with her own, Colette had reflected as the plane made its descent over the Irish Sea, with the Sugar Loaf etched against a clear blue sky and Dun Laoghaire and Dublin Port to her left, and the ferries gliding across a silver-sparkled sea beneath. Hilary and her humdrum existence in her father's business, running that lighting shop, and still living at home, while she was swanning around cosmopolitan London, meeting all kinds of interesting people in the course of her work in Dickon and Austen's, and having a terrific social life to boot. Far better than trad sessions, and evening classes, for sure. But Hilary wasn't like her. Hilary was easy-going, content to let life take her where it would. Colette on the other hand had always wanted to make something of herself. To be a mover and shaker. To show her parents that she too could be a force to be reckoned with in her field.

Colette knew that her parents had wanted her to study law and follow them into the legal profession. It had been their plan for her all along but she had rebelled. She had no intention of studying dry as snuff law tomes and arguing the toss about some legal point or other over interminable dinner parties such as she'd had to endure at home with her parents' legal friends and colleagues.

Francis O'Mahony had been horrified when Colette's mother Jacqueline had suggested their daughter go and stay with his sister Beatrice in London to get over a failed romance. 'That girl needs to knuckle down; she's been gallivanting around Europe, partying like the end of the world was coming and spending money like it was going out of fashion,' he grumbled. 'We all agreed that she was going to study law after her travels. It's time for her to grow up and get serious,' Francis had decreed at his most thunderously impressive. To no avail.

Colette had taken off to London and enrolled in a fine arts

college. Her father was somewhat mollified by her choice of career. It wasn't a common or garden career. Nothing worse than to have to say to his peers, many of whom had children studying law, that his daughter hadn't started university yet, or was only taking an arts degree. Every Tom, Dick and Harry had an arts degree. He had wanted more for Colette. Legal preferably but a career in the medical or financial fields would have sufficed. Fine arts would just about cut it. It was classy if nothing else.

Jacqueline was rather pleased. She knew in her heart of hearts that her daughter, although she had brains, was not cut out for a legal career. She would have spent her time flirting with the judges, she'd thought wryly, when Colette had sashayed into the Law Courts to meet her for lunch one day and had ended up with a flock of young legal eagles around her, much taken with her charms and the fact that she was Francis and Jacqueline O'Mahony's – the hot power couple everyone wanted on their legal team – daughter. The difference between Colette and her mother was that Jacqueline had had to fight to get to where she was in life. She had worked with her best friend Sally, Hilary's mother, in the local supermarket during their school holidays, and when she'd gone to university she'd worked as a hotel chambermaid to pay her way through her law degree because her father hadn't been able to afford the fees. Jacqueline had clawed her way up the ladder of success rung by rung. Colette had cruised through life never wanting for anything because her parents had been hungry to succeed and had indeed succeeded beyond their aspirations. Both of them had ended up raking in massive fees. Their sense of entitlement grew, as did Colette's, and the hoi polloi were now a different race.

When Colette had flown home for Jacqueline's birthday celebrations she knew that the first barbecue was for those very hoi polloi who peopled their life. The grandparents and aunts and uncles and cousins who had grown up in Artane. The Kinsellas had been Jacqueline's neighbours when she lived at home, and Hilary and Dee, who had been Colette's childhood friends, were coming.

Colette knew this was the 'duty' party. The one that was expected by family. But the more lavish one, the 'real' party where serious money would be spent and champagne would be the drink of choice, would be for their neighbours in Sutton, their golfing and bridge friends and their col-leagues.

Colette had been looking forward to showing off, espe-cially at the first party. She had a fabulous Dolce & Gabbana dress that screamed money, courtesy of her parents' more than generous allowance. She had told Hilary, who to Colette's complete astonishment had still been dating Niall Hammond, to bring him to the party. Colette couldn't quite see what Niall saw in Hilary. Hilary was just Hilary, dependable, loyal, unexcitingly normal. She had been more than miffed to hear that he had indeed phoned her friend and had passed on the chance to date *her* when she had last been home. Colette had been somewhat disconcerted to see the intimacy and frisson between her oldest friend and the hunky Niall. 'Are you sleeping with him?' she'd asked when Niall had gone to the marquee to get more drinks for them.

'Of course I am. I'm practically living in his flat,' Hilary laughed. She was glowing, she'd dropped weight, her hazel eyes were sparkling, and the new layered hairstyle suited her chestnut locks. Colette couldn't help the surge of envy that washed over her.

'Have you met the parents?'

'I have.' Hilary grinned. 'I was invited to Sunday lunch, the first time, and I was rattling, especially when Niall told me his mother only brought out the good china, and the Irish-lace tablecloth, for very special occasions. I was petrified I'd drop gravy on it or something. But they were lovely and made me feel at home and I relaxed and we actually had a good laugh. Now we get on very well. His dad has the same easy-going way as Niall and his mum spoils him rotten. Niall can do no wrong in her eyes and I was worried Margaret might see me as a rival – you know the way some mothers-in-law are? But she's very easy to get on with, thank goodness, although Niall's sister's a bit prickly.' Hilary grimaced.

'Older or younger?' Colette probed.

'Sue's at least ten years older. I've only met her a couple of times, she doesn't visit her parents that often. She's very career orientated and very superior. A bit up her own ass actually. Thinks she's an "intellectual". Looks down her nose at Niall's music and wouldn't be "seen dead" at a trad session. We won't be bosom buddies, for sure,' Hilary observed ruefully.

'So it's *serious*? Is this what you're telling me?' Colette was taken aback at the speed of Hilary and Niall's romance.

'Yep!' Hilary grinned. 'We're going to look at houses after Christmas!'

That news had put a dampener on her visit home. It was unthinkable that Hilary would be married before she was. Colette had gone back to London with a mission. It was time to reel Des in.

CHAPTER THREE

'Now, son, are you *sure* you're eating properly?' Nancy Harpur asked anxiously, wishing she could get her hands on her only son to give him a decent feed.

'Mam, honest, I am,' fibbed Jonathan, averting his eyes from the biscuit jar, the bread bin with the crusty baguettes and Maltana, and knowing that his small freezer compartment contained a packet of processed chicken Kievs, while his fridge had a chunk of mouldy cheese, a black carrot, two splits of champagne and a bottle of Chardonnay.

'What are you having for dinner today?' Nancy demanded quick as a flash.

'Chicken and veg,' he riposted. 'Lovely buttered carrots just like you make them.'

'Good boy!' she approved, appeased. 'So how is work going?'

'It's OK. Busy.' He nibbled on a bread stick, having no intention of telling his mother that he hated his job in the Civil Service and that his boss was a homophobic bully and he felt sick to his stomach going in to work every day. His mother didn't need to know *any* of that. 'I've got another interior design commission,' he said, changing the subject.

'And I'll be needing curtains made up. Gorgeous gold brocade. I'll bring the material down as soon as I've bought it.'

'Grand, I'll clear the decks so. I've been busy this last week with the sewing,' Nancy said briskly, delighted with his news.

'And I'm doing a lighting design course tomorrow, so I'm looking forward to that.'

'I'm delighted you're doing so well for yourself in Dublin. So pleased, Jon, you deserve it. You're a great lad,' Nancy praised, and Jonathan smiled. His mother was his greatest champion, always had been, and always would be. He adored her.

'How about we plan a weekend for you to come up soon and I'll bring you shopping, and to the theatre, and we'll have dinner somewhere posh?'

'Ooohhh lovely!' Nancy enthused. Going to spend a weekend with Jonathan was always fun from start to finish and it was a treat to spend time in the capital and go shopping in fancy Grafton Street, although Roches Stores on Henry Street was her favourite department store of all.

'Perfect. We'll plan it when I bring the curtain material down. Love ya, Mam.'

'I love you too, son,' Nancy returned and Jonathan smiled as he hung up the phone. He would take Nancy to BT and buy her a new outfit, although she would protest as she always did and say Clerys or Roches Stores would suit her just as well. He would bring her to those stores too. She particularly enjoyed shopping in the basement section of Roches, which had everything from china to bed linen, and other household goods and knick-knacks. On her last shopping spree there both of them had bought a set of little forks in a round wooden barrel to eat cobs of buttered sweetcorn with. 'Ever so posh,' Nancy had enthused, debating whether to buy fish knives as well. 'I don't be giving swanky dinner parties like you do.'

'Why don't you cook a dinner for some of your quilting friends? If everyone hosted a dinner every so often, it would be something for you all to look forward to,' Jonathan suggested, tossing the knives into the shopping basket.

'Aren't we all fed up cooking? That's why we go *out* for a meal,' Nancy retorted, putting the knives back on the shelf.

'Mother, you're absolutely right!' Jonathan agreed. 'Let's go to the Shelbourne for afternoon tea, and we can go to the pictures and have dinner afterwards in The Commons or the Troc, and spot the celebs and theatre folk and discuss what they're wearing. I love it when you pick holes in their crooked seams and hanging hems.' He grinned.

'Well honestly, Jonathan, some of those designers should be ashamed of the finishes on their clothes. Clothes that cost a fortune, I might add,' Nancy declared. 'I'd be embarrassed to send someone off wearing a dress or jacket with threads hanging and seams and necklines and armholes puckered. Some of those designers are right chancers, I can tell you, looking down their noses at us when they go to London and get too big for their boots. Remember one of those snooty ones, in the sixties, who designed for the jet set, and she was passing off the lace crochet as her own. And I happen to know the lady who made some of those pieces. Beautiful intricate work and she never got the recognition for it,' Nancy said indignantly. 'When you make it big with your interior design don't forget where you came from,' she added, wagging her finger good-humouredly.

'I won't, Mam,' he had said, fondly enveloping her in a bear hug right in the middle of Roches Stores basement.

Jonathan sighed as he filled the kettle. His mother had such faith in him. She had always encouraged his love of decorating as a child and let him wield the paintbrush, at first in their small back yard when there was more white-wash on him than on the walls. But as he'd grown older she'd taught him how to wallpaper and paint, and how to sew on her trusty Singer sewing machine. He had a flair for colour, and knew instinctively how a couple of bright cush-ions here, or a lampshade there, would lift a room and coordinate the colours on the walls and curtains. One of the best presents he had ever got was a subscription she had bought for him for *Interiors & Design* and he had devoured each edition, cutting out pictures and articles that particu-larly inspired him. He had folders, kept meticulously, divided and subdivided into furniture, fixtures and fittings, materials, colour schemes, and miscellaneous. They were his pride and joy. His best friend Alice shared his passion and they had spent many happy hours when they were children building doll's houses from the shoeboxes from her father's shop and decorating them to their hearts' content. Nancy loved to watch the pair of them sitting in front of the fire in the kitchen on a wintry afternoon, chattering away as they designed delightful little houses, while she worked on her sewing machine, doing alterations or making curtains to bring in an extra couple of pounds.

Jonathan made himself a mug of tea and found a stale

chocolate gold-grain biscuit and curled up on the bright green bean bag in the bay window of his ground-floor bedsit. He had had a ghastly day and the wraith-like tentacles of depression that he fought hard to keep at bay were tightening their grip on him. Normally he would have tasty food in his fridge. Smoked salmon, organic beetroot, feta cheese, a delicious hummus that he had whipped up himself, but it was a sure sign that depression was getting the better of him when he let the contents of his fridge go and lost interest in eating. He really should go and see his counsellor and therapist. It had been a couple of months since his last visit and Hannah Harrison would chide him gently for letting it go so long.

At least though he would be able to tell her that he had taken a stand against his boss Gerard Hook and his rampant homophobia. Gerard, a red-faced, fat-bellied, blustering bully, had made his life a misery since Jonathan had been transferred to the Finance Department. Gerard was in charge of his section and the first time he'd seen Jonathan he'd looked him up and down, noting Jonathan's red Paisley scarf wrapped cravat-like around his neck, and his highly polished winkle-pickers, and sneered, 'Quite the fashion plate, aren't you? Let's hope you're as good at preparing invoices as you are at fancy dressing.'

He was an odious man, and never lost a chance to make homophobic remarks in general office conversation. Jonathan had grown up with homophobia, but he'd hoped when he had moved to Dublin to work that things would be easier. And they were, in many ways. In fact it had been a life-changing liberation for him to meet so many lads just like him, who had endured the same miseries that he had growing up. It had been as though a burden had lifted from his shoulders. He was not alone, he was not a freak, there were others like him, and life could be a lot of fun.

He had found a spacious bedsit in a big old red-brick semi in Drumcondra that overlooked a small park and was only ten minutes from the city centre and his workplace. The landlord had told him he could decorate it as he wished, and he had painted the walls a buttery cream, and the skirting boards and architraves a rich burgundy. He'd made new chintz covers for the shabby old two-seater sofa, bought a new mattress for the single bed and dressed it in a cream candlewick bedspread and burgundy and green scatter cushions, and placed lamps around the room so that he would never have to use the stark centre light that gave the room such a cold glow. His landlord had been so impressed he had asked him to decorate the front bedsit upstairs, and had beefed up the rent for the new tenant, a young teacher called Orla, to cover the costs.

Orla was from Cork and as mad as a brush, and she and Jonathan hit it off from the start; and when he was not socializing in the George or the Front Lounge, they often went to the pictures, or ordered in a Chinese or Indian meal and drank copious amounts of red wine and discussed the current men in their lives.

Jonathan grinned, hearing his friend moving around upstairs as she prepared her evening meal. She was in foul humour and was keeping to herself. Orla had been dumped by a Garda she had dated for two months, prior to moving in to her new bedsit, and she was still furious. 'How dare that thick culchie from Kerry dump me before I had a chance to dump him! I'll show that chancer what he's missing. You're coming to Copper Face Jacks with me, minus the winkle-pickers and scarves. I'll dress you as butch as can be, because you're quite handsome, Jonny boy, and you've to be all over me. An Oscar-winning performance, OK?' She arched an eyebrow at him, daring him to argue.

'Have I any choice?' he retorted, entertained at the notion that he could make a straight, six foot Kerry man jealous.

'No! You can wear jeans, and a T-shirt and jacket and a normal type of leather belt, not one of those ones with the big buckles, and get your hair cut in a buzz cut.'

'Aahhh, that's going a bit far now, Orla,' he protested. He liked his casually tossed blond shaggy look.

'OK then, but let me blow-dry it and part it at the side.'

'Orlaaaaaaaaaa! A side parting, noooooooooo!'

'You can't look gay,' she protested.

'But I *am* gay!' he pointed out.

'I need you to be a manly man, just for one night,' she'd pouted. 'Pleaseeeeee.'

'Do with me what you will!' Jonathan had said resignedly and laughed when his friend flung her arms around him.

They had planned to hit the nightclub that weekend but fortunately for him Orla's period had arrived unexpectedly early and she was flattened with a migraine and, big no-no, her chin had erupted with three large spots. Not a good look to make an ex jealous, she'd informed Jonathan glumly before trudging upstairs to get something to eat, and take to the bed.

He might take to the bed himself, Jonathan yawned. He

needed to get in the right frame of mind for his course tomorrow. Today had been a tough day at work, and he still felt shaky after a run-in with Gerard, but at least he'd stood up for himself and let his obnoxious boss know that he was no longer prepared to be bullied.

He took the small notebook out of his pocket and flipped open the cover. Beneath the date and time that he had written in neatly were the words: *My grade 4, Gerard Hook, called me a shirt-lifter in public in the staff canteen, while I was on my tea break. My colleague Gwen Reilly was a witness and is prepared to verify my complaint.*

Jonathan reread the sentences. He would make a stand if he had to, but hopefully, Hook would tone it down now that he was aware that Jonathan wasn't prepared to take his odious guff any more.

It didn't get any easier. He'd had to stand his ground many times at school, and as a teenager and young adult, but today marked another turning point on his journey. Gwen had been laughing uproariously at one of his witticisms when he'd heard Gerard say in his raspy growl, 'Hey, you!'

Jonathan felt his stomach tie itself in knots but he ignored the other man, who had never used his first name since he'd started in the office.

'*You*! I'm talking to you,' Gerard said irately.

'I think he's talking to you, Jon,' Gwen murmured.

'I'm not answering to "you". I have a name!' Jonathan kept his back resolutely to his boss who was sitting at the table behind him.

The next minute Gerard was standing beside them.

'You lot are here more than fifteen minutes. Get back to your desks. What do you mean by *ignoring* me when I'm speaking to you?'

'Oh!' said Jonathan politely. 'I didn't hear my name being called. What can I do for you, Mr Hook?'

'Don't get smart with me, you little shirt-lifter.' Gerard was so incensed he was almost spitting.

The hum of chatter at their table had ceased and all eyes were on Jonathan. A strange calm descended on him and he took a small notebook he carried out of his pocket. Very slowly and deliberately he opened it to a blank page, looked at his watch, wrote down the time and date and began to write.

'What are you writing in that?' Gerard blustered, realizing he had overstepped the mark.

'I am writing down the time and date, and your gratuitous insult, Mr Hook, and if you persist in your bullying and disrespectful behaviour, I *will* be reporting you to the Personnel Department and may take the matter to my solicitor.' He stood up and with his head held high left the canteen and made for the men's loos. Once behind the relative privacy of a cubicle door he let the hot tears flow silently and tried hard to smother his sobs so that no one would know that he was crying. Many times he had cried silent tears; he would cry many more, he suspected. But he would never allow himself to be abused and bullied again. Thanks to his counsellor Hannah, he was working through the trauma of his childhood sexual abuse at the hands of his neighbour all those years ago.

He would make an appointment to see her soon and

speak to her of today's events. It would be interesting to see if this bully would continue his bullying, Jonathan mused as he moseyed into the small kitchenette and took the bottle of Chardonnay from the fridge. Gerard Hook was a typical playground bully. Jonathan had fought them many times before, often coming home with a black eye or a bloodied nose, much to his mother's dismay. Although she never brought up the subject, Jonathan knew that his mother knew and accepted that he was gay. It was a comfort to him that the subject had never come up for discussion. It was no big deal, as it should not be. He was Jonathan, her son, and that was all that mattered. He wondered would the day ever come when he would be accepted in society for who he was as a person, irrespective of his sexuality.

He poured himself a glass of wine and took a big note-book from his work shelf. He flicked through his notes on colour temperature and colour rendering and how important they were for commercial lighting. Office lighting was generally low-energy fluorescent in cool white. He hated the white strip lights in the office with a vengeance, with their irritating hum and constant flicker. He was more interested in domestic lighting, and especially how lamps, uplighters and downlighters could create a warm and cosy ambience. He always felt he'd achieved something when he persuaded his growing list of clients to change from harsh central lighting to diffused glows around the room. If only he could make a career out of his interior design business. It was his dearest wish and his greatest goal. That and resigning from his permanent and pensionable job and telling Gerard Hook he could get stuffed!

CHAPTER FOUR

Hilary stood outside the city centre hotel suite where the lighting design course was being held, rooting frantically in her bag for her registration document. She was sure she had put it in with a shopping list and two bills she had written cheques for that needed posting.

The door to the small foyer burst open and a tall, lanky man with a mop of blond hair flopping into his eyes, and carrying a large pink folder under his arm and wearing the pointiest shoes she had ever seen, hurried towards her, panting. Hilary paused from her rooting and grinned in spite of herself. Someone else late too, she thought with relief, glad she wouldn't have to slink in bashfully alone.

'Hi, is this where the lighting design course is? Are you doing it too?' He sounded breathless but he managed a smile.

'Yes, if I can find my registration letter.' Hilary resumed her rooting.

'You remind me of my sister, she carries a sack too,' he said, eyeing her large tote bag. 'We'll go in together, it's probably started. It's a quarter to ten and it was starting at 9.30 sharp! As it said in the letter. I'm Jonathan. Jonathan Harpur.'

'Oh! I'm Hilary Hammond' she responded, thoroughly irritated with herself and wondering if in fact she'd put the letter and bills in the dashboard of her car which was parked a good ten minutes' walk away.

'Right, deep breath then,' the man said, inhaling loudly before wincing.

'What's wrong?' Hilary asked.

'I drank a bottle of Chardonnay on an empty stomach, and feel a tad iffy,' he murmured, opening the large green door.

A group of around thirty people sat taking notes from the diminutive, bespectacled lecturer, who was pointing to an image on a large screen of a shop-floor display of fabrics, and talking about something called metal halide lighting. Hilary knew that shop or store lighting was completely different from domestic, especially where fabrics were concerned, and a light as close as possible to natural light was needed. Hopefully this was the point being made and they hadn't missed too much of the lecture and would be able to grasp what was being taught, fairly quickly.

All the seats at the back were taken and Hilary glanced at her companion, who grimaced and began to edge along the side. 'There's seats at the front, hurry along, please, we have a lot to cover,' the man said impatiently as everyone turned to look at them. Mortified, Hilary scuttled behind her new acquaintance who nonchalantly flicked his purple scarf over his shoulder as he strode along ahead of her. There were four empty seats in the middle of the front row and he sat on one of them and she sat down beside him and took out a large notebook from her tote, and then realized with a sinking heart that she had to go rooting for a pen. She scrabbled desperately in the depths of her bag as the lecturer eyed her irritably.

'Err ... em ... my pen,' she said weakly, catching her companion's amused gaze.

'I've two, take one,' Jonathan murmured, handing her a blue biro. 'Mary Poppins has nothing on you,' he added *sotto voce* as he clipped some pages to a clipboard and, pen poised, gazed expectantly at the lecturer.

Hilary giggled, earning another irate frown from the lecturer, before she lowered her head and opened her notebook as he began to discuss new developments in lighting technology.

'I'm more interested in domestic lighting, to be honest. Fitting out a store or display premises wouldn't be my cup of tea,' Jonathan confided as they sipped coffee and nibbled on dry pink wafer biscuits a couple of hours later at the coffee break.

'Umm, we do all types of lighting in my job, domestic and commercial. My dad has a lighting business and showrooms; I run it for him,' Hilary told him, trying not to gobble her biscuit. She was starving, having only had time for a half-slice of toast that Millie hadn't eaten. The girls were having a sleepover at her sister's and she'd had to pack overnight bags, as well as getting them ready for school.

'Really? Do you give discounts to friends?' Jonathan enquired. 'I have a new interior design commission. I need lights and lamps and shades and now I'm your friend.' He grinned at her and she laughed.

'I'm sure we could do business, Mr Harpur.'

'Excellent, Ms Hammond! Here's to a long and fruitful friendship.' He clinked his coffee cup against hers and winked. 'Look at the Mona Lisa over there, casting sultry glances at the guy in the brown cords. She's wasting her time. He plays on my team.'

'Gay?' Hilary arched an eyebrow.

'For sure. I should go over and flirt with him myself.'

'How do you know?' Hilary asked. 'He looks ... er ... em ...' She was going to say butch but stopped in case she implied that Jonathan wasn't. The minute she'd seen Jonathan's shoes, and the scarf draped artistically around his neck, she'd known that he was gay.

'You *always* know who plays on your team,' Jonathan assured her confidently. 'He's been eyeing me up all morning so Mona Lisa is barking up the wrong tree there,' Jonathan smirked.

Hilary laughed. Mona Lisa was a spot-on description of the slightly round-faced, dark-haired girl with the protruding eyes, who had introduced herself as Jacintha and informed them, as Jonathan politely handed her a cup of coffee, that she was an architect with a 'cutting edge' firm in Merrion Square. She believed in using the medium of architecture in a 'sculptural' way, she informed Hilary and Jonathan, who listened politely, as she earnestly declared that a lighting design course would add to the services she could offer to clients. She had looked down her superior little nose when Jonathan told her that he worked in the Civil Service. 'So you haven't been to uni full-time then? Just courses here and there?' Jacintha sniffed.

'I've been to the University of Life, and how,' Jonathan drawled with a theatrical sigh.

'And what do you do?' Jacintha had turned to Hilary who had been about to say that she worked in her dad's business when Jonathan cut in.

'Can you believe it, Jacintha? Hilary is the MD of her *own* lighting and electrical business, as well as a mother of two! This lady is a DY NA MO!'

'Oh! Right,' Jacintha said, casting a supercilious glance over Hilary who was wearing black trousers, black espadrilles and a white broderie anglaise top. Jacintha was dressed in a sharp, tailored grey trouser suit, worn with a red-silk cami that was stretched tightly across her bountiful bosom. She tottered on her skyscraper heels and carried a YSL briefcase.

'I suppose you have to keep up to date?' she observed, glancing around the room to see who else she might be interested in talking to.

'Indeed,' murmured Hilary, who was finding it hard to keep her face straight as Jonathan was standing slightly behind Jacintha and flaring his nostrils and arching his eyebrows.

'Are you into er . . . interior design too?' Jacintha sounded bored and was clearly making polite conversation.

'Of course,' Hilary shrugged. 'It's intrinsic to my business; good lighting can only complement and add an extra dimension to any room.'

'But with interior design you either have it or you don't, it's innate, unlike architecture which can be learned. Don't you agree?' Jonathan interjected smoothly, turning to Hilary.

'Absolutely.' She nodded emphatically. 'You *have* to have

a flair for sure.' Hilary only said that because she thought the other girl was so smug and dismissive. She had never given the matter much thought.

'I don't actually agree with you on that point. Enjoy your coffee,' Moon Face had retorted before drifting off to try her luck with Mr Brown Cords.

'I'm devastated!' Jonathan murmured and Hilary giggled. Her companion was great fun and really adding to her enjoyment of the course. 'Very patronizing, wasn't she? She nearly fell off her high heels when I said you were an MD.' Jonathan grinned.

'You weren't letting her get away with anything. She's so up her own posterior.' Hilary eyed the last biscuit on the plate longingly.

'Some people bring out the worst in me,' Jonathan confessed, taking a gulp of coffee. 'I must warn you, if we are going to be buddies, that I have a terrific inner bitch.'

'Oh me too,' Hilary grinned. 'And she could probably out-bitch yours.'

'Excellent!' Jonathan approved. 'I think we are going to get on like a house on fire. Now eat that last biscuit, you look as if you are in need of vittles, and then I really must go to Louisiana before we start back.'

'Me too, I shouldn't have drunk that second cup of coffee,' Hilary said as they made their way to the restrooms.

She touched up her make-up and brushed her hair. She was glad she'd come to the course. It was vital to keep up to date with developments and new lighting designs, but today didn't seem like work with Jonathan sitting beside her, whispering witty asides.

She felt she'd known Jonathan Harpur all her life. She felt completely comfortable with him and he seemed very relaxed with her. Easy! That's what they were ... easy together. A most unexpected bonus on this lovely sunny Friday, away from the business, and home, and all their demands.

'Do you know what would be great?' Jonathan said as he wolfed down a steaming bowl of Irish stew, while Hilary made short work of a succulent lamb shank. They were having lunch in a pub on the quays not far from the hotel.

'What would be great?' she asked, mopping up some gravy with a piece of bread.

'We could go to some of those lighting fairs together. Did you see the timetable of fairs Mr Personality gave us? Frankfurt, Belgrade, Moscow, Stockholm. Helsinki. The world is our oyster, missus.'

'I have a husband and two children,' she reminded him.

'A minor detail, my dear!' Jonathan said airily, giving a discreet burp. 'Sorry,' he apologized. 'I just feel so comfortable with you. I forgot we've only just been introduced.'

'Weird, isn't it? I feel as if I've known you forever.' Hilary replenished their water from the jug with the mint and lemon floating prettily in the middle, thinking that the colours would be a good match.

'Funny, I think that too. We're going to be great friends, you and me.' He smiled at her. 'And now I have somewhere new to source my lighting requirements, with the discount of course,' he teased. 'Seriously though, I can't wait to see your showrooms.'

'If you've nothing on this evening, you could come and

have a look,' Hilary said impulsively. 'My children are having a sleepover at my sister's and my husband is abroad working for a few days. I had planned to catch up on housework. I've nothing else on. I could rustle us up something for dinner.'

'Forget about rustling up, we can order in, Chinese, Indian, I'm all for the easy life. What do you want to go cooking for when you don't have to?' Jonathan remarked. 'And we could polish off a bottle of vino if you cared to.'

'I'm liking you even better!' Hilary grinned. 'But if you shift Mr Brown Cords in the meantime, I'll understand,' she joked.

'Now that is what I call a *true* gurlfriend,' Jonathan laughed. 'I just need to ring my other gurlfriend, Orla, and make sure she's OK. She lives in the flat above me and has been dumped by a Kerry man and is in the horrors as well as having bad lady pains. I don't want to drop her like a hot potato. Wouldn't be fair. And besides she'd have my guts for garters and make my life a misery. You order the coffee while I go and give her a bell.'

Jonathan seemed a very decent bloke. She liked that he was making sure that his friend was OK, Hilary approved, catching the waitress's attention and mouthing, 'Two coffees, please.'

They had just been placed on the table when Jonathan arrived back. 'All sorted,' he said cheerfully. 'I'm allowed to date you as long as I get her a cheeseburger on the way home.'

'And is there any significant other in your life?' Hilary asked, pouring milk into her coffee.

'Tragically, no. I'm all alone and celibate as a nun,' Jonathan sighed. 'I was with someone for a while but it didn't work out. He was sports mad and I couldn't hack it. Standing on the sidelines watching him play badminton and shuttling that cock over the net did my head in eventually. It's not even *real* tennis,' he grumbled. 'Do you know any sexy gay men at all?' he queried hopefully.

'Sorry, none that are unattached. I know one couple who are regular customers, and another guy who sources lights for his restaurants but he's seeing someone,' Hilary said apologetically.

'Never mind, I'm immersing myself in my work for the time being anyway.' He glanced at his watch. 'We need to get a move on. Lunch is on me,' he added firmly, taking out his wallet.

'No!' protested Hilary, rooting in her bag for her purse.

'Yes!' Jonathan gave her a stern look that made her laugh. 'Don't forget you'll be giving me a discount. I'm just worming my way into your affections.'

'Well I'm getting our takeaway tonight then,' she responded equally firmly as a lipstick and one of Millie's sparkly hairbands fell out onto the table.

'Right, Mary Poppins, sort yourself and that bag while I go and pay.

'I'm looking forward to the domestic lighting module. It sure beats the hell out of being stuck at work – it will be the happiest day of my life when I can resign from the Civil Service,' Jonathan confided when they headed for the exit.

'That's a big step to take,' Hilary remarked as they emerged onto the quays, the balmy breeze blowing their hair around their faces. The sun sparkled on the Liffey, a flowing, glittering ribbon of molten silver, and the scent of flowers from a street seller's stall perfumed the air. A seagull squawked from the *Jeanie Johnston's* masts and a small boat chugged towards the East Link Bridge, leaving a foamy swirl in its wake. She inhaled deeply and wished they had time to sit in the sun over a glass of wine and watch the world go by.

'We all have to take a leap of faith sometimes,' he said lightly, falling into step beside her.

'Giving up a permanent and pensionable job isn't a decision to be taken lightly.'

'Yes, Mammy!' Jonathan said drily.

Hilary laughed. 'That did sound a bit middle-aged all right,' she conceded.

'Don't worry, I want to have a good portfolio of clients, and I'm getting there slowly but surely and you know where you and I should look for business?' He steered her across Custom House Quay.

'Where?' She was intrigued.

'Lots of hotels are having spa areas installed, and proper lighting is crucial. That's the market we need to go after.'

'Well, would you believe, we've supplied lighting for several hotels doing just that,' Hilary said.

'Supplied the lighting!' He made a face. 'We should *design*, supply and *install*. There's a whole new market out there just waiting to be tapped in to.'

'Are you suggesting we work together?' Hilary exclaimed.

'You've said it, missus. Hammond and Harpur Interior and Lighting Design Specialists. What do you think?'

'I think it has a very good ring to it!' Hilary grinned. '"Sculptural", as Jacintha might say!'

'Oooohhh bitchy, I like it.'

Laughing, they made their way into the hotel, delighted with the unexpected bonus of new friendship that their design course had brought them.

CHAPTER FIVE

'I really think it's going to be me, Colette. I've just had an email from Daniel Burdell. Reading between the lines I think you and I are heading for New York.' Des was on a high as they sat in the back of the chauffeur-driven car that was taking them to Heathrow. They'd entertained the Japanese businessman and his little dumpling of a wife to afternoon tea in the exquisite surroundings of the stately home and now luxury hotel that Cliveden House had become. She wished she'd had time to wander around and admire the antiques and paintings but she'd performed her wifely duty and made small talk with their guests, and Des's potential client.

'Jerry Olsen is going to go ballistic! Tough luck, Jerry boy!' Des rubbed his hands.

Colette sighed. Was it the line of coke he'd taken before they left, or was he really in with a chance for the promotion that would see them relocate to the US? She hated it when Des took coke. He was hyper enough without it, but the drug made him edgy and manic.

'Let's not count our chickens before they're hatched,' she murmured, but her husband wasn't listening; he had resumed working on his laptop, tapping furiously as they sped along the M4. She gazed out of the car window noticing the iconic Round Tower and turrets of Windsor Castle in the distance. The flags fluttering in the breeze and great oak trees framing the view. In spite of her irritation with her husband, she still thought what a magical, otherworldly sight it was, conjuring up images of knights in shining armour jousting for their ladies. She had been to a weekend party years ago in a stately country house in Berkshire, soon after they'd married. A striking Piper painting of Windsor Castle hung in the gallery that ran the length of the house. Colette had thought it beautiful and had returned to gaze at it several times over the weekend incurring the displeasure of her husband.

'For heaven's sake, stop skulking here and come and mingle. We're going grouse shooting. Go and change,' he instructed.

'Go without me, I'm not sitting shivering in that damp weather waiting for you to shoot some poor unfortunate birds. I *told* you that I wasn't going shooting.'

'Some help you are,' he'd muttered angrily, stomping off, and she'd thought how exhausting it was climbing the social ladder sometimes.

Colette grimaced at the memory. They had found their niche in London – her aunt's connections had proved invaluable – and she was very comfortable with their place in the *haut monde*. If they went to New York it would almost be like starting afresh and those Waspy East Coasters were notoriously cliquish as she'd found on their frequent trips Stateside over the years. *And* they'd have to take Jasmine out of prep school and away from her little friends. It wouldn't be easy. But, on the other hand, she *loved* New York. And what a feather in their cap it would be, and how impressed her parents would be, if Des got this plum job and they ended up living on the Upper East or West Side of Manhattan? The Met, MoMA, the Guggenheim, the Morgan and L&M, and so many more cultural delights, all on her doorstep. Des would have Wall Street but they would be her pleasures.

Colette brightened up as they merged onto the M25 speeding towards the exit for Heathrow. She could see planes in their holding patterns circling in the distance and hoped there'd be no delays to their flight. It was rare these days to take off on time.

Now that she was on her way Colette had started looking forward to her trip home to Ireland. She wouldn't say anything about her husband's job interview until it was in the bag, though. It would be too ignominious if she'd spoken about it and then Des didn't get the position. Image was everything in your own home town.

She'd tell Des to drop her at Hilary's, and have a good chat with her friend about it. Colette wouldn't mind saying it to her. She knew better than anyone the person behind the bright, self-confident façade Colette put up. She could always depend on Hilary for advice. Besides it would be more enjoyable having a drink and a chat with Hilary than having to make polite conversation with Des's colleagues. He had reservations for dinner in Guilbaud's , but tonight she wasn't in the mood for fine dining, hovering waiters, and over-rich food. She actually had a strange longing for a kebab, she thought in amusement, remembering how Hilary used to go mad when she'd eat half of hers after a night out.

'I want you to drop me off at Hilary's when we get to Dublin. I'll take a cab to the hotel later,' she said as the driver swung around the roundabout and drove towards Terminal 1.

'But we're going to Guilbaud's.' Des looked at her, perplexed.

'I'm not in the form, darling. I'm tired. That dinner for the Americans took a lot of work and energy and I just want to flop with Hilary for an hour or two and wind down.'

'Fine, if that's what you want,' Des said, packing away his laptop. 'Have you told your folks we're coming over?'

'No, I'll ring them from the hotel tomorrow and we can arrange to meet up.' Colette refreshed her lipstick and ran a brush through her hair as they pulled up at the set-down area.

'They won't be too happy that you haven't let them know you're coming,' Des warned.

Colette shrugged. 'I know they'll be in a huff. I'll worry about that tomorrow.' She slid gracefully out of the car, making sure she had her copy of *Vanity Fair* in her Louis Vuitton travel bag. She would read her favourite magazine in the comfort of first-class on the short flight home. Now that she was at the airport she was dying to surprise Hilary and have a good girly natter.

'It was like being in an Aladdin's cave of lighting. They're beautiful showrooms – you should be very proud,' Jonathan remarked as he and Hilary divvied up spring rolls, crispy duck and lemon chicken and rice, in her kitchen. He had meandered around the showrooms, particularly enjoying the uplighters and downlighters and the glittering cascades of the sparkling chandeliers that were displayed artistically throughout.

'Thanks. I like to keep up to date with new designs but I like classic fixtures as well. It's all about keeping the balance right.' Hilary drizzled hoisin sauce over the shredded duck and added some cucumber and shallots.

'Were you always interested in lighting as a career?' He topped up their glasses of Bin 555, their second bottle, and followed Hilary outside to a patio enhanced by an array of planters overflowing with vibrant, fragrant blooms, and where she had set a round mosaic table beneath a pale green parasol.

'Oh nice,' he approved, glancing around appreciatively.

'I love being outside, now sit and eat,' Hilary instructed.

'The lighting career?' he prompted as he sat opposite her.

'Not at all,' Hilary laughed. 'I got lumbered with it. Dad has heart trouble and my sister was in the middle of her degree and I was just about to start university, so she couldn't give it up and it fell to me to keep the show on the road, and here I am well over a decade later.'

'And what would you have liked to have done?' Jonathan asked, licking hoisin sauce off his fingers.

'I wanted to study languages. I was good at French and Spanish at school. I became fluent in French when I worked as an au pair in Paris. I think all children here should learn languages in primary school. Nearly everyone on the Continent has two or more. They put us to shame.'

'*Mais oui.*' Jonathan took a bite of his spring roll. 'Hmm, this is *très bon* or even *muy bueno.*'

'You're bilingual,' Hilary remarked before taking a slug of her red wine.

'Tri, actually, Ms Hammond,' he said smugly. 'I know Irish as well, *ta* and spring roll *ana mhaith ar fad.*'

'I'm suitably impressed, *Monsieur* Harpur.'

'I'm only teasing,' he joked. 'I have schoolboy French and the only other Spanish I know is *la cuenta, por favor* and *ningún hombre podría compararse a ti.*'

Hilary chuckled. '"No other man compares to you!" You charmer.'

'You have to have the basics when you travel abroad,' Jonathan declared airily, leaning back in his chair and looking out over the shrub-filled garden. 'This is lovely and private. When I get a place of my own, privacy will be a huge priority for me. I always think the garden should be an extra room, so to speak. This one works extremely well.' He studied the verdant lawn edged with curving flowerbeds and an array of blossoming shrubs. The branches of an old apple tree and a damson tree on either side of a winding stone path met in a tender embrace creating a shady emerald archway that drew the eye to another raised seating area with a small water feature and a variety of ferns and bamboo. 'That's a charming feature down there,' he said.

'That was *my* baby,' Hilary said proudly. 'My Zen garden. That's where I go for a bit of peace and quiet, and to read whenever I get the chance, which is rare.'

'You did a great job of it, and the garden.'

'Well, I can't take responsibility for the rest of the garden as such,' she confessed. 'It was well matured when we bought the house. An elderly couple lived here, the McMillians. They were great gardeners and then the husband died and the wife had to go into a nursing home. She interviewed every person who put in an offer and chose us, because she felt we would look after her garden. She was a very feisty lady. I used to visit her in the home and take photos for her, and we had her visit for tea every now and again until she got too frail. It gave her great happiness to sit and look at the damson tree and apple tree, especially in the spring. Oh Jonathan, it's absolutely glorious with the arbour of frothy pink and white blossoms. It would be perfect for a wedding,' she sighed dreamily, feeling deliciously tipsy.

'You could rent it out as a wedding venue.'

'Now that's an idea, I must suggest it to Niall.'

'He's dishy,' Jonathan approved. He'd seen their wedding photo on the mantelpiece in the lounge.

'Umm, can't argue with you there.' She leaned over and topped up his glass before refilling her own.

'Are you happily married?' He smiled across at her.

'Very,' she nodded. 'Very, very happy.'

'You're lucky. I'd give anything to be in a stable, happy relationship,' Jonathan confided.

'It will happen, some day when you're not looking. He'll come into your life, and you can have a ceremony under my trees,' she grinned. 'But not in the autumn because you might get conked on the head by a windfall.'

'There's a good crop budding already.' He glanced over at the fruit-laden branches.

'We generally have a good harvest of damsons and

apples. The girls love picking them. Every autumn I used to make Mrs McMillian damson jam and apple chutney with her own fruit. She loved it. The girls used to bring it to her in a little basket with a bow on it. She passed away a couple of years ago.'

'You are a kind person, Ms Hammond,' Jonathan said, raising his glass to her.

'Not at all, I'm a grumpy wagon most of the time,' Hilary retorted, embarrassed.

'Perhaps that too, but kind nevertheless. And talented. Perhaps we could go into Zen garden design while we're at it.'

'Steady on, Harpur, we haven't got any clients yet.'

'Oh we will! Never you fear, we will. Today has revitalized me. We are going to go far, missus, you and me, I can feel it in me waters. This is the life.' He raised his glass to her.

Hilary lifted her face to the last rays of the sun as it began to set. She was feeling completely relaxed. It had been a gift of a day, so unlike her usual run of the mill stuff, and how rare was it for her to have the house to herself and to be able to sit drinking with someone she knew was going to become a dear friend. *And* tonight she was going to have the luxury of the bed all to herself. What bliss to spreadeagle herself to the four corners and sleep until she awoke of her own accord without the tyranny of the alarm clock or hungry children. She would nip across to the supermarket and get fresh croissants and the paper and sit out on her patio in the morning if it was fine and have a lazy relaxed breakfast before going to collect the girls from her sister's. She hadn't had a free night like this since she could remember.

The sharp, intrusive buzz of the doorbell through the patio doors was like a cold shower and Hilary gave an irritable tut, hauling herself out of the chair. 'Who's that now, I wonder? Someone selling something or other!' she grumbled. 'Excuse me until I put the skids under them.' She slipped her feet into her espadrilles that she had kicked off under the table and frowned as the doorbell shrilled again.

'Impatient, aren't they?' Jonathan remarked.

'Not as impatient as I'll be when I get to them,' Hilary retorted, hurrying into the house. The girls had told their friends they were having a sleepover, so it was hardly any of them, she thought, passing through the kitchen to the hall. She could see the outline of a woman dressed in pink through the stained-glass panel.

She composed her face to hide her irascibility and opened the door.

'Surprise! Surprise!'

'*Colette!* What are you doing here?' She stepped back, astonished. Colette waved at someone in the back of a glossy black car. 'Just let me wave Des off. He's on his way to a business dinner in Guilbaud's. I couldn't face it, so here I am! He said to say hello.' Colette flung her arms around her and Hilary hugged her back, her heart sinking. Trust Colette to arrive when the house was close to being a tip and she was half-tiddly.

'Where's everyone? The house is very quiet!' Colette glanced around.

'No one's here except me and a friend,' Hilary said, pointing out to the patio.

'Anyone I know?'

'No.'

'Get rid of them, and let's have a good old natter,' Colette ordered, handing her a bottle of Veuve Clicquot, and a gift bag with a bottle of Chanel No 5. 'I've loads to tell you, and I don't want to be making polite conversation with a stranger. And I'm *starving!* I could murder a kebab! I keep thinking about the ones we used to get in Ishmael's. I haven't had one for years.' She swanned ahead of Hilary into the kitchen and Hilary gazed at her friend's retreating back, thinking crossly: *And how high exactly do you want me to jump, Colette? Well, I'm not dumping Jonathan just because you've arrived on my doorstep without a by your leave!*

CHAPTER SIX

Colette strolled out to the patio, having glanced around the messy countertops in the kitchen with a slightly raised eyebrow, much to Hilary's chagrin. How typical of Colette to arrive unannounced and find the house in a mess. She hastily shoved the Chinese cartons into the bin and gave the countertop a quick wipe. She put the champagne in the fridge and couldn't help but spray some of the timeless perfume on her wrist and sniff it. Colette always bought her expensive gifts when she flew home for a visit, even though Hilary told her not to.

'You know me, I love spending, so why not spend on someone I care for?' she'd said once, having presented Hilary with a beautiful silk Dior scarf. And yet her friend would expect Hilary to do the hot potato act and get rid of Jonathan, so that she could be the centre of Hilary's attention for the evening.

'Hello there, I'm Hilary's oldest friend,' she heard the other woman say to Jonathan, holding out a languid hand. 'Colette O'Mahony. We haven't met before I don't think,' she said, not waiting for Hilary to perform the introductions.

Jonathan stood up courteously. He could sense the

blonde, petite, designer- dressed and immaculately made-up woman was merely being polite and was not best pleased to see him.

'Jonathan Harpur,' he reciprocated, returning the handshake with a firm grip. He hated limp handshakes.

'I don't remember Hilary ever mentioning you,' Colette remarked, glancing around at the detritus of their meal.

'That's because, until today, I had never met Jonathan,' Hilary said cheerfully, emerging onto the patio and handing Colette a glass of wine.

'Oh! Really? I suppose that explains it.' Colette sounded bored. She took a sip of her wine. If Jonathan hadn't been there she would have slugged it, but impressions had to be made, no matter how fleeting.

'I should be making a move.' He didn't resume his seat. 'I guess you ladies have some catching up to do.' He smiled at Hilary. 'I had a lovely day!'

'Yes, indeed we do! I haven't seen Hilary in yonks. Lovely to meet you,' Colette said sweetly.

'Don't go yet, Jonathan,' Hilary protested.

Jonathan saw Colette flash an exasperated glance at her friend but because Hilary was looking at him she didn't see it. 'Colette's brought a chilled bottle of champers, let's pop the cork and toast our new venture,' Hilary grinned at him, quite oblivious to the fact that Colette had a face on her that would stop a clock. His diva instincts kicked in. He didn't like this snooty friend of Hilary's who wouldn't even try and let on that she wasn't anxious to get rid of him. Why should *he* go? *She* was the one who had gatecrashed their party.

'Get you! You've just said the magic words "champagne" and "new venture".' He turned to Colette, casually dropping an arm around Hilary's shoulder. 'You're looking at ... wait for it ... ringing bells and whistles ... drum roll ... Hammond and Harpur Interior and Lighting Design Specialists—'

'And don't forget Zen garden design,' Hilary giggled.

'How could I, Mzzz Hammond?' Jonathan ramped up his gay persona, throwing his eyes up to heaven theatrically and running his fingers through his hair.

Colette looked at them, gobsmacked. 'That will be the day. Hilary, what do *you* know about interior design?' she derided. 'You two are obviously pissed,' she said crossly. 'I should leave you to it.'

'Don't be silly, kick your shoes off and sit down and get pissed *with* us. Will I order something from the Chinese? We've just finished ours.' Hilary saw the disgruntled expression on Colette's face and felt her deliciously tipsy feeling begin to fade a little.

'I don't fancy Chinese!' her friend said petulantly.

'Indian?' Hilary persisted.

'Too fattening, all that cream.' Colette dismissed that proposal.

'I have some steak in the fridge, a fillet. You could have it with salad and some ciabatta.'

'Fine,' Colette agreed, slipping out of her pink Chanel jacket and handing it to Hilary. 'I just need to freshen up, Heathrow makes you feel so—'

'Manky,' Jonathan chipped in.

'Well ... er ... yes, I was going to say hot and sticky.'

Colette stared at the upstart coolly. He *really* didn't know his place.

She marched into the house, her high heels clicking a tattoo on the wooden floor, and Hilary looked at Jonathan and gave a sigh. 'Sorry about this, Jonathan. She's my oldest friend, she lives in a posh gaff in London and she has a housekeeper, and how *typical* that she arrives when the house is a tip,' she fussed. 'And now I've to go and cook, just when we were having a delightful evening.'

'The house isn't a tip. It's a *home*! You sit there and I'll slap the steak on the pan, that's if you don't mind me rooting in your fridge and presses,' he added hastily.

'No, you sit and relax!' she protested.

'I wouldn't know what to say to her. She's *très* formidable.' He made a face. 'I'll cook and you get her tiddly and take the edges off her.'

'OK, there might be some cheese in the fridge that's gone a bit mouldy, it might be smelly,' she warned him.

'You should see mine,' he comforted. 'I've a carrot that's shrivelled up – at least I think it's a carrot – and a cucumber that's going to have to be poured out! Here she comes, get that wine down her. Are you sure you want me to stay? I feel I'm intruding.'

'Oh please do stay, Jonathan. You're not intruding at all. I was enjoying our evening so much. I'm not in the mood for "my wonderful life in London" tonight,' Hilary sighed, feeling a tad disloyal but irritated nevertheless.

'I'm doing chef,' Jonathan announced gaily when Colette joined them. 'Steak . . . medium, well done or rare?' He gave her a saccharine smile.

'Oh!' Colette was thrown. 'Um ... medium to rare, please.'

'No bother, sit and relax, ladies. Your champers will be out forthwith. Where are the glasses, Hil?'

'The press on the left-hand side at right angles to the sink,' Hilary instructed, sitting down at the table.

'Righto.' Jonathan cleared the dishes on the table and sashayed into the kitchen. Hilary hid a smile at his antics. He was really camping it up for Colette's benefit.

'How did you meet him? He's certainly making himself at home.' Colette frowned. 'I can't believe you only met him today and he's rooting around your presses already.'

'We met at a lighting design course. He's an interior designer and a potential new customer, and, I have to say, I haven't had as much fun in ages. I feel as if I've known him forever.'

'He's a typical queeny gay, isn't he? And—'

'Oh for God's sake, Colette!' Hilary interjected crossly. 'What's that got to do with anything! Say I'd met someone else, who was straight, you wouldn't be sitting there saying he's a typical hetero, would you?'

'You're very ratty, Hilary. I was merely going to say he's gay *and* pushy. Lots of them *are*.' Colette scowled, taken aback by her friend's rebuke.

'They're not another *species*, Colette.'

'I know *that*! I'm not homophobic, Hilary. There are lots of gay people in our circle. It's just you don't know him more than a day and he's making himself completely at home and I was surprised, that's all,' Colette said sulkily. 'I was hoping to have you to myself. I've *loads* to tell you.'

'What are you doing home anyway? I presume Jasmine's not with you?' Hilary changed the subject.

'No, it's too short a visit. Des had to come over on business so I said I'd come and see the parents and you, but you don't seem too happy to see me!'

'I *am*, I'm delighted. I wasn't expecting you, that's all, and I'm a bit the worse for wear; we've been drinking since we got home,' Hilary said in a more conciliatory tone.

'I wish *I* was plastered,' Colette said glumly.

'Why, what's wrong?' Hilary gave an inward sigh and prepared herself for a litany of gripes. She knew her friend of old. When Colette was worried about something, it was inevitable that she would dump on Hilary.

'Des seems to think he's in with a good chance for a big promotion, which means we'll be relocating to New York!' Colette made a face.

'Fantastic! But what's wrong with that? You *adore* New York!' Hilary exclaimed.

'Yes, for shopping and holiday breaks. Going to live there is a different kettle of fish. It's like starting out all over again to get anywhere on the social scene. And they're very cliquish on the East Coast. And then there's Jazzy. She'll have to get used to a new house, new school and a new nanny.'

'Oh yeah! That's true.' Hilary could identify with that. Jasmine was a precocious five-year-old who reminded her of the younger Colette. Always looking for the attention that her parents didn't have time to give her. Privileged, pampered, with everything she could want, her childhood was almost a replica of Colette's own, and Hilary was surprised

73

that her friend had behaved just as her own parents had. Surely she would have been determined to raise her own daughter differently from the way she had been raised herself, reared by nannies or palmed off to be minded by Sally and others. Motherhood had not diminished the me, me, me trait Colette had always exhibited. Nannies had played a major role in Jasmine's life from her birth. 'It's not the worst age to make a big change. Jazzy's young and adaptable.' Hilary sipped her wine.

'She's very demanding sometimes though.' Colette shook her head.

Only because you don't spend enough time with her. Hilary bit back the criticism, having seen Jasmine throw some magnificent tantrums in the past. 'When will you know if Des has got the job?'

'Sooner rather than later. Des seems to think he's got it, but I'm not going to say anything to Mum and Dad or anyone else until it's in the bag,' she added hastily. 'So say nothing, not even to Niall.'

'Mum's the word!' Hilary assured her as Jonathan stepped out through the patio doors with two sparkling glasses of chilled golden champagne.

'Ladies! Enjoy your champers.' He placed the two glasses in front of them with a flourish. 'Your steak is in the pan, and the salad is in preparation.' He bowed towards Colette.

'You've very accomplished, aren't you?' she drawled.

'*Very*!' he smirked and winked at Hilary before going back inside.

Colette's eyes narrowed but she said nothing. She had taken an instant dislike to Jonathan and he was doing nothing to reverse that. His faux chumminess merely served to increase her antipathy.

'How's Niall, where is he?' she asked casually. She was disappointed he wasn't here. She would have enjoyed boasting to him about Des's last bonus.

'He's in Moscow.'

'Why didn't you go?' Colette looked at her, astonished.

'Because I've two children in school and a business to run,' Hilary said drily.

'What a pain having to stay behind. I love going abroad with Des. He gets to do all the hard work and I get to swan around shopping and enjoying myself!' Colette said smugly.

'You have a housekeeper and a nanny and you don't work full days outside the home,' Hilary pointed out. *You don't work in the home either*, she thought nastily and then felt like a heel. She was being mean to her friend for no reason at all.

'True! My part time consultancy hours mean I can suit myself. Can't you get someone else to run your dad's shop?' Colette always called it the shop, never the showrooms or the business.

'Aah, I wouldn't do that to him and besides we're very, very busy – business is starting to boom with all this Celtic Tiger stuff. We're supplying a lot of hotels now. There are so many opening, I don't know where they're going to get the people to stay in them.'

'I know! London's buzzing! Des is making a mint in bonuses even if he is working practically 24/7. When you think of that terrible recession we grew up in in the eighties it's hard to believe. Dickon and Austen's have had to take on four new staff to cope with the demand for fine art.'

Hilary raised her glass. 'Here's to progress and good times!' she toasted, just as Jonathan emerged onto the patio with Colette's meal.

'I'll drink to that,' he declared, placing the steak in front of her. 'Here's a herb butter sauce as an accompaniment. I raided your herb garden, Hilary,' he said, pointing to the large fragrant herb-filled planter on the patio. 'I'll be back in a sec with the salad and more champers.'

'It smells divine.' Hilary inhaled the aromas wafting across the table.

'It tastes delicious,' Colette admitted grudgingly, chewing on a piece of the succulent tender steak, which was cooked just the way she liked it.

'I'll just raise my glass to good times and then I'll leave you in peace. I'm sure you have lots to catch up on,' Jonathan said diplomatically, placing Colette's artistically arranged side salad beside her plate and refilling their glasses.

'Aw, just sit down for another little while. Colette's interest is in fine arts. She's a consultant in a prestigious gallery in London, and she's always seeing famous people,' Hilary said, knowing that her friend loved name-dropping all the famous people who had been clients or who she'd met at viewings and launches.

Colette rose to the bait, as Hilary knew she would. 'Oh well last week, would you believe, I saw Johnny Depp and Helena Bonham Carter having dinner in San Lorenzo. I was dining with a client. Des and I eat there regularly—'

'Do you ever see Princess Di there?' Jonathan asked eagerly. He loved Princess Diana and followed her progress in *Hello!* which he always bought when she was on the cover.

'Often,' Colette shrugged. 'And I've seen her shopping on the High Street. Always immaculate and so stylish, even in her casual clothes.'

'Wow!' Jonathan sat down and sipped his champagne.

'And I was at a gallery exhibition recently and Helen Mirren was there. And I've seen Elton John too.' Colette speared a piece of cucumber and lettuce. Whatever Jonathan had drizzled over it, it was a crisp and very tasty salad.

'Helen Mirren, she is DIVINE!' Jonathan enthused and Hilary smiled to herself as Colette relaxed and continued to regale Jonathan with anecdotes about her well-to-do life in London.

Just as well Niall isn't here. He would have been bored out of his tree, she thought, having watched her husband's eyes glaze over often enough when Colette and Des set out to impress.

'I really must go,' Jonathan said a couple of hours later. Dusk had changed to darkness and the candles and lanterns that Hilary had lit illuminated the patio and garden in a flickering wave of light casting dancing shadows around them. Down at the end of the garden, Hilary's Buddha sat in Zen-like serenity under the benign gaze of a full moon. It was hard to believe they were in a city, it was so peaceful and private.

'Don't forget you have to bring your friend a burger,' Hilary reminded him, standing up to see him out. 'Will I call a cab for you?'

'Not at all, I'll get one over on the Howth Road, no problem at this hour of the night,' he assured her. 'Now where did I drop my bag?'

'By the kitchen counter, I think.' Hilary had a vague memory of him sitting on one of the stools with his bag at his feet.

'Very nice to meet you,' Jonathan said politely to Colette.

'Likewise,' she returned, equally polite.

Hilary linked his arm as they walked through the house. 'I'm going to have the mother and father of a hangover tomorrow and it will be all your fault, but I had a lovely day and thanks for staying, even though it turned into a bit of a monologue with herself,' she grinned.

'Umm, she's an interesting lady,' Jonathan said diplomatically, retrieving his bag, and Hilary laughed.

'Ring me tomorrow for a chat whenever it suits you. I'll be going to collect the girls around lunchtime. But not too early,' she warned. 'I intend to sleep my brains out.'

'Me too. I'm delighted to have met you,' he said, hugging her.

'Same here,' Hilary smiled, and his hug was warmly reciprocated.

'Now we can have a real heart to heart,' Colette exclaimed, delighted to see the back of the interloper. She had enjoyed impressing him with her tales of London life, but she was finally glad to have Hilary's undivided attention.

Oh no! thought Hilary. She was tipsy and tired, ready for bed. But Colette was re-energized and went into the house to locate another bottle of wine. 'Only a small glass for me,' Hilary protested weakly.

Ignoring her, Colette filled both glasses to the brim and sat down and said, 'Now what do you think? Should I have a facelift in London or New York? It would probably be better to have it in London so I'm fresh when we move Stateside? And do you think I should get a boob job done? Pinky and perky are beginning to droop a little,' she moaned, thrusting her pert bosom upwards.

'They look fine to me,' Hilary slurred. She wanted to put her head on her arms and lie down on the table and fall asleep.

'No they are not,' Colette assured her. 'When I'm wearing a strapless dress I can feel the tug of gravity.' But her words wafted off on the balmy breeze as Hilary's head sank to her chest and she gave a tiny snore.

Jonathan leaned back against the leather upholstery and let the sounds of Dean Martin singing 'Amore' wash over him. The taxi driver was listening to a late-night programme on the radio and was not inclined to talk, for which Jonathan was utterly relieved. He hated chatty taxi drivers.

Today had been a cracker of a day. A real surprise. The course had been interesting and informative but meeting Hilary had been the icing on the cake. She was the biz. He smiled to himself as the taxi whizzed through Fairview, the park dark and uninviting on his left a contrast to the bright lights of the thronged pubs and restaurants on his right.

It was a shame that friend of hers had called. What a diva! She had spent two hours monopolizing the conversation and he could see that Hilary was a tad cheesed off with her. And what a name-dropper! He had pretended interest out of politeness, and there were times when Colette *had* been interesting but she hadn't allowed anyone else to get a word in edgeways. It seemed she might be moving to the States, so perhaps he would never have to see her again. A relief, he thought. Especially as he just knew he and Hilary were going to be great pals. And he was definitely going to up his game in his lighting design on his latest commission. Actually he couldn't wait, Jonathan thought happily. He had some terrific ideas about how to progress his new project and his future career and Hilary was definitely going to be a part of it.

It certainly wasn't the evening she'd anticipated, Colette thought grumpily, waiting for the taxi she had called to arrive. Hilary was up in bed snoring, and she had been left to blow out the candles and bring the dishes and glasses into the kitchen and lock up. She was damned if she was cleaning up, although she did note that Jonathan had cleared up after cooking her meal, and he must have filled the dishwasher because there were no other dishes on the counter. He was a poncy little upstart who didn't know his place, no matter what Hilary said. He'd made himself at home and was far too familiar for someone Hilary hardly knew, in Colette's opinion.

The taxi driver flashed the lights when he arrived, seeing her looking out the window, so she gave a wave and switched off the sitting-room lamps and walked into the hall. She thought she should leave the light on in case Hilary came downstairs later. Her friend was well jarred and she could easily fall down the stairs in the dark. Colette pressed the keypad to set the alarm and closed the front door behind her.

'The Shelbourne,' she said crisply, settling herself into the back of the taxi.

'Off to a party, luv? Nice night for it,' the driver said chattily.

'No,' she said curtly, hoping he would take the hint and shut up.

'Nice houses around here,' he remarked, undaunted, driving along The Middle Third.

Colette ignored him and sat staring out of the window. She was fed up. She'd wanted to talk things over with Hilary. She'd wanted her best friend to be impressed with the great new opportunity that was opening up for her and Des. She'd wanted Hilary to offer advice and assure her that everything would work out well for them. Instead she'd had to entertain a stranger that she didn't particularly take to and make small talk for the entire evening.

Jealousy had raised its familiar head too, Colette admitted ruefully. When she'd seen how comfortable Hilary was with Jonathan, who had been lounging in the chair out on the patio when she arrived, she *had* been miffed to discover they'd only just met. And spouting all that guff about setting up in business together. That was drink talking for sure, she thought derisively. Hilary had enough on her hands with her father's shop. There was nothing of the go-ahead career woman about her. She was far too laid-back.

Jonathan should have left, no matter what Hilary said. He should have known that she was only being polite when she'd pressed him to stay. And Hilary should have *wanted* to be on her own with Colette. It was *ages* since they'd seen each other! It was just like when they were young. She'd had to stake her claim on Hilary sometimes because Hilary's other friends would squeeze her out. A hateful memory surfaced from deep in the recesses of her mind.

'Do I *have* to ask her to my party?'

Now why had *that* come back to haunt her? Colette thought crossly.

She gazed out of the window at the capital. Dublin had undergone such a transformation in the last few years. Even though it was well after midnight the city was teeming, vibrant with Friday night revellers spilling out of pubs and restaurants and heading for clubs and discos. The quays had changed totally from the way she'd remembered them, shabby, dilapidated and neglected. Now they were developed and revamped; modern office buildings and refurbished period houses gave an elegant, polished air that the capital had lacked for a long time.

Progress had certainly been good for her home town, she thought wearily, stifling a yawn. It had been a long week and she felt exhausted. And tomorrow she had to face her parents and make excuses for not telling them that she was coming to Dublin. She was glad she was staying in a hotel tonight and not having to make an effort to do any more talking. Des wouldn't be finished socializing until the early hours. He'd end up with his cohorts in the Horseshoe Bar in the Shelbourne, where the in-crowd gathered on a Friday night. If she was at home with her parents she'd have to sit up and talk and she wasn't in the humour. How strange life was, Colette mused. When she was young she would have given anything for her parents to have had the time and inclination to sit and talk to her, and now when they wanted to spend time with her she didn't care to spend time with them. Too late to turn back the clock now, Colette thought resentfully. Far, far too late.

CHAPTER SEVEN

'What do you mean you stayed in the Shelbourne? Why didn't you stay with us?' Jacqueline O'Mahony asked huffily when Colette phoned her the following morning.

'It was easier to be in town. Des is here for work, there was a meal in Guilbaud's for his Irish counterpart's retirement do and now he's gone to play a round of golf with some of the senior execs. I can meet you here in the Shelbourne or come over to Sutton.' Colette tried to hide her irritation with her mother. Surely *she* who was always so busy working, socializing and entertaining her own colleagues could understand what a business trip was like.

'Is Jasmine with you?'

'No, it's such a short *working* trip I didn't think it was fair to bring her.'

'That's a shame, Colette. Your father and I would love to see her, we get so little chance as it is, and after all she *is* our only grandchild,' Jacqueline said snippily.

'Well you're always welcome to come over to London whenever you want,' Colette said, resting against the big plump pillows of the queen-sized hotel bed, nibbling on a luscious strawberry from the fruit cup she had ordered for breakfast.

'You know how busy we are, professionally and socially,' Jacqueline retorted.

'Right back at you, Mum,' Colette riposted coolly. She heard her mother's sharply inhaled breath of exasperation.

'Well, let me see then – we're going to lunch in the golf club with the McAdams and dinner with the Reilly-Carrolls in town tonight. You could join us for either,' Jacqueline suggested, brightening up. How wonderful to be able to show off Colette. She was so knowledgeable about art and antiques and was always so elegantly turned out. And Des, although she found him rather brash and opinionated, was undeniably successful.

'Just as well we didn't stay with you then. You're quite booked up – we would have hardly seen you,' Colette said lightly, if a touch sarcastically.

'I wouldn't have made the arrangements if I'd known in advance that you were coming, Colette. I'm sure you must have had some idea of when you were arriving,' Jacqueline said sharply. 'It doesn't really matter about lunch, the club can fit you in without prior notice, but if you are coming to dinner I'll need to ring The Commons and advise them that we will have two extra guests.'

'Why don't you and Dad stroll over to the Horseshoe after dinner and we can have a drink with you here?' Colette suggested, not wanting to listen to her parents and the Reilly-Carrolls trying to outdo each other in loquacious legalese.

'I suppose we could do that.' Jacqueline tried not to sound

disappointed. She wasn't a fan of the Horseshoe Bar with its drink-fuelled, testosterone-filled atmosphere, and standing room only, thronged with journalistic hacks, minor celebrities, high-flying business tycoons, drunken politicians and legal eagles, all trying to outdo each other. 'Or you could come to brunch or lunch tomorrow? What time do you fly back?'

'Around 4.30.' Colette struggled to suppress a yawn.

'Well then come for brunch around 12.30 and that will give you plenty of time to get to the airport,' her mother said briskly.

'Let me check with Des, but I think that will probably work for us,' Colette said, relieved that she had got off relatively lightly.

'Excellent,' Jacqueline approved. 'I'm looking forward to seeing you.'

'Me too,' Colette reciprocated, feeling it was required of her.

'And your father will be delighted,' Jacqueline added.

'Bye, Mum, talk later.' Colette hung up and stretched, glad that their meeting was sorted and she hadn't got too much of a lecture over not staying with her parents. Her mother was annoyed but that was her problem. Colette wasn't going to let it affect her unduly. She had enough to worry about with this impending relocation and all it entailed.

She had pre-booked a facial and massage and she was going to have a leisurely day of pampering and shopping. A stroll along Grafton Street to Brown Thomas was just what the doctor ordered. She wondered would Hilary be interested in coming into town for lunch but then remembered that her friend was going to pick up the girls from her sister's. Hilary would have the mother and father of a hangover anyway, Colette reflected, remembering how Hilary was sprawled asleep when she had left her the previous night.

She hoped that lanky, queeny friend of Hilary's was suffering too. Colette scowled, still miffed at being made to feel she'd gatecrashed their private party. She wouldn't bother ringing Hilary to see how she was. She'd ring Lindsay Kennedy and Marcy Byrne instead and see if they were available for lunch. It would be good to meet and catch up with the Sutton gang and let them see how fabulous she looked and how well she was doing. Lindsay and Marcy were well-heeled ladies-who-lunch but they didn't have anything like her wealth, style or status, Colette thought happily, throwing off the bedclothes to go and find her trusty Filofax. She used a mobile phone in London and it was so handy, but they were only coming into vogue in Ireland and most of her friends and acquaintances were, unfortunately, still slaves to the landline.

Colette poured herself another cup of coffee and took it to the chair by the big window that overlooked St Stephen's Green. It was a glorious sunny morning, and the lush green of the trees, interspersed with frothy splashes of pink from late-flowering cherry blossom, was etched against a sapphire sky. A welcome foil to the lanes filled with slow-moving traffic that circled the Green. As bad as Piccadilly, Colette reflected, remembering how she and her teenage friends had invariably made their way to Grafton Street and the Dandelion Market on Saturdays, all those years ago.

Just across the park where a big shopping centre now stood, Dublin's most famous market had flourished. The old stables, mews and courtyards had hosted many fabulous stalls selling bang up-to-date fashions that had thrilled their youthful hearts. Colette even remembered seeing a very young U2 playing one of their first gigs in the courtyard, and had thought The Edge was the coolest guy she had ever seen.

She was happy then, and she hadn't even realized it, too busy trying to impress her peers, and worrying about who would marry her or fretting that she would be left on the shelf. Spinsterhood was something they had all agonized about. She wondered if Hilary hadn't made the first move towards marriage, causing her to panic, would she have ended up marrying Des?

She who, like her peers, had felt she was such a 'liberated' young woman of the eighties, with the world as her oyster, had still been unable to shake off the notion that marriage was the holy grail for a woman. Centuries of conditioning had not been eroded by the advance of so-called feminism, whatever feminists might like to think, she thought wryly, thinking of a banking acquaintance of theirs who had shot up through the ranks, was highly skilled and competitive, but was desperate to be married before she was forty when her 'successful high-flying career-woman' label would inevitably change to 'sad singleton who never got a man'. Better to be divorced even than to be one of them.

Hilary and Niall had married for love, and for years Colette had secretly envied them that. The way they looked at each other, the intimate little manner they would hold hands or hug or make each other laugh. No matter how much Colette had sparkled or flirted, Niall had only ever had eyes for Hilary, much to her chagrin because she had always fancied him.

The Hammonds' marriage was far different from hers and her husband's. She and Des were a *perfect* match. They always looked designer good; they had the same aspirations: to be wealthy, successful, and well placed in society. They each recognized what the other brought to their marriage and appreciated it, but were they deeply in love? Colette sighed. Love was for fools! Love hurt! And love didn't last. She had seen that at first hand, thanks to Rod Killeen. She preferred what she had, thank you very much, she decided briskly, flipping through the phone section of her diary to find Marcy Byrne's number.

'Honestly, Frank, Colette could have let us know she was going to be in Dublin for the weekend, and she could have brought Jasmine. She has no consideration for us after all we did for her,' Jacqueline groused, placing the breakfast dishes in the dishwasher. 'She makes no allowance for the fact that we rarely see our granddaughter. The child will soon be a *stranger* to us. Sometimes I think Colette's trying to *punish* us for something.'

'Don't be silly, Jacqueline,' Frank said irascibly. 'What would she be punishing us for? We gave her the best of everything. A car when she was eighteen, foreign holidays, college in London. All she ever wanted. We paid a fortune for that wedding in Rome! What's her problem?'

'She's always been the same, a little madam,' Jacqueline

declared. What kind of a family were they when their only child didn't let them know that she was coming for a visit, and instead preferred to stay in a hotel? She sighed deeply, staring out at the sea, framed by two spiky palm trees, that shimmered and glittered at the end of their immaculately kept landscaped gardens. A house, not much bigger than theirs, half a mile away, had sold for a million recently causing huge excitement at the golf club. Prices were beginning to climb after all the grim, grey days of the eighties recession and the economy was powering ahead. She and Frank were seriously thinking of buying a villa beside a golf course in the Algarve. The Sheedys had bought one near Albufeira and were always boasting about their fabulous views of the Atlantic, visiting several times a year and coming home with terrific tans and much improved handicaps. She and Frank had worked like Trojans for years: it was time to start winding down a little and enjoy their hard-earned affluence.

Someday this house and all their wealth would be Colette's, for all the thanks her hard-working parents were getting from their ungrateful child. It would be good enough for her if they left it all to charity.

They weren't close, she and Colette. They'd never had that great mother–daughter bond that some of her friends enjoyed. Jacqueline had got pregnant unexpectedly at the very worst time in her career, just as she was starting to make a name for herself. She and Frank had gone into business together, and O'Mahony and Co. were clawing their way up the legal ladder. A baby was the last thing Jacqueline had wanted. It was a huge shock to realize that she was not as in control of her life as she thought she was and that the rug could be pulled from under her arbitrarily, whether she liked it or not.

Jacqueline sighed, remembering how furious she had been that, despite going on the pill and taking responsibility for her life choice, her wishes had counted for nothing in the grand scheme of things. It was the same kind of fury she felt, even to this day, when she lost a court case.

She had always been a control freak, Jacqueline conceded, wiping her Italian marble countertops with more vigour than was necessary. That had come from being the child of a mother who had frittered away housekeeping money on bingo, horses and the slot machines in the sleazy arcades in town. Money that meant eating more cheap mince and beans than she could stomach, and going to school in her sister's hand-me-down uniform. When she grew up she would be in charge of her own life, the young Jacqueline vowed, after the umpteenth time of telling the gas meter man her mammy wasn't in when he came to collect payment. 'Good girl,' her mother would say. How could her mother get her to tell lies and then make her go to confession religiously every Saturday? It just didn't make sense.

It was her difficult childhood that had propelled her to achieve top marks at university, and that same drive fuelled her desire for success in her chosen career. And then she had fallen pregnant.

No doubt her newly conceived daughter had absorbed the energy of her mother's immense dismay, and the other myriad emotions Jacqueline had experienced. She had been sick morning, noon and night, which only added to her resentment.

She hadn't told her husband when a pregnancy test confirmed what she already knew. She had wrestled with the idea of going to England for a termination. She could have easily said nothing and Frank would never have known. But she loved her husband dearly, and she knew one of his dreams was to have *O'Mahony and Son,* or *Daughter* etched on a discreet gold plaque on their office door. The child was his as well as hers. Created by them both. It wasn't all about her. To her consternation, Frank had been delighted. An only child, he'd told her when they got engaged that he'd wanted a boy and a girl to make them a 'proper' family.

'But, Frank, it's crap timing.' She'd burst into tears. 'I can't take time off to look after a baby! We haven't planned it.'

'That's OK! We can get someone to mind it,' he soothed. 'We're getting a lot of referrals, we can afford—'

'Exactly, we're up to our eyes, and this is the last thing I need. Why is it the woman *always* has to make the sacrifices? That's my career up the Swannee,' she raged.

'You won't have to sacrifice your career. We'll manage fine. Working mothers are becoming the norm now, it's not like when we were growing up,' Frank reassured her. Their parents, family and friends had been thrilled with their news so she constantly had to stifle her negative feelings and keep them to herself, putting on a façade in the face of their anticipation and delight.

Childbirth had been the most long-drawn-out, painful, embarrassing event of her life. Jacqueline had felt a complete and utter failure looking at her daughter's screwed up little red face as she screeched loudly when placed in her arms, and felt no overwhelming bond, just exhaustion and irritation that her freedom was curtailed and life as she knew it had changed completely and she was now responsible for another being, whether she wanted to be or not.

Difficult as it was to admit now, all these years later, having a child had not brought a great deal of joy into her life. No wonder she and Colette weren't close, Jacqueline conceded. She had put her career before her child and now she was paying the price. And, much as it pained her to say it, her daughter was making the same mistakes with Jasmine. It was something she should try and diplomatically point out. Perhaps at brunch tomorrow, Jacqueline decided. If Colette wanted a better relationship with her daughter than the one she had with her mother, something had to be said.

Chapter Eight

'She sounds very nice and a bit of a laugh as well.' Orla munched on a slice of toast liberally smeared with pâté, snuggled up beside Jonathan on his bed as he told her all about meeting Hilary at the lighting design course the previous day.

Orla had made them breakfast. Jonathan had been too tipsy the previous night when he had arrived home with her cheeseburger to have a proper conversation and after yawning his head off yet again she'd sent him packing off to bed and told him she'd see him in the morning.

'Hilary is lovely, really down to earth, a bit scatty, and good fun. Just my sort of woman! And you should see her showrooms. FABULOUS, darling.' Jonathan took a slug of coffee and forked half a sausage into his mouth. 'The other one now, the Colette one, was a right little madam. I know she wanted me to leave, she kept giving me the evil eye, and if I'd felt that Hilary wanted me to go I would have, but I kinda felt that Hilary wasn't overly excited to see her. Colette was all Me! Me! Me! You know that sort,' Jonathan observed tartly.

'Oh dear! Me! Me! Me! And You! You! You! I'd say that was good,' Orla murmured wickedly.

'Cheeky hussy,' Jonathan grinned. 'Her clothes were gorgeous though, all designer, and the Louis Vuitton bag, and the Cartier watch. *Lashings* of dosh, I'd say. The husband works in finance and she works in fine art. Lots of name-dropping. Her parents are that legal pair that are always in the papers. The O'Mahonys.'

'Ooohh posh! You're coming up in the world, Mr Harpur.'

'Yes indeed, on the fringes of High Society! Hilary and I are going to be *THE* interior and lighting designers to go to,' Jonathan smirked.

'Right, Mr Interior Designer, I have to go. I've got basketball practice and I'm meeting the girls in town afterwards.' Orla took a last gulp of coffee and got off the bed.

'And how are your lady pains?' he asked solicitously.

She made a face. 'I'm dosed up with Solpadeine. The exercise will help. What are you doing for the rest of the day?'

'I've to go and buy gold brocade curtains, and source a glass coffee table and some lampshades. And then I'm meeting some of the lads in the George.'

'We probably won't see each other until tomorrow then. Brekkie and the papers in Omni around eleven? I'll drive.' Orla arched an eyebrow.

'Perfect,' he said as she blew him a kiss on her way out.

What a delightful weekend it was turning out to be, Jonathan reflected, lying back against his pillows as the sun spilled in through the big bay window and a lark sang in the branches of the minty green rowan tree that was bursting into soft-blossomed bud in the front garden.

How different he felt from the day before yesterday when he had been so demoralized after his confrontation with

Gerard. He'd made a new friend in Hilary, had a great time on the course and was eager to move forward in his design career. Optimistic, that's what he was, Jonathan decided, relieved that the feelings of depression he'd felt coming on had receded. It was hard work keeping the darkness at bay sometimes, but on days like today he felt ready for anything. He sprang out of bed and headed for the shower. Today was not the day to linger in the snug confines of his bed. Today was a day of purpose. He had things to do, places to go and people to see. And then tomorrow he and Orla would have breakfast together and sit reading the papers in a cosy booth in Bewley's in Omni, and then perhaps have a walk in the Botanics, and he would come home and work on his portfolio and his latest project in the afternoon. He wanted to bring his new client to approve the furnishings he'd selected, as soon as possible. He wanted to be ultra prepared.

Jonathan was carefully folding a selection of small swatches of material to put into his shoulder bag when the communal phone in the hall rang. He knew Tommy, the occupant of the bedsit beside his, was out, as was Orla, so he went to answer it.

Surprised, because they'd only spoken in the last two days, he heard his mother's voice at the other end of the line. 'Hello, love,' she said, but he knew by her tone something was up.

'What's up, Mam?' he asked, instantly alert.

'Some sad news, Jonathan. Poor Gus next door died yesterday evening. Took another massive heart attack. I waited until I had the funeral arrangements before I rang you and the girls. The removal's tomorrow evening and he'll be buried after ten Mass on Monday. You'll be down for the removal, won't you? I don't think Rita would expect you to take a day off work and I certainly wouldn't but tomorrow is a Sunday so that will be grand. I'll be there on Monday but we can all be at the removal tomorrow,' his mother said firmly.

Jonathan couldn't speak. He literally froze. His abuser was dead and his mother wanted him to go to his removal service. He couldn't do it, he just couldn't! He swallowed hard. 'Ma ... Mam,' he stuttered. 'I have something arranged for tomorrow. I'm not going to be able to make it.'

'Oh Lord, Jonathan. Couldn't you rearrange it? He was a kind neighbour. He was good to me. To us,' Nancy said in dismay.

'Mam, I have to go now, I'm meeting a client. I'll ring you this evening,' Jonathan fibbed, desperate to get his mother off the phone.

'Well, get a Mass card at least, and try and rearrange whatever you have on tomorrow, Jonathan. You should be there if at all possible,' Nancy urged.

'OK, bye, Mam, bye,' he said hastily and hung up. Jonathan was shaking as he walked across the hall and closed the door behind him. The memories came surging back against his will and he was instantly transported to that untidy, smoke-polluted sitting room with the brown tweedy sofa and the big chipped oval mirror over the fireplace. The memory of the curtains being pulled, the belt being unbuckled, Gus's raspy breath as he forced him to his knees brought tears to Jonathan's eyes. The recollection of the fear and revulsion that always overwhelmed him came back with a force that stunned him. And afterwards, when the hideous assault was over, he remembered Gus's finger held up in warning. 'Don't tell anyone about this now or I'll make things difficult for yer mammy, and I won't buy her any more cigarettes and ye wouldn't like that, now would ye?'

Jonathan would nod his head and run out of the house as fast as he could, down the small pathway that separated their two houses and into the shed at the bottom of his garden where he would fling himself onto an old quilt his mother had given him to play house with Alice. He would sob into his forearm, his body shaking with terror, revulsion, rage and helplessness.

For three years, Gus had made his life a living hell. If he didn't see Jonathan outside, he'd wait until he saw Nancy and say, 'Nancy, will ye ask the wee lad to run to the shops and get me a few fags and I'll get him to buy ye a packet too.'

'I don't want to go, I'm too tired,' Jonathan often protested, petrified and desperate at the thought of what would inevitably happen. On one occasion he had refused outright. His mother had gazed at him sternly and said, 'I'm surprised at you, Jonathan, that you wouldn't run an errand for a neighbour, and he not a well man. I thought I'd reared you better than that. I'll go myself.' She had gone to the shops in a huff and not spoken to him for the rest of the evening.

'Sorry, Mammy,' he'd muttered, suffused with guilt when he'd gone into the kitchen to say goodnight and seen her sewing a button on his good white Sunday shirt.

'Ah sure, it's not often you don't do me a favour when I ask you. We'll let bygones be bygones and forget about it,' Nancy said kindly, opening her arms to him. She'd hugged him tightly and he'd rested his head on her shoulder and so badly wanted to blurt out that Mr Higgins *wasn't* a kind man. That he was mean and dirty and made Jonathan do horrible things.

Shortly after his eleventh birthday, his neighbour had crooked a finger at him one Saturday afternoon when he was mowing the grass. Jonathan, being the man of the house, was responsible for keeping the front and back gardens neat and tidy and for putting out the bin. Nancy had gone to measure up a woman for a dress she was making for her and his sisters were doing housework, making sure the dusting and polishing was done to have the house spick and span for Sunday. 'I want a few fags, laddie. G'wan to the shops and get me some – here's ten shillings. Get yer ma a packet as well.'

Jonathan had taken the money without a word, hurried to the shop to complete his purchase and walked home, his heart thumping, his stomach knotted so tightly he could hardly breathe. Instead of knocking on the front door as he usually did, he shoved the cigarettes and change through the letterbox, making sure to keep Nancy's packet in his pocket. He leapt over the garden wall in a bound and hurried into his own front garden to complete his grass cutting, comforted by the fact that the door to their small front porch was open should he need to make a run for it.

Gus opened his front door scowling. 'Come over here you and bend down and pick up these fags. Why didn't ye knock on the door?' he growled.

Jonathan ignored him. He thought he was going to vomit, but he knew he had to make a stand. There was something very wrong with what that man made him do. His mammy wouldn't like it if she knew, he was sure of that.

'De'ye hear me, lad?' said Gus, raising his voice a little. His face crimson with temper.

'I'm not going into your house ever again,' Jonathan shouted, brought to breaking point. 'Ever! Ever! *EVER!* And I'm not doing that thing you make me do. You're a bad dirty bastard!' he cursed.

Gus came down his path like a bull. 'Shut up, ye little runt. Shut up, I tell ye! De ye want the neighbours to hear? Now get in there and pick up those fags and go into the front room like ye always do and no more of yer guff!'

In desperation, Jonathan picked up the gardening shears and pointed them at Gus. 'Get away from me or I'm telling my teacher on you—'

'Don't ye ever tell anyone or ye'll be mighty sorry. I'll say you're a little liar,' Gus ranted, astonished at this utterly unexpected onslaught. Seeing Mrs Johnston, another neighbour, coming along the road towards them, he turned on his heel and stomped, puffing and wheezing, back into his house, leaving Jonathan trembling like a leaf.

'That's a nice job you're doing, Jonathan. If I gave you a shilling would you do mine?' his neighbour asked when she got to his gate, oblivious to the incident that had just occurred.

'You don't have to pay me, Mrs Johnston,' he managed shakily, knowing his mother would be annoyed if he took payment from a neighbour for cutting her grass.

'Well I'll tell you what then, seeing as you're a kind boy, I'll make an apple tart for you and you can share it with your mammy and sisters. But you've to get the biggest slice,' she said, giving him a wink.

'Thanks, Mrs Johnston,' he answered shakily, darting a glance at the Higginses' house. The door was closed and he couldn't see the bulk of his tormentor silhouetted behind the lace curtains.

'Grand, I'll go and make the tart so,' Mrs Johnston said, walking on to her own house.

Jonathan waited.

Would Gus reappear?

If he did, Jonathan was ready to run. His palms were sweaty as he gripped the lawnmower and began to push, keeping a wary eye on that hated red door with the paint flaking off it, and the dull, blackened brass door knocker that hadn't seen Brasso in years. The door remained resolutely closed.

Was that it? he wondered. Was that what it took? To overcome his paralysing fear and stand up to the bully? Was the nightmare over? He finished cutting the grass and wheeled the lawnmower out the gate to Mrs Johnston's, still half expecting his tormentor to come after him. But of Gus there was no sign. Jonathan could hardly believe it.

The following morning at half ten Mass he saw his neighbour dressed in his Sunday best walking up the aisle to receive communion as usual, his wife and two daughters following behind him. Dread enveloped Jonathan. It was certain that the two families would meet, as they often did after Mass, either in the church grounds or jostled together in the small corner shop that sold bread, milk and the Sunday papers. The old familiar stomach-knotting anxiety reclaimed him and he could hardly swallow the Host when he went up to receive.

'Good morning, Nancy, morning, girls, morning, laddie,' Gus greeted them affably as the crowds spilled out of the small church into the bright sunshine.

'Morning, Rita, Gus,' Nancy responded cheerily. 'A lovely day, thank God.'

'Did ye get the few fags I sent in yesterday?' Gus asked, ignoring Jonathan completely.

'I didn't but thank you, Gus, you really shouldn't have. Jonathan, you should have told me Mr Higgins was kind enough to buy me cigarettes,' his mother chided.

'Sorry, I forgot,' Jonathan said truculently, glowering at Gus.

'You're very kind, really.' Nancy smiled at her neighbours.

'Not a bother,' Rita assured her. 'Sure isn't Jonathan the grand wee lad going to the shop for Gus here when he runs out of smokes. We can always depend on him,' Jonathan heard Mrs Higgins say. His stomach lurched.

'Any time you need a message just let us know,' Nancy said firmly. 'Isn't that right, Jonathan?'

'I'm just going over to say hello to my teacher.' Jonathan's voice was almost a squeak but he raised his gaze to Gus, hoping against hope that the man would understand the implied threat.

Gus's eyes narrowed but he pretended not to hear and turned to salute another acquaintance, while a friend from the quilters' group accosted Nancy.

Jonathan pushed his way through the Mass-goers to where his teacher, Mr Dowling, was surrounded by some of his pupils. Jonathan wanted Gus Higgins to see that he would follow through with his threat to tell his teacher if Jonathan was ever put through a torturous episode again.

'Hi, Mr Dowling,' he said, glancing over to see his neighbour casting surreptitious glances in their direction.

'Aahh, Jonathan,' said the young master kindly. 'How are you today?'

'Fine thanks. I just wanted to say hello.' Jonathan liked the new teacher who had recently taken over from Mrs Kelly who had gone to have a baby.

'Done your ekker yet?'

'Yes, on Friday,' Jonathan grinned, liking that the master called his home exercises ekker and not homework. Mr Dowling was a Dub and that's what the Dubs called homework.

'Excellent. Good man. The day is yours then. Enjoy it,' his teacher approved.

'Thanks, sir.' Jonathan felt strangely, uncharacteristically, light-hearted. If that dirty, disgusting thing ever happened to him again he *would* tell Mr Dowling. And if Gus Higgins did anything bad to his mammy he would tell him that too. Mr Dowling was kind and very knowledgeable. *He'd* know what to do. Jonathan saw his best friend Alice waving to him and hurried over to her.

'Let's have a picnic down at the river and plan our new secret club,' she said excitedly. 'I've a new Five Find-Outers book from the library, it's brilliant. *The Secret of the Spiteful Letters.*'

'And I've a Secret Seven,' he said happily. Today was turning into a very, very good day.

'Anthony Kavanagh and Darina Keogh want to join too. Will we let them? We could make badges and have a password and your shed could be our secret den,' Alice burbled. 'We could solve crimes, even a murder if we had to!'

'And practise our invisible writing,' Jonathan chipped in enthusiastically. 'And we could make lemonade and bring biscuits, for a feast.'

'I wish we could have ginger beer and anchovy paste.' Alice linked his arm. Enid Blyton's midnight feasts always sounded exotic and delicious to their mind.

'I wish we had a dairy to go to where we could have buns and cream cakes,' Jonathan said wistfully as his fears and anxiety receded and the prospect of an exciting afternoon beckoned.

For weeks after the encounter with Gus, Jonathan would feel sick to his stomach every time he walked past his house. Several times he saw Gus coming home from work, or at Mass. The man ignored him completely. Jonathan hardly dared to believe that the ordeal was over but as the months passed and the warm, bright days of summer ceded to autumn's glory, he began to relax and committed the memory of those horrendous episodes to the far reaches of his mind. He was happy at school, in Mr Dowling's class. Mr Dowling didn't allow any name-calling, fighting or bullying, and the next two years were the happiest of Jonathan's life, before he started secondary school and had to begin standing up for himself all over again.

The memories of his 'lost years', as Jonathan called them,

brought fresh tears to his eyes as he sat on the bean bag in his bay window and wept brokenly at the grief and bitterness that engulfed him. Many nights he had lain in bed imagining how, now, as an adult, he would confront Gus Higgins with his abuse and tell him that he was going to bring a court case against him. It gave him pleasure to conjure up the shock, fear and apprehension that Gus would feel when Jonathan told him he was reporting him to the guards. And when Gus would say as he surely would, 'You're a liar and no one will believe you,' Jonathan would play his trump card.

'I'll tell them about your birthmark!'

The satisfaction that much anticipated encounter would bring was a balm to his wounded spirit through the years. And now he was to be denied justice.

If only he'd had the guts to carry it through instead of putting it off. Now it was too late. The bastard had got away with it, and Jonathan was back in his private hell, the hell that no one knew about except Hannah Harrison his counsellor, and Kenny Dowling, his much admired teacher from primary school, whom he had met in the Front Lounge years later, and instantly recognized, and wondered how he had never copped that he was gay. They had spent a couple of hours drinking and catching up and Kenny was as nice a man as Jonathan had remembered as a child. Every so often they would bump into each other and have a chat. Kenny had a partner, Russell, an artist, and they often invited Jonathan back to their house, or for a meal out, or to go to a concert.

One night, when Russell had gone to bed, he and Kenny

were talking about an abuse case that had come to light with a mutual friend. 'Anything ever happen to you?' Kenny asked casually.

'Yeah,' Jonathan sighed, and then it all came out in a torrent of bitter bile that shook him to his core.

'That fat bastard. I remember him. A married man with kids and they say it's us gays who abuse kids,' Kenny swore, coming to sit beside Jonathan and putting an arm around his shoulder. 'I always felt you had a secret sadness. I could see it in your eyes. I should have made an effort to see what was wrong. I just had to be extra careful about boundaries, you know yourself. I'm sorry, Jonathan, I let you down.'

'No you didn't. You gave me peace and security in your class and soon after you started teaching us the abuse had come to an end. In fact I threatened the slimy toad that I would tell *you*, and after that he never did it to me again. So you did save me from it.' Jonathan gave a shaky laugh.

'Look, you have to go and see this wonderful woman, Hannah Harrison. She's a terrific counsellor. She practises just off the canal in Harold's Cross,' Kenny had said, getting a pen and paper to write down the details. 'Promise me you'll go to her – she'll work wonders for you. She's a holistic, metaphysical healer as well as a psychologist,' he urged. 'She's different, but brilliant, and I should know, I've been to a few.'

It had taken six months before Jonathan made the appointment. It was the best thing he had ever done for himself. Hannah, an elfin, brown-haired woman in her late forties, had a calm, reassuring presence. She had such beautiful eyes, blue with flecks of grey and violet around the iris, full of warmth and kindness. The kindest eyes he had ever seen, apart from his mother's. She had listened patiently as he poured out his story to her, interjecting a comment here and there and, when he had come to a faltering halt, she had made him a cup of tea.

'Today is the day you have made a fresh start,' she said firmly. 'Today is the day you go forward with your life and begin to clear and release the past. Today is the day you let go of the burden of guilt and secrecy. Today is the day that you say to yourself that no blame attaches to you in *any* way, shape or form for what that man did to you. Do you understand that? Today you go free.'

Free, Jonathan thought bitterly, remembering his counsellor's words; freedom was an illusion. Now here he was back to where he'd started, having to lie to his mother just as he'd lied as a child, so as to protect her from knowledge that would crucify her.

Nancy would think badly of him if he failed to show up for the removal service. In a small country town like Rosslara, neighbours looked out for neighbours and stood by them in their hour of need. That was a given. So did he put his mother's wishes first? Did he allow her to unwittingly reopen a wound he had long fought to heal? Or did he protect himself and stay away? That was his choice. Jonathan stared unseeingly through the shining windowpanes as his demons returned with a vengeance and the day that had promised so much faded away.

CHAPTER NINE

'Ooooohhhh!' Hilary groaned, squinting at the blinding disc of sun that assaulted her when she blinked open her eyes. The shrill jangle of the phone on her bedside locker jack-hammered through her head.

'Hello!' she croaked, her mouth dry.

'What's wrong with you?' Her husband's concerned tone jerked her awake.

'Oh! Niall! Hi. Nothing's wrong, just bit of a hangover,' she confessed.

'Ha, can't leave you for a day or two and you get rid of the kids and go on the ming!' he teased. 'Where did you go? Did you have a night with the girls?'

'No I didn't go anywhere. Actually I met a really nice guy on the course and brought him over to see the show-rooms, and then we came back here for a Chinese, and then Colette arrived out of the blue, so we opened another couple of bottles and now I'm paying for it,' she moaned.

'*Oh*! Should I be worried about you bringing strange men back to the house when I'm away? Is he still *there*?' Niall couldn't hide his surprise.

'No he's not!' Hilary suddenly realized how her description of the previous evening must have sounded to her exiled husband. 'Jonathan, that's his name, is a lovely chap but he'd fancy you more than he'd fancy me if you get my drift.'

'Oh right! That's a relief. I was beginning to wonder would I have to jump on the next Aeroflot to London and get myself home and tell him to put his dukes up and fight it out,' he said good-humouredly.

'Ha! I don't think it's ever going to come to that with any man. If you saw how I looked now even you would flee. How's Moscow?'

'Raining, chilly, crowded and getting dark. What's it like at home?'

'It looks like a gorgeous day out.' She yawned. 'The sun is shining right in on my face. You know the way our room gets the sun in the morning. Not good in my present condition.' She burrowed under the relative darkness of the duvet, with the handset.

'How's Colette?' Niall enquired.

'Herself,' Hilary said drily. 'She's probably annoyed that I didn't send Jonathan packing and devote the evening to her. You know what she's like.'

'Indeed I do. Go back to sleep for another hour and have a bacon sandwich when you get up and you'll be fine,' her husband said kindly.

'I love you.' She yawned again.

'I love you too. Give my love to the kids. I'll ring tomorrow. Same time. Bye.'

'Bye,' she said and heard the click as Niall hung up. She

put the handset back in the cradle and turned on her stomach and pulled a pillow over her head and promptly fell asleep.

The phone's jingle woke her again and a bleary glance at her clock told her that she had been asleep for more than an hour and a half. Her sister's cheery greeting brought her wide awake. 'Morning, Sis, hope you enjoyed your lie-in.'

'Hi, I did, it was great. I'll be over in the next hour or so,' she said hastily, not wanting Dee to think she was taking advantage of her.

'No need. I was ringing to ask if it would be OK for the kids to come to the pictures this afternoon and I'll drop them back this evening?'

'Are you sure?' Hilary couldn't believe her luck. What a treat to have a *whole* day to herself. Pity she was feeling so grim.

'I've no choice. There's great excitement – they were plotting it in bed last night. You know what they're like when they all get together. I promised them McDonald's as a treat afterwards because I'm a big softie, ha ha. So they'll be fed.'

Hilary laughed. 'You, a softie?' she teased. 'You're as hard as nails. Are you sure though? Do you want me to come over and go with you?'

'Don't be ridiculous. There's no point in both of us having to endure an under-twelves!' her sister retorted. 'Make the most of the few free hours. I'll get you back another time, don't worry. You sound as if I've just woken you up. Go back to sleep, you lucky wagon. See you later.'

Hilary smiled as she hung up. Only another mother could

truly understand how precious was a lie-in without children clamouring for attention.

Her stomach rumbled and she realized that she was feeling slightly better *and* peckish. Why was it that you were always hungry the next morning after eating Chinese? Hazy memories of the night before drifted back. Laughing at Jonathan's wit. Colette not even trying to hide her irritation when she saw him sitting outside. Weaving her way to the fridge to get more wine. She couldn't even remember going to bed. Had she even locked up, she wondered, flinging back the duvet, a frisson of anxiety penetrating her dehydrated fug. She vaguely remembered Jonathan saying goodbye but not Colette, she thought, brow furrowed, trying to remember as she went downstairs.

The alarm was on. The light was on in the porch. The lights were off everywhere else and the kitchen looked very tidy. That was Jonathan, she was sure. Colette didn't do cleaning up, she had people to do it for her, Hilary thought guiltily, wondering what must Jonathan think of her, drinking like a fish and getting pissed.

Her bag was slung under a kitchen stool and she bent down and groaned as she hauled it up. She rooted for her notebook and found Jonathan's number scrawled on the back of her notes. She should ring him and apologize, she thought, a tad mortified. She sat at the breakfast counter and dialled his number from the kitchen phone that hung on the wall. It rang for ages and she remembered vaguely that he had told her that it was a communal phone. He was probably out, she figured, about to hang up, when the phone was answered.

'Hello?' a muffled voice said.

'Hi, could I speak to Jonathan Harpur, please,' she said politely.

'It's me. I'm Jonathan.' He sounded strange.

'Oh. Oh hi, Jonathan. I didn't recognize your voice. It's me, Hilary. I just rang on the off-chance of finding you in, to say sorry that I got um . . . er . . . a bit tipsy last night. I'm not usually such a lush, in case I might have given you the wrong impression on our first date, so to speak,' she explained hastily.

'Oh! Hilary! That's fine. No problem,' Jonathan said, clearing his throat.

'Are you OK? Are you under the weather too? You sound a bit weird.'

'Umm. Yeah, I'm fine,' he sniffed, and she sensed that something was up.

'Sure you're OK?' she probed kindly, not wishing to be intrusive.

'Yeah . . . no . . . no! Hilary, something happened and I just don't know what to do.' He burst into tears, unable to continue.

'Hey, Jonathan. What's wrong? Will I come over? I've a couple of hours free that I wasn't expecting,' she offered.

'No, it's OK, I don't want to put you out.' She could hear him gulping.

'Do you want to come up to me, then? I could nip over to the shop and get us something for brunch? I haven't eaten yet.'

'Ah no, I really don't want to put you out,' he repeated, composing himself.

'Don't be daft. Get your skinny ass over here *pronto*!' she instructed and heard him give a small chuckle.

'Bossy, aren't you? Are you sure?'

'Certain!' she reiterated firmly.

'Thanks, Hilary. You're a pal, and I need one right now,' he said gratefully.

'A pongy pal,' she smiled. 'I have to go and have a quick shower. I reek of alcohol and I stink! See you in about twenty minutes. Can you remember how to get here?'

'Yeah, I remember. Thanks, I owe you,' he said and hung up.

Galvanized and wondering what on earth was the matter with her new friend, Hilary opened the fridge, took a long slug of orange juice straight from the carton and hurried upstairs to shower. The hot water sluicing down over her shoulders felt good and she lathered soap over herself and began to feel much more human. She dried herself swiftly, pulled on a pair of jeans and a T-shirt, towelled her hair dry and ran her fingers through it to shape it and applied a sliver of lipstick before grabbing her purse and house keys.

Her stomach was growling as she walked briskly down the tree-lined street and around the small green, surrounded by neat cottages, to make her way to the shops. The supermarket was busy and she threw croissants and baby tomatoes, mushrooms, bacon bits and grated cheese into her basket, chose two coffee slices and two cream doughnuts from a selection of luscious-looking cream buns, grabbed a newspaper from the stand and stood in the queue thinking how lucky she was to be so near to shops, pharmacies and a DART station.

She and Niall had bought their cottage when house prices were low, just before they got married, and had extended and renovated it over the years. Now, in this first year of the nineties, house prices were rising and houses in their area were much sought after. It might not be a posh pad near Kensington, she reflected, placing her groceries on the belt, but it had been a good buy and it suited them down to the ground, despite Colette's pronouncements that Hilary and Niall should 'relocate and upsize to somewhere – 'a little more upmarket – like Howth, Sutton or the seafront'.

Hilary liked where they lived. There was a good mix of young families, single professionals and older people who had lived in the area all their lives. She particularly loved the fact that because there were so many cottages they weren't overlooked. And, unlike Colette and Des, they at least had their own garden, and a big, well-laid-out *private* back garden at that, Hilary reflected, stuffing her purchases into plastic bags and handing the cashier a twenty. Colette and Des had no front garden to speak of and shared a very overlooked communal garden at the rear of the Holland Park mansion. Hilary loved her privacy and wouldn't swap with Colette for anything, and had no intention of going more 'upmarket', thank you very much, she reflected, thinking how even more snobby her friend had become over the years.

The sun was warm on her face, dappling through the bursting, blossoming emerald foliage of the trees, and children played on the green, laughing and squealing as they raced around in the fresh air.

She glanced down the street when she got to her own small cul-de-sac and saw no sign of a car parked behind hers in the drive. She'd have time to set the table outside and start their brunch before Jonathan arrived.

She unpacked the shopping and made herself a cup of tea to keep her going, wondering what on earth was wrong with him. He was clearly very upset by something. At least he felt he could come and talk to her, even this early in their friendship. She stood at the cooker, inhaling the mouthwatering aromas as she fried off the bacon bits and mushrooms and filled the croissants with them, before adding the sliced baby tomatoes and cheese and wrapping them in tin foil. She slid them into the preheated oven. They wouldn't take long to cook.

Was it boyfriend trouble? Or was it because of his homophobic boss? Jonathan had told Hilary of his encounter with his horrible manager and how upsetting it had been. It must be so difficult being gay and suffering snide comments and abuse from intolerant, unkind, uncharitable people, in every strata of society. She'd never given the topic much thought but if any of her children or her nieces or nephews were gay and were treated badly when they were older she'd be horrified. Life was hard enough without being judged because of sexual orientation, which was a personal matter as far as Hilary was concerned. Love was precious and if you loved someone and they loved you back how lucky were you in a world that was often hard to live in.

Hilary brewed a pot of fresh coffee, enjoying the welcoming smells wafting around the kitchen, and was setting place mats and cutlery on the patio table when the doorbell rang.

Jonathan, pale and miserable, stood on the step, shoulders drooping, eyes red-rimmed. A far different Jonathan from the funny, vibrant, eager and enthusiastic young man of the day before. Her heart went out to him and it was the most natural thing in the world for her to open her arms and give him a comforting hug. 'What's the matter?' she asked, leading the way into the kitchen.

'Oh Hilary, my life is a mess.' He shook his head. 'Something happened to me when I was a child. I thought I had managed to put it behind me but something's come up and I feel I'm right back where I started,' he added shakily.

'Ah no!' She rubbed his back as he slumped onto a kitchen stool, her heart sinking. 'Abuse?' she asked hesitantly.

'Yeah.' His lip wobbled.

'Oh Jonathan, I'm so sorry! I don't know what to say,' she said helplessly. 'Can you talk about it? Can you tell me what's happened to upset you?'

'I don't want to offload on you, Hilary. God, we've only just met and here I am bawling in your kitchen.' He gave her a wobbly smile, tears brimming in his eyes.

'That's what friends are for! And we're friends,' she said firmly, deciding to abandon her plan to eat outside. 'Let me pour you a coffee. I have a few cheese, bacon and mushroom croissants in the oven, if you're able to eat.'

'I felt a bit sick earlier, but the smell is very enticing,' he said, wiping his eyes with the back of his hand and perking up a little bit in the warmth of her cherishing.

'Sit there, and I'll dish them up. I'm starving,' she confessed. 'I felt very ropy this morning and haven't had anything yet, and the reason I rang you was to apologize for acting like an out-and-out dipso. I haven't drunk that much in yonks.'

'Would you stop! I wasn't that far behind you, you've nothing to apologize for. I hope it's the first of many a night on the tear for us,' he said with some of his old spark as she handed him a mug of coffee.

She laughed. 'My nights on the tear will be few and far between, unfortunately. I have a husband and children to factor in.'

'Minor detail,' he said airily and she was glad to see a bit of colour coming back into his cheeks. She served up their brunch and sat beside him at the counter. 'This is lovely,' he said, forking melted cheese and some bacon and mushroom into his mouth.

'My children love it.' She savoured the flaky croissant, feeling ravenous.

'I'd say you're a great mother.' He took a gulp of coffee.

'Oh I don't know so much – you should hear me screeching at them in the mornings to get down for their breakfast.'

'My mother had a wonderful roar,' he smiled. '"Jon-aaAAATHANNN!" It would wake the dead.'

'You've very close to her, aren't you?' His conversation the previous day had been peppered with mentions of Nancy.

'Yeah,' he sighed, putting down his fork. 'And that's part of my problem.'

'Tell me,' she invited.

And he did, the whole tragic, sad, appalling saga, right up to where his mother had phoned him and told him she expected him to be at the removal. It emptied out of him in halting, angry, grief-stricken bursts.

'You can't go! You just can't go,' Hilary said emphatically, tears trickling down her face. She was devastated for her friend.

He reached over and squeezed her hand. 'No one's ever cried for me before,' he said.

'Haven't you told *anyone*? Your sisters even?' she asked, wiping her eyes with some kitchen towel.

'No, I never told them. I couldn't bring myself to, or my mam, they'd be gutted.'

'If something like that happened to one of my children, I'd *want* to know,' she said fiercely.

'Don't forget my father was dead and Mam was working her fingers to the bone to make ends meet for us and give us a good upbringing,' he reminded her. 'I couldn't bring myself to tell her. I didn't *know* how to tell her. I was afraid she might not believe me. And besides I was petrified of what he might do if I told her. He always threatened me that he would make life hard for her if I said anything. That used to scare the living daylights out of me.'

'But when you grew up and when her life became easier, would you not have said it to her? It would have been healing for you not having to carry the burden of secrecy,' Hilary persisted.

'My counsellor points that out too, when she tells me it's my choice and I should do what's right for me, but can you imagine how tormented Mam would be? Her life would be in upheaval. She'd never have a moment's peace of mind again. And, she would have still had him living beside her until now.' He shook his head. 'Hilary, I just couldn't do it to her, even though I was tempted to tell her many times and I know that she would never hold it against me. I know she would chastise me for keeping it from her for so long. But why would I allow that bastard to destroy two lives? Because her life *would* be destroyed. She'd be tortured with guilt . . . wouldn't you?' He eyed her glumly.

'Yes! I'd never forgive myself for allowing it to happen—'

'No! No, Hilary, you can't say that. You wouldn't "allow" it. Mam didn't "allow" it to happen. It was him and his cunning, and his deviousness. He was such a calculating bastard. All paedophiles and sexual abusers are. And I was good at hiding stuff, too. A lot of abused children are. They feel it's their fault and they don't want to upset their parents. So I attach *no* blame to my mam in any way,' he said emphatically.

'I know you don't, Jonathan, I'm just reacting as a mother. I'd want to know,' she pointed out.

'And I'm just reacting as a son who loves his mother very much,' he said gently. 'She's almost seventy now. She deserves a peaceful old age and I want her to have a tranquil, untroubled life. She's sure as hell earned it.' He sat up straight. 'And you know something? She's going to have it. Thanks for letting me talk this through with you, Hilary. I was angry with her when she phoned me expecting me to go home tomorrow. But I bloody well will go. It will be good to see that coffin. Damn good. I hope the fucker died screaming!'

'Are you sure you'll be OK to go? It might all be too much for you when you get there,' Hilary said dubiously.

'No. I won't let it overwhelm me. I will *not* be that bastard's victim any longer. He's had enough of my energy. I *choose* to go. I choose *not* be a victim.' He looked at Hilary and threw his eyes up to heaven and smiled sheepishly. 'God, I sound like a self-help book!'

'No! You sound like a very brave man who is taking control of his own life. You should be proud of yourself, Jonathan. Your mother couldn't have a kinder, more loving son.'

'Isn't it amazing?' We've only known each other two days and I feel as if I've known you forever.' He smiled at her.

'I know.' Hilary laughed. 'I was telling Niall about meeting you on the course yesterday and about you coming back here last night and he was wondering should he fly home and duke it out with you, until I reassured him and said there was more chance of you fancying him than me.'

'And what did he say?' Jonathan asked warily.

'Ahh that was grand. He was relieved I hadn't fallen for someone,' she joked. 'Niall takes people as he finds them. You'll like him and he'll like you,' Hilary assured him, refilling his mug of coffee. 'Oh and I have something for you,' she exclaimed. 'I'll be back in a sec.' She went into what was once the small kitchen in the original cottage but which now housed two desks and two computers, hers and Niall's. She rooted in her desk drawer and located two lighting catalogues.

'Here you go,' she said, brandishing them in front of Jonathan. 'I thought these might give you some ideas for your latest project.'

'Brilliant!' he exclaimed, flicking through them eagerly.

'Ohhhh I love these,' he said, pointing to a waterfall pendant light. 'And those sconces would be *perfect* for what I'm doing now!' Hilary watched as he poured over the catalogues and was so relieved that the grey look had gone from his face and some colour had come back. He had looked so miserable and forlorn when he'd arrived; she'd been worried about him.

'Hil, you're a dote!' He jumped off the stool and enveloped her in a hug. 'First for letting me come over and unload on you, and second for this. I was supposed to be going into town to have a look at furniture and fittings but after getting Mam's call I just fell to pieces and couldn't hack it. But hell, I'm going to go to town and my client's rooms are going to get the best damn makeover any designer ever came up with. Thanks so much for these. And thanks for reminding me that there's much more to my life than what Gus Higgins did to me all those years ago.' He hugged her again, tightly, and she returned the hug with equal warmth.

'Why don't I go with you?' she suggested on the spur of the moment. 'The kids won't be home until this evening. I'm a free woman! To hell with housework, and the massive pile of ironing I was going to do. You can give me some pointers on the design side of things. I need to up my game a bit.'

'Are you sure?' Jonathan's eyes lit up.

'Yep, when do I ever get the chance to go to town, child-free, on a Saturday?' she grinned. 'Just let me get my bag.'

'The Mary Poppins one?'

'No, smarty, I have a smaller one with only two side pockets,' she retorted as he began to clear their dishes. 'Put them in the sink. I have to empty the dishwasher – I'll do it later. Let's go,' she instructed gaily.

Hilary loved the idea of expanding her interests to include interior design projects and she knew, from their conversations the previous day, that Jonathan would be able to teach her a lot. And it would be fun!

Hilary felt privileged that Jonathan had trusted her, and felt comfortable enough with her, to divulge his appalling secret. She knew without the shadow of a doubt that, if she ever needed him, his would be a shoulder she could cry on. Different indeed from the friendship she shared with Colette, who hadn't even had the manners to phone and thank her for supper, or apologize for arriving without a by your leave and imposing on her evening with Jonathan, Hilary thought acidly. Intuitively she knew that she would get far more support from her friendship with Jonathan than she ever would from her friendship with Colette, as old as it was.

She remembered a quote of Aristotle's that she had written in her notebook of quotes, a notebook she had kept since her schooldays. *Friendship is a single soul dwelling in two bodies.* That would be her and Jonathan, Hilary reflected, transferring her keys and wallet into her smaller bag while he rinsed the dishes under the tap. A friendship had been born between them and she was very grateful for that gift. She would value it and so would he. Colette took Hilary's friendship for granted and didn't value it at all, and she was getting a bit fed up with it. One of these days, Colette might find out that Hilary was no longer available to be at her beck and call when it suited her. Hilary had new fish to fry and fry them she would, she thought in amusement, spraying some perfume on her wrists and slicking some lipstick across her lips, looking forward to her unexpected jaunt to town with Jonathan.

CHAPTER TEN

Jonathan pushed away his half-eaten breakfast and gave a deep sigh. All around him the hum of chat and laughter, the clatter of cutlery against china and the smell of Bewley's coffee could not give him the feel-good experience Sunday morning breakfast in Omni always did. Orla lifted her head from the *Sunday Tribune*. 'You OK, hon?'

'Yeah I'm fine,' he fibbed. 'Didn't sleep great last night.'

'You're not finishing your brekkie?' she asked, fork poised.

He laughed and shook his head. 'I'm leaving room for a Mammy Dinner! She's cooking a roast for me so she can "feed me up", so she said, so help yourself.'

Orla speared a sausage and hash brown. 'I *love* hash browns!' she raved, eating with relish. Do you want another cup of coffee?'

'No thanks. I think I'll head, if that's OK with you. I want to get on the road.' Jonathan tried to keep his tone light. His stomach was knotted, he felt faintly queasy.

'No prob,' his friend said distractedly. Orla's topknot had just come askew and she was tucking her long auburn hair back into the tortoiseshell comb that kept it in place. She didn't realize just how agitated he really was, he thought. He had never told her about his past. He hadn't told any of his friends about his childhood secret. He just wanted to be normal with them and not have them feel sorry for him. Dublin was his future, he'd reasoned. He never wanted to look back.

But sometimes, in spite of your best intentions, you had to, he thought morosely, folding up his paper neatly and taking a last slug of coffee. 'Are you going to stay the night at home and come back early in the morning or will you drive back tonight?' Hair sorted, Orla tucked into the cream cake she had treated herself to.

'I'm going to come back tonight. It's bad enough having to get up on Monday mornings to go to work without having to get up at the crack of dawn and drive for an hour and a half from Rosslara to Dublin, in bumper-to-bumper traffic.' Jonathan grimaced. He stood up and leaned over and kissed her. 'Be good!'

'Don't be a spoilsport,' Orla grinned. 'I'll be as bad as I get the chance to be. Ciao, baby, drive carefully.'

'I will,' he assured her before making his way in between the tables in the crowded restaurant to the exit. Eating breakfast in a café had become the new fad in Dublin, a sure sign that the grinding recession that had banjaxed the country in the last decade was over, he reflected. It was all so ... nineties ... so cosmopolitan. It was far from hash browns he'd been reared, but now a fry-up wasn't considered a fry-up without them.

Sunday was the only day they had had a cooked breakfast when he was growing up. It was such a treat to come home from Mass, dressed in his Sunday best, and have his mother put the rashers and sausages on the pan and to listen to them sizzling and spitting while she fried bread on another pan. How they would all tuck into this once-a-week treat with gusto, and then, because it was Sunday, have a chocolate gold-grain biscuit afterwards, to dunk into the second cup of tea. Now every day was a fry-up day, it seemed.

The weather had changed, and it was spitting rain as he hurried through the car park wishing he could just go home and flop and not have to face the ordeal ahead. He was committed to attending the removal now, he thought ruefully, having phoned his mother the previous evening to assure her that he would be coming and would give her a lift to the church, much to her delight.

He was veering from being bullish and determined to apprehensive and subdued. He had tossed and turned all night, his thoughts whirling, trying to keep his anger at bay and his disgust with himself that he had never confronted his abuser.

Higgins would look him in the eye as brazen as you like and greet him as though nothing had ever happened in the past. 'You're looking well, laddie, the big smoke is suiting ya, isn't it, Nancy?' he'd said the last time Jonathan had been home, and he and Nancy were walking up their garden path and Higgins had been coming down his, clomping along breathlessly, leaning on his cane. Jonathan, as usual, had been furious at his nerve but because his mother was with him he had forced himself to say hello.

'Wimp!' he'd chastised himself privately, wondering if Nancy hadn't been with him would he have confronted Gus

Higgins or told him to fuck off. Now it was too late. His pervert neighbour was going to his grave and Jonathan would never have the satisfaction of seeing fear in his eyes, or apprehension, at the anticipated knock on the door from the guards. His chance was gone because he hadn't had the guts to deal with the perpetrator of his abuse, Jonathan castigated himself, *loathing* himself for his failings.

Right now he felt very sick and fluttery in his stomach. He got into the car just as the drizzle turned into a sudden downpour. He and Orla had driven to Omni in their own cars so that he could head off after their breakfast. He was sitting at the traffic lights at McDonald's when a thought struck him and he cursed loudly. The bloody curtain material – he'd forgotten to bring it. His mother had assured him she had cleared the decks and was all ready to commence making them. What an idiot he was; now he'd have to drive back to Drumcondra. 'Prat!' he cursed himself, heading right towards town instead of left as he'd intended. The traffic was heavy even though it was Sunday as he sat opposite the Skylon, idling in neutral, and he realized irritably as he saw people streaming along the wet footpaths, decked in their county's colours, and cars with flags fluttering out of their windows that there was a match on in Croke Park and he was going nowhere fast. By the time he got to the bedsit he was fit to be tied.

A note was stuck under his door. *Kenny rang and asked for you to call him back. Tom.*

He hadn't made plans with Kenny and Russell and forgotten about them, had he? Jonathan thought, frazzled, rooting in the jam-jar he kept coins in for the phone.

'Hey, dude, were you looking for me?' He pretended to be bright and chirpy when Kenny answered the phone.

'Hi, Jonathan. Yes! Um ... I was just wondering did you hear about Higgins? Did your mum call you?' Kenny asked kindly.

'Yeah, she did.' Jonathan sighed heavily. 'I'm just on my way home. I had to come back here because I forgot the friggin' curtain material she's expecting. How did you know?' He was surprised that his former schoolteacher would have heard about his abuser's death. Kenny had taught the Higgins girls a long time ago.

'Sylvia O'Connell is coming up to Dublin during the week and we always meet up when she's in the city and she said she was going to a funeral on Monday and I asked was it anyone I knew and she said it was Higgins. She knows his wife from playing bridge.'

'Oh, right!' Mrs O'Connell had taught him in third class. She and Kenny had been young teachers together and they had got on well. She had eventually become the headmistress of the primary school and Kenny still kept in touch with her.

'I just wanted to make sure you're OK. Did you say you're going home?' Kenny asked.

'I told Mam I'd bring her to the removal. She expects us to be at it. You know what it's like, us being next-door neighbours and all.'

'Jonathan, could you not make some excuse? That's going to be hard on you. It's OK to put yourself first in a situation like this.' His friend sounded perturbed.

'I *did* make an excuse, but you know, Kenny, I'm not

running away from it, him, or myself any more. I'm Jonathan Harpur. Not a victim! Not a gay! I'm me, a human being, and people can like me or lump me. And his power over me has ended. I'm not letting it continue now that he's dead,' Jonathan explained agitatedly.

'Well said, buddy, well said,' Kenny approved. 'Stay where you are and I'll be over in half an hour. I'm going with you.'

'No! No! No!' Jonathan protested. 'I'll be fine. I'm not putting you out and dragging you down the country on a Sunday.'

'Harpur, do as you're told,' Kenny said in his best teacher's voice. Jonathan laughed in spite of himself.

'You're OK, Kenny, I really appreciate your offer—'

'Half an hour, Harpur! Have your shoes polished and your hair brushed.' The phone went dead.

Jonathan shook his head and smiled. How lucky was he to have friends like Kenny and Hilary? Hilary had offered to get a babysitter for a couple of hours and come with him but he wouldn't hear of it. He knew too that if Orla had known about his history she would have offered to come with him too.

He put the kettle on to make himself a quick cup of coffee before Kenny arrived, glad that he wouldn't have to face the ordeal alone. To have someone at his side who knew what had happened to him and who understood his torment was a blessing Jonathan was very grateful for. He felt his spirit revive and his courage flow back. With a good friend beside him he could face what was to come and close that horrible chapter of his life once and for all.

Chapter Eleven

Half an hour later almost to the minute he said he'd be there the loud beep of Kenny's Peugeot announced his arrival. Jonathan saw with surprise that Russell was with him.

'In case you have to be dragged off the coffin shouting obscenities,' Kenny's partner said irrepressibly when Jonathan opened the car door and carefully laid the curtain material, which he had wrapped in drifts of tissue paper, in the back.

'You and whose army?' he retorted. 'It would be the talk of the town, wouldn't it? Pity I'll have to behave myself. Lads, you're very kind. Are you sure about coming?'

'*Think where man's glory most begins and ends, and say my glory was I had such friends.* Who said that, Harpur?' His ex-teacher glanced over his shoulder and raised an eyebrow.

'Eh ... Kavanagh ... no ... Yeats.'

'Well done. Enough said. Get in the car, shut the door and sit back and relax,' the older man instructed.

'I never remember you being this bossy when you were teaching me,' Jonathan remarked, stretching himself out across the seat and clipping on his seat belt.

'Tell me about it,' groaned Russell. 'I live with it every day.'

'You love being bossed about,' Kenny retorted and they smiled at each other. Jonathan, listening to their teasing banter, wondered if he would ever be lucky enough to have a partner of his own. One that he could be so at ease with. Someone who would know him inside out and accept him, warts and all, and vice versa. What a comfort and joy it must be to have someone to share your life with. So far he hadn't met anyone he could have that deep connection with, but he lived in hope. He was ever the optimist, he thought with a wry smile.

'Son, you should have told me you were bringing friends!' Nancy exclaimed when the three of them walked into the kitchen through the back door. She had been scraping carrots and was caught by surprise.

'He didn't know, Mrs Harpur. It was a spur of the moment decision. I'm Kenny Dowling, his old—'

'Mr Dowling! You're welcome. I remember you well. You were very good to my boy when he was at school.' Nancy wiped her hands on her apron and greeted him warmly.

'And this is Russell McDowd, my—'

'I'm a friend of Kenny and Jonathan's. Lovely to meet you, Mrs Harpur,' Russell interjected kindly, not sure if Jonathan's mother was ready to hear the term 'partner' in relation to another man.

'Delighted to meet you, Russell. I'm ever so pleased Jonathan is making good friends in Dublin. Now just let me do a few more spuds for a bit of mash and there'll be *plenty* for the dinner. Jonathan, put the kettle on and make your friends a pot of tea.' Nancy bustled around putting mugs on the table before taking a bag of potatoes out of her small pantry.

'Please don't go to any trouble, Mrs Harpur,' implored Kenny. 'Couldn't we go out for a meal and save you the bother?'

Jonathan laughed as he filled the kettle. 'Kenny, you're getting a Mammy Dinner. There'll be no going out for a meal. You might as well save your breath to cool your porridge.'

'But we arrived unexpectedly, we can't impose—'

'Whist now like a good lad. It won't take me a minute to peel these,' Nancy said firmly, ignoring his protests. Russell couldn't hide his amusement. It had been a long time since Master Kenny Dowling had been told to whist.

The rain battered furiously against the kitchen window and a faint growl of thunder grew into a roar as it raged across the sky. The smell of the roast, and the mushy peas that simmered in the small pot on the cooker filled the homely kitchen as the three friends sat around the table drinking tea and chatting easily with Jonathan's mother. When the food was ready, Nancy carved the pork while Jonathan lashed yellow globs of butter onto the carrots and the boiled potatoes, mashing the spuds into a fluffy white cloud, with a good portion of cream for added texture and flavour. He slid the crispy golden roast potatoes out of the oven, while Nancy plated up the inviting dinner. She smiled, gratified, as the three men devoured it.

'That was *scrumptious*, Mrs Harpur. You can't beat a Mammy Dinner, as Jonathan calls it,' Russell complimented her, scraping the last bit of mushy peas, mash and gravy from the plate.

'You need to cook proper dinners. It's all very well going

to these fancy restaurants and bistros and having your pâtés and your bruschettas and risottos and the like, but meat, veg and potatoes is good for you,' Nancy declared, placing a large serving of home-made apple tart and cream in front of him. 'Eat that up now. It was very kind of you to come and save me from myself, I'm a divil for apple pie.'

'Me *too*!' Kenny enthused, spooning a mouthful of feather-light pastry into his mouth. 'Jonathan, we'll be coming to visit more often.' He grinned across the table at his friend.

'You come whenever you want. Jonathan's pals are always welcome. Now I'm going up to get ready. I want to be at the church before the hearse arrives. We'll meet the girls there; they were in Galway for the weekend. I hope they'll be back in time. Put the dishes in the dishwasher, son, before we go, so we can come back to a tidy kitchen,' Nancy instructed, hurrying out of the room.

'Yes, Mother,' Jonathan saluted.

'She's a sweetheart, Jonathan. She idolizes you.' Kenny cleared the table.

'I know. She's the best. And I'm glad I never told her what happened. She's contented with her life now and I want it to stay like that.'

'For what it's worth, I think you're right,' Russell said quietly. 'Although I think she would be very supportive of you. More than mine was,' he added with a hint of bitterness.

'Oh! What happened, or do you prefer not to talk about it?' Jonathan ventured, placing the saucepans into the dishwasher.

'I told my mother one of the Christian Brothers was making me touch him on his privates and I got a hard clip around the ear and was told not to tell filthy lies about a holy man. She never forgave me for it either and often asked me had I told the priest in confession that I'd been telling lies.'

'That's terrible,' Jonathan said sombrely.

'She couldn't believe that a "man of God" would do such things. The Church is sacrosanct in her eyes. All this talk of abuse is the work of the devil to bring down the Church, that's what she told me a while back. There's no point in going there. She believes what she wants to believe and she certainly doesn't believe me.' Russell's face darkened.

'Do you go to counselling?'

'Indeed I do. What would we all do without Hannah?'

'Aw she's amazing. She makes you feel so good about yourself. She's at a conference in Birmingham this weekend but I've booked an appointment next week.' Jonathan wiped down the countertop vigorously wishing he could wipe away his past as easily.

'Well, the only thing that gives me any satisfaction is that I frightened the shite out of the old cockroach before he died. I met him on the street and of course he didn't recognize me, but I told him who I was and he *still* didn't remember me. Can you believe that?' Russell grimaced. 'I was of no conse-quence to him at all. The fact that he ruined my childhood was not a consideration in this "man of God's" life. I could have clocked him. I nearly did actually. Anyway I told him I was reporting his abuse to the guards and I told him he'd want to watch over his shoulder wherever he went out because one day myself and some of the other lads he abused were going to get him and bring him somewhere quiet and beat the living daylights out of him. He wasn't so brave and omnipotent then, I can tell you. He nearly scuttered himself and couldn't get away quick enough. Died of a stroke two months later.'

'Nice one, mate!' Jonathan approved. 'I'd always *planned* to confront Higgins. I used to imagine all the things I'd say to him. I used to imagine how terrified he'd be of going to prison but I could never bring myself to do it. I kept putting it off and now he's gone and kicked the bucket, the dirty louser.'

'Forget about him, he has to meet his maker. And after what he's done, rather him than you or me,' Russell advised, patting him on the back affectionately.

You have to meet your maker! The words went round and round in Jonathan's head as he stood outside in the rain holding an umbrella over his mother while they watched Gus Higgins's coffin being wheeled from the hearse to the door of the church to be welcomed by the priest.

He thought he would feel more emotion but mostly what he felt was numbness throughout the short service. It surprised him, especially after the grief and rage he had felt in the previous twenty-four hours since hearing the news of his neighbour's demise. Perhaps it had been good to go through those emotions then instead of having them surging through him in public and having to try and stay composed, he mused as the soloist sang 'Nearer My God To Thee'. At the end of the service a sudden unexpected emotion churned his gut and he felt queasy again. He knew he was going to have to walk past the coffin of his hated abuser. He had a fierce longing to give the coffin a good kick. That would cause a fair bit of scandal around the place, he reflected with dark humour, imagining what the neighbours would say if he gave in to his urges.

He followed his mother and sisters up the aisle to pay his respects to Rita and her daughters and never glanced at the coffin, keeping his eyes firmly focused on the arrangement of roses and lilac on the altar. He even managed a sympathetic smile when Rita thanked him for coming. Jonathan had often wondered if Gus's wife had any idea what her husband got up to in her absence, but she had always been open and friendly with Jonathan whenever she saw him and he didn't think she could have been that good an actress. She seemed genuinely grieved at the loss of her husband, which vaguely astonished him as Gus was a loud, lazy, dictatorial couch potato and he couldn't for the life of him see why anyone would miss him and grieve for him.

He felt a huge sense of relief when he finished shaking the bereaved family's hands and reached the end of the pew. He followed Nancy down the aisle towards the door of the church, and freedom.

'We're going to head back to Dublin now, Mam,' Jonathan said when they emerged out into the daylight. The rain had stopped and the evening sun was flirting with the clouds.

'Ah could you not come back for a quick cuppa with the girls?' Nancy urged.

'I could get a cup of tea,' Kenny said easily. 'A quick one, Jonathan, for the road.'

'Sounds good to me,' Russell agreed.

'Right, I'll go with Rachel and I'll have the kettle boiled in no time and I have a fresh cream sponge to go with it,' Nancy said happily, tucking her hand into her eldest daughter's arm.

'Home-made cream sponge, I'm in heaven.' Russell rubbed his hands together and Jonathan began to relax now that the stress of the dreaded ordeal was over. He was glad he'd gone to the removal, he thought as he sat in the kitchen drinking tea with his family and friends. The girls were laughing at Russell's camp humour and he didn't feel he had to make an effort to make conversation.

He had triumphed over his fears and apprehensions and faced up to his past and it hadn't been as hard as he'd thought it would be, thanks to the support of his companions. And he hadn't let his mother down. *That* gave him great satisfaction. Nancy was the best mother anyone could wish for. She had made his friends so welcome and had served up a feast at no notice at all. He was fiercely glad she had no knowledge of what had happened to him, he thought gratefully, watching her chuckling at Rachel's good-natured teasing. He had *chosen* never to tell her. For him it was a good choice, he knew. Hannah was right: knowing you had choices in the decisions you made was very empowering.

'You're a great lad, Jonathan, thanks for coming and it was lovely to meet Kenny again and Russell is a grand chap.' Nancy hugged him tightly when they made their move to go. 'Don't be strangers now, you and Russell,' she said to Kenny, following them to the garden gate. 'And if you could find a nice fella for Jonathan, so that he could be as happy as you and Russell are, I'd go to my grave contented,' she added matter-of-factly to Kenny.

'Leave it to us, Mrs Harpur,' Russell assured her while Jonathan stared at his mother, gobsmacked.

'Go and find yourself someone like Russell or Kenny here,

Jonathan. We all need love in our lives,' his mother advised, leaning on the gate. 'Safe journey now.' Nancy waved at them as Kenny started the engine. She blew them a kiss and Jonathan rolled down the window and waved back at her until they turned left at the top of the road and she was out of sight.

'And there was me afraid to let you introduce me as your partner, Kenny,' Russell chuckled.

'Pick your jaw off the ground, Jonathan. Mothers *always* know and always want you to know that they know! She wants you to be happy, so go on ... be happy.' Kenny laughed over his shoulder at Jonathan's stunned expression.

Jonathan stared out at the tree-lined, winding country roads he had travelled as a child and knew that this chapter of his life was over. It was time to move on and let the past go. He had a lot to look forward to. And his mother would welcome his partner if he was ever lucky enough to find one. Where he had thought there might be hurdles, there were none, he thought ruefully when the car picked up speed, leaving Rosslara behind them.

He had to do it. Jonathan knew if he didn't he'd feel he'd let himself down for the rest of his life. It was bad enough that he felt he'd wimped out with Gus Higgins; he couldn't let the feeling of being a coward eat away at him a second time in his life.

'If I faint drag me out,' he murmured to his friend and colleague, Mary Helen.

'Why, what are you going to do?' she asked, perplexed, as he pushed back his chair and stood up.

'Watch!' he grimaced. They were in the staff canteen and the sun, shining through the big old-fashioned sash windows, added to the buzz of chat and conviviality of the mid-morning tea break. Jonathan took a deep breath and walked over to the adjoining table where Gerard was holding forth. 'Mr Hook, I'd like a word.' His voice was admirably steady. He had thought he would be quaking but a strange calm seemed to have enveloped him.

'I'm on my tea break. It can wait until we're back at work,' his boss said rudely, casting a wary glance at him.

'Actually, Mr Hook, it won't,' Jonathan said firmly, raising his voice an octave as a hush descended on the people at the two tables. 'Last Thursday when I was on my tea break you spoke to me in very derogatory terms. I told you that if it happened again I would report you to Personnel. Having given the matter, *and* your vile remarks, some consideration over the weekend, I would now like you to apologize to me here, in the canteen, where you originally made those remarks in the presence of my colleagues and others.' He stared at the man in front of him, willing himself to remain composed.

'Now, now, now, there's no need for that kind of thing. If your feelings were hurt it wasn't meant,' bristled Gerard as an audible gasp came from Jonathan's workmates.

'I beg to differ. You *did* mean what you said and you *did* mean to belittle me. Your apology, please, or I will go to Personnel *and* the union!' Jonathan said icily, enjoying the other man's discomfort.

Gerard blanched. He wanted no truck with the union. 'Very well then,' he muttered, almost inaudible. 'Sorry.'

'I don't think my colleagues heard that,' Jonathan said coldly.

'Sorry,' Gerard barked angrily.

'Apology accepted,' Jonathan retorted and turned on his heel to walk back to his table. Mary Helen was grinning from ear to ear. Aidan Corrigan gave him the thumbs-up and began to clap. His other colleagues followed suit as, beet red, he sat back down beside them.

'Well done. I'm proud of ya, Harps.' Mary Helen patted him on the back.

'Good on you, Jon,' said Aidan.

'Very well said,' applauded Laura.

'That will teach him.' Maria held her mug up in toast.

'He's puce,' giggled Rebecca.

'Good enough for him,' snapped Tara.

'Way to go, mate.' Matthew gave him a high-five.

Jonathan basked in the glow of their praise. He might not have settled his score with Gus Higgins *mano a mano* but he'd got a public apology from Gerard Hook. He'd faced down another bully. Whatever his boss might think, Jonathan was more of a man than he'd *ever* be.

Today was a good day. He'd ring Hilary and tell her what he'd done. She'd be pleased for him. And so would Orla. His next session with Hannah would be interesting too. His counsellor made him think outside the box, that was for sure, he thought ruefully, remembering how Hannah had responded when he'd said that he didn't think much of a God who would allow such terrible things to happen to his so-called children.

'God, the Universe, Our Source, or whatever you choose

to call the loving energy that created us, has given us the freedom of choice to make our own decisions about how we live our lives. We cannot blame "God" for man's inhumanity to man. But the immutable laws of the Universe are very clear – and this has nothing to do with religion – every deed or thought we put out comes back to us. Good or bad. Everything is perfectly balanced. As Edwin Markham's classic quote says, *There is a destiny that makes us brothers; no one goes his way alone. All that we send into the lives of others comes back into our own.'*

'Do unto others what you would have them do unto you,' Jonathan said gloomily, remembering the biblical quote from his catechism.

'That's another way of putting it,' Hannah said crisply.

'Jonathan, did you ever ask yourself why you are here? What is your purpose? Did you ever think that you chose to incarnate with your parents and your family, for example? A specific soul group that you are part of since the beginning of time? Did you ever think that perhaps it's not what happens to you that's important, but the way you *deal* with it? This abuse has happened to you but you can choose how you let it affect your life. You can choose victimhood or victory. That choice is yours!' she'd said in her gentle, matter-of-fact way.

Jonathan knew the choice he wanted to make. His life was changing for the better and so was he.

CHAPTER TWELVE

Des Williams punched the air exuberantly before replacing the phone on the cradle. 'Yes! Yes! Yes!' he trumpeted, barging into the hotel bathroom where Colette languished in a bath of frothy soapsuds sipping a G&T and flicking through *Vanity Fair*.

'What?' She glanced at him irritably. She hated his habit of bursting into the bathroom without even knocking.

'We're married. So what?' he'd retort when she would chastise him for his lack of finesse.

'We're going to New York, baby! I got the job! Graydon Taylor *himself* just phoned me. Jeez, he works 24/7, even on weekends! I've to fly over on Tuesday for a briefing – that's why I got the call. Jerry Olsen, eat your heart out!' Her husband was fizzing with excitement, striding up and down, eyes glittering in anticipation at what was to come. 'This brings us way up! *Way* up! This is the big time! Mega bucks, baby, mega bucks! Let's go celebrate.' He leaned down and kissed her hard on the mouth.

Colette's stomach gave a strange little lurch. When Des said this was big time stuff, she felt a flutter of apprehension. He would expect a lot of her. She would have to compete with all the other corporate wives in the multinational company that was now dictating where they lived. New York society was a whole new ball game. She'd be up against wives who knew each other. Women who had contacts and a whole social network behind them. She would be starting from scratch again as the outsider and it was daunting. Not that she'd ever let on to anyone that she was intimidated, Colette thought, returning her husband's kiss.

'Congratulations, darling, I knew you'd get it,' she said loyally. 'You're head and shoulders above Jerry Olsen. You played a blinder.'

'So did *you*, my sweet. They were mightily impressed at that dinner we gave. Ginny Olsen doesn't have any of your sophistication or savoir-faire and they could see that. You could carry anything off. Image matters. Never forget that, baby. We're a team, a great team. The Yanks won't know what's hit them,' he grinned, taking a slug of her drink.

Colette was warmed by his praise. Des was right, they *were* a team, and a premier division one at that, and it was something he always acknowledged. 'Come on, I'm taking my gal for a champagne dinner. We'll be able to announce it to your folks tomorrow.'

'I'll enjoy that!' Colette stretched languorously, the water rippling like warm silk over her smooth body.

'Me too.' Des grinned at her. 'Papa will have to admit, his daughter married a go-getter of the highest order.'

'He does think I married well.' Colette soaped her limbs with Miss Dior bath lotion.

'He looks down his aquiline legal-eagle nose at me, don't kid yourself,' Des scoffed. 'When he's visiting our pad on the

Upper East Side and our summer rental in the Hamptons he'll change his tune!'

'Imagine what the Palmer-Hicksons will say! They'll be sick as parrots.' Colette perked up, thinking of how a couple they socialized with but didn't particularly like would react to the news of Des's promotion.

'We'll invite them to New York for our house warming! And Barty and Cecily Herne, and the Goffs!' Des sat on the side of the bath and flicked suds at his wife.

'Oh *yeess!* Tamara Goff is such a snooty cow sometimes, showing off with that place in the South of France. The Hamptons will trump that any time. She'll be pea green! Oh bliss, I can't wait to tell her. This is going to be fun.' Her exhilaration and the thought of outdoing the more competitive members of their social set ignited and she felt a burst of adrenalin. 'I might take a trip to Paris and buy a few pieces. We'll probably have to do a lot of entertaining.'

'Good thinking. Those American wives will recognize class when they see it. I'm going to order us up a bottle of bubbly! To get us in the mood! Back in a sec.'

I'm going to live in New York! Colette thought dreamily, her earlier misgivings evaporating as she finished her G&T and waited for Des to come back with the champers. There was no stopping her now. The notion of her friends' envy made the G&T taste even better.

'So Des got the promotion, that's great news, Colette. What an adventure. Jazzy will find New York a big change,' Hilary commented when Colette revealed her momentous news the next morning. Colette was all ready for a long chat despite the fact that her friend was in the midst of preparing Sunday lunch for her in-laws.

'She's very adaptable,' Colette said touchily. Trust Hilary to be negative.

'I know she is, I was just saying,' Hilary said mildly. 'It's different when you have children. I could have gone to Moscow for a while when they opened the duty free and Niall was there for weeks. Bahrain is next on the list so I might get over for a week.'

'Well we'll be going to *live*!' Colette said edgily. Hilary's jet-setting opportunities were only minor compared to hers, and Niall Hammond was a minnow in comparison to Des.

'It's a big step. How do you feel about it?'

'Thrilled. Absolutely thrilled. What an opportunity. Des is going to make *pots* of money. And the investment opportunities ... the sky's the limit. You can really climb the ladder there. What's not to love going to live in New York?'

'Well good for you, Colette. You know I wish you all the best,' Hilary said warmly.

'Thanks, Hil.' Colette softened a little. Her friend had such a good nature that Colette knew that Hilary truly meant her good wishes, unlike some of her two-faced friends. 'Actually I'm a bit apprehensive as well, to be honest,' she confessed now that the initial buzz of breaking the news had worn off.

'I can understand that. It's a huge, life-changing event,' Hilary empathized.

'I know. And Des expects so much of me. All that entertaining and networking. That can be hard-going. He's even making plans for our house warming and we haven't even moved! And if it's tough-going keeping up with the Joneses here and in London, it's a thousand times worse over there. I've seen some of them in action. I swear to God, Hilary, it's not for the faint-hearted. He wants me to get onto charity boards and committees. You know they're such a big deal over there. I'll have to work my ass off. I'll have no time for myself!' Only to Hilary would Colette confide her trepidations.

'Oohh wouldn't be too into that now, myself. Just having to buy clothes for all those events would be my worst nightmare. But you're used to that kind of lifestyle, it will be no bother to you,' Hilary said bracingly.

'Umm,' Colette sighed. 'I wish we could have had time for a real chat – why didn't you get rid of that Jonathan yoke on Friday night? He was very insensitive. He should have known we would have liked a private conversation,' she rebuked petulantly.

'Don't be like that, Colette. I didn't know you were coming and I couldn't do the hot potato act to Jonathan. He's a very nice guy,' Hilary reproved.

'He doesn't know his place! I could hardly get a word in edgeways – he had an opinion on everything and he took charge of your kitchen as if he owned it, and you hardly know him,' she retorted huffily, not used to being demoted to second place by Hilary.

'Sometimes you just know who's going to be a good friend and he's going to be a good friend of mine,' Hilary said firmly. *And you were the one who took over the conversation*, she thought crossly but kept it to herself.

'Well I *am* your oldest friend! And we don't get to see each other that often any more. You never come to London now.'

'We'll see each other at Rowena's wedding next month!' Hilary pointed out.

'Aw hell! I forgot about that. I hope Des will be around for it. I'll check it out. Anyway I'd better go. We're calling in to Mum and Dad's for brunch before going to the airport, and I'm not finished packing yet. I'll ring you before the wedding,' Colette said hastily, glancing at her watch. 'Just wanted to tell you my news, byeee.'

Colette had completely forgotten about Rowena Ryan's wedding, she tutted, neatly folding her clothes into the Louis Vuitton case that was open on the bed. Rowena, an old school chum, was the last of their set to get married. She was having a glitzy late-June wedding and her father, a well-known developer, had hired out the new Mont Clare Hotel in Merrion Square for a two-day bash.

Colette was looking forward to showing off in the wildly expensive black off-the-shoulder Christina Stambolian gown that Des had bought her for her last birthday. It was one of her 'investment pieces' as he liked to call them and he had been as proud as Punch when she had worn it to a gala night where he had been hosting a table for charity. 'Princess Di has nothing on you,' he'd enthused when she'd modelled it for him. Des was a generous husband. He never begrudged the money she spent on style. He actively encouraged her and she knew it was because it reflected well on him and the lifestyle he was able to afford. No way would Niall Hammond ever be able to afford Christina Stambolian and Catherine Walker gowns, and trips to Paris, for Hilary to buy a designer wardrobe, even though he had a very good job, Colette thought smugly, packing away her toiletries.

Hilary was too chunky for couture fashion anyway. It would be wasted on her. She was at least a size 14 compared to Colette's petite size 10.

If Des couldn't go to Rowena's wedding she'd go on her own, but she hoped her husband would be able to accompany her. It would be the ideal opportunity to let all their Irish friends and acquaintances know they were moving Stateside and impress them.

'Get a move on, sweetie, I've paid the bill!' Des strode into the room looking extremely debonair and sporty in his pale blue Lacoste shirt and tailored cream trousers. Preppy, very American, she thought happily, observing his tanned good looks with pleasure. He reminded her of a young Robert Redford with his tawny blond hair, blue eyes and square jaw. She *had* married well, Colette comforted herself, remembering the brown-eyed, black-haired, well-built medical student who had broken her heart. He could never carry off a preppy look – he was far too untidy with his curly hair tumbling into his eyes, and his odd socks because he'd dressed in a hurry. But she felt a pang of longing remembering their lusty love-making, knowing that her husband had never brought her to the heights of happiness that Rod Killeen had ... or the depths of despair, she thought crossly, wondering why *he* had come into her head after all these years.

Des shrugged into his navy blazer, slotted some floppy disks into his portable-computer bag, zipped it up and slung it over his shoulder. 'I want to send a fax to London and NY. I'll send a porter up for the luggage and I'll meet you in the lobby. Don't be long,' he instructed briskly. He was anxious to get back home to London to make a start on his preparations for the big move. Colette felt herself begin to tense up as he hurried out the door. He'd be like a coiled spring, edgy and restless for the foreseeable future, and *that* she was not looking forward to.

She glanced out of the window across to St Stephen's Green. A myriad of pink, blues, greens and yellows daubed against an azure sky. A Monet painting framed by green railings. The Victorian park looked spectacular in the morning sun, the early summer bedding splashes of riotous colour against the green hues. It was a timeless, picturesque sight that brought back happy memories. She had strolled around that park often with Rod, walking through the impressive Fusiliers' Arch, and diagonally across to her favourite sculptures, the *Three Fates*, when they were heading to O'Briens on Leeson Street for a teatime drink on Fridays to celebrate the start of the weekend. What a relatively simple and unsophisticated life she'd led then, Colette mused, thinking how much her life had changed and how much it was going to change with the move to New York.

Who knew, in a few months' time she might be looking out onto Central Park, the most famous park in the world. She might even see Jackie jogging around the reservoir, as was the ex-First Lady's wont, Colette thought with a thrill of anticipation at seeing the most stylish woman in the world and one that she greatly admired. Jackie Kennedy Onassis too, was a connoisseur of fine art. She had made a superb job of renovating the White House when she was First Lady. New York was a treasure trove of antique stores. Perhaps, in the future, Colette might even open a gallery and have a fine art business herself. She was certainly well qualified to do so. She had a lot to offer. She should stop feeling anxious about her place in New York society.

No one who knew her would ever think she was prone to moments of insecurity. They wouldn't *believe* it of her. Only Hilary knew the *real* Colette. She could always tell her friend her true feelings and worries because Hilary was no threat to her in any way, shape or form. Colette knew that she was brighter, slimmer, prettier, more elegant, and more success- ful and infinitely wealthier than her childhood friend, and always had been, and that was the way of it. And that was why she could show her insecurities. She supposed it was like having a sister. Hilary was the sister she had never had. If she needed a bit of bolstering in the Big Apple she could always phone her.

She took one last look at the view, wondering when she would see it again, before snapping shut the locks on her case, just as a young porter arrived to collect their luggage.

Their chauffeur-driven car was waiting at the hotel's entrance and Colette smiled at the doorman as he held open the door for her. Had she ever, in all her sauntering around one of Dublin's premier locations, thought that she would take a chauffeur-driven car for granted? When they were in New York, Des always used a Town Car and put it on expenses. They had come a long way from taking yellow and black cabs and she squeezed his hand as he got in beside her. 'Let's go impress the legal eagles with the news. I'm so proud of you, Des. You deserve it.'

'Thank you, darling.' He leaned across and kissed her. 'A lot of it is down to you too. We worked our butts off, and it paid off, and the best is yet to come.'

The best is yet to come. She liked the sound of that, Colette decided, wishing that that little knot in her tummy she always got when she and Des were meeting her parents would disappear.

CHAPTER THIRTEEN

'But we'll never get to see Jasmine! We hardly get to see her enough as it is,' exclaimed her dismayed mother when Colette revealed their momentous news an hour later as they sat down to eat in the sunny conservatory that overlooked the shimmering, silver-blue sea.

'Cut back on work and come and spend summers in the Hamptons with us,' Colette said smartly, knowing full well that work and 'the Firm' were sacrosanct.

'We can't do that, we're up to our eyes in work, you know that,' Jacqueline said tetchily, handing her a platter of crab, prawns, oysters and scallops.

'Delish,' Colette approved, spooning portions onto her plate before handing the platter to Des.

'Your father got them fresh in Howth.' Jacqueline smiled at her husband.

'Nothing but the best for my little girl.' Frank passed her a bowl of crispy Caesar salad.

'Thank you, Dad,' she said coyly. Her father had always spoiled her rotten. She was the apple of his eye.

'So you're off to New York, Des. Big step! They'll work

you hard over there.' Frank eyed his son-in-law over the top of his bifocals.

'Nothing I can't handle,' Des said a touch defensively. He wasn't particularly fond of his in-laws. They always made him feel a mite inferior. They thought they were so smart, so intellectual, and so successful. Their smugness and sense of entitlement knew no bounds. Jacqueline in particular seemed to have forgotten her roots and acted the lady to the manor born. She had looked down her pointy nose at his mother and her travel agency business. It hadn't stopped her looking for a free upgrade to the Caribbean for a flight once though.

'But poor Jasmine, having to leave all her little friends.' Jacqueline nibbled on a prawn while Frank poured a chilled Sauvignon Blanc into the sparkling Waterford crystal glasses.

'She's young, she'll adapt.' Colette repeated her mantra, trying to hide her irritation.

'And what about her nanny? Will you bring Elisabetta with you?' her mother enquired.

'We haven't really discussed it yet,' Des shrugged.

'At least Jasmine would have some continuity and some sense of security if you did. I'll never forget how devastated you were when Denise Boyle left us so unexpectedly and with no notice. I was very put out about that,' Jacqueline observed, remembering the upset her thoughtless nanny's abrupt departure caused the family all those years ago. 'You were very fond of her. It took you a long time to get over her going. You were obnoxious to the next girl who came. She didn't stay very long as I remember. You were a little minx then,' Jacqueline remarked.

Colette's face darkened at the memory. She had adored Denise and her going had had a lasting impact on her.

'Maybe I was a little minx because I had reason to be,' she said irately, shooting a look at her father who could have come to her defence but was keeping out of the discussion. 'And don't forget you and Dad were never at home. You were too busy with the Firm! I couldn't compete with that,' she added tartly.

'Don't be like that, Colette. You know we always gave you the best of everything. How ungracious of you,' reproved her mother coldly.

'The best of everything except your time. So stop getting on to me about Jazzy. I spend more time with her than you did with me.'

'You know, Colette, sometimes you just have to let things go. It's the same thing over and over with you,' Jacqueline said wearily. 'Who else do you know got a car for their eighteenth birthday, and a year off, with a generous allowance to travel around Europe, and then had their fees paid for an expensive London college? Certainly not Hilary, or Rowena, or any of your other friends. That all came from *our* hard work. Money doesn't grow on trees, you know. Your father and I started off with nothing ... nothing! And when we go you will be a millionairess, so build a bridge and get over it, Colette. I'm heartily sick of this "poor little me, I was neglected growing up" emotional blackmail nonsense you go on with! It's utterly offensive and unwarranted,' Jacqueline exploded, pushed to her limit.

Colette stared at her mother whose face had a blotchy crimson hue. Jacqueline *never* lost control of her temper. One of the reasons she was a superb barrister in the courts. She could never be goaded.

Des kept his eyes on his plate, annoyed at the way the conversation was going. He must remind his wife to tone it down a bit. She didn't want her inheritance left to charity, which could very well happen if she pushed her mother far enough. Des had great plans for Colette's inheritance.

'When do you start working on Wall Street, Des?' Frank changed the fraught topic of conversation with practised ease, warily noting his daughter's dour expression.

'I've to fly over on Tuesday for a few days. I'll know more then.' Des shucked an oyster into his mouth. 'Superb quality,' he remarked smoothly, glad the fracas was over.

'Fresh off the boat,' Frank replied with faux joviality, thinking how *dare* that pushy social-climbing upstart imply that Frank and Jacqueline would not serve anything but the best. It was far from oysters for lunch that Des Williams was reared.

'I'm looking forward to bringing Colette to taste the best clam chowder *ever* in Harbor Square in Nantucket. The Tavern, I think it was called. The seafood on the East Coast is excellent quality, of course. I was at a clambake in the Hamptons two years ago – never tasted anything like them. So succulent. Have you ever been to that neck of the woods?' Des eyeballed Frank. Mr Know-It-All was not going to get the better of him.

'Er no. New York, Chicago and New Orleans are our haunts. But I tell you the jambalaya and filé gumbo and crawfish pie down in New Orleans are *sensational*! Have you ever tried them?' his father-in-law batted back.

'I wouldn't be a fan of pastry with fish. It takes from the delicate flavour, I find. The same with filé.' Des speared a prawn and dipped it into the Marie Rose sauce. 'I would be more of a purist.'

'Interesting,' said Frank. '*I* would find that the Marie Rose sauce quite *overpowers* the prawns but clearly that's not the case with you. I find prawns so delicate that even a *soupçon* of Tabasco or garlic can overwhelm the taste. I—'

'Well we hope to take a summer rental in the Hamptons, or Nantucket or Cape Cod, so you'll have to come for a week or two,' Colette interjected hastily, wishing her father and husband would stop trying to outdo each other. It was always the same. They were decidedly childish, she thought crossly, glaring at her husband who was scowling at Frank's masterly put-down. He glared back at her.

'Of course we'll come visit. I believe it's a very picturesque part of the States.' Frank topped up Colette's glass and went to top up his son-in-law's.

'Not for me, thank you, Frank. *I* have a lot of work to do when I get home. I try not to drink too much at weekends.' Des placed his palm over the glass. 'But *you* go right ahead.'

Frank's nostrils flared at the implied insult.

'Will you rent out the flat?' Jacqueline made an effort to be polite after her outburst.

'We haven't discussed that yet, either,' Colette said snootily.

'You'd get top dollar. It's a prime location. And within walking distance of Kensington Palace – the Princess Di factor will bump up the rent. Go to one of those high-end letting agencies,' Frank said authoritatively.

As if we wouldn't think of that ourselves, thought Des derisively. *Prat!*

'If we rent it out we won't have a base in London,' Colette pointed out.

'Stay in a hotel.' Her father helped himself to some smoked salmon.

'We'll see.' She would make up her own mind about what she wanted to do with her home without her parents sticking their oar in. Frank had been put out when she had inherited the flat from his sister. He had planned to make a very fine profit from the sale of it, if Beatrice predeceased him, which he was sure she would because she was ten years older than him and in poor health. She had married a very wealthy English stockbroker, and thereafter had considered her family in Ireland way out of her social league. She and Frank had not been close. Beatrice had seen something of herself in Colette, and, being childless and lonely, had been glad of her niece's company when Colette had come to live with her to get over her romantic setback.

It galled Frank that Des Williams had waltzed in and ingratiated himself with his sister and ended up living in that magnificent flat, while half of what was left of Beatrice's estate had gone to various charities. He had ended up getting far less than he had anticipated. There was no love lost between him and his son-in-law, and it gave him no small sense of satisfaction that Colette had kept her own name after marriage because she preferred it to her husband's surname.

Des was a wide boy, in Frank's estimation, and not the man he would have chosen for his daughter to marry. He had made damn sure to ring-fence his own estate into a trust for his daughter and granddaughter and that devious little shit wouldn't be getting his greedy mitts on any of it when the time came.

'Will you buy a place or rent in New York?' Jacqueline laid down her knife and fork. She wasn't feeling very hungry any more and she was annoyed with herself for losing her temper with her daughter. This damn menopause was knocking her for six. She was too young for it. It was a shock to realize that she was, if not wholly menopausal, very much peri. These mood swings and short-tempered outbursts that she was prone to lately were unexpected and unnerving. Time to go on the HRT, she thought gloomily.

'We'll rent for a while until we get settled in and then we can start scouting for somewhere we'd like to live. Or perhaps we'll just rent in New York and buy somewhere along the coast.' Colette thawed a little.

'Greenwich Village is lovely.' Jacqueline offered a placatory smile. 'Or Chelsea.'

'I'd like a view of the Park,' Colette admitted.

'You'll pay for that,' Frank scoffed.

'It's something to aspire to.' Des glanced at his watch. 'We need to keep an eye on the time. The car will be here in twenty minutes.'

'I would have given you a lift to the airport,' Frank protested.

'Not at all, Frank. I have a driver and car 24/7 when I'm here on business.' Des couldn't hide a note of self-importance. 'I'm sure you'll be wanting to get in a round of golf. I played a damn good eagle in Foxrock yesterday. I heard on the grapevine that there was a bit of a ruckus between a consultant and a doctor in your clubhouse recently, and it's being called "the kickboxing club" by the Southsiders.'

Frank's mouth tightened into a thin line. 'Is that so? I never listen to idle gossip.'

'Amusing though.' Des wiped his mouth with his linen napkin.

'Do have a cup of coffee while you're waiting for the car,' Jacqueline urged, getting up from the table to bring the coffee percolator from the kitchen. This brunch had been a disaster from start to finish. If they couldn't even have brunch without sniping at each other how would they manage a week together in the Hamptons or wherever? 'We will get to see Jasmine before you go, won't we?' she asked when the gleaming black car pulled into the circular drive.

'Yes, Mum. How about I bring her over for Rowena's wedding and we'll stay with you,' Colette suggested, ready to make amends.

'Oh darling, that would be wonderful. I'm sorry I er ... lost my temper. I'm a little stressed lately. Time of life business, I think. Very inconvenient,' she murmured when Des had excused himself to use the bathroom.

'Oh!' Colette was surprised. It was almost inconceivable to think of her soigné, poised, imperturbable mother suffering the ignominy of the menopause.

'I know you felt I had some shortcomings as a mother and perhaps you're right. Don't make the same mistake with Jasmine,' Jacqueline said awkwardly as her son-in-law came back into the room.

'Jasmine is well looked after,' Colette said stiffly.

'I know, and so were you, but not enough by me, it seems. I just don't want her to be at loggerheads with you, like we are now, in years to come,' Jacqueline said wryly, proffering her cheek for a kiss.

'That won't happen,' Colette said firmly but she hugged her mother more affectionately that she normally did before turning to her father to kiss him goodbye.

'That little jumped-up chancer. The bloody nerve of him to talk to me like that. Why she married him I will *never* know. She knew from the start I didn't like him. She married him to spite me, and after all I gave her.' Frank was fuming as he strode around the conservatory.

'Don't be ridiculous. Why would she want to spite you?' Jacqueline said wearily, a hormone headache throbbing at her temples.

'He didn't even try to be civil,' Frank raged. 'With his smart comments. Did you hear him about the fracas at the club? Jeering he was. Sneering and jeering. But I got him good with the prawns. *Smothered* in sauce they were, the pretentious little spoofer. And he thinks he's going to make enough to live Uptown NY. *Ha!* He has as much chance of that as I have. He'll be out of his league with the big boys over there, the little braggart—'

'Will you *listen* to yourself, for God's sake. You're a highly respected senior counsel and you're acting like a ten-year-old. There's a pair of you in it. Cover up what's left of the food and put it in the fridge. I'm going to lie down. I've got a headache.' Jacqueline had had enough. Why couldn't a simple brunch go right? Why was there always such an *edge* when they were all together? Why could Colette not see how *lucky* she was rather than focusing on her imagined deprivations? Didn't she realize they were the envy of many, and rightly so. And as for Des, what was his problem trying to outdo Frank all the time? They had much more in common than they both realized. Perhaps that was it. They were *too* alike.

Colette had clearly resented her advice when they were saying goodbye. Wouldn't even acknowledge the idea that she might be making the same mistakes with Jazzy that Jacqueline had with her.

The family who had it all they certainly were not, she thought sourly, making her way upstairs to the sound of her husband clattering dishes into the dishwasher, in high dudgeon.

'That was a damn ordeal! Your pater is a pain in the butt.' Des was thoroughly cantankerous as the car sped to the airport.

'You were as bad,' his wife retorted.

'I won't miss them when we go to America,' he growled.

'And I'm sure they won't miss you,' Colette snapped. 'Don't forget, Des, my family's money enables us to live where we live. Aunt Beatrice was more than generous to me, and Dad lost out. So give him a bit of leeway.'

'You know something, Colette, you *will* have your view of the Park and he can stick his attitude because I'm going to make a damn fortune on Wall Street,' Des vowed, turning away from her to stare out of the window.

I married someone just like my father, Colette reflected,

gazing at the runway lights lit up at right angles to them. An incoming flight flew over them with a roar that almost deafened her. *And as far as Jazzy is concerned I'm turning into my mother.* Jacqueline's parting remarks had touched a nerve. Her daughter was left mostly in the care of her nanny, no matter that Colette was in denial about it. She was repeating the mistakes her mother had made with her. She would have to make more of an effort with Jasmine. Perhaps she too had inherited her mother's lack of maternal instinct and that was difficult to acknowledge.

Hilary was a very good mother, Colette conceded morosely. She gave her girls a lot of attention. She cooked proper dinners and baked for them and helped with their homework, just like Mrs Kinsella had done for her. Colette left all that sort of thing to Elisabetta, the Italian nanny.

When she was a little girl being cared for by Sally, she'd been *consumed* with envy at the way Hilary's mum always had scrumptious buns and tarts baked, awaiting their arrival home from school. Colette could still remember the aroma of freshly baked bread, and beef stew or roast chicken, wafting out from the kitchen to greet them. The Kinsella household had been a happy one. The fun they all had decorating at Halloween and Christmas, the excitement rising to fever pitch. Sally making sure that Colette was involved. Jasmine should have those sort of experiences. She hired a firm in to decorate the flat every Christmas, Colette thought guiltily.

This should be an exciting time in her life, but today's episode had left her thoroughly disgruntled and brought up truths that she didn't want to have to face. She would buy her daughter something particularly nice in the duty free.

Jazzy loved earrings and bling. Des could sulk in the executive lounge. She would go shopping. As well as treating Jasmine she'd treat herself too. What was the point of having pots of money if you didn't spend it? Colette felt the anticipation of a spending spree begin to build. If comfort couldn't be found in a visit to her parents it could be found in glitzy shops or even Dublin duty free.

'Mummy, Mummy, what did you buy me?' Jasmine raced into the hall when she heard her parents' key in the front door.

Colette smiled when she saw her daughter, her silky golden curls bobbing up and down, her periwinkle-blue eyes sparkling with anticipation. She was a little beauty, Colette thought proudly, sweeping the five-year-old up in her arms.

'Hello, sweetheart,' she exclaimed, hugging her tightly. Jacqueline hadn't been a hugger; Colette hugged Jasmine all the time. Perhaps she'd been too hard on herself comparing her mothering skills, or lack of, to her mother's, Colette decided.

'No kiss for Daddy?' Des dropped a kiss on top of his daughter's head. 'I'm going to change and go into the office. Lots to do before I go Stateside,' he threw over his shoulder, striding along the parquet hallway with his luggage.

'Would you like some tea, Ma'am?' Elisabetta asked, emerging from the kitchen.

'Love some, please, and will you sort out the luggage?' Colette said, carrying her daughter into the lounge and plopping her down on the plump pale lemon-and-blue sofa that faced the enormous sash windows. The rays of the early evening sun cast glimmering prisms of light onto her Waterford Glass chandelier. That, and their paintings, would be coming to the States. That chandelier was a very impressive heirloom. Those snooty Uptown Wasps wouldn't be able to fault her for her style and elegance, Colette decided, sinking wearily onto the sofa. She was tired after travelling and wouldn't have minded a nap.

'Where's my present?' whined Jasmine. 'I want it *now!*'

'Don't be naughty,' chided her mother, taking the small earring box and the bag with the jangly charm bracelet out of her handbag.

'Is that all?' Jasmine was astonished, grabbing the box eagerly. 'It's very small!' Her pretty little face darkened.

'See what's in it,' retorted Colette crossly, remembering such a scenario in her own childhood when Jacqueline had presented her with a silver Claddagh ring after an absence away and she had been disgusted.

Perhaps she should get pregnant again, even though she dreaded the idea, Colette mused. She had always longed for a sibling. An only child could so easily end up becoming spoilt and precocious, just as she had been, Colette thought with a rare moment of self-awareness. Hilary's two were great companions and after all she could afford a nanny. She'd bring up the subject with Des when they were settled into their new life in the USA, she decided as her daughter studied her new earrings and bracelet and looked decidedly unimpressed.

CHAPTER FOURTEEN

'Bloody black tie! I hate wearing monkey suits!' Niall Hammond gave a hurricane-force sigh that blew tendrils of Hilary's hair across her nose.

'Stop giving out and just go to Black Tie and get fitted and book it today. This day next week we'll be going to the wedding,' she said drowsily, nestled in against him on an unseasonably wet Saturday morning.

'The time is flying by – the girls will be on their school holidays before we know it. Do you think we could risk a quickie? I heard them going down to watch TV.' He slid his leg over hers and she felt him harden against her.

'You opportunist, you,' she grinned, turning round to face him. 'We did it last night.'

'I'm a healthy young man with healthy young man urges,' he grinned back, cupping one of her breasts and lightly stroking her nipple with his thumb until she gave a smothered groan and felt a lusty surge of desire. She loved morning sex when she was relaxed and rested and horny.

'Mammmm!' Sophie thundered up the stairs, followed by her sister.

'Contra and Ception,' Niall said drolly, drawing away as

their daughters tumbled into the bedroom after a peremp-tory knock on the door.

'Mam, she said the F word and then—'

'Liar, liar pants on fire, *you* said the F word first!' Millie was outraged.

'Stop it this minute! Dad and I were trying to have a lie-in because we work so hard during the week and you two self-ish girls have spoiled it. I don't want to hear another word. Stop telling tales.'

'But—'

'Out! Out! Out! And close the door behind you and feed the cat while you're at it,' Hilary said crossly.

'I suppose you're going to do sex!' Millie accused, thor-oughly disgruntled.

'*What*?' Hilary couldn't believe her ears.

'Kelly Maguire said parents do sex on Saturday morning. Eewwww!'

'Kelly Maguire has too much to say for herself. We were trying to have a snooze – impossible in this house,' Hilary snapped. 'Now go away.' She pulled the duvet over her head and tried not to laugh.

'At least I wasn't inside you.' Niall threw his eyes up to heaven when the door closed behind their squabbling off-spring.

'Well what's stopping you now? After all it is Saturday morning and according to Kelly Maguire sex is what we are supposed to be doing!'

'I've lost my nerve,' her husband laughed, tracing his hand down over her hip and drawing her to him.

'Doesn't feel like it to me,' murmured Hilary as he entered

her, remembering how they would spend Saturday mornings in bed riding each other ragged before they'd had children.

The doorbell rang and Niall cursed as Hilary tensed. 'Hurry,' she urged, wrapping her legs around him, knowing it would only be moments before they would be interrupted again.

'I can't!' he groaned.

Hilary pushed him away, wriggled out from under him and got out of bed. 'Who is it?' she asked, opening the bedroom door when she heard Millie race up the stairs.

'A boy is looking for money for a line cos he's doing a five-mile walk for charity.'

'There's change on my locker,' Niall said grumpily.

'Here, give him this,' Hilary sighed, handing her daughter some coins. 'And if any more boys come tell them we've sponsored already.'

'OK, Mam. Can I have a banana? I'm hungry.'

'Yeah! I'll come down and sort breakfast in a little while. Now don't keep that boy waiting at the door.'

'I'd better get up,' Hilary sighed as guilt set in.

'Ah hop in for another five minutes, I've hardly seen you this week, you can have my banana if you want,' Niall urged, throwing back the duvet.

'Niall! Five minutes, but let's forget the conjugals, *my* nerves wouldn't stand it,' she agreed, snuggling in to him. 'This day next week we'll be up early dolling ourselves up to have a whole day to ourselves.'

'Aawww, did you have to remind me of it *again*? Couldn't you bring your new gay friend – they love weddings and dressing up,' he suggested with an air of studied casualness.

'Niall! Don't describe Jonathan like that. It's so disrespectful. I mean would you say "bring your heterosexual friend" if I was bringing Colette or someone? And don't come if you don't want to,' she added huffily, trying to shuffle off his arm that was tight around her.

'Don't get in a snit,' he appeased. 'I just thought he might like to go, seeing as he's into fashion and the like. That's a lovely dress he found for you.'

'Yes it is,' Hilary agreed, mollified. She had mentioned to Jonathan in one of their tri-weekly phone calls that she had to go shopping for a dress for an upcoming wedding and she was dreading it.

'Where are you going to go for it?' he asked.

'Oh I don't know,' she sighed. 'I suppose I should go to Brown Thomas or Switzers. It's a posh do. I'd far prefer to go to Arnotts or M&S. But Colette will be wearing some designer outfit. I suppose they'll all be wearing designer gear. It's that sort of a wedding.'

'Well we can't have you looking like a Mary Hick in front of Little Miss Muffit,' he joked.

'Stop it,' she giggled. 'Colette's not that bad and she *is* my oldest friend!'

'If you say so I'll take your word for it. She didn't like me at all. She's one of those friends who likes to have your whole and undivided attention and I'd be far too exuberant and irreverent in company for her. I'd want as much attention as she did,' he said humorously. 'Is your sister going shopping with you?'

'God no, we'd end up rowing. She hates shopping even more than I do. She'd tell me I look good in a sack just to get me to buy something,' Hilary said gloomily.

'And what about Niall?'

'Are you mad! We'd be divorced!'

'I'll come with you then,' he'd offered. 'I *adore* clothes shopping.'

'Would you? That would be a bit of craic! We'd have a laugh.' She'd been delighted with his unexpected offer.

He'd been indefatigable, walking the legs off her, plucking dresses that she hadn't even noticed off the racks. Making her twirl and parade in front of mirrors but never satisfied with what he saw.

'How come you know such poshies?' Jonathan asked, having taken pity upon her and agreed to her suggestion of a coffee to revive them. They chose the Westbury as it was near by and, after the noise and bustle of Grafton Street, Hilary enjoyed the calm serenity of the first-floor lounge as they sat eating cream cakes and drinking strong, aromatic coffee.

'Rowena was actually a friend of Colette's,' she explained, offering Jonathan an éclair. 'Their parents are legal friends and Rowena and Colette went to the same stage school—'

'That figures,' Jonathan said archly. 'I bet Madame always got the principal role.'

'You shouldn't be so pass-remarkable,' Hilary said, defending her friend.

'Sorry. I just took agin her when she pooh-poohed our plans for our proposed interior design project. She was quite derisive.' Jonathan grinned unrepentantly. 'You were saying about Rowena?'

'For some reason we always clicked. She likes trad so she'd often come to a session with me when Niall was playing. She's lovely. You'd like her. She's real dreamy and ethereal and doesn't give a toss about keeping up with the Joneses type stuff. And Pete, her fiancé, is sound. He's a floor manager in RTÉ. That's where they met. She works in RTÉ's make-up department but she hardly wears any herself.' Hilary licked some cream off her finger. 'Her father is loaded! He's building them a big pile in North County Dublin.'

'Lucky girl,' sighed Jonathan, who longed to have a house in the country.

'Do you know something – we're doing the lighting. I must introduce her to you, I bet she'd love some advice about decorating,' Hilary said, topping up their coffee and settling back in the comfortable armchair, legs stretched out in front of her.

'Don't get comfy,' Jonathan warned. 'This is just a pit stop.'

'I can't face any more,' she moaned. 'Let's forget about it or else go back and buy that red-and-black dress in Pamela Scott. I liked that one.'

'Hmm, it wasn't bad but you could do better, I *know* it! The right dress is out there for you and we are going to find it.' Jonathan was relishing the challenge.

'But my poor feet are killing me,' she protested.

'Now, now, Granny, take a deep breath and centre yourself. I've got a place in mind where I think you could be lucky and it's not far,' he coaxed. 'Humour me.'

He had brought her to a small boutique off Clarendon

Street that she didn't even know existed and made for a rail of colourful cocktail and evening dresses, flicking through the hangers with a professional eye until he made a selection. 'You're so tall you should *revel* in it,' he proclaimed, handing her a hanger with a rich cerise V-necked dress that flowed elegantly to the knee. 'I have a feeling about this,' he said excitedly. 'Get in there quick.' He led the way to the dressing room.

'And perhaps this wrap to finish it off?' the assistant offered helpfully, producing a gossamer-fine, silky cream wrap from another rack.

'Ooohhhh! Yessss!' approved Jonathan. 'Perfect.'

And it was perfect, thought Hilary gratefully. The ruched panelled V-neck showed off her tan and hid a multitude at the midriff and flowed gracefully over her hips to her knees. Sheer silk stockings and cream high heels and a clutch finished the wow factor and her husband's eyes had widened in appreciation when she'd modelled it for him. 'Verrrrry niceeee!' he declared appreciatively as she pirouetted around for him.

'That chap has great taste,' he added a touch grudgingly. 'He's quite the all-rounder, isn't he?'

'What's that supposed to mean?' Hilary looked at him, surprised.

'Nothing, he just seems to be accomplished at everything he does,' Niall remarked.

'You hate coming shopping with me for clothes.'

'I know,' her husband conceded with a wry smile. 'I couldn't have done better myself.'

'Nor could I,' Hilary acknowledged, loving the way the

ruches hid the round curve of her tummy, and emphasized her shapely waist. Left to her own devices, she would never have found as stylish and flattering a dress and knowing that she looked really good was an added bonus. It was going to be a big shindig and every social diarist in Dublin had been invited. Rowena had confided to Hilary months ago that the wedding was turning into a huge impersonal gala-style event and she didn't know half the people who were coming. 'I would have loved a wedding like yours – it was such a terrific hooley and so intimate. I swear to God, Pete and I just want to take to our heels and forget the whole thing,' she said miserably, the very antithesis of the happy bride-to-be.

'Great idea, if they want a lift somewhere I'll drive them,' said Niall when Hilary had told him of Rowena's comment. Hilary knew if she did agree to his suggestion that Jonathan accompany her to the wedding her husband would actually be delighted. Niall and her new friend had yet to meet but they had spoken on the phone and enjoyed some banter and she was very confident that when they did meet they would get on very well.

'Maaaam? Tipsy is coughing up a fur ball! I thinking she's choking,' Sophie yelled up the stairs.

'Why is it always "Maaaam"? Why is it never "Daaad"?' grumbled Hilary, getting out of bed for the final time.

'Any chance of a cuppa while you're at it?' Niall tried his luck.

'Every chance and I'll have a grilled rasher sandwich while you're at it,' Hilary retorted, tying the belt of her dressing gown around her as Sophie's yells reached a deafening crescendo.

'I'm coming, stop panicking,' she called exasperatedly, hurrying down the stairs to deal with the cat, the fur ball and her two hungry daughters.

An hour later as they all sat finishing their brunch, the phone rang and Sophie answered. 'Hi, Auntie Colette, I'll get Mam for you,' she said cheerfully. Hilary went out to the kitchen and tucked the extension line under her ear.

'Hi, Colette,' she said, setting about filling the dishwasher with the dishes her daughters had carried to the sink.

'Hi, Hil, I was just wondering, Des is going to have to fly out ten days before we'd planned because something's come up Stateside and I'm dreading leaving on my own ... is there *any* way you could come over for my last couple of days in London? It's the last time we'll see each other for *ages!*'

'Gosh, Colette, I don't know if that's on the cards. Niall is up to his eyes, and we're fairly busy at work too,' Hilary exclaimed, thinking how typical of Colette to think that Hilary could just drop everything and fly to London for a few days.

'Aww, I feel very sad and unsettled. It's such a *huge* step moving to the States and I'd really appreciate your support,' Colette said despondently.

'But you've plenty of friends in London,' Hilary pointed out.

'Oh they're all working or vacationing and besides you're the only one who knows what I'm like when I get into a tizzy!'

'Look, we'll talk about it at the wedding, OK?' Hilary suggested.

'Thanks, Hil, I think we're sitting at the same table. I did ask Rowena to put us at the Fitzwilliams' table, because Shay and Des have a lot in common and they get on well and we have mutual friends in London but she said her mother was doing the table plans and she wanted the Fitzwilliams at Kenneth Reilly's table. Honestly, Rowena should have *some* say!' groused Colette petulantly.

'Right!' Hilary said drily. Typical of Colette that she didn't even know how insulting she sounded, implying that sitting with Hilary and Niall was less than desired. Shay Fitzwilliam was a high-powered banker, jet-setter and go-getter, and it would be right up Des's alley to schmooze with him at Rowena's wedding.

'And seemingly Eric Dunne's ex-wife is kicking up a right royal row because he's bringing that tarty blonde PR one he's hanging around with, as his plus one!' Colette prattled on, oblivious.

'Fireworks so.' Hilary filled the knife and fork container. 'Poor Rowena. Listen, I have to go, we'll see you at the church on Saturday, OK?'

'Great, and think about what I said, we could have a lovely few girly days,' Colette chirruped.

'Will do,' Hilary replied, wondering what her friend would say if she said ask Shay Fitzwilliam's wife to come over to London and cry on *her* shoulder. She hung up, annoyed. Colette was always the same. Me, me, me. Hilary decided not to tell Niall about the conversation or let him know they were seated at the same table. He put up with Colette out of loyalty to Hilary but he had no time for Des. 'A self-important spoofer,' he'd called him after their first encounter. Nothing over the years had helped change his opinion. Listening to Des bragging about the promotion in the States, as he undoubtedly would, would do Niall's head in. And then he'd get grouchy. Perhaps her husband's suggestion that she ask Jonathan to accompany her wasn't such a bad idea after all. What was it about weddings? They could be such ordeals. And somehow Hilary had the feeling that Rowena and Pete's wedding wasn't going to be the best wedding she was ever at.

CHAPTER FIFTEEN

'Now there's macaroni cheese, chicken casserole and some goodies in the fridge. And the phone number of the hotel is by the phone in the hall if you need it. Don't let the girls stay up too late and—'

'Mam, Auntie Colette is on the phone for you.' Sophie bounced into the sitting room where Hilary was giving last-minute instructions to Carla, their babysitter.

'Sorry, Carla, excuse me for a minute.' Hilary went out to the hall and took the receiver from her daughter. 'Hi, we're just getting ready to leave and—'

'Hilary, I have a HUGE favour to ask,' Colette interrupted.

'What's that?' Hilary asked warily.

'Elisabetta, Jazzy's nanny, had a tummy bug and couldn't travel – could Jazzy please stay with your two? I'll give the babysitter the extra cost for minding her. I'm really stuck. Mum tried a few of her friends' daughters but they were all doing something. I suppose it *was* short notice.' Colette sighed theatrically.

'Umm well, I'd better check it with Carla, she's the one who's babysitting,' Hilary replied, nonplussed.

'Oh she won't mind, I'm sure. A few extra quid will go down a treat,' Colette said airily.

'Let me check it out with her,' Hilary said firmly. Trust Colette to have a drama at the last minute. She walked back into the sitting room where Carla was French-plaiting Millie's hair. 'Listen, Carla, and feel free to say no if you want to, my friend Colette is on the phone. Her little girl's nanny couldn't travel from the UK with them and she has no one to mind Jasmine and she was wondering if you would look after her too. She'd pay you extra, needless to say.'

'Aw Mam, nooo! Not Jazzy, she'll ruin everything. She'll want to play her games her way and she's just *too* bossy,' Sophie protested vehemently.

'Now don't be like that, Sophie. Jasmine's younger than you and she's an only child. She has no sister to play with,' Hilary reproved.

'I don't mind, Hilary, it's fine with me,' Carla said obligingly, giving Millie a cuddle. 'Don't worry, I won't let this Jazzy boss anyone around cos *I'm* the boss.' She winked at Sophie.

'Are you sure?' Hilary didn't want her treasured babysitter to feel pressurized.

'It's all good,' Carla assured her. 'Go and enjoy the wedding and don't rush home.'

'You're a pet,' Hilary said warmly, knowing how lucky she was to have a terrific babysitter. The girls loved her, she'd been their babysitter since they were very small and Hilary felt very confident leaving them in her care. She went back to the phone. 'That's fine, Colette. Drop Jazzy over,

Carla said she'd mind her. I'll get Niall to pump up the airbed and she'll make it up for her tonight.'

'Super duper, I knew I could depend on you,' Colette said gaily. 'Sorry we can't give you a lift into town, Mum and Dad are sharing the car with us. How are you getting in?'

'Taxi.'

'OK! We'll see you with Jazzy in twenty minutes or so.'

'Nope, we'll see you at the church. The taxi's booked to come in the next ten minutes and I'm not paying him to keep the meter running,' Hilary said firmly.

'Oh!' Colette wasn't expecting this. 'Right then! I'll just drop Jazzy in and pay your babysitter,' she said a touch acerbically.

'Fine, I'd better go and root out the blow-up bed. See you at the church.' Hilary hung up and went in search of Niall to tell him the latest.

'Typical,' he retorted when she thrust the navy-and-red blow-up bed and air pump at him.

'Just pump it up, Mr Dishy, and hurry, the taxi will be here any minute,' Hilary urged.

'I want to sleep on the pump-up bed,' Sophie announced.

'No, I do, it's my turn, you slept in it the last time,' Millie protested.

'Don't start,' warned Hilary, beginning to feel harassed. It was always the same when Jasmine was coming to stay. 'If there are any rows I'll tell Carla to put the two of you in our bed and Jazzy can sleep in one of yours and we'll sort it when we get home. Do *not* misbehave and annoy Carla, OK? Now I mean it,' she said sternly.

'OK!' her daughters agreed sulkily.

'Don't be like that, girls. Behave yourselves. Give your mother a kiss and tell her to enjoy herself, and don't spoil her day,' Niall ordered as he began to pump up the bed, his black shoes gleaming. He looked so handsome in his black tie gear, Hilary thought appreciatively, glad that he had backed her up.

'Have fun, Mammy.' Sophie flung her arms around her and Hilary hugged her. 'You look gorgeous,' her daughter approved.

'I love you, Mam, sorry,' Millie said as the doorbell rang.

'I love you too, pet.' Hilary gave her a kiss, so glad that her children generally were very good-natured and not prone to holding grudges.

'It's your taxi, Hilary,' Carla called.

'Bring us home some wedding cake.' Millie slipped her hand into Hilary's as Niall gave the bed a few last pumps before following them down the stairs.

'They're good kids,' he said proudly, waving at them from the taxi as they stood on either side of Carla blowing kisses enthusiastically.

'Yeah, we're very lucky.' Hilary nestled in against him.

'Carla will have her hands full when the little madam arrives. I give them five minutes before a row starts.' Niall put his arm around her.

'Carla won't stand for any nonsense. She's a brick! And one thing I do know, Colette will pay her well over the odds. She's not stingy.'

'True and good for Carla but she'll earn it today.'

'But you and I are going to knock as much fun out of today as we possibly can. Let's watch all the Joneses outdoing each other!'

'Yeah, let's see how the social elite behave. I'll try not to belch and eat with my mouth open,' he teased.

'Spoilsport. Could you imagine the faces of Jacqueline and Frank if you let off a magnificent rasper?' she chuckled.

'Don't tempt me, Hilary, don't tempt me,' her husband laughed as the taxi headed for the Southside.

'Mummy, I don't want to stay here, I want to go to the wedding.' Jasmine scowled at her mother. 'I want to be a flower girl!'

'You have to stay here with Millie and Sophie—'

'But I don't *want* to!' Jasmine stamped her foot.

'Jazzy, behave,' Colette hissed. 'Carla, thank you very much,' she said, handing the babysitter an envelope. 'We're very obliged to you. See you. Be a good girl for Carla, Jazzy,' she cautioned, hastening out the front door.

'Muuummaayyyyyyy!' wailed Jasmine but Colette kept going without looking back.

'Don't cry, Jazzy, we'll mind you,' Sophie, ever the soft heart, said kindly.

'I don't want you to mind me, I want my mummy,' screeched Jasmine.

'Well your mummy's gone,' Carla said calmly as the car disappeared from view. 'How would you like to go to Howth on the DART to see the seals and we'll bring a picnic?'

'That's a silly idea! I don't like your stupid DART. I go on the tube, you know. I live in London.'

'Good for you,' Carla smiled. 'But we're going on the DART and we're having our picnic and you can tell us all about living in London.'

'We're going to live in America. We're going to Disney-land,' Jazzy informed her.

'You're lucky,' Sophie said enviously.

'Well we *are* very rich, you know.'

'Are you?' Sophie was wide-eyed.

'Stop boasting,' Millie said crossly. She had been so look-ing forward to their jaunt with Carla, but now they were going to have to listen to Jazzy bragging about everything!

'Right, girls, let's get a move on. There's a DART at ten past two, let's be on it,' Carla said briskly, much to Jasmine's disgust. She didn't like that this strange girl was bossing her around. But there was something about her firm manner that led Jasmine to believe that Carla wouldn't take any nonsense so throwing a tantrum wouldn't get her any-where.

'I like you,' she said sweetly, changing tack. 'I'm going to sit beside you on the DART.'

'I want to sit beside Carla,' Sophie declared truculently.

'You can sit beside me going, Jazzy, and you can sit beside me coming home, Sophie, OK?' Carla said in a tone that brooked no argument.

'You look nice. Have you dropped weight?' Colette eyed Hilary up and down before air kissing her as they stood on the steps of the church watching the photographer pose the bridal couple for a family photo.

'I think it's the dress, it hides a multitude,' Hilary remarked as Des leaned over to kiss her before shaking Niall's hand.

'Hey, buddy, how are you?' he said.

'Great, thanks. Congratulations on the promotion,' Niall reciprocated.

'So where did you get the dress? It's very flattering – you can't see your love handles,' Colette remarked as she stood on her tippy toes to kiss Niall.

'Thanks for the backhanded compliment,' Hilary said drily.

'Oh you know what I mean. This is a Christina Stambolian. Diana wears her clothes. She has the most fabulous boutique in Beauchamp Place. It cost a fortune but how and ever. Do you like it?' She glanced coquettishly at Niall and did a seductive twirl in her figure-hugging black off-the-shoulder creation that was the height of style and sophistication.

'Very nice. It shows off the sunbed tan!' he drawled.

'Actually it's St-Tropez,' she smiled sweetly, but she was irked at his smart remark. She turned back to Hilary. 'Would you look at all those mutton dressed as mutton, all those polka dots and big collars. Is Paul Costelloe the only designer anyone goes to here?'

'Well he designs for Princess Di too,' Hilary reminded her tartly.

'And he designs lots of air hostess uniforms,' Colette sniffed, unimpressed, as she surveyed the array of fashions on show. 'Paula Devlin looks positively mumsy and she's younger than us! And what on earth is Shauna Finley wearing? She looks like a puff adder! And look at her hair. An eagle could nest in it. And Martin Kerr looks as though his dress suit came out of mothballs – probably too mean to buy a new one.' Colette gave a running commentary on their fellow guests.

'I've heard he's got a gambling problem. When I was play-ing golf in Foxrock the last time I was here they told me he'd lost a fortune and remortgaged the house to boot. Had to let his golf club membership lapse.' Des added his tuppence' worth.

'Rowena looks beautiful, so waiflike and otherworldly,' Hilary pointed out, uncomfortable with their unkind, small-minded gossip. 'She's like a medieval princess. A friend designed her dress and she made a terrific job of it,' she added admiringly as Rowena caught a glimpse of them and waved.

'I believe her mother was furious! She wanted her to go to the Emanuels, or to Phillipa Lepley, like I did,' Colette said smugly. 'Oh look, there's Charlotte Wesley, I must go and say hi. Come on, Des, let's tell them your news.' Colette's eyes gleamed at the chance to boast to an old adversary on the social circuit.

'What are they like?' Niall groaned. 'They're never happy unless they're dissing people. They're *so* superior. And we're stuck with them for the day. I'm starving. Will we slip off and get a chippie, or coffee and a sandwich? It will be hours before we eat if this photographer has his way. They're all heading to Merrion Square for more photos – we won't be missed.'

'Brilliant idea.' Hilary tucked her arm into his. 'I married a genius. Let's go add another pound or two to my love han-dles.'

'She can be such a bitchy little madam. That's why I said about the sunbed,' Niall scowled.

'I know, you're very loyal.' Hilary laughed. 'She doesn't mean it. It's just her way. You have to look beyond it. She has to feel good about herself by pointing out other people's flaws. I've never seen her as bad as today though. They were cutting people to ribbons. I'd say it's because she's getting really anxious about the move.'

'You're the loyal one. I would have ditched her long ago.' Niall guided her across the street.

'Dee says that too but I see that hurt little girl behind all that veneer. Jazzy's exactly the same. The way you're brought up moulds you. Our parents gave us their time as well as their love. Colette always had to compete with Jacqueline and Frank's work. Growing their firm was more important to them than anything else and she was a lonely, sad little girl who hid it all behind that façade of bravado and that's why I don't take too much notice of her disparaging remarks. And she can be great fun when we're on our own and she's not trying to impress anyone.'

'You're a big softie, that's what you are.' Niall stopped and pulled her into his arms and kissed her soundly in the middle of the footpath.

'*And* I love your love handles,' he teased when he raised his head.

'And I love you,' she sighed happily as they resumed their stroll to the nearest coffee shop.

'Let's ask Carla if Jazzy can sleep in the other room, cos I'm really sick of her.' Jasmine stiffened as she heard the whispers behind the bedroom door. She had gone to the bathroom to brush her teeth and left her two companions getting into their pyjamas in their bedroom, while Carla made them all hot chocolate.

'We can't do that, it would be mean,' said Millie, sighing deeply. 'We just have to put up with her! Mam says she's just spoilt because she has no sister to play with and she doesn't know how to share and we have to be friends and be kind to her.'

'Well I just don't like that girl. She ruined our day!' Jasmine heard Sophie say indignantly. Her heart gave a very painful twist and she wanted to cry. How *dare* those girls talk about her like that? As if she wanted to be friends with them. She had *plenty* of friends in London. Her nanny was always bringing her to play in the park with them. She wished Elisabetta was here to give her a cuddle and tell her everything was all right. If only she hadn't got sick Jasmine would have been staying at her Grandma Jacqueline's, in her lovely room with the huge rocking horse and ginormous doll's house that she loved playing with. It used to be her mummy's bedroom when she was a little girl. But her grandparents were at the wedding too and she was feeling very alone, as she often did.

Jasmine took a deep breath and swallowed hard and pushed open the bedroom door. Millie got a bit red in the face but Sophie just looked cross. 'I think I might ask Carla if I can sleep in the other room on that bed. You know I have my *own* room at home and at Grandma Jacqueline's. With all my *own* toys. I don't like sleeping with other girls and I don't really like sharing if I don't want to,' she announced defiantly. 'It must be horrid to have to share your room and toys and wardrobe and everything. You see, if you were rich like me you'd have your own bedroom each.'

'Oh!' Millie said, astonished at this display of bad manners.

'Well my daddy has a very good job and we have plenty of money too,' she retorted.

'But are *you* going to Disneyland?' Jasmine demanded triumphantly.

Sophie folded her arms across her chest and stared at her. 'Didn't your mammy tell you that caring is sharing?'

'My mummy lets me do what I *like*. And *I* don't share and *I* don't care,' Jasmine said haughtily and grabbed her dressing gown and marched downstairs leaving the two sisters speechless at this display of impudence.

CHAPTER SIXTEEN

'. . . and needless to say, Niall, I'll be in the right place to keep an eye open for investment opportunities and I can give you the nod!' Des scraped the last bit of strawberry roulade from his dish and ate it with relish.

'Is that not considered to be insider trading?' Niall leaned back in his chair, wishing he was anywhere but where he was. The other man had out-talked everyone else at the table, taking charge of the conversation and directing it back to himself and his 'golden opportunities', every chance he got.

'Oh come on, now, it's not as if you're going to be investing millions,' scoffed Des. 'Everyone gives a few tips here and there. They don't go after us for helping out small fry. They're only interested in the big players. Mind you I got a great tip two years ago that made me the guts of half a mil. It's all about who you know.'

'Thanks, I'll keep it in mind,' Niall said politely, thinking what a patronizing gobshite the other man was.

'Now the boring speeches,' yawned Des as the father of the bride clinked his fork against his champagne glass and called for silence.

'Did you think any more about coming to London to be with me for my last couple of days?' Colette leaned across Niall to speak to Hilary.

'I'm not sure how I'm going to be fixed. The girls will be on holiday so I'll have to sort them out,' Hilary murmured, not wishing to be rude when Rowena's father was speaking.

'Oh please try,' she begged. 'My nerves will be shot, you know what I'm like when I get in a tizzy. We'll have some fun. I'll bring you to San Lorenzo for lunch, Di might be there.'

'Couldn't your parents go over if I can't make it?' Hilary whispered.

'You must be joking, take time away from their precious court cases?' snorted Colette, who had been lashing into the champagne they'd been served non stop since they'd arrived at the hotel that afternoon.

'Shush, you pair! ' ordered Niall.

'Oohhh I love bossy men,' giggled Colette. 'Excuse me, I have to go and pee.'

'I think I'll slip out too and smoke a Robusto. Superb flavour. Woody but not too strong. Join me if you like,' Des invited.

'Thanks, I don't care for cigars, but you go right ahead,' Niall replied, clapping at a lame joke the bride's father had attempted.

'Oh you're familiar with Cuban cigar brands?' Des looked surprised.

'Duty free *is* my business,' Niall said coolly.

'Oh of course, I must get you to get me a few cases at cost price!' Des replied, ever the opportunist. 'See you later.'

'God, they're so rude, I was glad they went out. She's pissed,' Hilary remarked when the speeches were over and people began to stretch their limbs and head for the bar.

'I wouldn't mind getting pissed myself. It might be the best of food and drink here but this is more like a corporate do than a wedding and two hours non stop of Des's waffling is doing my head in.' Niall glanced at his watch. It had gone nine. He'd been right about the food, it had been 7 p.m. before the meal was served, although there had been champagne and canapés for the guests when they'd arrived from the church.

'We'll stay until about eleven and slip away,' Hilary soothed. Her husband was right, the wedding was big, brash and corporate and she had no desire to sit listening to more of Colette's tipsy giggling. She need not have worried – the other couple never came back to their table. There were far too many High Society guests to mingle with and impress.

Hilary and Niall stayed chatting for a while to the other guests at their table before drifting up to the bar to order more drinks, where they met some of Pete's relatives who felt completely out of their depth at such an elite gathering. Niall and Hilary introduced themselves and they all ended up having a great bit of banter and a laugh.

'We were dropped like hot potatoes,' Niall murmured into her ear later as they smooched to 'It Started With A Kiss'. They could see Colette and Des chatting animatedly to Barbara and Ronan Dolan, a high-profile couple who owned several hotels, including a very luxurious spa hotel in Sandy Lane. 'I bet they're angling for an invite to Barbados,' Niall speculated, watching Des nodding in agreement with something Ronan said. The dance floor was heaving and the heat was overpowering. A girl weaving around boisterously to the music bumped into Hilary, her stiletto heel stabbing into her foot. She apologized carelessly before being swallowed up in the swaying crowd.

'Will we head off? My feet are killing me. These shoes are torture,' Hilary suggested, grimacing in pain.

'I thought you'd never say it.' Niall couldn't hide his relief that the ordeal was coming to an end.

'Right, let's say goodnight to Rowena and Pete and make a move.' The bride and groom were chatting to Pete's mother and sister and Rowena hugged Hilary when she saw her. 'Listen, Pete and I have decided that when we move into the house we're going to dress up in our wedding clothes and have a party with all our *real* friends. Niall, will you bring the bodhrán and we'll have a proper hooley with people we know and love?'

'Sure,' he said easily. 'Great idea.'

'This is mad, we don't know half the people here.' Rowena glanced around the room and made a face.

'Oh listen; talking about the house, I have just the chap for you to help you decorate. You'll love him,' Hilary said. 'I'll get him to meet us in Illuminations when we're planning the lighting system and see what he has to say. His name is Jonathan Harpur, he's fun,' Hilary said enthusiastically.

'Brilliant, I'd love that. The parents-in-law want us to go with Coburn and Taylor, they decorated their house, but it's like a luxury hotel and it's not the look I want for our house. I want a home! I'd love to meet this Jonathan chap,' Rowena agreed eagerly.

'Right, I'll sort it when you're back from your honeymoon. We're going to head off now and we just wanted to say thanks for a lovely day.'

'No, thank you for coming, Hilary. I'm sorry we didn't get to spend any time with you.'

'Don't worry your head about it, I'll see you soon.' They hugged again and then someone else arrived to claim the bride's attention and Hilary and Niall made their way along the side of the dance floor.

'I presume they aren't going to collect Jasmine tonight?' Niall nodded in Colette's direction.

'I wouldn't imagine so, but I'd better tell them we're going,' Hilary said, pushing through the throng.

'We're slipping away, Colette.' She tapped her friend on the shoulder.

'Ooohhh, sweetie,' gushed the other woman, 'you can't leave yet, we've hardly had a drink together. Niall, we have to dance.'

'No, we're going.' Hilary was firm. 'You won't be collecting Jasmine tonight, I take it?'

'Do you mind if we don't, lovie? It's a bit late and we'll be here for another while. I'll pick her up in the morning and we'll have coffee and a chat. Bye, sweetie, bye.' She kissed Hilary, waved at Niall and turned back to Barbara and Ronan.

'Sweetie my ass,' Niall said caustically as they stepped out into the refreshingly balmy breeze to hail a taxi. 'You're supposed to be one of her closest friends and she made no effort, apart from sitting at the meal with us, to spend time with you, and she wants you to go to London in case she's in a "tizzy" when she's leaving. She has some nerve. Don't you dare put yourself out for that one any more. She uses you, Hilary, always has, and you deserve far better than that.'

'We'll see how I'm fixed,' Hilary murmured, relieved when a taxi pulled in, putting an end to the conversation. She hated it when her sister and husband implied that she was some sort of doormat in regard to Colette. They had been friends for many years. She was used to her and her ways, although there were times, such as today, when Colette *did* behave badly and make her feel used. She was pushing it . . . hard.

All of the O'Mahonys were social climbers who had forgotten their roots, she thought crossly, thinking of how Jacqueline never invited Hilary's mother to her really posh soirées. Sally had been a very kind friend down the years, minding Colette for Jacqueline when she was young, but the more successful Jacqueline grew the looser the tie of friendship became. Now it was only the annual party at Christmas for the 'second tier', as Hilary privately called the gathering, which included Niall and herself, who were invited out of duty and faux largesse. Was that the way her friendship with Colette would end, she wondered as they drove through the thronged city streets, crowded with weekend revellers.

She *would* go to London, she decided impulsively. She would use Colette to have a few days away. It would be nice to lunch in one of the chic restaurants in Kensington and then go for a stroll in the park, up to that beautiful palace that she saw so often in news reports of Princess Diana. And she could treat herself to some beauty treatments and a shopping spree. It had been ages since she'd been on one and she could do with updating her wardrobe. A mini break would do her all the good in the world, Hilary decided, cheering up somewhat. *And* it would give her an opportunity to tell Colette that she was behaving like a selfish little princess and it wasn't acceptable. Hilary cut her a lot of slack, but not any more. It was time she made a stand.

'Grandma, Grandma!' Jasmine flew into her grandmother's arms around 10.30 the following morning when Jacqueline unexpectedly arrived to collect her. Hilary had been expecting Colette so she had been surprised to find her elegantly turned-out mother on her doorstep, her navy Merc parked outside.

'You were a dear to keep Jasmine, Hilary. I hope you don't mind me coming so early but I want to spend time with her before they go away to the States, and I'm afraid both Des and Colette are a little under the weather – it was a very late night. She asked me to tell you that she'll phone you when she gets back to London,' Jacqueline said in her beautifully modulated voice that had no hint of her Dublin origins.

'That's fine, Mrs O'Mahony. Jazzy's had her breakfast, and she was a very good girl,' Hilary said kindly, handing the other woman Jasmine's overnight bag and thinking that the little girl cuddled into her grandmother was the spitting image of Colette when she was younger. She was glad to see the obvious bond between grandparent and grandchild. Jacqueline was mellowing as the years went by, it seemed.

'Well cheerio then and thanks again,' Jacqueline said briskly, taking Jazzy by the hand and making for the door. 'Enjoy the rest of your Sunday.'

'I will and you too,' Hilary said politely, thinking, as the Merc drove out of sight, how rude it was of Jasmine to not even say thank you and how lacking of Jacqueline not to insist upon it.

'So they've got bad hangovers – serves them right. At least we didn't have to listen to them yakking about who they met and mingled with last night,' Niall said, pouring her a mug of fresh coffee he'd just brewed. 'Come on, the girls are out the back on the swings – let's take our papers outside and relax and we'll go to Clontarf Castle for lunch and not bother cooking today.'

'You're on,' she agreed, picking up the *Sunday Tribune* Niall had bought earlier.

Her daughters were swinging happily at the end of the garden, the sun was warm on her face, Niall was sitting opposite her flicking through a Sunday supplement; she was a very lucky woman to have such a happy family life, Hilary thought gratefully, thinking of Jasmine going back to her grandmother's house to parents that clearly did not have her happiness as a priority in their fast-paced lives. She wouldn't swap her life with Colette's for all the tea in China, that was for sure.

'Darling, I'm *soooooo* sorry it's been so long. Honestly, it's all been *maaad!*' Colette trilled gaily down the phone two months later.

'Is that so, Colette?' Hilary said tartly. 'You went off to London without even ringing to say goodbye. You never even thanked me for having Jazzy to stay for Rowena's wedding. You dropped Niall and me like hot potatoes that day, to lick up to the so-called movers and shakers. How rude was that? *And* I thought you wanted me to come over and stay for a couple of days, when you were leaving. What happened to *that* plan? You went to America and didn't even pick up the phone to contact me. Some friend you are, Colette O'Mahony.' Hilary couldn't hide her anger. She had been sizzling about Colette's behaviour for weeks and she was going to give vent to her feelings. This time she'd really had enough! She'd had this conversation in her head for the last two months: now it was for real and she was glad to have her say.

'Oh!' Colette was taken aback by Hilary's unexpected onslaught. 'Well, things were *so* hectic, and so many people wanted to see me before I left, and then Carole Curtis arranged a dinner in San Lorenzo the night before I went and I couldn't very well turn it down, and it was all just craaazy! But listen, you'll have to come over to New York sometime this year. Apart from the humidity I *adore* it here. We are having a ball, we've got a fabulous apartment in Tribeca and we've spent a few weekends in the Hamptons and Nantucket. We've made some great friends; I don't know what I was worried about. And Jazzy *loves* it and *loves* her new au pair.' Colette ignored Hilary's outburst completely as she always did when they rowed.

'That's great, Colette, I'm delighted for you,' Hilary said flatly. 'Just a word of advice about your new friends. To have a friend you have to *be* a friend, which is something you don't know *anything* about and—'

'Oh don't be huffy with me, Hil. You know you're my *best* friend and I hate it when you're cool,' Colette begged.

'Well you've a funny way of showing friendship, that's all I can say,' Hilary retorted. 'You should be *ashamed* of yourself for treating me like this after all these years. I've been a bloody good friend to you.'

'I know. I know, I'm terrible, the worst friend ever,' Colette agreed gaily. 'Listen, I have to fly, that's the doorman buzzing me. A Town Car has arrived to bring me to the Met. I'm meeting the owner of a *fantastic* art gallery, Madeleine van der Post, for lunch. We'll talk soon. I'll fax you my address and phone number,' Colette cooed. 'Love to all and when you come to the Big Apple I'll give you the time of your life and I'll make it up to you, I *promise*—'

'Don't bother your arse, Colette, because I won't be coming to the Big Apple,' Hilary said furiously. 'I've had it with you, lady. You can go and get lost! You're no friend of mine!' She slammed down the phone, livid at Colette's bad behaviour.

Colette O'Mahony Williams could frig off for herself. She'd had more than enough of her.

'Phew!' Colette murmured, staring at the phone. She hadn't expected Hilary to be *quite* as mad as she was. Surely she must have realized how crazy the last months had been. She could be *totally* unreasonable sometimes. She'd expected a lecture for not being in touch but this was the first time Hilary had ever hung up on her. *And* said, *You're no friend of mine! That hurt!*

'Narky cow!' she muttered crossly, flinging herself on the sofa, and picking up the latest copy of *Vogue*. Hilary would get over her temper tantrum and call her back. She was never able to sustain a row. She wouldn't keep this one going, Colette thought confidently, settling down for a read of one of her all-time favourite magazines.

Typical of Colette to ignore her anger and rebukes and pretend everything was fine, Hilary raged, flinging knives and forks from the dishwasher container into the cutlery drawer. Typical of her to take no responsibility for their friendship whatsoever. Typical! Typical! Typical!

'I hope you told her to stick her invite,' Niall said at supper that night when the girls were in bed and she told him about Colette's phone call. 'Colette has proved my point over and over. She doesn't *know* the meaning of the word *friendship*. There's an old saying, *There comes a time when you have to stop crossing oceans for people who wouldn't even jump puddles for you*. That time is now, Hilary. Forget her, she couldn't give a toss about your friendship and the sooner you recognize that the better.'

'Ah stop, Niall, it's just the way she is,' Hilary said, his words making her feel uncomfortable. She hated acknowledging the truth of what he was saying. It made her feel a failure.

'That's all I'm saying, I'm off to bed, I'm whacked and I've an early flight.' He kissed her and walked out of the kitchen.

Hilary sat with her hands around her mug of cocoa. Much as she hated agreeing with him on this, she knew her husband was right. Colette was on the other side of the Atlantic, had been there two months without making contact. She was building a new life, just as she'd done in London. They had nothing in common any more and it was time to admit that she and Colette had never had a *real* friendship. They were more a habit, she thought in surprise. And a bad one at that. She wouldn't be crossing the Atlantic, physically or metaphorically, for Colette any time soon. It was time for letting go.

When Hilary hadn't phoned three months later, Colette couldn't stand it any longer. Even though she was up to her eyes settling in to her exciting new life, attending functions, networking for all she was worth, finding her way around the city, every time she got a phone call she still expected it to be Hilary. They'd often gone for two months or more without getting in touch, but never as long as this, and usually it would be Hilary who would ring.

It was almost Christmas, and Hilary hadn't even sent a card. Unheard of! Colette had sent a card, and a parcel, to the Hammonds, with three fabulous Marc Jacobs leather handbags, and a Ralph Lauren wallet for Niall that she'd got in the Black Friday sales after Thanksgiving. But not a word of thanks from Hilary. And she had made sure to enclose a card with her New York address and phone number. Colette was rattled to say the least.

On Christmas Eve, before heading out to brunch at Tavern on the Green with her parents, who had flown over to celebrate the season with them, Colette slipped into the bedroom and dialled Hilary's number from the phone on her bedside table.

To her dismay, Niall answered. Colette swallowed. Pretend everything's normal, she told herself. 'Niall, Happy Christmas,' she said brightly.

'The same to you. Who's this?' he asked.

'It's me, Colette,' she almost squeaked.

'Oh!' His tone was chilly, and her heart sank.

'I just wanted to wish you all the compliments of the season and make sure the parcel arrived OK. Is Hilary there?' she persevered.

'Hold on and I'll see if she wants to talk to you.' She could hear the sound of Bing Crosby singing 'White Christmas' in the background, and one of the girls calling Niall, looking for matches.

Probably to light a candle in the window, an old Irish custom on Christmas Eve, Colette thought, feeling lonely and homesick for her home town. Would Hilary talk to her? If she didn't it really was the end of their friendship, and Colette, for the first time, began to realize what a loss it would be to her. Hilary was like her big sister. Always there in times of trouble. Always a shoulder to cry on, or a sounding board for advice. Her heart was thumping when she heard the phone being picked up. Would it be Niall to tell her that Hilary didn't want to speak to her?

'Hello.' Hilary's voice came down the line and Colette exhaled, not realizing that she had been holding her breath. The relief was so immense she forgot she was going to act breezy and unconcerned.

'I'm sorry, Hilary,' she blurted. 'I didn't mean to hurt you. Please say you're still my friend.'

'Crummy timing as always, Colette,' Hilary said. 'I'm up to my elbows in stuffing.' But Colette knew she was teasing.

'Do you forgive me?' she ventured.

'Just about, but don't do it again,' her friend warned.

'And would you have let Christmas go by without ringing me?' Colette asked, still amazed that Hilary had held out for so long.

'It's a possibility, for sure,' Hilary answered. 'But we'll never know now, will we?'

'You never sent a card.'

'Did you deserve one?'

'I suppose not,' Colette conceded. 'Did you get the parcel?'

'Yes. I was undecided whether or not to put it under the tree,' Hilary said coolly.

'Oh!'

'But now that you've phoned and apologized, a first, I may add, I probably will.' Hilary softened. 'Now I really do have to go. I've to fit in visits to the parents and I'm way behind schedule. Happy Christmas, Colette. I'm glad you rang.'

'Me too. Happy Christmas, Hilary. I'll call you in the new year,' Colette said eagerly.

'Do that,' Hilary agreed. 'See you.'

'Bye, Hilary. I'm glad we're talking again.'

'Me too. Talk soon.' And then she was gone, and Colette heaved a sigh of relief. Hilary was still a bit cool, but at least they were back on track, and that was all that mattered.

'You're a big softie.' Niall shook his head.

'It's Christmas and she made the first move and I don't like holding grudges.' Hilary resumed chopping parsley and thyme. The kitchen was filled with the aromas of Christmas, herbs, spices, candle wax, pine, and a tape of seasonal songs and carols added to the festive atmosphere in the Hammond household.

'She won't change, you know,' her husband warned her.

Hilary laughed. 'I know that, Niall. I'm not a complete idiot. Someday we'll drift apart or she'll push me so far there won't be any turning back, but that's not today, and I'm glad she phoned. It shows she values the friendship at some level, and that's all that matters for the moment. Now be a good husband and pour me a glass of wine, because you're driving tonight, and I want to get into the Christmas spirit,' Hilary instructed briskly.

'Ho! Ho! Ho!' grinned Niall, pouring a glass of Merlot for his dearly beloved.

'Ho! Ho! Ho! to you too,' laughed Hilary, raising her glass to him. 'And to absent friends,' she added before taking a sip of the ruby liquid, glad that there was no longer an estrangement between her and Colette.

PART TWO

Millennium Year 2000

BOOM!

CHAPTER SEVENTEEN

'I'm really sorry, Jonathan, I thought we would have been out of here ages ago. Someone collapsed so the clinic's running way behind and Mrs Hammond's not been seen yet. I'll be with you as soon as I can,' Hilary murmured into her mobile as she stood in the busy hospital corridor outside the warfarin clinic where her mother-in-law was waiting to be tested.

'Why couldn't "The Secretary" bring her?' Jonathan asked snippily, referring to Hilary's sister-in-law, Sue. He called her 'The Secretary' because she was always banging on about being the PA to a busy property developer, or, as Jonathan called him, 'A-Builder-with-Attitude'.

'She's too busy and couldn't take the time off work,' Hilary said flatly.

'Oh and *you're* not too busy and it's OK for *you* to take time off work and Mrs H is not even *your* mother,' Jonathan grouched.

'Stop giving out, I'll be with you as soon as I can,' Hilary retorted. 'See you.' She hung up, switched her phone to vibrate mode and slid it back into her bag.

'Hilary dear, why don't you go ahead. I know you have a

meeting to get to. I'll get a taxi home,' Margaret urged when Hilary went back into the waiting room and sat down beside her mother-in-law.

'Not at all, Gran, I rang Jonathan and told him I'd be a bit delayed and he can do his designer bits until I get there.'

'He's a lovely lad, I'm very fond of him.' Margaret smiled, her grey eyes twinkling.

'Me too.' Hilary smiled back, thinking what a beautiful complexion her seventy-five-year-old mother-in-law had. Nivea Crème was her secret, Margaret assured her. She had used it since she was a young woman.

'I feel bad about delaying you, dear. I know you're busy,' the old lady fretted.

'Don't worry about it at all,' Hilary soothed. She didn't want Niall's mother feeling under pressure. Margaret Hammond was a kind, gentle lady and a great mother-in-law and grandmother. She had welcomed Hilary into the family with open arms. Early in their relationship she'd confided to Hilary that of all the girls Niall had brought home, Hilary was the one that Margaret had hoped he'd marry. When the grandchildren had been born, Niall's parents couldn't have been happier and Margaret had been a very hands-on grandmother. When her husband had died, she had become even more immersed in their family, and sometimes Hilary felt she had two mothers.

Sue, Niall's sister, could not be more different and the relationship she had with Hilary was superficial and distant. She made fleeting appearances at family events but her lifestyle was so busy and all-consuming, family were way down the ladder. Brash and self-absorbed, Sue took no responsibility for her now elderly mother's care, and as Margaret grew more frail, needing frequent doctors' appointments, it fell to Hilary and Niall to do the lion's share of caring. If she hadn't been truly fond of her mother-in-law she would have been a bubbling cauldron of resentment, Hilary reflected when Margaret was finally called for her blood test.

Her own mother was recovering from a bad dose of flu and between visiting Sally and cooking meals for both sets of elderly parents, as well as being up to her eyes at work, Hilary was feeling fraught and stretched. It was Sophie's' birthday at the weekend and her daughter wanted to host a sleepover for five of her friends. A daunting prospect.

I'll think about it tomorrow, Hilary thought, doing a Scarlett O'Hara on it and hoping against hope that Margaret might get away with a month before being tested again. She had been taking antibiotics and steroids for a chest infection and they played havoc with her warfarin.

It wasn't to be, and Hilary's heart sank when the nurse gave them an appointment for the following fortnight. Sue would have to bring her mother to that appointment and that was the end of it, Hilary decided, not relishing the thought of the phone call she would have to make to her sister-in-law.

'I know you're in a hurry so we won't stop for coffee,' Margaret said when Hilary helped her into her coat.

'Are you sure?' she said, feeling a bit of a heel. She knew her mother-in-law loved their cup of coffee and scone after her warfarin test, but she really needed to drop her home and get to Castleknock to meet Jonathan and their new client.

'We'll do it again,' Margaret assured her, slipping a pair of black-leather gloves onto her thin hands and grasping her walking stick firmly. She had broken her ankle in a fall and was only recently out of plaster and was a little unsteady on her feet. Hilary had offered to get her a wheelchair but Margaret wanted to get along under her own steam. If you gave in to yourself it was another step on the slippery road to dependency was her reasoning.

'I'll tell you what, let me get a few cream cakes on my way home and I'll pop in for a cuppa later with the girls,' she suggested, taking her mother-in-law's arm and tailoring her pace to suit Margaret's.

'Lovely! I'll have the fire lighting. I haven't seen them since last week.' Margaret perked up. Since Niall's father had passed away two years previously she was lonely and loved company. Her granddaughters were her pride and joy and Sophie and Millie loved her dearly. But they were busy at secondary school now, their lives full, of study, sport and girly sessions with their friends. Sometimes she hardly saw them herself, if she was working down the country on a project, Hilary thought ruefully, hoping she hadn't got clamped in the hospital car park.

It was over an hour later that she swung into the circular drive of a large, detached, double-fronted, red-brick house in Castleknock and saw Jonathan's black BMW parked beside a massive SUV.

Hard to believe that Jonathan was now driving a top-of-the-range BMW. Hilary smiled, remembering a couple of boneshakers he'd driven in the early days of their partnership. He had come a long way from his studio flat, and his

Civil Service job, in the past ten years. He had used every contact Kinsella Illuminations had provided – builders, electricians, quantity surveyors – to claw his way to the top. There was so much building going on, extending the commuter belt, he'd ended up decorating a slew of show houses along the east coast, from Dundalk to Gorey, while she'd handled the lighting design, and as their portfolio grew over the years of the Celtic Tiger, their work had multiplied.

She pulled up behind the BMW and glanced in her mirror and frowned. She certainly looked stressed, she thought, noting the deepening lines around eyes and mouth. She needed to touch up her lipstick. She applied a slick of Mulberry Rose, sprayed some L'Air du Temps on her wrist and got out of the car. A squally gust blew her hair into her eyes and she shivered. It could very well snow, Hilary thought, looking at the leaden sky and the banks of dark clouds that were rolling ominously in from the east.

A young woman with a baby in her arms answered the door. Early twenties, foreign, had to be the au pair rather than the client, Hilary surmised. 'Ello, madam,' the young woman said politely. 'Madam ees expecting you. Let me take your coat and show you upstairs. Zhat ees where zey are now.'

'Thank you.' Hilary followed her in to a wide, bright hall, papered in an elegant grey, green and gold stripe above the white dado rail and painted a pale mint green below. Very nice, Hilary thought, admiring the sparkling chandelier and the gleaming bevelled wall mirror that made the hall look even more spacious and light.

The baby smiled a huge toothless grin at her as she

followed the au pair up the grey-and-gold-carpeted stairs and Hilary's heart melted. She had a sudden, overpowering longing to cuddle the baby and feel its soft downy head against her cheek, nestled in against her. *Oh for God's sake!* she thought wildly. *Haven't you enough on your plate without getting broody?*

'Ah there you are!' Jonathan appeared at the top of the stairs immaculately turned out in his D&G ruby shirt, black trousers, and a black-and-ruby scarf knotted casually around his neck. His blond hair was perfectly highlighted and styled and Hilary felt guilty that she hadn't made more of an effort with her own appearance. She was wearing a taupe trouser suit and black cami and a string of pearls but her indulgences at Christmas and the Millennium New Year celebrations had resulted in her piling on at least half a stone in weight. The waistband of her trousers was digging in to her. Her boobs were stretching the cami, which clung to her spare tyre, and she knew she had a VPL. At least she smelt perfumed, she thought ruefully, catching Jonathan's gaze at her cleavage. She looked down and saw her glasses and a tissue tucked into her bra and managed to whip them out and shove them in her handbag before a slender young woman in jeans and a lilac cashmere jumper emerged from the bedroom Jonathan had come from. 'Hi, you must be Hilary.' She smiled. 'I'm Andrea Keirns. Thanks for coming—'

'Terribly sorry I'm late. I got delayed at a clinic with my mother-in-law,' Hilary explained, hastily shaking hands.

'No worries, Jonathan and I have had a wonderful time plotting and planning,' Andrea said gaily, holding her arms out for the baby. 'Yolanda, will you go and make us coffee, please, and serve it in the library,' she instructed her au pair.

'Yes, madam,' the girl said dutifully, her long black hair swinging behind her from its high ponytail as she hurried downstairs.

'I adore what you did with Rowena's house. Her parents are friends of my mother's,' Andrea raved. 'As I was telling Jonathan, this house was the family home, but my dad passed away several years ago and my brother is in Australia and it's got too big for my mother to rattle around in on her own – it's got five bedrooms – so me and my husband have sold our house and bought this one and Mum's moved into the mews at the end of the garden. We want to do a big makeover and update it. I'd love to have a lighting system installed with dimmers and spots, and something similar, but *different*, to Rowena's,' Andrea explained chattily. 'But needless to say I don't want her to think I'm copying her,' she added hastily. 'I absolutely love the way you put the lights in the wall at floor level in the hall and landing, and the lights up the stairs. That was *gorgeous*!' Andrea enthused. 'And besides you designed that a few years back, it's at least eight or nine years ago if I remember, so when we get ours done it will be even more contemporary, which is the look I'm going for.'

'Expensive though, as I'm sure Jonathan has told you. All the walls will have to be chased and replastered,' Hilary pointed out, shooting a look at Jonathan who gave a slight shrug.

'Oh that's no problem, we've remortgaged to get the job done. It's fine,' Andrea said airily. 'I want to put *my* stamp

211

on it and totally modernize it. All white walls, very mini-malist, and wooden floors.'

'Well off-white,' Jonathan cut in smoothly. 'With feature walls and splashes of colour in the accessories. You don't want it to look *too* cold. I'm thinking crimson, mint green, and grey cushions, throws and lampshades to suit the look Andrea wants.'

'Very nice,' agreed Hilary, privately thinking what a shame it would be to change the relaxing pastel colour palette that Andrea's parents had decorated the house in. It had a warm, welcoming feel and it didn't need a whole lot of refurbishing, Hilary thought, eyeing the expensive luxury deep-pile carpets and the tasteful drapes and blinds. Even the softest of lighting could not completely take the cool look from white, no matter what colours accessorized the house. White was fine for hot sunny climates, she reflected as a sudden squall of rain hurled against the landing window and the dreary gloom outside emphasized the snug warm interior space she was standing in. House makeovers on TV had certainly caught people's imaginations, but sometimes they were OTT and looked disastrous. Hilary had long ago learned that most clients knew exactly what look they wanted and it was up to her and Jonathan to advise and facilitate rather than impose their own tastes on a project.

'Jonathan tells me you're working on a lot of leisure centres and spas. I love going to Powerscourt Springs. Have you ever been?' she asked eagerly.

'Oh indeed we have!' Hilary laughed. 'When it opened a few years ago Jonathan and I hot-footed it down to Wicklow to see what all the fuss was about.'

'We did a lot of "research" in Powerscourt Springs. Well that was our excuse,' Jonathan grinned. 'There's a lot of new places springing up – if you'll excuse the pun – but Powerscourt Springs led the way in health farms in Ireland, it was the first, and to my mind it's still the best. Those views of the Sugar Loaf and the Wicklow countryside ... wow ... and that Tranquillity Room with the recliner couches – I have to admit, it was my inspiration for a few places I've designed myself.'

'Me too,' confessed Hilary. 'I wouldn't mind being there right now, sitting in that lovely lounge, wrapped in a towelling robe, looking out at that horrible weather, waiting for a facial or massage.'

'Ooohh yes,' agreed Andrea. 'Or tucking into their gorgeous lunches. That walnut bread—'

'Stop!' commanded Jonathan. 'You're making me hungry. We need to focus on the job in hand,' he added briskly.

'Right well I'd like really soft lighting in our bedroom and en suite. Also I'm very tempted to break down the walls and have a freestanding claw-foot bath with antique fittings. I think that's a fabulous look too. All white to match my white-lace Egyptian-cotton bedlinen. And I want white voile draped over the four-poster and white louvre blinds—'

'I'm sure Jonathan has advised that you'd need to factor in steam removal so damp won't become a problem if you go down that route,' Hilary interjected, ever the pragmatist.

'Indeed,' Jonathan affirmed. 'I've made all these points to Andrea, but this of course is just a preliminary discussion.'

'Of course.' Hilary smiled at her partner and he gave her a tiny wink.

'And you know the way they play that very calming music in all the treatment rooms in spas? I'd really like to have a sound system installed as well,' Andrea declared, waving a perfectly manicured hand in the air. 'I don't think Rowena has one.'

'We can give you a quote for that too – we've worked with a firm who install them,' Jonathan assured their client, who was seriously determined not only to keep up with the Joneses but to outdo them.

It was all about impressing and outdoing people these days, he thought, amused at the notion that he, who had grown up in a small semi in a country town, decorating doll's houses made out of shoeboxes, was now working in a business that catered for the most affluent of Irish society. *It was far from health farms and claw-foot baths and sound systems you were reared*, he thought, looking forward to telling his mother about his latest client. It would be interesting to see if Andrea and her husband would follow through with all their proposed renovations when they got their quote.

Listening to Jonathan and Andrea discuss colour schemes for the refurbished bathroom Hilary felt some of the tension she'd been aware of begin to recede, and she slipped into working mode and took her big notebook from her briefcase and began to take notes and draw diagrams of the various rooms.

Margaret Hammond stared out at the sleeting rain bouncing off the circular cream-and-brown ceramic table on her patio. Her garden, though rain-battered and windswept, was well kept, thanks to the gardener that her son paid for to come once a fortnight. Niall was a generous son, she couldn't deny, but he expected a lot of Hilary. Her daughter-in-law had her own demanding job; surely he could have taken an hour or two off to bring her to the clinic. There was no point in Margaret expecting her daughter to take the time off. Sue was so absorbed in her own life she had no time for anyone else.

Margaret sighed as she struggled to open the cap of her paracetamol container. She felt very arthritic today, always did when it rained. Old age was unforgiving and unrelenting and a cause of great worry to her. She could feel her body deteriorating. Her eyesight was beginning to fade, her hearing getting poorer. The breathlessness caused by her heart congestion was increasing. The water tablets she took were affecting her potassium levels and had to be adjusted and it was just one thing after another, she thought glumly, as the urge to pee increased and she hoped she'd make it to the loo without wetting herself.

What would happen, she wondered, limping back into the kitchen, if she just stopped taking all her tablets? If she thought she would go quickly to her eternal rest she'd do it, Margaret thought defiantly, wishing she had the nerve. Death did not worry her. It was the way of her going that concerned her. Her great fear about stopping her tablets was suffering a stroke and being trapped in her body. Her other great fear was ending up in a nursing home.

She knew Hilary and Niall would do the best they could for her. Sue would think a nursing home was the perfect solution ... as long as she didn't have to pay ... How had she reared a daughter who was so ... so indifferent and self-absorbed? Margaret shook her head. She had been too soft on her children and her husband. Done too much for them. It was as much her fault as theirs that Sue and to a lesser extent Niall were somewhat selfish.

She could see in her daughter-in-law the same giving nature she'd had. She saw how Niall and her granddaughters often took Hilary, and all she did for them, for granted. Niall was content to let Hilary run the household and ferry the girls to their various appointments. Margaret had done the same with her family while her husband had concentrated on his job. The difference was, she hadn't worked outside the home. Hilary was a woman with a career and a very successful career at that. She had elderly parents of her own to keep an eye on. She just couldn't be running after her and bringing her to clinics and appointments.

But what other options did she have than to accept her daughter-in-law's assistance, Margaret brooded, finally managing to get her tablet carton opened. She studied the pile of white rectangular tablets. It was a pity they were quite sizeable pills, difficult to swallow a large amount. An overdose caused liver damage, she'd heard. Would that be painless? What would happen if it didn't work? She filled a glass of water and shook two tablets into her palm, and swallowed them.

Coward!

It's a sin to think like that.

If you didn't have warfarin and the likes you'd be dead anyway – it's the tablets that are keeping you alive. You are being kept alive through artificial means.

'Oh stop it!' she said aloud, angrily wiping the tears from her eyes. She didn't normally give in to self-pity but she felt low and fed up today. The come-down from her steroids had kicked in and she missed the artificial energy they gave her. It was disappointing, too, to have to go back to the clinic in two weeks' time. Even if she got a taxi herself, she would still have a long walk to the clinic along hospital corridors, without the comfort of someone beside her if she took a wobbly. But she couldn't impose on Hilary's kindness any longer. She would have to find some long-term solution. It was time to face facts and deal with her situation, instead of sticking her head in the sand, Margaret decided.

She made herself a cup of tea, buttered a slice of bread and cut a hunk off a block of Cheddar cheese. A spoonful of tomato chutney and an apple completed her repast and she carried her cup and plate into her sitting room. It had grown so overcast and gloomy with the rain the room was almost dark. She switched on a lamp, the opaque light casting a warm glow over her armchair. She was tired after her early morning start; a fire would be a nice treat. Normally she didn't light one this early but she deserved some little perk, she told herself, spiritedly placing firelighters and some turf and briquettes from the wicker basket beside the fireplace into the grate. In minutes a comforting blaze threw out a satisfying heat, the flickering flames crackling companionably in the hearth.

'I'm very lucky, I'm still living in my own home, I have my independence and a good pension,' she told herself, trying to raise her spirits with her little pep talk. After her lunch and a nap in front of the fire she would do her physio exercises and give some considered thought to making herself even more independent and taking some pressure off her much loved daughter-in-law. Perhaps it was time to give serious consideration to going into a nursing home, even if it was the last thing she wanted to do.

CHAPTER EIGHTEEN

'More money than sense,' Hilary remarked later that afternoon as she and Jonathan pored over a diagram of Andrea's house, discussing the optimum placement of lights to suit Jonathan's interior design plan and Andrea's desires. 'Imagine remortgaging to spend an absolute fortune on redesigning that lovely house. They could have paid off their mortgage and borrowed from the Credit Union, and they wouldn't be paying a massive amount of interest for the next twenty years.'

'We're not all sensible like you, daahling.' Jonathan took a slug of coffee and stretched. 'I'm in hoc up to my eyeballs with my mortgage and 2000 car, but I just adore driving around in my lovely new shiny BMW.'

'But you don't have kids and college fees ahead, you're a free agent, and besides that penthouse you bought has increased in price with all that renovation you've done on it. You'll more than double your price for it the way things are going. Property prices are still going *way* up. People won't be able to get on the property ladder soon,' she pointed out.

'That's the Celtic Tiger, babes. Economy expanding more than 9 per cent. One hundred per cent loans from the bank, plenty of people will be buying, and we'll be saying no to more jobs than we'll be saying yes to,' Jonathan predicted confidently. 'I mean look at how you've had to employ two extra people in the showrooms and three more electricians. It's all taken off everywhere you look.'

'Yeah I know, it's incredible how much the business has grown in the last few years, but you make sure you save some of your dosh – we nearly had to close during the last recession in the eighties. I remember my parents being very worried, so I'm saving some of mine for a rainy day.'

'We're doing well, aren't we though?' Hammond and Harpur Interior and Lighting Design Specialists couldn't have happened at a better time. What a stroke of luck for us that the economy's booming and people have massive amounts of dough to spend.' Jonathan grinned. 'Imagine we have a *waiting list*! Imagine I was able to afford to take a *career break*!'

'That's the great thing for you, Jonathan. You have the safety net of the permanent and pensionable job to go back to if things go belly up.'

'I don't know if I'd ever go back; imagine being behind a desk after doing this. No thanks.'

'At least you have the option.'

'Not one I want to take. I love flying by the seat of my pants.'

'It's been mad for sure.' Hilary sighed.

'But fun, a lot of the time, Hil?'

'Yeah!'

'You're in fierce bad form today. What's up, Dac?' he said in a Bugs Bunny voice and she laughed.

'Ah nothing ... everything. Getting stuck at the clinic with Gran H pissed me off. Niall pissed me off because he won't have it out with Sue about doing her bit and I'll have to ring her myself. And I have five teenagers coming for a sleepover tomorrow night, and Niall's got a gig tonight so I've to do a big grocery shop. And then to crown it all I've to go and inspect the 2nd fix on the Horizon House Hotel project next week and I just know that little fart of an electrician is going to muck me around again. He thinks he knows everything and he can't stand the fact that a woman is telling him what to do,' Hilary moaned.

'When are you going? I'll rearrange consults if I have any and come with you,' Jonathan offered.

'Ah you're grand, I'll deal with that little muppet,' Hilary said grimly.

'Look, we haven't seen each other properly for ages. I'll drive us down to Wexford and you can offload on me and I'll tell you all about my new romance!'

'Your what?' Hilary asked, her bad humour forgotten.

'I've met someone new,' Jonathan smirked.

'Right!! Spill!' Hilary refilled their mugs from the percolator of coffee he'd made when they got back to the office.

'Well he's younger than me—'

'Aren't I always telling you to go with someone your own age or someone older for a change?' Hilary threw her eyes up to heaven.

'No, listen. Leon, that's his name, is very mature. He's a dad.'

Hilary raised an eyebrow. 'Married?'

'No!' her friend exclaimed indignantly. 'He was with a

girl for a couple of years and she got pregnant. They never got married and they've separated and she married someone else a few years ago. His son is eight. Leon hasn't come out to his family yet. He's lovely though, honestly. You'll like him.'

They always are, thought Hilary, but she kept that view to herself. 'Where did you meet him?'

'Would you believe I went into a small bistro in Dalkey. I was visiting a client to show her some swatches and I was too early so I went to a little place off a side street to have a cappuccino and a wrap and it was jammers. I sat at a counter and he was sitting beside me, and I dropped a book of swatches and he picked it up. And then we got chatting. Turns out he's a carpenter. We've quite a lot in common actually.'

'And this was a month ago and you're only telling me *now*?' She couldn't hide her surprise. Usually Jonathan would be on the phone immediately after meeting someone new.

'I'm taking your advice; I'm playing it cool. Not rushing anything. I think this could work out, Hil,' Jonathan said, eyes alight.

'Oh Jonathan, I'd love if it did. You so deserve to find someone nice. Someone who will give you as much as you give them. Not a taker or a freeloader – you've had enough of them.' Hilary jumped up and threw her arms around her dear friend and gave him a hug. Her greatest wish for him was that he would find the love of his life and be in the loving relationship he so longed for.

'Aw thanks. Fingers crossed I don't mess up this time. I

don't think Hannah could take any more sob stories ... or you either,' he grimaced. 'Cripes, look at the time, I'd better get out of here, I've to go and meet Davy King in Woodies to mix a particular shade of duck egg blue to go with a fabulous flock wallpaper. It cost a fortune. A hundred and ten sterling a roll, and they needed ten rolls so I *have* to get the paint just right. See ya, darlin'. We've sorted the 2nd fix in Wexford so I'll drive us down next week. Give the gang my love and tell Sophie to have a great sleepover. Give Smokin' Sue hell!' He jumped up off the chair, put all his work designs neatly into a folder and gave her a hug before pulling on his black pure-wool coat and leather gloves.

Hilary laughed. 'I'll phone Sue, all right, for all the good it will do. Give your mother my love and have a good weekend with her.'

'I will. Bye, ducks.' And then he was gone, like a whirling dervish, coat flaps flying open behind him, scarf blowing in the wind as he crossed Illuminations' car park to his shining new pride and joy. He waved as he drove past and she waved back before turning to the paperwork on her untidy desk.

Hilary sighed at the mess of papers that needed her attention. She was not an organized person, not like Jonathan whose desk in his home office was immaculate. Everything filed neatly and colour-coded. It was time he came and did one of her office tidies. He did it every six months or so and would stand over her until every item on her desk was cleared and order ruled once more, until a lack of time and organization would start the whole process off again. Hilary had a secretary who was so busy with

Illuminations business she didn't have time to keep her boss's desk as tidy as each of them would have liked.

Perhaps Hilary could come in for an hour on Sunday and put manners on the place, she decided, pulling out the file for Horizon House to remind herself of the lighting layout. She was studying it intently when her direct line rang. Her husband's number flashed up.

'Hi, sorry, I'm only getting a chance to ring you now. We had the managers over from Dubai and Moscow for a meeting and then I took them to lunch and you know yourself,' he sighed. 'How did Mam get on?'

'She's got an appointment in two weeks because of being on the steroids and antibiotics; they really muck up her blood.' Hilary was not in the mood to hear about Niall's busy day. She had enough work of her own to deal with.

'Rats!' he groaned. 'I won't be here. I have that trip to Canada to visit the concessions in Montreal, Ottawa, Halifax and Winnipeg, remember? That's a nuisance. Can we reschedule for when I'm back?'

'No!' she said irritably. 'That's not an option with warfarin. And I have a client consult that morning so Sue's going to have to do it. I've been asking and asking you to get in touch with her about your mother's appointments and you haven't and I'm sick of it,' she snapped.

'Keep your hair on, I'll ring her when I get a chance,' he growled.

'You've been saying that for ages, Niall. If you don't ring her I will,' she warned.

'I hear you,' he retorted. 'I'll call her today. Anything else strange or startling?' he said, changing the subject.

'No, don't forget Sophie's friends are coming to stay on a sleepover tomorrow so I have to do a shop later. Are you coming home or going straight to the gig tonight?'

'I'll shower and change here and go from work; no point in getting stuck in the rush hour twice. So don't worry about dinner for me.'

'I wasn't,' she said drily. 'I was going to order a Chinese – I haven't time to cook.'

'OK, look, I have to go. I'll try not to wake you up when I get home.'

'OK, bye,' Hilary said unenthusiastically and hung up.

Don't worry about dinner for me. Niall was a hoot, she scowled. Did he really think she was sitting in her office worrying about what to give him for his dinner? Friday night was Chinese night. The only cooked meal he'd be getting this weekend was on Sunday, unless he cooked it himself. Sophie wanted to order in pizza for her friends so Millie and she and Niall could have pizza too. Hilary was planning to cook two joints of roast on Sunday so she could do a dinner for Gran H and her own parents as well, with enough for a dinner for them on Monday. She'd stock up on a few Butler's Pantry meals for her freezer the next time she was passing one of their branches. That would give her a bit of leeway even if it was expensive.

Niall *had* better ring his sister, Hilary scowled, or Ms Susan Hammond Kelly would be getting an irate phone call from her and she didn't care whose feelings would be hurt.

Niall scrolled down through his phone until he got to his sister's number. He sighed deeply, tapping his pen impatiently against his desk as he waited for Sue to answer. He was exasperated having to make the call. He knew his sister of old, knew that she would make excuses about being 'up to her eyes', saying she couldn't take days off 'at the drop of a hat'. And 'couldn't their mother not take a taxi to her various appointments'. The phone rang out and went into voicemail as he knew it would.

'Sue, it's me. Please call me back sooner rather than later. Thanks,' he said crisply. He deliberately didn't say why he wanted her to ring him back and left the message suitably vague hoping that the request might make her think something was up and she would ring to see what was wrong.

They weren't close siblings. Sue was ten years older than him. His mother had suffered several miscarriages before conceiving him. Sue, who had been especially spoilt by their father, had not been impressed with the mewling little stranger who had taken her parents' focus off her. She had left home to share a flat with friends when he was eight and they had nothing in common except their parents. After their father's sudden death she had been happy to let Hilary and Niall provide her mother with the comfort and practical aid that Margaret so badly needed. Gradually Margaret had come to depend on them, taking great solace in the company of her grandchildren. Sue had been happy that she was able to continue to live her life unhampered by the needs of her aged mother. Her free and easy life was coming to an end, Niall thought grimly. Hilary was generally very easygoing but when she got a bee in her bonnet about something it was time to look out.

*

Sue Hammond Kelly's' lips tightened as she listened to her brother's message. What now? she thought irascibly. Was something wrong with their mother or did Niall want something of her? His message was very ambiguous, but he sounded bossy rather than stressed. One way of finding out what was up, she decided, punching in a number on her office landline.

'Hello.' She heard her mother's voice with a flash of relief. Margaret was at home in her own house so all must be well.

'How are things, Mam?' she asked casually. 'How's the chest infection?'

'Ah, Sue, I'm not too bad at all. How are things with you, dear?'

'Oh I'm up to my ears as usual. Mr Barrington is phenomenally busy. He's developing a big shopping centre in the Midlands and is trying to get planning issues sorted and it's all go, I can tell you. I never have a minute.'

'Ah God love you. Poor Hilary is up to her eyes as well. We couldn't go for our usual coffee after my clinic appointment because she had to go to a meeting,' Margaret confided.

'Poor girl,' Sue yawned. 'And how did you get on at the clinic? Did you get four weeks out of it?'

'Unfortunately not,' sighed her mother. 'The steroids and antibiotics have it all out of kilter so I've to go back in two weeks' time.'

'That's a shame,' Sue said sympathetically. 'Look, I'll pop over some night after work for an hour or two, so take it easy. I'll bring some pesto chicken soup and some brown rice. That will build you up. Talk soon, Mam. Cheers.' She hung up and stared out of the window. She knew now why Niall had phoned. He needed her to bring their mother to the clinic. For some reason Hilary mustn't be able to do it. Hilary was her own boss. It was much easier for her to take time off than it was for Sue. Mr Barrington *hated it* when she took days off. He even rang her at home, often at ten or eleven at night, wanting her to organize something for him that couldn't wait until the morning.

Hilary had a much easier life than she had, with her big house and garden, and her two bright children. Margaret thought she was the bee's knees and was always going on about Hilary and Niall's great careers. And she never shut up about Sophie and Millie. It drove Sue up the wall. Her mother didn't mean it, she hoped, but it was almost as though subconsciously Margaret thought Sue was a lesser woman for not having children.

All this fuss about kids was so irritating. Sue had always been upfront about taking the responsible decision not to have children that she didn't *want*. And *still* society pilloried her, she thought crossly, remembering all the times relatives and neighbours, and indeed her parents, had asked when she was going to have a child. And wasn't she leaving it a little late?

'I don't want sprogs,' she would say bluntly and see the faintly incredulous expressions on their faces.

'Ah you'll feel differently when you hold your own in your arms,' or similar was thrown back at her. Eventually she'd told people that Cormac, her husband, had had the snip and it just wasn't going to happen.

It had been a relief when Niall had married Hilary and

they'd had children. It had taken a lot of pressure off her. Sue liked the freedom being childless gave her. She could do her yoga, and Pilates, and hill walking, and keep the figure she worked so hard to maintain. She didn't have one spare ounce of fat on her body, she thought proudly. Not bad for a woman in her early fifties. Her only vice was smoking, but smoking helped keep her weight down. She could mix with the movers and shakers and the political elite her boss socialized with, and be completely confident that she looked her absolute best. But it was hard work. Niall needn't think he was going to start dumping their mother on her. Let *him* take the morning off if his precious Hilary couldn't. After all she was only *pretending* to be a career woman with her itty-bitty lighting carry-on. Sue *was* one.

CHAPTER NINETEEN

Jonathan hummed to himself as he cruised along the M50 in his brand-new Beemer. He was dying to take his mother for a spin in it. She'd be chuffed, he thought proudly. He was fairly chuffed himself. He smiled, loving the smooth way the car purred along in the fast lane. Had he ever thought when he started out working for himself that he would be able to afford a brand-new car? And a BMW at that.

The last ten years of slogging and studying and double jobbing had paid off and he couldn't be more pleased. For the first time in his life, he was in a very confident and comforting place. He was successful in his chosen career, he was happy in his own skin and finally after years of meeting Mr Wrong he was convinced he had found Mr Right. The new Millennium couldn't have started off any better. Maybe after all the brickbats life had thrown at him it was now his time to fly high.

It hadn't been easy, and that was what made this new phase of his life all the richer. He had enrolled in as many extracurricular interior design courses as he could manage and studied hard. His experience with his homophobic boss, at the beginning of the nineties, had been the catalyst for all the changes in his career. That very difficult time had been a blessing in disguise really, he reflected, gearing down to queue to pay his toll.

Jonathan sat, engine idling, while the driver two cars ahead fumbled for coins, remembering how Hannah often said that life's challenges were always a doorway to a 'growth experience' and that it was the way the challenge was met that was just as important to the soul as the challenge itself. Well he had certainly met Gerard Hook's challenge head on, dealt with him and moved on. It was that particular episode that had been his motivation to go for every single work interview he could, to get out of Hook's department.

Taking a career break had certainly been a leap of faith. But something else that Hannah had said to him during one of his counselling sessions had resonated deeply with him. She had told him that when someone knew that something was very right for them and they stepped away from the security of all they knew *that* was when doors opened for them. And open for him they certainly had, Jonathan acknowledged, remembering that nerve-wracking first month when he had taken his career break and there had been no monthly salary to pay his mortgage. But that very week he'd been paid handsomely for the refurbishment of a large three-storey house in Ranelagh – owned by his ex-landlord – that was divided into five one-bedroom flats. He had redesigned the five living quarters in different styles and colours, depending on where they were in the house and what their aspect was. Then he had got a professional photographer to shoot the end products and he couldn't have been more pleased with the results. His subsequent new glossy portfolio looked most professional and prospective new clients were impressed. James, the landlord, also owned two adjoining B&B's near Liberty Hall in the city centre, which he wanted to upgrade into a boutique hotel. He had offered the interior design job to Jonathan and Jonathan had given the lighting contract to Hilary.

It was their first collaboration and it sealed their friendship. They bounced ideas off each other, learned from each other, and had a lot of fun in the process. Slowly and steadily Jonathan's list of clients grew, as word of mouth continued to put business his way. The economy was booming, development was rampant and Hilary and he were perfectly placed to take advantage of the boom. He couldn't have wished for more in his career. All he'd needed to make life perfect was a companion to share it with.

This time he was not going to rush into anything, Jonathan promised himself, knowing his tendency to fall headlong into a relationship, give his heart and soul and more, and be brought crashing to earth when it all ended in tears. 'You should strive to have more *equality* in your relationships, Jonathan,' Hannah would advise him patiently when he would come for counselling, and to pour his heart out to her after yet another heartbreak. 'Stop giving *everything*. Allow yourself to be the recipient too, so that it's not all one-sided. Expect more. You are *worthy*, Jonathan, so worthy of all that you desire.' How often had she said it to him?

And that was the key, he admitted. Even all these years after his childhood abuse he felt, deep down, that he wasn't *deserving* of goodness and until he let go of that mindset he would never be open to the right relationship. Jonathan knew Hannah was right. But he fell into the trap of being the giver every time because he was so desperate to find Mr Right. He wanted a relationship like Kenny and Russell had. He wanted the same sort of loving, nurturing, restorative bond Hilary and Niall, and many of his friends, shared. He wanted not to be lonely any more.

He was really trying hard not to make the same mistakes this time, with Leon. He had even declined an invite to go and see *The Talented Mr Ripley* this Sunday with him, even though he would have loved to go on a date to the cinema. Jonathan had a crush on Jude Law and Leon had confided that he really fancied Matt Damon, so it was a film both of them would have enjoyed. The old Jonathan would have agreed to go on the night out immediately; the new, more aware Jonathan was being more restrained.

'Perhaps during the week,' he'd suggested casually when Leon had issued the invite. 'I've plans for Sunday.' He'd hoped against hope that Leon would agree, and he'd been secretly delighted and relieved when his new crush had said easily, 'Sure, whenever suits you. Just let me know.' Now *that* was progress, Jonathan assured himself, very pleased that he was finally following Hannah's advice and taking things slowly.

It would be great too to be able to tell his mother that there was someone new on the scene. One of Nancy's fervent prayers was that someone kind and loving would come into his life and make him happy. Nancy was a wonderful mother, Jonathan thought gratefully. He was looking forward to spending the weekend with her and to seeing his sisters and his niece and nephews.

It was hard to believe that Nancy was almost eighty. She was still sprightly and looked years younger than her age. She cooked and baked and did her own shopping, in spite of her children's protestations. 'Thank the good Lord I can look after myself for now and when I can't and I need looking after you can look after me,' Nancy assured them spiritedly. But age had slowed her down and she couldn't see well enough to sew any more, so she had turned to knitting blankets and hats, scarves and gloves and socks for children in orphanages around the world. She was in a knitting club, was a member of a bridge club, she had choir practice every Friday evening, and Jonathan often teased her that she had a better social life than he had.

It gave him great satisfaction to see his mother so relaxed and contented in her retirement after all the years of hard work and sacrifice. They were so lucky that Nancy was healthy and robust for her age and rarely had to go for the medical appointments that often accompanied ageing. Jonathan only had to take time off work once, to bring her to an optician, and only then because she was getting drops in her eyes that would have blurred her vision.

Every so often she would take the bus to Dublin and he would meet it at Busáras and watch her step jauntily onto the concourse with her neat travel case, looking smart and lively, and his heart would lift at the sight. Nancy would spend a weekend with him and enjoy a trip to the theatre or a music recital or art exhibition before getting the bus home after lunch on Sunday. Rachel or Maria would meet her in

Rosslara and have her tea ready. Life had turned out well for all of the Harpur family, Jonathan reflected gratefully, swinging onto the slip road to exit the M50 and head for home.

An hour later he drove off the motorway and went south. He could see the church spire of St Anthony's in the distance and he took another left turn that would bring him to the winding roads of home. It was almost 5.30 but still bright, although dusk was beginning to encroach. Nightfall wouldn't come for another hour or so. He'd made good time. Jonathan loved arriving home before dark. It made the weekend seem longer. The lengthening days since Christmas lifted the spirit with the promise of spring and summer to come. The rain had eased the further west he'd driven, the setting sun flashing orange-yellow between the bare-branched trees and hedgerows. Already the winter barley was covering the rich loamy soil of the fields with a faint film of green. He touched a switch and the electric window slid down smoothly and he inhaled the fresh country air. The birds were chirruping and singing before settling down for the night and in the distance he could hear the drone of a tractor as it ploughed ruler-straight furrows in the winter-rested earth.

His mobile phone rang and the Bluetooth kicked in. 'Hello, Jonathan Harpur,' he answered, sliding the window up again, and hoping it wasn't a client. Some of them could be very demanding, expecting him to be at their beck and call 24/7.

'Hi, it's me,' came the greeting from an unexpected caller. Jonathan's heart soared.

'Hi, Leon.' He couldn't disguise his pleasure at hearing his new friend's voice.

'So where are you? Driving somewhere, clearly.'

'Correct! As we speak, I'm about half a mile from my mam's.'

'Oh! You've gone home for the weekend?'

'Excellent deduction, Sherlock,' teased Jonathan and they both laughed. 'So what are you up to?'

'I've just finished up putting in bespoke wardrobes in a new extension and if I say so myself they look pretty damn good.'

'It's great when you're happy with the way something turns out, isn't it?' Jonathan enthused.

'Yep, although you're lucky, you work for yourself. I'm very tied to the building contractor I work for. We're starting a new build next week in Rathfarnham, miles from where I live, so that's going to be a bummer of a commute.'

'You should aim to work for yourself,' Jonathan encouraged.

'I'd love that! Who knows, we might work together sometime. Hey, if you'd like, I can show you the wardrobes so you can see the quality of my work. We don't hand the house back to the owners until the week after next when the painters are finished,' Leon suggested.

'That would be great, I'd love to see them! I'll check my diary and see how I'm fixed.' Jonathan remembered to sound laid-back even though he was over the moon at the idea of meeting up with Leon.

'So will you be back Sunday then?' Leon asked casually.

'No, Monday morning. I always like to spend a decent

chunk of time with Mam when I come home and it takes the pressure off my sisters and gives them a free weekend because even though she's very feisty and independent, they keep a great eye on her, so it's good for them to have time for themselves,' Jonathan explained.

'And here was me thinking you had a big date with some-one on Sunday,' Leon confessed.

'I do, I've a big date with the ladies of the knitting club. I'm hosting a Spanish tapas supper night for them. Anyway, I've arrived now so I'll let you go, and I'll give you a shout early next week, OK?'

'Great, enjoy your weekend.' Leon sounded disappointed that their conversation was ending.

'You too. Byeee.' Jonathan hung up as he pulled up outside his old home. His heart was singing. Leon had phoned *him*, and had presumed Jonathan had a date, so it must have both-ered him that he'd declined the Sunday night invite to the cinema. He *had* to be interested. He wouldn't have phoned otherwise. And he was making all the running, even inviting him to check out his work. And Jonathan had played it cool and hung up first. He was particularly proud of his *I'll let you go*. That sounded ever so casual. 'Way to go, JI I, way to go. You're learning at last!' he murmured, turning off the igni-tion and taking his Nokia out of the hands-free cradle. Letting someone else make the running was *so* empowering. Hannah was right. He should have listened to her long ago.

Nancy must have been on the lookout for him because she appeared at the door, beaming. Jonathan's heart rose at the sight of her as he opened the small iron gate that he had painted Mediterranean blue for her the previous autumn.

Maybe at last her prayers were to be answered and he had finally met someone he could spend the rest of his life with. 'Hello, Mother mine.' He dropped his overnight bag and wrapped his arms around her, loving the familiar scent of Avon cream and Max Factor powder that was part and parcel of her.

'Hello, son, welcome home.' Nancy greeted him as she always did, returning his hug. 'I have the kettle boiled and the fire's lighting so come in now and sit down and relax yourself,' she urged. 'You must be tired after the drive.'

'No let me make the tea. You go and sit down and relax *yourself*,' Jonathan instructed. 'I have the lemon chicken all ready to go in the oven and it will only take fifty minutes.'

'I would have cooked a dinner for you, you know that.' Nancy shut the door behind him.

'I saw this recipe and I wanted to try it out, and besides you deserve to have a dinner cooked for you after all the years of cooking for us. It's time for you to sit back and take it easy.' Jonathan took the tin-foil-covered dish out of a carrier bag, and set it on the kitchen counter, before turning on the oven and filling the kettle.

'Go away out of that now,' Nancy said firmly. 'Sure what am I doing only enjoying myself. You're the one who's working hard. Inside to the fire and do what you're told.'

'Yes, Mammy!' Jonathan pretended meekness and Nancy laughed, ushering him into the sitting room while she made them a cuppa.

Jonathan looked well. Even, dare she say it, happy! Nancy mused, pouring a good strong brew of tea into his favourite

mug. Perhaps she was foolish to be worrying about him.
Tossing and turning at night every time she heard one of
those reports on the news about a new child-abuse scandal.
There were so many of them now. Nearly every second day,
reports of horrendous abuses covered up by the Church. She
felt so disappointed, so betrayed ... so angry with the Pope
and the cardinals and the bishops. The hierarchy! Enabling
these crimes against children. Enabling the rape of children.
It was more than shocking. It was pure evil. And the Pope,
that very same Pope she and most of the country had fallen
in love with nearly twenty-one years ago, the one who had
said, 'Young people of Ireland, I love you!' had done nothing ... nothing except have these evil men moved from one
parish to another, allowing them to carry on with their vile
abuse. Nancy could not get her head round it. And it was
terrible that all the good priests who gave so much to their
parishioners, and who were true men of God, had to suffer
because of those rotten apples.

Nancy's brows knitted in a frown as she stirred in a
heaped spoonful of sugar and added milk to Jonathan's tea.
Of course it wasn't only clergy that abused children, there
were many wicked paedeo ... paedo ... she couldn't pro-
nounce the word, but abusers of children was what they
were, and the more she heard, and the more she read about
this shocking crime, the more she worried something might
have happened to her own precious son. It was something
she could not get out of her head lately.

Nancy sighed and cut a slice of biscuit cake for Jonathan.
He seemed happy today but she had seen him, over the
years, down and depressed, in a dark mood that he would

try and hide from her. Sometimes he went on antidepressants, she knew, because he had told her a few years back when he had been glum and gloomy and she had nagged him to tell her what was up with him. 'A touch of depression,' he'd said. 'I must go back to my doctor and get some antidepressants.'

'Why are you depressed?' she'd asked. 'Is there something wrong in your life? Are you not happy? Is there anything I or your sisters can do to help?'

'No, Mam, nothing at all. It's just me. Some people are prone to it and I'm one of those people.'

She'd asked the girls had he ever said anything to them about the reasons behind those dark moods and they had said no. Mind he'd improved a lot since he'd started working for himself. Maybe he hadn't been happy at work, she'd surmised, and gradually she had let go of her worries as she saw how contented he was in his new career. But lately, with all these disturbing headlines, she had started to worry that something had happened to him, something she didn't know about, something he had hidden from her and carried alone, and *that* she couldn't bear.

After dinner, when they were settled beside the fire and he was relaxed, she was going to ask him out straight whether anything had ever occurred when he was young.

Nancy had a fierce knot of anxiety in her stomach. She remembered him coming home from school several times with a black eye or a bloodied nose after being in a fight. 'Did you give as good as you got?' she'd ask and he would always assure her that he had. Fighting in the playground was part of growing up, she knew that, just as she knew

that she could not go and fight his battles for him, much as she longed to. How she'd wished her husband was alive to teach Jonathan to box, and to do manly things with him.

She'd signed him up in a judo club, which he'd surprisingly enjoyed, and it had given her some solace that he could defend himself better against the bullies who tormented him for being different. He might have been different but he was more of a man than any of those little thugs were, Nancy had cried, tossing and turning at night in bed, worried sick about him and wondering should she go and speak to the headmaster. She had mentioned this to Jonathan and he had begged her not to. 'They'll only call me a sissy and it will make it worse, please don't. I can sort it myself.' Reluctantly she'd acquiesced to his wishes and felt even more of a failure as a mother. When he'd got the job up in Dublin, she didn't know whether to be glad for him or sad. Sad that he was leaving home but happy that he was escaping from their small rural town where his wings were clipped and he would never be able to soar to the heights he wanted to. But Dublin had been good for him. Made a man of him and let him have the life he wanted.

In the last few years she'd stopped worrying so much about him. She knew he had a great circle of friends and that was a huge comfort to her. If he could just find a partner to companion him through life she would die a happy woman, Nancy reflected. That, and if she knew that there was nothing in his past that he hadn't shared with her.

She dreaded asking him had anything bad ever happened when he was young and she dreaded what she might hear even more, but if she was any sort of a decent mother it was

a question that had to be asked. Better to know than to remain in ignorance and let her son carry a burden alone. The time had come to either put her fears to rest or never know a minute's peace of mind again.

Jonathan Harpur was a really nice guy, Leon Kyle mused, sitting in the Friday evening snarl-up on the M50 and wondering what idiot had designed the toll bridge that narrowed to two lanes causing huge tailbacks.

Jonathan was a talented interior designer, for sure. He'd shown Leon some of his commissions and Leon had been more than impressed. It would be good to keep in with him. His new buddy might be able to put some nixers his way. What a pity he had to go down the country and visit his mother. It would have been nice to socialize with Jonathan this weekend in some of the capital's gay haunts. Leon exhaled a deep breath. He had to be careful where he was seen. None of his family knew that he had gay tendencies. They would all be shocked. He was butch, manly, played soccer, had a child, and not one of his family or friends knew that his life was hell on earth and he hated himself. He hated that he preferred men to women, he hated that he hadn't the guts to come out, he hated *himself* for preferring men. He hated that he had to sneak around and tell lies and watch that he didn't slip up. He certainly wouldn't be able to introduce Jonathan to his family and friends and definitely *not* to his eight-year-old son and ex-partner. They would wonder who was this exotic creature with the flamboyant scarves and sharp dress sense, who was as gay as Christmas. Nope, introducing Jonathan would be out of the question but there

was nothing to stop him having a good time with Jonathan, discreetly, now and again. Nothing at all, Leon decided, flinging his coins into the basket and gunning the engine, impatient for the barrier to rise.

Chapter Twenty

Hilary glanced at her watch. She needed to get a move on. It had started to sleet again. She'd pick the girls up from school, nip in and have the promised cuppa and cake with Gran H, drop the girls home and do her supermarket shop. She'd just go to Nolan's in Clontarf. Driving out to Sutton to go to Superquinn on a wet Friday evening was not on – she was too tired and she had too much to do. Her cleaner, Magda, had not come back from Latvia after Christmas and had sent a text saying that her mother was ill and she would not be returning to Ireland, much to Hilary's dismay. She needed to sort out getting a new cleaner too. She should have got the mini-maids in to get the house shipshape before Sophie's friends arrived but she wouldn't have a snowball's chance in hell of getting them at this late stage.

Her desk phone rang, and she dithered. It was someone who had her direct line number. She should answer it, she supposed. It might be her mother or Margaret.

'Hello?'

'Sweetie! It's *so* good to hear your voice. I miss you!' Colette chirruped down the line.

'Colette, hey, what are you doing ringing me at work?

You usually ring in the evening, what's up? Is everything OK?' Hilary asked, surprised at the call.

'You'll never guess, Hil, I had to tell you. Who do you think is working in Manhattan Eye and Ear, a couple of blocks away?' Colette asked dramatically.

'Who?' Hilary asked, trying to pretend she was interested. Colette's timing was the pits.

'Rod Killeen!' Can you believe it?' Colette was giddy with excitement.

'Who?' Hilary wracked her brains. The name sounded vaguely familiar but she couldn't place it.

'Hilary!' exclaimed Colette indignantly. 'Rod Killeen, the skunk that *broke* my heart!'

'Oh yeah, sorry.' Hilary glanced at her watch. She needed to be getting a move on. 'What are the odds of that? Did you meet him or something?'

'God no!' Colette shuddered. 'Imagine the shock if I'd bumped into him unexpectedly. No, Janine Winthrope told me that her husband was attending an Irish eye specialist in Manhattan Eye and Ear. She *adored* Dr Killeen's accent, she told me. "Killeen?" I said. "Rod Killeen?" "Why yes," she said. "Do you know him?" Do I know him?' Colette scoffed. 'That lying, two-faced toad devastated my life. If only Janine knew. I wonder did he marry that red-headed dumpling?'

'What differences does it make now, Colette?' Hilary asked with as much patience as she could muster. 'You're happily married to Des. You have a fabulous lifestyle. So what if he married that girl?'

'I know,' sighed Colette. 'But I'd just love him to know how well I did in spite of him. Do you think I should inveigle

Janine into throwing a party and inviting him? Oh I could swan in in style and leave him standing there with his mouth open to see what he could have had!'

'No, Colette! Not a good idea,' advised Hilary firmly. 'The past is the past. Leave it there. What's the point, after all these years?'

'I suppose you're right,' the other woman said dejectedly.

'I *am* right, lovie, now I have to fly or I'm going to get stuck in the rush hour. Sophie's having friends over for her birthday and I'm way behind schedule. I'll call you next week. Remind me to tell you about Sue and her carry-on. You're so lucky you don't have in-laws and elderly parents to contend with. Mind yourself.'

'OK, you too. Are you sure you don't think – you know, for closure – that I should—'

'Positive!' Hilary said sternly. 'Bye, Colette.'

She shoved her diary into her bag, grabbed her mobile phone and stood up. She had a lot to do before she'd be able to put her feet up and flop in front of Graham Norton with a well-earned glass of wine. Niall need not worry about waking her when he got in from his gig. She'd be dead to the world because she was absolutely knackered.

Was it just her that was finding it hard to cope? Other women seemed to manage their juggling much better than she did, Hilary mused as she edged cautiously out into the already heavy Friday traffic. Was she just not good at coping with stress? Women were bombarded with images of designer-dressed career women in skyscraper heels breaking through corporate glass ceilings, juggling career, motherhood and home-making with apparent ease. Carrie

Bradshaw and Co. were far removed from ordinary women, although in fairness, the portrayal of Miranda the lawyer in *Sex and the City* when she'd had her baby was real enough. But a noughties-type character from a TV programme she certainly was not, Hilary thought, suppressing a yawn. If any of her friends rang right now and suggested a night out on the tiles, drinking cocktails, they'd get short shrift. Women could *not* have it all, no matter how much feminists liked to believe it. Women were spread too thin. She couldn't give her all to her family *and* her job and there was certainly no room for downtime for her.

Andrea Keirns's baby had ignited a surge of unexpected longing in her that surprised her. What on earth would she want a baby for at this stage of her life, fifteen years after having Sophie? Madness, she thought, as she crawled along in bumper-to-bumper traffic.

Her life had been much less stressful when the girls were babies. She had enjoyed being at home with them, enjoyed bringing them to visit their grandparents, enjoyed picnics and walks on Bull Island, or Sutton Beach. She'd even had time to read. She'd been an avid reader once. If she had a baby now she certainly wouldn't be jaunting off for picnics and the like and as for reading books . . . ha ha!

Colette was something else, she reflected, amused at her friend's phone call. How lucky was she if the only thing she had to worry about was trying to show an ex-boyfriend that she had done well for herself? Sometimes Hilary thought Colette had married Des on the rebound. Rod had been her first love and she had fallen for him hard. Hilary had listened to a lot of crying and ranting in those days. She grinned, remembering how she'd even been involved, against her better judgment, in a stakeout of Rod's flat, one wet December afternoon.

Time had not healed the wound of rejection in Colette's breast, despite the fact that she'd had a hectic social life in London. It only seemed like yesterday that Colette had come back to Dublin on a Christmas visit and had spent an hour griping about her ex, Hilary reflected, her thoughts drifting back to their early twenties when the trauma of a broken love affair had knocked Colette for six.

'I wonder, is he still living in that flat in Ranelagh? Will we drive over tomorrow and check it out?' Colette had suggested, eyes glittering with anticipation.

'Why? What's the point? You don't want him to think you're running after him. Forget him, Colette,' Hilary retorted.

'Please, Hilary! *Please*! Let's drive over and see if he still lives there?' Colette begged. Knowing she would get no peace until she agreed, they had set out on a wild, late Saturday afternoon in December, in Hilary's ramshackle Toyota, driving through the wet suburbs on the Northside to the tree-lined, narrow street of red-brick houses on the Southside of the city. They'd parked a few doors across the street from where Rod lived, in a ground-floor flat, with two other medical students.

As rain lashed against the car windows, they had sat with hats pulled low over their faces and scarves up to their noses. 'Just in case Rod sees us,' Colette fretted. The downstairs of No. 27 was in darkness. Upstairs in the window of a first-floor flat the lights of a bushy little Christmas tree twinkled gaily, casting sparkles of light into the gloom. Pools of orange light radiated from the street lamps, reflected in the puddles of water around their bases. People came and went into their warm, lamplit homes, doors opening, light spilling out into gardens, then closing on the dark, damp night where Colette and Hilary kept their lonely vigil fortified by a flask of coffee and Twix bars.

'I think we should go,' Hilary said gently an hour and a half later, as she wriggled uncomfortably in her seat, pins and needles shooting up her leg from her cramped position.

'Just five more minutes,' pleaded Colette miserably and so they sat for another half-hour until their patience was rewarded and Rod's motorbike roared up the street, with a black-helmeted pillion passenger, arms wrapped tightly around his waist.

'Fat cow!' Colette burst into tears as Lynda climbed off the back of the bike and Rod chained it against the railings.

'She's not *tha*t fat,' protested Hilary, who was feeling particularly plump having demolished two Twixes, and whose jeans were digging into her waist due to a combination of PMT fluid retention and a week of Christmas parties that had ruined her pre-Christmas diet.

'Yes she is,' sniffled Colette. 'Look at the wobbly arse on her. If I had an arse like that I'd shoot myself.'

'Oh stop it,' snapped Hilary. 'I have a fat arse too. Think how that makes me feel hearing you go on like that.'

'*Oh!* Well at least you don't have a bust like the Dublin Mountains.'

'Wow, that makes me feel a million dollars,' Hilary snorted.

'Oooh look! Bastard! Bitch!' Colette burst into tears as her Rod switched on the Christmas tree lights and enfolded his girlfriend in a loving embrace. Their silhouettes etched against the twinkling glow of the multicoloured light, the pair snug and warm from the deepening rain that was now hammering down on the top of the car. The little tableau of domestic bliss was almost cinematic, Hilary thought, wishing she was at home in front of the fire with her book and a glass of wine. But her heart softened as Colette's whimpers turned into full-blown sobs, and she started the car engine and said kindly, 'Come on, we're getting out of here. There's no point in prolonging the agony.' Colette had cried the whole way home.

And to think that now, years later, knowing that Rod Killeen was working in a hospital a few blocks away from her could send Colette into a tizzy. It surprised Hilary. Her friend was a strange girl where men were concerned. Every man was subject to the famous O'Mahony charm. Even Niall, Hilary thought wryly, having witnessed Colette's flirty behaviour with her husband on numerous occasions. Colette *had* to be the Belle of the Ball. Rod had ditched her, and that had been a first; Colette usually did the dumping. Clearly she had never got over it. What did she want to return to the past for when she had made a very good life for herself with Des? Why open up old wounds? If that was the greatest of her troubles she was doing very well, Hilary sighed, swinging right onto Vernon Avenue.

She parked on double yellows outside Thunder's and raced in to buy a selection of gooey cream cakes. She deserved a treat after the hectic week she'd had, she thought, damping down the guilt when she bought a creamy coffee cake as well. She'd need a sugar lift to keep her going – it would be ages before she had her meal.

A motorist shook his fist at her as he manoeuvred past her car and she muttered, 'Ah shag off!' She hadn't blocked him or anyone. She'd half parked on the pavement – it was the car on the far side of the road that was causing the problem. *You're the very one who'd be giving out if it was the other way round.* She acknowledged her double standard, twisting the key in the ignition, relieved that the lights were red and she was able to scoot out in the gap in the traffic.

Her daughters were standing under an umbrella, scowling, when she finally drew up as near to the school gates as she could. She tooted at them and they hurried to the car, grumbling as they threw their bags in and climbed in. 'We were waiting ages, Mam!' Sophie reproved, flicking raindrops off her blonde ponytail.

'My shoes are leaking,' moaned Millie, plonking herself into the front seat beside Hilary.

'I'll give you the money to get a new pair,' Hilary sighed. 'We're going to Gran H's to have a quick cuppa and a cream cake. I didn't have time to go for coffee with her this morning after her warfarin.'

'Cream cakes, yummy.' Millie cheered up, twiddling the knobs to change the radio stations until she heard Whitney Houston belting out 'My Love Is Your Love'.

'Aw turn off the radio and play Christina Aguilera – it's in the deck,' Sophie protested, starting to hum 'Genie In A Bottle'.

'No, I'm listening to this,' Millie retorted.

'If you start arguing I'm switching back to RTÉ,' Hilary declared.

'Mam, because it's my birthday sleepover I don't suppose we could go to Wes?' Sophie asked hopefully. 'After all I'm fifteen now.'

'You suppose right. You're too young,' Hilary said firmly, not in the humour for having an argument about being allowed or not allowed to go to a popular disco. It was such a nuisance The Grove, a disco in their neck of the woods, had closed a couple of years back. It was an institution and going there with a gang of friends had been a rite of passage for local teenagers for several decades.

She and Colette and their friends had felt so grown-up the first time they'd gone to the famous disco. They had been in Seventh Heaven to finally walk past the bouncers through the hallowed doors. Thereafter the weekly night out had been the highlight of their teen years. They had bopped their hearts out to The Rolling Stones, The Doors, The Eagles, Thin Lizzy, Bruce Springsteen; the music had been class, she remembered with a smile. She would have had no problem with her daughters going to The Grove, but Wesley FC in Donnybrook was a different kettle of fish and not comfortingly near like the disco in Raheny had been. And she hated driving over to the Southside when it was her night on collection duty.

'Mam, it's not fair! Millie's allowed to go.' Sophie's remonstration interrupted her reverie. 'Some of the girls—'

'Millie's seventeen. I'm not going to argue about it, Sophie.'

'But—'

'*No!*' She glanced in her rear-view mirror and saw her youngest daughter sitting with a mutinous expression on her face and felt like slapping her. Sophie knew the rules. Knew she wasn't going to be allowed to go to Wesley until she was sixteen, and until then would have to make do with her youth club and sports club discos.

'You're not missing much, it's not *that* great,' Millie assured her. But Sophie was not to be mollified.

'I didn't ask you, did I?' she said rudely.

'Be like that then,' Millie snapped.

'You're just so rude.'

'And you're—'

'Girls! Be *quiet!*'

Whitney Houston's melodic tones filled the air as Hilary's daughters obeyed her dictate. 'Take that puss off you in Gran's,' Hilary warned as Sophie stomped up Mrs Hammond's garden path ten minutes later.

'Take a chill pill, Mam!' Sophie scowled.

'Less of your cheek, miss,' Hilary snapped.

Had she been as moody and stroppy when she was a teen? she wondered when she'd dropped the girls home an hour later before going to do her supermarket shop. She'd been hoping Sophie would get out of her huff and offer to come shopping with her and queue at the meat counter while Hilary shopped around the narrow aisles of the old-fashioned supermarket. And then unload the trolley for her at the checkout. But neither of her daughters had offered and she felt grouchy and tired, with the beginnings of a headache. She circled the large car park hoping to get a spot near the door. Luck wasn't on her side and she had to park at the far end and got drenched before she made it to the shelter of the shop.

By the time she put her key in the front door, fifty minutes later, Hilary was starving and weary to her bones. She was going to put away the shopping, order their Chinese take-away and pour herself a big glass of red and that was it for today. The housework could wait until tomorrow.

The house felt warm and welcoming and she tried to over-look the two school bags dumped on the hall floor beside the hallstand. Millie's leaking shoes were left in the middle of the floor where she had stepped out of them. God Almighty, was it too much to expect them to put their stuff away when they came in from school? Laden with bags, she shoved open the kitchen door and felt a rush of anger at the sight that greeted her. 'Ah for God's sake, you pair, look at the state of the place! The least you could have done was filled the dishwasher,' Hilary ranted, seeing the breakfast dishes still on the kitchen counter.

'It needs to be emptied,' Sophie muttered from where she lay sprawled on the sofa in the family room.

'Well why didn't you empty it? Do I have to do every bloody thing in this house? Sophie, you empty it and put those dirty dishes in it and, Millie, you get over here and help me unpack the shopping.'

'Why can't she do it – most of this stuff is for her sleep-over,' Millie grumbled, unpacking mini Twixes and Crunchies. 'I have to study.'

'You could have studied while I was doing the shopping instead of lolling on the sofa watching rubbish on TV.'

'I was tired, Mam!'

'And I'm not?'

'Oh give it a rest.'

'Don't talk to me like that.'

'Well you're just *so* cranky,' Millie retorted furiously.

'Maybe if I got a bit more cooperation in this house I wouldn't be so cranky. Perhaps if my daughters got up off their backsides and gave me a hand now and again instead of behaving like two lazy lumps, I wouldn't be so cranky. Did you ever think of that?' Hilary raged, giving vent to her frustration.

'Why don't you just go and get someone to replace Magda?' her eldest daughter said exasperatedly. 'It can't be that *hard* to get a cleaner.'

'Listen, madam, it's far from cleaners you were reared. And let me tell you when I was your age, myself and your aunt used to spend *every* Saturday cleaning Granny and Granddad's house from top to bottom. Hoovering, polishing, cleaning windows and floors, scrubbing the bathroom, shining the brasses. You pair don't know you're alive. Tomorrow morning this house is getting cleaned thoroughly so be prepared to get up early and roll up your sleeves.' She banged the press door having flung all the goodies for Sophie's party into the Tupperware containers.

'This is all *your* fault.' Millie turned on Sophie. 'What do you need a sleepover for? You're not ten any more.'

'Oh just shut up you.' Sophie slammed the dishwasher door closed and stomped upstairs.

'Sophie, have you tidied your bedroom, and is that bathroom of yours clean?' Hilary yelled.

'It's fine, I'll do it tomorrow.'

'You certainly will do it tomorrow if your friends are coming over,' Hilary assured her.

'They won't mind. Their bedrooms are just as untidy.'

'Well *I* mind. I have some *standards*. I don't want them going home saying our house is a tip,' Hilary shouted up the stairs and was sure she heard a muttered, 'Oh piss off.'

Hilary's lips thinned and she was ready to run up the stairs and have it out with Sophie for her lack of respect. No one in her family respected her, she fumed, spraying Jif into the sink and scrubbing the tea stains around the plughole. They made it look so easy on those silly TV ads, for household cleaning agents, that assumed women were morons. She scrubbed aggressively, venting her annoyance on her dirty sink, and deciding that first thing on Monday morning she was getting a new cleaner.

How nice for Niall to be out playing at a session on Friday night, leaving her to sort everything for the weekend as usual. He needed to cop on to himself a bit more and muck in. She was damned if she was doing his or the girls' washing this weekend, she decided, throwing tea towels and dishcloths into the washing machine. And he could press his own trousers while he was at it. That was a bit passive-aggressive, she thought crossly. She should just have it out with him. Hilary hated rows, and it *would* turn into a row because Niall would get defensive and irritable, knowing she was right, and there'd be an atmosphere, and sometimes it just wasn't worth it, she thought glumly, fed up with everything and everyone. Did Colette realize just how lucky she was with her housekeeper, and her Town Cars to whisk her wherever she needed to go? And her long weekends in Nantucket? Some people had all the luck. She tied a knot in the ponging bin bag and hauled it out to the black bin, another chore Niall should have done, Hilary fumed resentfully.

When she finally ordered their takeaway, all the shopping had been put away, the hall had been cleared and the living room was relatively tidy. She was starving. She made up the shredded crispy duck pancakes while a sullen Millie dished out the lemon chicken, egg fried rice and chow mein.

Millie took her plate and marched out into the hall to take her meal upstairs. Hilary took a deep breath, ready to remonstrate with her. Meals were not allowed to be eaten in bedrooms. But she stopped. Her daughter looked pale and tired, she had her period, and there had been enough shouting and arguing. It was Friday night. They were all tired. Enough was enough. She took her own plate to the sofa, and Sophie followed her and sat in the armchair. They ate their meal in silence, lost in their own thoughts.

Colette lay sprawled on her queen-sized bed, the sun slanting through her apartment windows, reflecting on the Murano glass vase that held an arrangement of peony roses. Normally the sight would give her pleasure but she was too troubled to notice the beauty and simplicity of the arrangement. She studied a photo of herself and a smiling, brown-eyed, straight-nosed, square-jawed, broad-shouldered young man with his arms around her. It was the happiest time of her life. She had been in love, in lust, completely confident in her allure for Rod. And then, out of the blue, he'd told her he was ending it. He wanted to 'concentrate on his studies'. Bitterness rose in her at the memory.

Concentrate on that little fat bogger was more like it. Had he married his red-headed nurse?

Tears slid down Colette's cheek. Rod had confirmed what she had always known, that men could not be trusted. No man was capable of being faithful. She couldn't be sure, but she suspected Des had the odd dalliance or two. He hadn't given her any reason to think so, but she had her suspicions. Extra-long hours at the office. Working out more than usual. A keener attention to his appearance.

She wouldn't ever let on to Hilary though. Some things you had to keep to yourself. No doubt Hilary trusted Niall one hundred per cent. She was a fool. Who was to say he didn't dally with some of the women who enjoyed his music sessions? Colette had seen how they'd responded to his easy charm. She'd caught him giving her the once-over a few times. If she put her mind to it she could seduce Niall Hammond, Colette thought dismissively, wiping her eyes. It wasn't seducing men that was the problem, it was keeping them that was difficult.

Hilary was right though. If she had any sense she would stay well away from her ex-boyfriend. To go down that road again was more than she could bear.

CHAPTER TWENTY-ONE

'Well that was tasty, son. Very tasty indeed – you're a dab hand at the cooking,' Nancy praised, wiping the last bit of sauce from her plate with a piece of Vienna roll. Although she had enjoyed the chicken dish, her stomach was unsettled at the thought of what was to come.

'It's so simple to prepare and it's all cooked in the one dish,' Jonathan explained, scoffing a crispy potato quarter. 'Just line a dish coated with olive oil with sliced onions and mushrooms and a few lemon slices. Put the seasoned chicken breasts on top. Mix a couple of quartered spuds, some trimmed green beans, garlic, seasoning, and a drizzle of oil. Cook for fifty minutes and Bob's your uncle. Actually it was Hilary who gave me the recipe. It's one of her "life-saver" dinners as she calls them.'

'I wish I'd known that recipe when I was working,' Nancy chuckled, remembering how she would race home at lunchtime and cook a meat, potatoes and veg dinner before hurrying back to work. 'I'm very fond of Hilary, she's a lovely girl.'

'I know,' Jonathan agreed affectionately. 'She's the best in the world and I'm lucky to have her as a friend.'

'And she's lucky to have you too,' Nancy declared, placing a large helping of apple crumble, drenched in steaming creamy custard, in front of him.

'Ooooh yum! You spoil me rotten.' Jonathan tucked in with gusto, delighted that she had made his favourite childhood dessert. 'So tell me all the news, scandal and gossip,' he grinned when she sat back down opposite him.

'Ah it's quite enough around here these days. Poor Nellie Murphy passed away last week and she was lying on a trolley in A&E for two days before they got a bed for her. It's a disgrace,' Nancy grumbled. 'All them chancers up in the Dáil never have to wait in A&E departments. Into the Mater Private and the Blackrock Clinic with them. There might be a boom but it's not making any difference to the likes of us.'

'Ah yes, the golden circle. The privileged few will always be looked after. Will it ever change?' Jonathan spooned honey-sweetened apple into his mouth.

'And we've plenty of chancers here too, I can tell you. You know that fella Donnie Quill over on Hawthorn Street? He works for the Health Board. Well Maura Flynn who lives beside him – she's in the knitting group and she's a nurse – she saw himself and another fella, brazen as you like, unloading a hospital bed from his trailer and storing it in his garage. And they cost *thousands*! And he's getting petrol from somewhere too because Maura sees him filling the two cars with it. You know the wife, Antonia, a real snooty one that wouldn't pass the time of day with you if you met her on the street, a right little consequence. Well Maura has the measure of her. "Did your car run out of petrol *again*?"

Maura says, ever so airy-fairy when Donnie was filling it with petrol, and Antonia was raging!' Nancy chuckled, and Jonathan laughed, enjoying his catch-up with the various goings on in Rosslara. 'Terrible, isn't it, to be robbing the Health Board like that?'

'Robbing *us* like that! It's our hard-earned taxes that pay for it.' Jonathan began clearing away the dishes. 'But don't forget, what goes around comes around.'

'And seemingly he was fiddling the gas company for years. Could have blown up the street interfering with the meter. Ah the world is gone to the divil.' Nancy wiped the table. 'The news is full of terrible things. How can people do the things they do to each other?'

'Man's inhumanity to man is endless indeed,' Jonathan sighed, filling the dishwasher.

'If I asked you something would you tell me the truth, son?' Nancy said hesitantly, filling the kettle to make another pot of tea. Her heart started to pound.

'Eh ... yes ... of course I would.' Jonathan looked at her in surprise.

'Good,' Nancy said weakly. 'That's good to know because I want to ask you something.'

'Right, fire ahead.' Jonathan frowned, seeing how troubled his mother had become, and wondered what was up.

Nancy took a deep breath. 'When you were young did anyone ever do anything bad to you? Anyone at school, the teachers, or the priests or the brothers? Were you ever abused?' She studied his face intently, her blue eyes filled with concern and dread.

It was as though time had stood still in his mother's

kitchen. Jonathan was acutely aware of the silence between them. The aroma of the meal they'd just eaten lingering in the air, the kettle beginning to hiss as it boiled. The steady tick-tock of the clock on the wall and the light of the moon glimmering through the frosted-glass panes in the back door lent an almost surreal air to the moment. Nancy stared at him expectantly, her hands clasped so tightly together her knuckles were white.

Jonathan swallowed hard, his heart pounding. 'No, Mam, no priest or teacher or brother ever did anything to me when I was young,' he answered truthfully.

'Oh thank God for that, Jonathan. I've been so *worried* about it. Every time I hear something on the news now, about child abuse, I wonder did anything like that happen to my lovely boy. I was afraid something had, and that you had to carry it alone. And I thought that was the cause of your sad moods.' Nancy's blue eyes glistened with tears and she fished up her sleeve for her handkerchief.

Jonathan put his arms around her. 'Don't ever worry about me, Mam, I'm fine. Honest.' He struggled to keep the emotion from his voice. He wanted to cry.

'Did *anything* ever happen to you? I know you got into fights and scraps. I used to cry myself to sleep worrying about you when you'd come home with a black eye or bloodied nose. Did anyone ever abuse you, Jonathan?' She drew away from his embrace and looked up at him.

It was the moment he could have told her. His mother was no fool. She'd finally put two and two together. But how could he tell her that the neighbour she had lived beside for so many years of her life, and who she thought of as a good person, someone on whose door she could have knocked in times of trouble, was the very one who had abused him. If Jonathan told his mother that Gus Higgins had perpetrated the crime she feared, her peace of mind would be shattered for the rest of her life. Much as he longed to blurt out the truth he knew that he couldn't. She too would become a victim of Higgins if she knew the reality and that he would not allow. But it wasn't fair either to palm her off with a flat denial, he reasoned.

'Something did happen,' he said quietly.

'I knew it. I *knew* it. When I started going back and thinking about it I knew *something* must have set off those depressions. Oh Jonathan, why didn't you come to me, why didn't you tell me,' Nancy exclaimed, aghast, her face crumpling into tears.

'Aah now don't cry, Mam! Let's bring our tea in beside the fire and we'll talk about it and then I want you to put it out of your mind, because I have,' he said firmly.

'Did he hurt you? Was it anyone we knew? What age were you?' Nancy sobbed.

'No, no, no, no one we knew,' he lied. 'Go in and sit down, and I'll bring in the tea.' He hated seeing his mother cry, hated the way her shoulders had sagged when he'd confirmed her worst fears.

What would he say had happened him? He thought frantically, pouring their tea into mugs and sugaring and milking them. He couldn't tell her anything like the truth. That would devastate her completely. He'd have to make up some story that wouldn't be too disturbing for her but yet ring true.

He shucked some chocolate rings onto a plate and put everything onto a tray and carried it into the sitting room. Even in his distressed state the sight of the soft light, the terracotta lamps spilling their warm pools of colour around the snug sitting room that he had decorated for his mother, gave Jonathan immense satisfaction. The fire was crackling in the grate, the yellow-orange flames flickering and dancing, casting shadows thither and yon. He had been so looking forward to lazing in front of the fire, but now both of them were upset and the evening was not turning out as he'd expected.

'Now, Mam, here you go, and I want you to stop agonizing or I won't talk to you about it, OK?' He handed Nancy a mug of tea and offered her a biscuit. 'Come on, take one. The world hasn't come to an end.' He tried to lighten the mood.

'You should have told me, Jonathan,' Nancy said miserably.

'Mam, you had enough on your plate when we were young, and besides I dealt with it.'

'But it sent you into depressions. I'm your mother, you should have come to me,' she protested.

'Well I know that, but part of the depression thing was because I realized I was gay and I didn't want to be. I just wanted to be "normal".' He did air quotes. 'Whatever "normal" is. I *hated* being different. I just wanted to be ordinary.'

'And what happened to you and what age were you? Were you a child?' his mother asked fearfully.

'No, no, no,' he assured her, knowing that he was

chickening out but comforting himself that it was for the best possible reasons. 'Look, I was a teenager and I was walking down by the train depot and this fellow jumped me and shoved me down Leyden's Lane and ... well basically he touched me up.'

'God above, that must have been so frightening. You never think of it happening to boys or men. You always think of women when sexual assault is mentioned. It's shocking.' She shook her head. 'You should have gone to the police.'

'It was different in those days. Now I would,' Jonathan assured her.

'And did the judo help?'

'Oh ... oh ...em ... it sure *did*,' he said hastily, forgetting when he had concocted his story that he was trained in martial arts and his mother would have expected him to defend himself. 'I was able to flip him over my shoulder when I had a chance to manoeuvre and then I gave him a good kick before I took to my heels.'

'And you didn't know who he was?'

'Not a clue. Whoever he was he had a couple of bruises when I was finished with him. I never saw him again.'

'Thanks be to God I sent you to those classes.' Nancy began to relax a little as she sipped her tea and nibbled on a biscuit.

'They were such a help and I got great confidence from knowing I could use what I was taught if I got into a tight corner,' Jonathan said reassuringly.

'Well thanks be to the Holy Mother the priests and brothers didn't abuse you, although I have to say we've always had very nice priests in this parish. That I know of,' she added doubtfully.

'We have, they're sound. Father McManus is exceptional,' Jonathan agreed, knowing how kind the parish priest was to the elderly of the parish.

'You should have told me though. And I'm sorry I didn't realize the difficulties you were going through about being gay. I didn't really know what being gay was, when you were young. Things like that weren't spoken about in our day. And being gay meant being happy and carefree,' she added wryly. 'I just thought you were a gentle child who liked playing with girls and doing girlish things. I thought that was because you had no male influence in your life, because of your daddy dying when you were just a toddler. And then when I *did* realize what it was all about I wondered was it because of anything I did or didn't do.' She gazed at him, distraught. 'I feel I failed you.'

'No, Mam. You didn't, *ever*. You did great. Even if Dad were alive, I'd still be gay. It's who I am.' He knelt beside her chair and took her hand in his. 'Don't ever think like that. We all have to walk our own path in life and this is mine.'

'And do you hate it? Is it a burden to you? Are you unhappy?' she asked earnestly.

'I did hate it at first. I hated myself, and it *was* a burden when I was young and had to hide it, especially here in Rosslara,' he admitted. 'And when I started working first, I had a boss who was homophobic and he gave me a very hard time—'

'I hope you reported him,' Nancy bristled.

'Oh I sorted him, don't you worry!' Jonathan said grimly. 'But I've made great friends in Dublin. Hilary and Kenny and Russell, you know them. And I go to a great counsellor called Hannah Harrison. You'd love her, Mam. She's amazing. She's made me look at everything so differently. If my boss hadn't bullied me, for example, I might have got stuck in a rut in the Civil Service, but because of him I was determined that no one would treat me like that again and it motivated me to do the interviews and climb up the grade scale. So Hannah says that on a soul level he was a great teacher for me in many ways. His homophobia made me stand up for myself and gave me the kick in the ass I needed to move upwards.'

'Oh! Well that's an unusual way to look at it, I suppose,' Nancy said dubiously.

'Yeah, she makes you think about stuff differently.' Jonathan stood up and went and sprawled on the sofa. 'She believes in reincarnation. And she says we come to teach each other lessons in life to advance ourselves spiritually.'

'And do you believe in reincarnation?' Nancy asked, thinking that she would have chosen for her husband to live, and not to have spent most of her adult life as a widow, if she'd truly had a choice.

'I think it makes sense, really. I've read a good few metaphysical books, and yes, it explains a lot.'

'Even why you're gay?' Nancy ventured.

'*Especially* why I'm gay,' Jonathan laughed. 'I've been straight in other lives. It's all about the challenge and how you deal with it and you know, Mam, right now I'm doing fine. I truly am, so you've no need to worry about me. As

Alice Walker, one of my favourite authors, said, *We have to own the fears we have of each other, and then in some practical way, some daily way, figure out how to see people differently than what we were brought up to.* That makes such sense to me. It can refer to anything in life, religion, politics and cultural differences. Fear of each other causes so much turmoil and violence in the world.'

'Exactly!' exclaimed Nancy. 'She put it very well. It's all about fear, isn't it, that homophobic stuff? I mean *who* could be afraid of you?'

'I can be pretty fierce,' Jonathan teased. 'Isn't it wonderful to be able to sit and talk like this. I'm so lucky to have you, Mam.'

'And I'm so lucky to have you, son. Just promise me you'll never keep anything from me again,' Nancy said sternly.

'I promise,' he assured her, utterly relieved that she had believed his story. It was a relief to be able to put her mind at rest too about how he felt about his life path. The evening wasn't a disaster after all, even if he had held back on the most horrendous events of his childhood, he decided. He had not betrayed himself. He had *chosen* not to inflict emotional carnage on his beloved mother.

'And you know something, Mam, I don't define myself by being gay. That's only *part* of who I am. I am a man, like any other, with a successful career, my own home, great family and friends, who happens to be gay. I never feel I have to introduce myself by saying, "Hi, I'm Jonathan and I'm gay." I hate the fact that people feel they have to "come out", or others feel that gay people have to be "outed". It's no one's business really. I mean you would never dream of introducing yourself as "Nancy who's heterosexual", would you? All that stuff pisses me off big time.'

'And rightly so, why wouldn't it?' Nancy agreed. 'The next time I go with the parish group to an event where we meet new people I must introduce myself as "Nancy the heterosexual". That would make a few jaws drop,' she laughed, tickled at the notion.

'All these labels we hide behind. Straight, gay, upper class, lower class, highbrow, lowbrow, black, white, they're all designed to make us forget that we are all equal, all one from the one Source, even the ones who abuse us. That last one takes some getting your head round, I can tell you.' Jonathan made a face.

'But why does it happen? Why does all this evil exist in the world?' Nancy sighed.

'Hannah says it's because we've all forgotten who we are and why we were created. She calls it "the vale of forgetting": we come back to earth and forget what we've come back to do. Life's hard knocks are one way of getting us to remember.'

'I like the sound of this Hannah. She has an interesting take on life.' Nancy stretched her feet towards the fire.

'You can say that again. She puts it up to you to stop feeling sorry for yourself, and really makes you look at it all from another perspective.'

'I didn't have time to be sorry for myself, but you know, before your daddy died, I wouldn't say boo to a goose and I depended on him a lot when we married. Too much really. And when I was widowed I *had* to stand on my own two feet and just get on with it, so his death made me a much stronger person. Was that his gift to me, I wonder? Was that the life path I decided upon, do you think?' She stared into the flames with a faraway look in her eyes.

'You see, when you start looking at things differently *everything* changes,' Jonathan exclaimed. 'It's not easy and you have to try hard but when it works, it works.'

'She sounds like a lovely lady who talks a lot of sense. In fact I might pay her a visit myself sometime,' Nancy declared, throwing a briquette onto the fire and sending a shower of sparks up the chimney.

Jonathan stared at his mother, astonished. Nancy had surprised him with her openness and acceptance of the esoteric teachings Hannah shared with him. He hadn't been so accepting the first few times she had volunteered them. He had argued truculently with her many times, affronted that she could suggest that Gus Higgins was a 'teacher' on a spiritual level. But she had always given him time to absorb what she said and told him only to accept what resonated with him. *When the pupil is ready the teacher will come.* Even when you were nearly eighty, it seemed.

'You'd love her and she'd love you.' He smiled at his mother and she smiled back at him and Jonathan felt the tension drift out of his body and his eyelids began to droop as he lay against the plump Gigli-print cushions he had accessorized the sofa with.

He had lied every which way to his mother about his abuse but his intention had been good. He had saved her from a grief that would have ruined her old age. That was more important than anything. But he had shared his feelings with her and that made the huge bond they had even stronger. Articulating how he felt about being gay, as he just had, had been very empowering. He was a human being who deserved to be treated with dignity and equality, just the way his mother treated him, and if people didn't like it they could lump it. And he wasn't a victim, he was *victorious*. Yes, victorious Jonathan Harpur who had put the past behind him and was ready to embrace his future, a future that hopefully he would spend with Leon at his side. Jonathan slept peacefully on the sofa, and Nancy, content that she had broached the subject she had been dreading and had not had her *worst* fears realized, closed her eyes and joined him for forty winks before the *Late Late* started.

Nancy lay in the warm hollow of her bed watching a sliver of moonlight through a chink in the curtains. She felt strangely at peace after her heart-to-heart conversation with Jonathan. He was a very strong person, this son of hers, she thought proudly. And a very *good* person. Why could people not see beyond the labels they hung on each other? Why could they not see the human being with the kind and loving heart? 'Queers' they called men like her son. How hurtful and derogatory. But they were the queer ones with their closed, judgemental minds and hard hearts. Jesus would never call anyone queer, she reflected, knowing that much of the hardship her son and others like him endured was in the name of so-called 'religion'. 'Sure you wouldn't say those awful names, Jesus?' she said aloud to the picture of the smiling Sacred Heart that rested on her bedside locker. Her eyes lit up and an idea popped into her mind. *Exactly,* she thought delightedly. 'Thank you, dear Lord, for putting the idea into my head.'

She lay drowsily against her pillows watching the moonlight disappear as the wind began to rise and the spitter-spatter of rain against the window lulled her to sleep.

CHAPTER TWENTY-TWO

'Good morning, light of my life.' Niall nuzzled in to her and Hilary felt him harden against her.

'I was asleep,' she griped, annoyed at being woken up.

'I'll wake you up,' he murmured, cupping her breast in his hand. Hilary's heart sank. She just wanted to go back to sleep. Niall had been drinking the previous night at his gig and she could smell the stale scent of beer off him and she just wasn't in the mood for sex. All she craved was deep, uninterrupted sleep.

'Can we do it tonight? I'm bushed. I just want to go back to sleep,' she mumbled, turning over on her front and burying her head under the pillow.

'We have a house full of teenagers tonight,' he reminded her, disappointed.

'Aw crap, I forgot about that. Tomorrow then,' Hilary slurred drowsily. She was asleep in seconds leaving her husband frustrated and disgruntled.

The sound of the smoke alarm jerked her rudely from her slumber. For crying out loud, she thought in exasperation, how many times have I told him to keep the kitchen door closed when he's grilling? She glanced at the clock and saw that it was nearly eleven and groaned. She hadn't meant to sleep in so late: Sophie's friends were coming and the house had to be cleaned. Hilary yawned. She supposed it might be too much to expect that the girls had made a start on their chores.

She threw back the duvet and grabbed her dressing gown and slid her feet into woolly slippers. It was raining. She could hear it hurling against the window and when she pulled up the blinds she saw the wind bending the bare branches of the rowan trees that lined her street so that they looked like old crones with long streaming hair. Rivulets of water flowed down the windowpane, the sky was dour, threatening sleet or worse, and she was glad she didn't have anywhere to go today. Once the house was clean she was going to come back to bed and read the latest Anita Shreve. She had treated herself to it ages ago but had never had the time to get into it.

She climbed the circular staircase that led to the recent attic conversion where the girls now slept in their own rooms, with a shared shower room and toilet. The square landing area that separated their bedrooms was a cosy lounging space, designed by Jonathan, with a small two-seater sofa, bean bags, a bookcase, coffee table and TV. Did her daughters have any idea of how privileged they were? Hilary wondered, remembering the bedroom with the one old-fashioned wardrobe and chest of drawers she had shared with her sister.

They had been so thrilled when Sally had bought a dainty dressing-table unit with three oval gilt-edged mirrors that could angle. That had been the height of sophistication and they had painted their room in a creamy lemon and got new gold-coloured curtains that matched the colour of the gilt on the mirror and had been delighted with their new-look room. They wouldn't have been able to fit a bean bag, let alone a sofa or bookcase, into their little kingdom.

She saw the remains of Millie's Chinese meal on the table, grains of rice like confetti against the dark green carpet. The cleaning up hadn't begun yet, she thought grimly, marching into the bathroom to pull up the blind before entering Sophie's room. Her daughter was curled under the duvet; blonde hair streaming over the pillows, her favourite battered old teddy bear poking out from under the quilt cover.

'Sophie, get up.' She shook her daughter none too gently.

'Whaaa ... uuuuhhh?' Sophie blinked open a bleary eye and raised a tousled head from the pillow.

'Get up and start tidying up. Look at this bedroom. It's a disgrace. And so is that bathroom. There's make-up marks all over the sink—'

'Breakfast in five. Sophie, do you want a fried egg?' Niall appeared at the bedroom door, a tea towel slung over his shoulder.

'Yeah, Dad. Mam, will you chill—'

'Those girls are not coming up here unless you clean up, do you hear me? Pick those clothes up off the floor and put them in your linen basket and put a wash on and make sure there are no knickers and tights pickling under the bed.' Hilary was in no mood to be told to 'chill'.

'*Maaam!*' hissed Sophie and suddenly Hilary was brought back to a similar scene in her own teenage years and remembered Sally using the exact same phrase. *Oh God! I've turned into my mother*, she thought, horrified. *I'm a middle-aged mother of teenagers, saying middle-aged things*. Her existential shock was interrupted by the arrival of her eldest daughter.

'What's going on?' Millie demanded. 'I was *trying* to have a lie-in. It *is* Saturday after all.'

'I told you we were doing a house clean today. You get that bathroom sorted – it's a disgrace!' Hilary retorted.

Niall threw his eyes up to heaven, exuding irritation with the three women in his life. 'Millie, do you want a fried egg?'

'Yep.' She stretched.

'Hilary?'

'No thanks.'

'Right, be at the table in five minutes,' Niall said crossly, annoyed that there was an atmosphere to ruin his Saturday morning. Hilary followed him down the stairs. 'Let's all lighten up a bit,' her husband suggested as she poured herself a cup of coffee while he began to fry the eggs.

'That's easy for you to say, Niall,' she grouched. 'I'd a very long day yesterday and when I came home from doing the shopping the pair of them were sprawled on the sofa watching TV and the breakfast dishes weren't even washed. I can't do *everything* by myself. I work too. I need support.'

'I support you,' he said indignantly, flipping an egg and causing greasy spatters to land on the countertop and floor.

Not enough, she wanted to say but she bit back the retort. 'Did you phone Sue?' She wiped the countertop.

'I left a message but she didn't get back.'

'She's going to have to pull her weight, Niall.' Hilary couldn't hide her annoyance.

'I hear you, I hear you,' her husband snapped, cracking

another egg onto the pan for Sophie, who liked her egg sunny side up.

'Well sort Gran's clinic visit between you because I have a client consult in Drogheda that morning and I won't be available.'

'I told you, I'll be in Canada.' Niall glared at her.

'Not my problem,' Hilary retorted. 'And she has an appointment with her geriatrician, her heart specialist and the optician in the next few weeks. I've marked the dates on the kitchen calendar. You can give them to Sue.'

'You know something, Hilary,' Niall said coolly as he plated up the breakfast, 'I've told you before there's no need for you to work as hard as you do, and I wish you'd ease back because you're becoming a real grouchy pain in the ass.'

'So you want me to be a stay-at-home housewife?' she demanded, stung by his criticism.

'Frankly, yes.' He stared at her.

'You know, Niall, it was the money that *I* earned that built that attic conversion, and it's the money that *I* earn that means we can have that extra holiday abroad and a decent car each. Don't forget that. *And* I'm contributing to the account for the college fees. All I'm asking for is some co-operation and for everyone to muck in, and for your sister to take *some* responsibility for her own mother, like I do for my parents. Not unreasonable, I would have thought. And as for giving up work or cutting back, *you* cut back and job share or something and *you* can be a stay-at-home husband.' She took her plate and marched over to the dining table fuming. She wasn't being unreasonable ... was she? She frowned, buttering a slice of toast.

'Mam, can I have the money for my shoes? I'm going to go into town with Jilly this afternoon.' Millie strolled into the kitchen in her PJs and fluffy slippers and put her arms around her dad who was absorbing his wife's backlash.

'Sure,' Hilary said calmly, and could see her daughter looking at her, waiting for the caveat 'when you've finished cleaning'. But she said nothing, squeezing ketchup onto her plate and taking a sip of coffee, for all the world like she hadn't a care. Sophie flounced into the kitchen, glowering at her. Hilary ignored her and ate some white pudding and mushrooms.

'Dad, we've decided we're going to go to see *The Talented Mr Ripley*. Will you give us a lift to the cinema?' she wheedled. Jude Law was her new pin-up. All her class thought he was 'to die for', and they were longing to see his new film.

Ha! thought Hilary. *Glad I got out of that one.*

'How can I refuse the birthday girl, even though it was your birthday last Monday?' Niall smiled at Sophie, handing his daughters their plates and taking his own and sitting down at the table beside Hilary. 'Breakfast OK?' he asked warily a while later, unused to her uncharacteristic silence.

'Lovely,' she said with faux breeziness, taking another slug of her coffee and finishing off the last of her sausage. She stood up and went over to the counter and poured herself a refill. 'Anyone else want some?' she asked, waving the percolator.

'No thanks.' Niall wolfed into his fry.

'Uhhh . . .' grunted Sophie.

'Can I have more OJ, please?' Millie asked, scrolling down through her texts. Hilary handed her the carton.

'Excuse me, all,' Hilary said politely, removing her plate from the table and putting it in the dishwasher.

'Where are you going?' Niall looked at her, surprised. The Saturday morning fry-up was traditionally a long leisurely meal when the family caught up with each other's various goings on.

'Back to bed.'

'Are you *sick*?' he asked, perplexed, because she had just eaten everything on her plate.

'Nope, just tired,' Hilary responded coolly. Out of the corner of her eye she saw the girls look at each other, clearly incredulous. *What about the cleaning*? she half expected them to ask. She didn't give anyone the chance to say anything else. She took her mug of coffee from the counter and walked briskly from the room. She opened the front door, lifted the morning paper from the mat in the porch and tucked it under her arm and went upstairs. She felt a giddy sense of liberation when she put her mug on her bedside locker and plumped up her pillows.

Niall's shirt was on the floor. She picked it up and brought it to his laundry basket in their en suite. It was almost full. She had planned to do a wash today and leave his shirts at the laundry for ironing. But her plans had changed, Hilary thought grimly. She was taking the day off. Time out. Let them all manage without her for a day.

She gave herself a quick freshen-up, patted some moisturizer onto her face and padded back to the bedroom. The rain was hammering on the roof, an angry impatient beat. A low growl of thunder echoed from the east. *Perfect* day for a duvet day, Hilary thought sliding into bed. Paper or book?

She dithered. Flick through the headlines and then settle down with the Anita Shreve, Hilary decided, snuggling down against the pillows and giving a luxurious stretch, watching the steely melancholy sky continue to unleash its volley of rain. It was strangely soothing to watch, snug beneath her downy quilt, and now that she had decided to step back and let the household get on without her she felt the tension she had been holding in every atom begin to float away.

'Er ... will I start hoovering?' Sophie poked her head round the door ten minutes later.

'Suit yourself,' Hilary said, looking out over the top of her glasses.

Sophie looked so gobsmacked Hilary nearly laughed.

'Em ... what time are you getting up?'

'I'm not.' Hilary bent her head to her book.

'But what about my sleepover?' her daughter bleated plaintively.

'Dad's here, he can make up the salads to go with the pizza. I'm taking your advice, Sophie. I'm chilling. Now close the door like a good girl, I'm at a really terrific part in my book.' Hilary repositioned her glasses and began to read with studied interest, much to Sophie's consternation.

'The door, pet,' Hilary reminded her sweetly, grinning when her daughter shut it with a decisive bang.

'You're not getting up at *all*?' Niall demanded five minutes later after Sophie relayed the news to him.

'Nope,' she said equably. 'Duvet day!'

'You can't have a duvet day today. Sophie's having a sleepover,' he protested.

'And?' She arched an eyebrow at him.

'Well ... well ... things have to be done, the food. The house needs hoovering,' he blustered.

'Sophie's fifteen. I don't need to hold her hand. Hoover if you want. It's entirely up to you. Oh and here.' She rooted in the drawer in her locker. 'Give this to Millie for her shoes.' She handed him some euro notes. 'Can I get back to my book now, please?'

'Do what you like,' her husband said exasperatedly.

'I certainly will,' Hilary said.

'Have you got PMT?' he demanded, completely thrown by her totally uncharacteristic behaviour. She almost laughed watching him stand, legs planted apart, hands on his hips, jaw thrust out aggressively.

'No, I feel perfectly fine. Please close the door when you go out,' she said, rolling over onto her side towards the window, with her back to him, precluding any further conversation. There was silence for a moment and then she heard him leave the room. She felt as she'd felt the one and only time she'd mitched off school with a friend one wintry December day, when they had gone to see the first *Star Trek* movie on a weekday afternoon, so desperately infatuated with Mr Spock and Captain Kirk they couldn't wait until the weekend. The movie had been disappointing, she remembered, with none of the humour and panache of the TV series; nevertheless it had been beyond exciting sitting in the darkened cinema with all the other devoted Trekkies, watching a shot of the *USS Enterprise* fill the huge wide screen of the Savoy. A sense of decadent exhilaration had filled her then, as she thought of her fellow classmates stuck at their desks studying geometry, and a similar feeling of decadent self-indulgence enveloped her today, lying in bed after midday on a Saturday when there was so much to be done. Let them at it, Hilary thought languorously as the words blurred on the page. She was stepping away from life's daily grind for once, and if they weren't careful she'd take tomorrow off as well.

CHAPTER TWENTY-THREE

Colette stretched cat-like on the luxurious emerald-green cushions on her lounger and gazed at the fine white silky sands and the translucent turquoise waters of the Caribbean. She was alone. Delightfully, desirably solitary at last. Jazzy was at boarding school. Her husband and, most thankfully, their house guests had flown back to New York on the private jet Des had hired to fly them all down to Turks and Caicos for the weekend. She'd had a stress headache since the previous night that had only begun to ease when the limos had pulled away from the villa and disappeared round the curve of road on Grace Bay that led to Providenciales Airport.

She glanced at her diamond-encrusted Baby Graff watch. The plane should be taking off in the next few minutes and the relief she felt at not being on it couldn't be described. She was taking a scheduled flight in two days' time to JFK via Miami, first-class of course. 'I need that time to myself, Des,' she'd insisted when he'd pointed out how expensive it was to hire a private jet, and a luxury villa in TCI, and then have to pay for a first-class flight back to New York when there was no need.

'I don't care, I'll pay it out of my own money,' she retorted. 'And that's rich to say that to me, considering *you* were talking about hiring the *Gulf Stream*, which is way, *way* more expensive than the *Bombadier*,' she snapped. 'That's crazy money you're spending on those stuck-up Wasps.'

'Look you have to spend money to get money. You know what these people are like. It's all about the image. Don't forget Chuck Freemont knows Bernie Madoff and Steve Cohen *personally*. These are the biggest big cheeses in wealth and hedge fund management you could meet and I *want* an introduction. If you think we're doing OK now, babes, we will be on the pig's back when we start investing with these guys.' Her husband's eyes gleamed with anticipation.

'I know who they are,' she retorted. 'I read the *Journal of Finance* and the *Wall Street Journal* too,' she added tartly, irritated that Des sometimes forgot that she wasn't some ditzy blonde airhead who was only interested in lunching with the 'girls'.

'Well then you know that Cohen's SAC had 70 per cent returns riding the high-tech wave last year and the year before. *70 per cent*, Colette. The guy's a financial genius! I want to work with him! Madoff's another one; the returns on his investments are high, high, high! Hell, some of my clients can retire because of the fortunes his company has made for them,' Des retorted. 'I've worked my butt off for the last ten years and climbed higher than I ever thought we would over here, and now it's time to make a killing and if your pa had any sense he'd listen to me and invest a million with Madoff.'

'Des, we've had this conversation before. None of the

major Wall Street firms invest with him, none of the major derivatives firms trade with him. They think his numbers don't add up and he's not legit. I'm warning you, don't risk our money and all we've worked for on a gamble with him.'

'For crying out loud, he's a former non-executive chairman of NASDAQ . He runs a multibillion-dollar operation. Of *course* he's legit. You're dad's a wuss not to take an opportunity if it comes his way and so would I be,' Des scoffed.

'Whatever, Des, just play it safe,' Colette said wearily.

'Colette, did you ever think we would be living in a swanky apartment on the Upper East Side, or own a condo in Aspen, and three villas to let in Florida, or have a house in Nantucket, or a share portfolio that would make your pa's eyes water? Have I not managed our investments *very* well over the years?'

'I suppose so,' she conceded. 'And we're doing fine, so why do we need to be inviting these' – she was tempted to call them freeloaders, but he would go ballistic – 'these acquaintances, on a weekend trip that's costing a fortune? I mean spending over a hundred thou for a weekend's entertaining is *way* over the top.'

'Contacts, honey, contacts. Money is no object to them – we must let them see it's no object to us. Perception is everything. It's time to take it up to the next level. This weekend will pay for itself one hundred times over, for the contacts we will make, trust me,' he said expansively.

Her husband was right: contacts were everything, Colette admitted. Mixing in the right circles opened doors that led to opportunities that they had taken every advantage of. The first few years of their life in New York had been an absolute whirlwind as she and Des had, with a forensic determination, climbed the career and society ladder for all they were worth. Her background in fine art, her judicious name-dropping of British artists, film stars, jet-setters, and even royalty, 'clients she'd had dealings with' in Dickon and Austen's, lent her authenticity and had impressed some of the people she had begun to socialize with.

It amazed Colette how the Americans adored the Royal Family and she had put that awe to impressive use when she had showed society matrons photos of Kensington Palace and the Orangery and formal gardens, and more or less implied that she had met Princess Diana and other royals who 'lived just down the road from her in Kensington', and who 'dropped into' Dickon and Austen's to buy paintings and sculptures.

When the shocking news broke that the Princess had died in a car crash in Paris, she had received many calls from her American acquaintances and friends expressing their shock, dismay and grief. Indeed, Colette had been, like millions, stunned at the news. She had held a discreet 'memorial lunch' on the day of the funeral to which she had invited the guests she and Des had decided were most useful and influential. Gratifyingly when word got out that she was hosting such a lunch an invite became quite the prize.

Dressed in a Chanel LBD and her highest Louboutins, and wearing a single piece of jewellery – a gold Paloma Picasso necklace – she had welcomed her guests to view the funeral on their enormous TV. Her maid had served Cristal champagne with beluga caviar, and Perugian white truffles, and, for afters, delectable petits fours from Duane Park Patisserie in Tribeca, an occasion of sin Colette had happened upon when she had first moved to New York that served the most exquisite hand-made French delicacies.

That little social gathering had led to Des meeting the husband of one of her guests at a soirée they had been invited to, and a job offer at JPMorgan that had increased his earnings eventually to the seven-figure sum he was now on. She had been over the moon when they had finally moved into a rental apartment on the Upper East Side. That was when Colette and Des knew they had it made.

'Sherman McCoy and Gordon Gekko have nothing on you, Des,' his father-in-law had commented sardonically, walking under the elegant long green canopy at the entrance to their building, to be admitted by Ryland, one of their liveried doormen, into the foyer of their posh new residence.

'Hell, don't say that,' Des exclaimed as they glided silently upwards in the sparkling mirrored elevator. 'Look what happened to them! Those "Masters of the Universe" went belly up and I know people the likes of whom those characters were based upon, Frank, and I'm *not* one of them.'

'Excellent,' said his father-in-law wryly. 'That's good to hear. Colette and Jasmine are in safe hands.'

Frank and Jacqueline had flown over to New York to spend a long weekend with them in their new fifteenth-floor eyrie, with its parquet floors, Italian marble bathrooms, 'European'-style kitchen and a view in the lounge, from a corner window, of 'the Park'! It was still a view, corner window or not, Des had assured her proudly.

It was hard to believe that was almost five years ago,

Colette sighed, as a boat drifted by on the aquamarine sea, red sails billowing in the trade winds. She reached out to take a sip of her G&T, luxuriating in her solitude. She had been as ambitious and eager for success as Des in those early years. She had revelled in their glitzy lifestyle that often saw her change her outfit five times a day to cover a coffee morning, lunch, launch, cocktail party and dinner she was regularly invited to.

But in the last year or so she had begun to weary of the constant treadmill their lifestyle subjected them to. Des worked practically seven days a week and was expected to be contactable by his boss 24/7. The more money he made the more he wanted. Last year's bonus always had to be topped.

She was constantly entertaining his clients or potential clients as well as their social set – at home, or in Nantucket during the summer months. Or co-hosting gala events with some of her peers for this charity or that one. Colette exhaled deeply. The charity circuit was not for the faint-hearted. The events she'd attended or organized in Dublin and London had not prepared her for the cut-throat viciousness that was a fundamental trait of the immaculately coiffed, face-lifted, plastic-surgery-enhanced, designer-dressed socialites who frequently reduced each other to tears of fury and jealousy – in private of course – despite the air kisses and gushy greetings of endearment. The patrons of the New York charity scene made piranhas look tame, Colette reflected glumly, taking a rather large slug of her cool, refreshing drink.

The breeze whispered against her face and she felt some of the tension flow out of her limbs. She hadn't realized just how stressed she was until she was alone. Wilted, that was how she felt, completely wilted from making small talk to people she hardly knew, and being constantly on the look-out to see that their every need was being met.

Chuck Freemont and his fat-thighed wife Dorothy had guzzled champagne from the minute they'd arrived on Friday evening, and had eaten their way through every expensive titbit put their way, as well as polishing off an entire box of hand-made chocolate liqueurs that had been placed in their guest suite.

Shirley, stick-thin wife of Brandon van der Graffe, Des's boss, had eaten nothing, except a few birdlike nibbles of lettuce and a couple of flakes of organic Irish salmon. She was constantly disappearing into their suite and looked suspiciously glassy-eyed throughout the weekend. She was edgy, anxious and deeply unhappy, and it was well known that coke was her only comfort. It was well known also that Brandon maintained an ultra glamorous young mistress in a pied-à-terre in Chelsea.

Des had looked a tad glassy-eyed, too, before the men had headed off to play golf and the women had settled to be massaged and beautified in their suites by a bevy of therapists Colette had employed on the Saturday afternoon. That had gone down very well, she thought, satisfied. And tomorrow she was going to have one of the therapists come over and massage her from head to toe, and give her a de luxe facial and to hell with the cost. She had worked her ass off this weekend being the perfect hostess. She deserved it.

Her taut, flat stomach gave a delicate little rumble and she realized she was hungry. She had had hardly any appetite for the rich food served by the chef who came with the villa, being far too stressed to actually enjoy a meal. That was no bad thing. She had to keep a strict watch on her calorie intake, she was determined to maintain her superb figure. Despite her spinning and cardiovascular workouts, and her jogs around the reservoir in Central Park, her tush was not as high and pert as it had once been.

There was some salmon and lobster left; she could have that with a salad but she'd have to get it herself. She had sent the staff home when they had cleaned up after the delicious lunch they had served to her departing guests. She'd eat soon and this time she'd enjoy every morsel of her food. How liberating not to have to talk to anyone, or keep an eagle eye out to make sure glasses were replenished with champers, costly wines and brandies. No one to worry about but herself. A rare and prized occurrence. Bliss!

She lay languidly in the balmy trade-wind breezes listening to the rhythmic, soothing swish of the gentle waves lapping against the curve of white-sanded beach fringed with palm trees and watching a gleaming white cruise liner glide serenely towards North Caicos. Colette drifted off to sleep.

When she awoke the sky was crimson, the setting sun a globe of molten gold dipping into a gilded sea, the fronds of the darkening palm trees silhouetted against the sky. She had slept for over two hours and she felt surprisingly refreshed. She slipped her sandals onto her feet and wrapped her sarong around her. She was *starving*.

What she'd really love was one of Ishmael's kebabs, Colette thought longingly, remembering the mouthwatering late-night feast she and Hilary had often shared on Baggot Street, after a night out in one of the ritzy nightclubs on the Lesson Street strip. The spicy sauce dripping from the wrap into her mouth. Colette smiled, remembering how sophisticated they had thought they were queuing for Zhivago's in a dingy lane off Baggot Street, or waiting for Maurice peering out through the peephole in Samantha's to give them the once-over. Barbarella's, Sloopy's, Lord John's: the nightclub names from her youth came flooding back and she suddenly felt a fierce wave of loneliness for home.

Where had that come from? Colette wondered, wishing she had Hilary here to share memories with and to confide how drained she was and how disenchanted she was becoming with life in the Big Apple. Hilary was the only one in the world she could admit that to and not feel a failure. There was not one friend or acquaintance on this side of the Pond that she could make that pronouncement to, secure in the knowledge that it would not be wafted along in Chinese whispers to all and sundry. Hilary would hate her lifestyle, Colette thought, remembering how her friend would far prefer to go to a trad session than a sophisticated nightclub.

They hadn't been in touch for ages. They had drifted apart over the past few years, having nothing much in common, each of them immersed in their own busy lives and careers. What she wouldn't give to have Hilary here now sharing a bottle of wine, and a meal on the moonlit deck, so that she could have a good old moan about Des and his never-ending, relentless pursuit of wealth and success. And to confide that she and Jasmine had just as prickly a relationship as Colette had with Jacqueline. Her teenage daughter was in boarding school in Upstate New York preparing for university. They were currently fighting about which one she should apply for. Colette had suggested Sarah Lawrence but Jazzy wasn't having any of it. 'I'm not going to a finishing school for young ladies,' she sneered dismissively. 'I want to go to Berkeley.'

'You are going to an East Coast university, miss, so you can forget about Berkeley,' Colette assured her, much to her daughter's disgust. When Jazzy had heard that Des was renting a jet to come down to the islands she had thrown a tantrum and insisted she wanted to come on the jaunt, despite it being term time. Another row had ensued, and now she wasn't talking to either of her parents. Did Hilary have as much trouble with Sophie and Millie? she wondered. The last time she had seen them, a few years ago, they were so sweet and polite and she had been mortified by Jasmine's thoroughly bad behaviour in comparison.

She walked past the shimmering pool and masses of fragrant flowering shrubs towards the villa, wondering why she had thought of Hilary and their carefree, giddy nights of so long ago. It seemed like another lifetime, and so far removed from the world she inhabited now.

She knew why she had thought of the succulent kebabs of her youth. She knew what this whole weekend had been building towards, knew why she had wanted to be completely alone. She hadn't given in to it for months, not even with the stress of the Christmas season and all the entertaining that had entailed, but this weekend had left her feeling utterly fraught, as she knew it would. Des had ratcheted up the pressure in the weeks leading up to it until she had wanted to scream, 'Leave me alone, for God's sakes!' But she hadn't, she'd calmed him down as she always did, and planned everything to the nth degree and now, thankfully, it was over and she could have her reward.

She flipped the switch for the lights and strolled into the kitchen. 'Don't rush, savour it,' she murmured, pouring herself a glass of fruity Merlot. She couldn't face another flute of champagne. She wanted substance. Colette opened the massive fridge doors and surveyed the array of food in front of her. She moved aside the conch salad to get to the platters of lobster and salmon. She placed them on the kitchen counter and took a crusty baguette from the ceramic bread bin, her mouth watering. She hadn't had bread in *ages*. She rarely allowed herself to eat white carbs. Colette cut the bread lengthways and slathered creamy butter all over it and bit into it so that she left teeth marks. It was gorgeous! She took another huge bite and stuffed some lobster and a hunk of salmon into her mouth so that her cheeks were bulging. A slug of wine and then more bread and lobster. Oh the comfort of it. The reward of it. How she deserved this solitary indulgence for all the stress she had endured. She felt exhilarated and utterly reckless and free as she feasted, until she could feast no more and she lay bloated, and bleary-eyed from drink, on the fat-cushioned chintz-covered sofa in the lounge.

Guilt, self-hatred and disgust consumed her and Colette wept bitter tears before running to the toilet to purge her body of the vile food she had consumed. Shaking and sweating as she retched, she vowed that this truly was the *last* time and she would go on a strict diet and she would never, *ever* binge again.

Later as she lay in bed curled up in a ball, revolted with herself, she realized that there wasn't one person in the world she could confide in. Not her husband, not her mother, not even Hilary. Her pride wouldn't let her. What did that say about her? Colette had never felt so lonely in her life. She sat up and got her Filofax out of her bag and studied her diary. It was fairly crammed but there were a few appointments she could lose. She wanted to go home to Ireland. It had been two years or more since she'd visited. She had been to London a few times last year but hadn't gone back to Ireland. Jacqueline and Frank had flown over to them. They were more inclined to come on mini breaks to New York, so going back to Ireland had not been a priority for Colette.

It would be good to talk to Hilary. Even if she couldn't tell her everything that was going on in her life, she could vent about some aspects that were driving her mad. And it would be a relief to step off the treadmill for a while. Her spirits lifted somewhat. A trip home was just what she needed. She would check her dates with Des and book flights tomorrow.

Worn out and sore and bloated from her food binge, Colette lay back against the pillows and fell into a restless sleep.

Des Williams felt the effects of the Ambien begin to hit as he lay on his massive queen-sized bed, naked apart from a soft towel around his hips, enjoying the sensuous movements of his lover's oil-slicked hands across the tightly bunched muscles in his neck and shoulders. He was beyond exhausted. If Skylar was hoping to get some tonight, she was going to be disappointed, he thought sleepily, groaning when her thumbs went deep into his deltoid muscle. Sex was the last thing on his mind. All he craved was sleep. Deep, deep sleep to revive him for a 6 a.m. start the following morning. The weekend had gone beyond his expectations; he had felt as high as a kite when the sleek long-range jet had raced along the runway at Provi Airport, lifting and soaring over the glittering waters of Grace Bay heading northwards over the vast Atlantic in a direct route to La Guardia.

His companions were relaxed, chatting animatedly as the stewardess handed out flutes of sparkling champagne to start the two and a half hour flight home. He was looking forward to casually mentioning to work colleagues that he had leased a jet to fly friends, including his boss, to a villa in TCI. He was a player now; this weekend had put him on another level. Colette had played a blinder; she deserved her two extra days to wind down and it would give him a chance to spend some quality time with his mistress, and get her off his back about how little attention he paid her.

Win! Win! Win! was Des's last thought before the Ambien took effect and he began to snore, much to Skylar's disappointment. Wall Street high-flyers were a disaster in the bedroom, she thought morosely, but the new diamond pendant hanging between her rounded silicone breasts was sufficient to keep her by Des's side for the time being. She wiped her hands on the towel that covered him, and turning onto her back, propped herself up against the pillows. She flicked on the TV, poured herself a glass of ice-cold bubbly from the bottle of Cristal nestling in the ice bucket and settled down to watch a rerun of *Sex and the City* and speed-read a manuscript that she hadn't got around to. She had an acquisitions meeting first thing in the large publishing company she worked for, and she needed to be on top of her game. An agent had assured her that this was the next Norman Mailer and she fervently hoped it had something to recommend it. Her last acquisition had been a dud, although she blamed sales and marketing for not doing more. Just as well she had a wealthy lover to pay her rent, Skylar thought wryly, even if he did blow ass in his sleep, and snore.

Dorothy Freemont cold-creamed her face in her extravagantly appointed pink bathroom. She had enjoyed the feel of the sun's rays caressing her skin on the weekend jaunt to TCI, but she could do with some refreshing, she thought, noting the broken veins on her nose and cheeks.

Chuck was already asleep in his suite. He had polished off a lot of alcohol this weekend and had been quite smashed when they landed in La Guardia. If Des Williams thought pouring drink down her husband's neck was the way to get into their set he was sadly mistaken. Dorothy pursed her lips. The wife Colette was nice enough if somewhat edgy. In fact she reminded Dorothy of herself all those years ago, when she and Chuck were giving it their all to get ahead. Yes indeed, she had once been as beautiful and pert and blonde as Colette was now, but the ravages of stress, kidney problems and arthritis, and the medication she had to take, had slowed her body down and caused her to put on weight, far more than she had ever carried, and she had seen the younger woman looking at her and wondering how she could let herself go so. Give Colette another twenty years and it would be interesting to see what she looked like in her sixties, Dorothy thought.

As for the husband, he'd hardly noticed her. Des had made the fatal mistake of patronizing Dorothy while schmoozing Chuck, the entire weekend. *Only the wife!* she could see him thinking. *Give her a few beauty treatments and expensive chocolates and she'll be fine.* Jackass! He didn't get that *she* was an equal player in all that went on in Freemont Enterprises? Clearly not! And that was a *big* mistake. Des Williams and his jittery wife, although they did not know it, had just been relegated to the Freemont Z list, Dorothy decided, slathering on more Crème de La Mer before donning a black-velvet sleep mask and retiring to her enormous canopied bed with her little pug Frow Frow.

Chapter Twenty-Four

'What is it?' Jonathan asked early on Monday morning when his mother handed him an envelope with a card in it. They had finished their breakfast and he was standing on the lawn in the back garden scattering crumbs for the birds. It was a glorious morning. All the cloud and rain and cold from the previous few days a mere memory as a weather front from the south chased away the northern polar air. There was even a touch of heat in the sun and the crocuses sprinkled around the garden in splashes of Van Gogh-like colour opened to its warm caress. The birds were singing and his heart lightened at the sound. His overnight bag was in the hall and he was almost ready to leave for Dublin. He wished he could stay longer but he and Hilary were heading to Wexford and he needed to get on the road.

'Open it,' Nancy said, her eyes glinting with pleasure.

'It's a book mark!' he exclaimed when he opened the card and saw what it contained. 'Oh! There's a photo of me in the middle. What's this about?'

'Read it!' His mother smiled at him.

'Before I formed you in the womb, I knew you through and through.

I chose you to be mine, before you left your mother's side;
I called to you, my child. To be my sign.'
'And the other one,' Nancy prompted.
'"For I know the plans I have for you," declares the Lord,
Plans to prosper you and not to harm you,
Plans to give you hope and a future."'

Tears blurred Jonathan's eyes. 'Oh Mam!' He could hardly speak.

'I got it done on Saturday morning. You know the small print shop in Castle Mall? I gave them the quotes and your photo and they suggested the book mark. Isn't it nice? I wanted you to feel good about yourself. God created you and God knows you and that's all that matters. It was a quote I heard at a funeral recently and I thought it was *perfect* for you. And of course the one from Jeremiah was one of the readings at Rachel's wedding, if you remember.' Nancy was thrilled with herself.

'Oh Mam, I'll treasure it forever. It's the most precious gift I've ever been given.' He enfolded her in a hug.

'And you and your sisters were the most precious gifts *I* was ever given and you make me proud and contented. And I know the good Lord is proud of you and never forget that, Jonathan,' Nancy said steadfastly, if somewhat muffled against his chest.

'I won't,' he whispered. 'I won't. And I'll always try to make you, my sisters and the Lord proud of me.'

'I know you will and I have no fears for you. You are a WONDERFUL and decent person and let no one tell you otherwise.' Nancy's arms tightened around him and they held each other in a loving embrace as the robin and blackbirds sang their song from the branches of the heavenly scented purple Daphne that bloomed so magnificently in the sun-drenched garden.

'Oooh I was like an Antichrist, Jonathan. They didn't know what to make of me. I would have put my own mother to shame. In fact I parroted some of the things she said to Dee and me.' Hilary grinned as they cruised along the N11 in Jonathan's Beemer. 'I stayed in bed the *entire* day with my book. It was *bliss*. Niall was running around like a headless chicken. He couldn't get his head round it at all. I got up and threw on a tracksuit when the girls came back from the pic-tures, organized the pizzas, had something to eat myself, accompanied by a large glass of wine, and then tootled off upstairs again and finished my book. I must give it to you, it was a terrific read.' Hilary stretched her legs and enjoyed the comfort of the soft cream-leather seat, the luxury of not having to drive, and time to natter to Jonathan in comfort.

'Way to go, m'dear!' Jonathan approved. 'We all need to have our diva days now and again. And to have a diva day *and* a duvet day. Double whammy. No wonder they didn't know what hit them.'

'And I was a right diva, I can tell you. You should have seen Sophie giving me the wary eye every so often when I was dishing up the pizza and salads. I don't know what she thought I was going to do but she couldn't have been more helpful, making sure everyone had enough and tidying up afterwards. The group she hangs around with are grand kids so they all mucked in anyway. And then I disappeared and left them to it.'

'And what did Niall have to say?' Jonathan indicated and overtook a juggernaut, enjoying the turbo dart of speed for the manoeuvre.

'He's annoyed with me. Who wants to be nagged on their weekend off? But shag it, Jonathan, I need more help than I'm getting. I'm struggling,' she sighed. 'I need to get another cleaner because the house is on the slide and I don't have the time to do it. I've booked to get the minis in later this week to blitz the place.'

'Good thinking. I do that every so often. It's a gift.'

'It's Niall's attitude that really bugs me,' Hilary grumbled. 'He actually asked why didn't I give up work.'

'You're *joking!*' Jonathan looked across at her, shocked.

'I'm not. He said there was no need for me to work, and fine, there isn't. He's got a great job and salary and we could well manage on it, but I know he just wants me to be there minding the house, bringing his mother to her clinics – and don't get me wrong, I'm very fond of her, you know that – because it would all be so *convenient* for him. And this all because I blew my top.'

'I can understand why you're finding the juggling hard. It would be beyond me. When you add elderly parents into the mix it's such an increased pressure. I just have Mam to think about, and my sisters are great for keeping an eye on her, but you have your own mam and dad *and* your mother-in-law. That's not easy. Did he ring Smokin' Sue?'

'He left a message!'

'And did she get back to him?'

'What do you think?' Hilary said drily. 'She won't get back. I know her. And knowing him he won't ring again unless I nag him. It's doing my head in,' she groaned.

'Umm ... that's not very proactive. I don't know if you think this is good news or not so.' He glanced across at her, an eyebrow raised.

'What?' she asked warily.

'Gina Grant's secretary phoned me. Gina and Shaun would like to meet us with a view to having a bespoke spa installed in their house, or rather mansion ...' he corrected himself.

'The Grants? The Grant Insurance Grants? Gina Grant the Charity Queen?'

'The very ones,' Jonathan said smugly.

'He's a multi-multimillionaire. He has his own heli-copter.'

'He is and he has ... *and* ... he want us to design his own personal spa!'

'Imagine being rich enough to have your own spa! I couldn't think of anything nicer than being able to have a facial or a massage whenever you wanted.' She sighed wist-fully.

'Me neither. The luxury of it. So are you up for it? It will just be something on a smaller scale than what we've done with the hotels.'

'Of *course* I'm up for it. Niall will just have to get over himself,' Hilary declared. 'This is *too* good an opportunity to miss. I wonder where did Gina hear about us?'

'I think she's related by marriage to Cecily Porter, who owns Horizon House. So we must have got a good report. You can't beat word of mouth.'

'It's great, isn't it? And all because we did a random lighting design course together. Imagine that was ten years ago!'

A Time for Friends

'I have the grey hairs to prove it,' Jonathan teased. 'Now you know we'll have to charge them an arm and a leg.'

'Why? We haven't even been on site yet. We don't know what it's going to cost.' She looked at him, surprised.

'That's immaterial. If we don't go high they won't feel they've got something special. The more they spend, the more they can boast about it. That's the way it works in that clique. Don't let the Joneses keep up with you, whatever you do. Now they'll have their own inhouse spa *and* a helicopter and a fleet of expensive cars and, and, and ...' Jonathan explained patiently.

'It's all a bit mad really, isn't it? I wouldn't like that type of lifestyle and all that goes with it. I'm happy enough with my attic conversion,' Hilary chuckled.

'Not just any old attic conversion ... *A Harpur*-designed attic conversion,' Jonathan reminded her as they drove across the bridge over the Avoca River at Ferrybank and into Arklow Town. 'The river looks choppy and high,' he observed, watching the waves whack angrily against the quays, the morning sun casting prisms of light that turned the water into a dazzling, silver, undulating sheath.

'Bad place for flooding here; I hope the tide hasn't risen before we come back. I wonder will we ever be able to afford our own helicopter?' Hilary bantered.

'Never say never. Ready for coffee?'

'I sure am,' Hilary replied. Jonathan had picked her up en route from Rosslara and she had just eaten a banana, knowing that they were stopping for refreshments before they got to Gorey.

Joanne's Hot Bread Shop was comfortably warm and the

303

scent of freshly baked bread wafted around them enticingly as they walked past the mouthwatering displays of cakes and breads. They tucked themselves into a little alcove at a table for two and scanned the menu.

'Scrambled eggs and a slice of bacon for me,' Hilary decided briskly.

'And a croissant and a scone and jam for me, please, and a pot of coffee for two,' Jonathan said to the waitress who had arrived to take their order.

'Do you think I'm neglecting family? Am I being selfish, Jonathan?' Hilary asked when the waitress had delivered their breakfast to them and Hilary had poured their coffee.

'*No!* Not at all!' he exclaimed. 'You're a very giving mother and wife, Hilary. Too giving sometimes, that's your problem. So I'm glad you had your day of protest. It does them no harm to get a reminder sometimes that you aren't Superwoman. Do you *want* to give up work?' He smothered his croissant in butter and jam and bit into it.

'No, I really enjoy it. It's just the juggling that I find hard-going and the fact that Niall is keeping his head in the sand about Margaret, and is allowing Sue to get away with doing feck all! My time is as precious as hers, or his, and neither of them gets that and it makes me furious,' she seethed. 'They seem to have the impression that I'm just dabbling in work, that it's some sort of friggin' *hobby*!' Her voice rose indignantly.

'We don't want to scare the natives, dear,' Jonathan said soothingly, noticing two middle-aged women at another table looking in their direction.

Hilary giggled. Her friend was so good at injecting humour when she got a bit fraught. 'But you know what I'm saying!' She bit into a slice of buttery toast.

'I do. I see exactly where you're coming from and if you want my advice, I would set my boundaries. Tell Niall, Sue and the girls that you have a career that's important to you and you need them to respect that. Tell them that they all have to pull their weight because you're not doing it all by yourself any more.'

'I know you're right and I *do* say things and they muck in for a while and then they forget and we all slip back into our old ways. I'll just have to keep nagging,' she grimaced. 'Anyway enough of me, tell me about *your* weekend. How's your mam? And any update on the new romance?'

'Well now that you ask,' Jonathan grinned, bursting to tell her his news. 'There *has* been a development and you'll be proud of me and so will Hannah.'

'Tell me all,' demanded Hilary eagerly, replenishing their coffee cups.

'He phoned me and for *once* in my life I played it cool,' Jonathan laughed, before telling her all about the events of his weekend.

'Isn't it great that we can tell each other *everything*,' Hilary said an hour later, tucking her arm into her best friend's as they walked up the hill at the side of the coffee shop to the car park. 'I never feel I'm being disloyal to Niall if I say something about him, and you're the only one I'd say things about him to.'

'Real friendship is such a gift, isn't it?' Jonathan smiled down at her. 'You know everything about me and I know everything about you and we can say what we like to each other.'

'I know. I say things to you I wouldn't dream of saying to Niall or anyone else. Even though I love him dearly.'

'Well of course you're not going to talk to him about your boobs and ass going south, and having to cross your legs when you sneeze! He doesn't need to know about your leaky bladder,' Jonathan teased.

'Give over, that was only once when I had the flu and I got a simultaneous coughing and sneezing fit,' she protested, getting into the car.

'Just keep doing the exercises,' he cautioned, clipping his seat belt on.

Less than half an hour later they were on site and Hilary was fit to be tied. The electrician had ignored her plans and had taken short cuts wiring the spa area that were totally unacceptable.

'Peter, this isn't on,' she said to the builder who was standing with his arms folded frowning at her. She turned to the electrician who was standing beside him glowering at her.

'Rory, I told you where I wanted the spots. And those dimmer switches for the floor lights were to be separate from the wall lamps. You can't have them all running off the one switch.'

'Ah now you're only complicating things. I've been doing electrics for years. I know what needs to be done and how to do it – don't get your knickers in a twist,' the florid, thickset electrician said patronizingly.

'He does have a point,' the builder remarked. 'This is all a bit complicated and time-consuming.'

'Is that right?' Hilary gave him a withering stare. 'Well I'm the lighting designer on this project, and I'm doing what the owner has asked me to do, so it's like this, Peter, I'm getting my client on the phone right now and you can discuss it with her. It's her money that's being spent here and as far as I'm concerned, you, Rory, are not doing what you've been asked to do, or paid to do.'

'Now wait a minute—'

Hilary ignored him and dialled Norah Clancy's number and gave her a brief rundown of the situation.

'Put that little toad on to me,' Norah commanded. Hilary handed Rory the phone and had to turn away and hide a smile as she heard the blistering tirade he had to endure.

'Here, she wants to talk to you.' The electrician handed her the phone back with bad grace and stomped off.

'Yes, Norah?' Hilary said.

'I gave him what for and told him if he wasn't able to do the job I'd get someone who was. Whatever expenses you've incurred coming down today invoice me for them. He'll be paying. And if he hasn't done what you want the next time you're down, he's off the project. I'll tell Peter Ryan I want someone new on the job. OK?' Norah said briskly.

'Fine. Otherwise it's all starting to take shape. Talk soon.' Hilary hung up. Her client was a woman who took no crap, and Rory Tobin had made a big mistake thinking he could get away with ignoring both her and Hilary's design.

'Peter, tell your electrician to follow the plan we all agreed on or there'll be financial consequences. Norah's going to be talking to you herself,' Hilary said coolly. 'I'll be getting on to the architect as well. He needs to know what's going on here as does the quantity surveyor.'

'God help me with the lot of ye,' the builder muttered. 'Right, I'll get it sorted.'

'I'll see you in a week then.' She marched out of the building and left her hard hat in the prefab. Jonathan was standing on top of the grassy bank watching the sun glistening on the sea.

'Sorted?'

'Yep,' she scowled. 'Thank God Norah's a strong woman and knows what she wants. Tweedledum and Tweedledee aren't too happy though.'

'Oh I think the filthy look you gave them and the ear-bashing from Norah will keep them in their boxes for a while. The place is going to be fabulous though. I can't wait to decorate. That floor-to-ceiling wall of glass where the relaxation room is going to be will be stunning. What a view! We'll come down for an overnighter when it's up and running.'

'Wonder will Norah give us a discount,' Hilary grinned.

'I wouldn't hold my breath. She's one tough cookie! She reminds me of Maggie Thatcher, with a hint of Bette Davis thrown in. You know, the permed blonde hair and the ruby-red lipstick and the square-handbag look.'

'Well she'd need to be a tough nut to deal with that pair.' Hilary took her wellies off and threw them into Jonathan's boot and slipped on her shoes. It was a nuisance that she'd have to come back the following week but that was the way it went sometimes. 'Thanks a million for driving me down,' she said gratefully, leaning back against the soft leather headrest.

'No probs. I wanted to see what the place was looking like with the windows in anyway. I can visualize it all much better now. I need to get cracking on sourcing my materials and fixtures and fittings.'

'Well I could have driven us. It was a treat being chauffeured.'

'That's what friends are for.' Jonathan handed her a bottle of water and took a swig out of his own.

'Speaking of "real friends" I got an unexpected text from Colette earlier. I haven't heard from her in I don't know how long!' Hilary glanced over at him.

'What does Little Miss Me Me Me want?' Jonathan derided, reversing out of the parking space.

'She told me she was in the Caribbean—'

'Well for some, isn't it?'

'Don't be like that,' Hilary chided. 'She said she was lonely and missed home and is planning a trip before the summer and hopes we can meet up.'

'Something must be amiss and she needs your advice,' Jonathan remarked as they emerged from the narrow secondary road onto the N11 and headed for the Gorey bypass.

'I hope it isn't,' Hilary said firmly. 'OK, she's not the best friend in the world and never has been but I hope life is good for her and I'll meet up with her when she's home.'

'You're the biggest marshmallow going, Hammond! And don't forget, the only people who appreciate a doormat are people with dirty shoes.'

'Yes, Jonathan.' Hilary smiled. 'And even though I could say things about pots and kettles, I won't.'

'No don't,' he grinned back at her and put his foot on the

accelerator. They sped along making the most of their time together and had a thoroughly enjoyable natter.

The only people who appreciate a doormat are people with dirty shoes. Hilary couldn't help remembering Jonathan's acid comment while she sat in Buswells Hotel sipping a second cup of coffee waiting for her sister-in-law to arrive. Sue had chosen the hotel near the Dáil for their meeting, and Hilary had watched several well-known politicians making their way in and out over the past hour as she fumed about Sue's lack of respect. Typical. She was always late when they arranged to meet. Sue being firmly of the opinion that her time was far more precious than Hilary's. If she hadn't wanted to finally have it out with her about her lack of assistance with Margaret, Hilary would have walked. It helped that by the time her tardy sister-in-law arrived she was steaming.

'Soooo sorry for keeping you.' Sue swept across the foyer, the long lilac tie-dye scarf wound around her neck floating out behind her. Her heels were impossibly high, her trouser-leg creases knife sharp and she was impeccably made up. 'We were meeting with some TDs over in the Dáil bar and I simply couldn't get away,' she gushed, giving Hilary an air kiss on both cheeks and looking her up and down rather dismissively.

'You did pick the time and the location, Sue, and I've been here for over an hour. I've had to postpone a client consult,' Hilary said coldly. That was a fib but she wasn't letting Sue know it. She had kept three hours free. She knew her sister-in-law of old.

'Well I'm here now. Just let me order a peppermint tea and then I'm all ears,' Sue said airily, catching a waiter's eye with an imperious wave. It was a wonder she hadn't clicked her fingers, Hilary thought irately as Sue gave her order without even bothering to ask if Hilary would like a fresh beverage.

Hilary took a deep breath. 'I'll get straight to the point, Sue. I'm pressed for time,' she added pointedly. 'I can't continue to bring your mum to her warfarin clinic *and* her various medical appointments. I have parents of my own to take care of, and a demanding job, as well as a husband, children and a house to manage. I—'

'But I simply *can't* take time off willy-nilly, Hilary. You've got to understand *I* have a very demanding boss and a *very* demanding job indeed,' Sue cut in indignantly.

'I appreciate that,' Hilary said smoothly. 'That's why I've worked out a rota for you and Niall, and *of course* I will bring Mrs Hammond to some of her appointments because I love her and she's a wonderful mother-in-law and grandmother. I just want you and Niall to pull your weight. After all Gran H is *your* mother.'

'I know she's my mother,' Sue snapped. 'But you have a sister to help you out. I don't!' She played a trump card.

'You have Niall,' Hilary retorted.

'He's not much use,' Sue said insultingly.

'Well the pair of you'd better work it out between you,' Hilary snapped back.

'I don't like your tone, Hilary.' Sue glared at her.

'Deal with it, Sue,' Hilary said sharply. For once in her life she wasn't going to be the pacifier. She wasn't going to swallow down her irritation and have heartburn for three days after their encounter. She was sick and tired of being taken for granted by the pinched-faced, self-absorbed woman opposite her. She was done trying to be nice. With Sue nice got you nowhere. She was fed up pandering to her and her moods and her airs and graces. Hilary took a typed-up sheet of paper out of her bag. 'Here are your mum's appointments for the next three months, including her next warfarin appointment. Niall will be away for that and I have an appointment but it's ten days away so you have some leeway to schedule it in. Sort the other dates with Niall and I will fit in as best I can,' she said crisply.

'Are you suggesting I take time off? Annual leave?' Sue exclaimed, aghast, taking the paper between her finger and thumb.

'It's what *I* have to do, Sue,' she retorted. '*I* take time off to bring *your* mother to her appointments. I'm up to my eyes. I can't do it any more.'

'But your job is much more flexible than mine.'

'Actually it's not. And even if it was, that's not the point. It's not up to *me*. And let me tell you something else, Sue, you might as well prepare yourself. As time goes on there are going to be more appointments and more demands on your time, so you'd better get used to it. I will help out as much as I can but you need to start taking your share of the burden. You could start by cooking Margaret a meal every second weekend or inviting her over for dinner. Niall and I pay for the garden to be maintained; you could contribute to having her cleaner come an extra day. *I* actually shouldn't have to be sitting here saying these things to you, Sue. And because they have to be said, it's Niall that should have been saying them. I don't want to fall out with you but frankly I'm sick of your self-absorbed behaviour and I'm heartily sick of being taken for granted. I have a family to rear, and parents to look after myself. I would love to be able to go to the gym and go hill walking and partake in all the activities you have time for. I don't even have time to read. So, Sue, there comes a time when you have to step up to the plate and your time is now. OK?'

Hilary stood up and stared at her shocked sister-in-law. 'I'd love to stay and have another coffee,' she said acidly, 'but I had to reschedule because you were late. I think it's disrespectful to keep someone waiting so I have to go now to be at my next appointment on time. Work out the dates with Niall and try not to make your mother feel like a burden.'

'I *really* don't like your attitude, Hilary.' Sue was furious at the way she'd been lectured. 'In fact I strongly object to it and—'

'Sue, build a bridge and get over it,' Hilary retorted. 'You've got away with it for years because I took so much on. Your mother deserves a lot more from you than what she's getting and if I have to point that out to you, that's such a sad reflection on you. Now I'm going. Bye.'

She hurried out of the hotel without a backward glance and headed towards Pearse Street. She'd taken the DART into the city, unwilling to deal with bumper-to-bumper traffic and the hassle of looking for parking. She didn't care if Sue was mad with her, as Hilary knew whatever polite façade they had kept up over the years there would be no coming back from today's encounter. She scowled, jaywalking across

Kildare Street. Frankly she didn't really care any more. The older she got the less inclined she was to put up with crap from people and Sue was full of it. You couldn't like everyone. And she didn't particularly like Sue. So be it – she wasn't going to lose sleep over the disintegration of their flimsy relationship. She had too much on her plate as it was.

The nerve of her sister-in-law, Sue raged, lighting up a cigarette on the steps of the hotel as she stood under the flag-bedecked awning trying to compose herself. Just who did she think she was, lecturing her about her responsibilities? Her boss would not be best pleased when she started taking mornings off to bring Margaret to her clinics and medical appointments. Niall was going to have to do as much as she did. He needn't think he was getting away with it. And she was going to tell him that in no uncertain terms, she decided, taking her phone out of the side pocket of her bag and dialling his number.

Hilary had to run to catch a DART just before it pulled out of the station and she sank into the seat breathless, relieved that she hadn't missed it and wasted even more time on Sue. Her sister-in-law was probably taking deep angry drags on a cigarette somewhere, fuming at what had been said to her. Tough, it had been a long time coming. Too long. Hilary scowled as the train pulled out of Pearse.

'Sue phoned me. She was most upset at what you said to her. Did you *have* to start a row?' Niall demanded down the phone a little while later as the train crossed the Liffey into Connolly.

'I didn't start any row. She's upset because she has to get her skinny ass in gear and take some responsibility for her mother, Niall,' Hilary hissed indignantly. 'She's got away with it for years because *I* was there doing what she should have been doing. So tough if she's upset. She's a grown woman. It shouldn't be up to me to have to tell her how to behave. And if I may say so, it's only because *you* didn't have the guts to do it that I had to, so don't give me a hard time about this, Niall, because I'm not taking it. Niall, you need to cop on a bit and start backing me up on this. I take responsibility for looking after my parents; you and Sue need to start taking more responsibility for your mother. Bye!'

She hung up and stared unseeingly out of the window as a flood of passengers boarded at the station. Her husband had some nerve ringing her because Sue had gone whinging to him obviously. Well it was time the two of them got used to the idea that she wasn't going to be a pushover any more. A doormat she was no longer prepared to be and if they didn't like it they could both lump it.

Millie and Sophie were going to the pictures with their cousins and having a pizza beforehand. Hilary had planned on cooking steak, onions and mash for herself and Niall. And she had decided to take the opportunity to discuss her reasons for taking the duvet day with him, and sort their issues once and for all, but as she drove home from work, tired and irritable and still simmering with resentment at her husband's high-handed attitude, she decided she was damned if she was cooking and took a detour to McDonald's. She ate her Big Mac and fries in a drive-through bay, and finished her meal off with a McFlurry ice cream and apple pie. She licked her fingers and shoved the cartons into the paper bag they had been served in and turned on the ignition. She was going to buy *Hello!* and pour herself a glass of wine and flop on the sofa and Niall could look after himself, she thought grimly, reversing out of her parking space.

'Where's dinner?' Niall asked grumpily an hour later, surprised at finding Hilary lying on the sofa flicking through a magazine, a big glass of red at her side and not a sign of a meal being prepared.

'I've had mine earlier. I got a McDonald's. There's steak in the fridge if you want it or order in, whatever you prefer.' Hilary didn't lower her magazine.

'Well thanks for telling me you weren't cooking. I could have got something at work,' he said indignantly.

'It was a spur of the moment decision. I wasn't in the humour for cooking,' she retorted.

'No, be honest about it, you're just pissed off at me and you're getting your own back, that's what's going on,' Niall scowled.

'That too,' Hilary said coolly.

'Well that's childish in the extreme.'

'You can look at it like that if you want to, Niall. I'm just taking a night off and putting myself first for a change.' Hilary took a sip of her Shiraz.

'You're good at that,' he said nastily.

'I am *not!*' Hilary retorted indignantly, sitting bolt upright. 'You go and frig off for yourself! *You're* the one that's good at putting yourself first! I never say anything to you about the nights you're off out playing music. *And* I've been very good to Margaret. *And* I do most of the running around after the girls. So don't give me that crap.'

'And do I say anything about the time you spend with Jonathan? And all the jaunts you go on with him that aren't work?' Niall demanded.

'Now *you're* being childish,' she retorted.

'No I'm not. You spend more time with him than you do with me.'

'Don't be ridiculous,' she snapped.

'Well you do. It's Jonathan this and Jonathan that,' he said sulkily.

'Yeah well if I do, and I dispute that, at least Jonathan doesn't treat me like Wee Slavey and he looks out for me.' Hilary glared at him.

'Oh shut up, Hilary, I've enough going on at work without coming home to this. I'm off to have a pint and a meal in peace and quiet.' Niall grabbed his car keys.

'Great, I'll get some peace. And I might even give Jonathan a ring,' Hilary said childishly, flopping back down against the cushions and picking up her magazine.

She heard the front door slam and exhaled. She was glad the girls hadn't witnessed their little spat. She and Niall were sniping at each other a lot recently. Hopefully he'd take on board what she'd said about Sue taking more responsibility for Margaret, and things would settle back down again.

Niall did have a point about Jonathan, she admitted grudgingly. She did spend a lot of time with him. Just as well her best friend was gay – Niall might even accuse her of having an affair. But that was the perfect thing about her friendship with Jonathan; there were no issues like that to deal with.

Let her husband cool down over his pint and pub dinner; Jonathan was right about the way she let her family treat her. She was too easy-going and people took advantage of that. He'd be pleased that she'd stood up for herself, finally, and what was even better was the fact that she didn't care any more if Sue was annoyed with her. She wasn't going to get an ulcer worrying that the other woman might never talk to her again. That would be a plus, she thought defiantly, amused at her newfound bolshiness. She hoped it would last.

And if she was changing so was Jonathan, she reflected. She was impressed by how he was handling his new relationship. He wasn't throwing himself in headlong. He wasn't giving everything and expecting little in return. He was playing it cool and letting Leon do the running. She would give anything to see her much-loved friend with the man of his dreams. Perhaps at last it was going to happen and not before time.

CHAPTER TWENTY-FIVE

'Are you sure I can't drive you to the airport?' Hilary offered as she neatly folded a set of plans they had been working on and placed them in the large green folder on her desk.

'Not at all, Hil. Go home and spend time with the girls. You said you were going to.' Jonathan scrolled down through his phone for the number of the taxi firm he used. He gave them the address and glanced at his watch. 'I've loads of time before check-in. I'll have a coffee and a mosey around while I'm waiting for Leon, and get myself in holiday mode.' He and Leon were going to London for a short post-Easter break that had been arranged on the spur of the moment. He still couldn't quite believe that it was happening.

'Are you excited?' Hilary asked him fondly, delighted that his new relationship was progressing so well.

'Yeah! And a bit nervous. I really think this is it, Hilary. At long, long last I think I'm going about it the right way, taking things slowly and really enjoying being friends first. We get on very well. We've got so much in common. He's fun to be with and I fancy the pants off him. Tonight's gonna be the night.'

'I hope you're staying somewhere nice.' Hilary sat back in her chair and stifled a yawn.

'He wanted us to book a Jurys Inn, but I wanted somewhere a little bit more special, so we're taking cheap flights, and I'm paying for the hotel. That's why we're flying Ryanair,' he grimaced. 'Imagine having to stand queuing, and then being told the gate has changed and then that mad gallop to get seats when you're boarding. Only for love, I tell you, only for *lurv*!' he declaimed, throwing his hands wide in a Shakespearean gesture.

Hilary laughed at his theatrics. 'So where are you staying?'

'The Franklin.' He sat down on the edge of her desk. 'It's a lovely, quirky, five-star townhouse hotel just off the Brompton Road. I love it. The rooms are fab, all designed very differently to suit their size and shape and orientation. I get great ideas when I'm there. It's got an honesty bar and a pretty little garden. And Knightsbridge is just a stone's throw away. Harvey Nicks, Harrods, the V&A across the road – what more could you want? And I just can't wait to show the Brompton Oratory to Leon, he'll adore it. You know all that over-the-top High Renaissance Baroque-style architecture, and the stunning murals and paintings. *Fabuloussss*!!' Jonathan was giddy with excitement.

'Sounds amazing. You're going to have a brilliant time and you deserve it.' Hilary jumped to her feet and gave him a tight hug.

'Well it's only for three days. It was all he could get off, but it's fine because it's our first time away together.'

'London is perfect for a short getaway; I used to love

visiting Colette before both of us got married. Haven't been in ages. I might suggest a trip to Niall sometime.'

'You should. You could do with a romantic break away. I can't believe *I'm* going on a romantic break. I have butterflies in my stomach,' he confessed.

'You'll be grand when you meet up with Leon. Look, here's your taxi. Have a ball, Harpur!'

'Will do, Hammond!' Jonathan gave her a last hug, draped his scarf around his neck, grabbed his case and carry-on bag and sashayed out the door to the waiting taxi. Hilary laughed and waved, delighted that her best friend was so happy and carefree.

Jonathan sat in the back of the taxi and checked to make sure he had his passport, sterling and mobile phone charger in his Italian-leather shoulder bag. Even though he had double-checked everything before he left his apartment he just wanted to make absolutely sure. He had left his passport behind once on a trip to Barcelona and had only discovered it was missing at check-in. He was always *extra* careful after that expensive little episode.

He couldn't quite believe that he and Leon were going to London. *And*, even better, at Leon's suggestion. They had been out for a drink on the Wednesday before Easter and Leon had asked him what he was doing for the bank holiday weekend. As it happened, Nancy was coming to stay with him on Good Friday until Easter Sunday. They had a tradition in the last few years of Jonathan taking his mother to all the Easter Ceremonies in the Pro-Cathedral, culminating in the sung Midnight Mass. Although he wasn't religious,

Jonathan loved the heart-soaring poignancy of the famous Palestrina Choir, as did Nancy.

'I have the week after Easter off – what would you think of hopping over to London for a few days?' Leon had suggested.

'I'd *love* it,' Jonathan had agreed enthusiastically, secretly delighted that it was Leon who was proposing the trip. As they had got to know each other over the past couple of months he had allowed himself to fantasize about having a future with the easy-going, fun-loving carpenter with whom he got on so well. They had snogged but not taken it any further and Jonathan, who was a romantic at heart, felt that Leon wanted their first real intimacy to be something special. Clearly the trip to London was going to be the next step in their relationship and he couldn't wait.

They hugged at the airport when they met up half an hour later. 'Nice threads, Jon,' Leon admired, running his hand over the arm of the jade, single-breasted deconstructed jacket. 'You can't go wrong with Armani. You'll score in that for sure!' he grinned.

'Ya think?' Jonathan said flirtily.

'I *know*! I can't wait to hit the clubs!'

'We've so much to fit in.' Jonathan fell into step beside him as they made their way to the Ryanair check-in desks. 'I've booked us a table for dinner tonight, at Bibendum. You know, the Terence Conran restaurant? It's so near our hotel we can walk to it. The Michelin Building's just eye-poppingly fab, wait until you see it, and we can have a wander around Habitat too! We can have a pre-dinner drink in the Oyster Bar there. It's epic! It's real art deco. And you'll love the Franklin too. I booked a double. You're *sure* you're OK with that?' Jonathan wanted to reassure himself that he and Leon were thinking along the same lines.

'Yeah, cool. We'll hardly be there anyway. We've places to go and people to see, and only three days to pack it all in,' Leon grinned.

'There's nothing to stop us going over again later in the year,' Jonathan remarked, pushing his case ahead of him with his foot as they moved along in the queue.

'Now you're talking! We could go to Barcelona too, that's such a great city for gays.'

'For anyone, gay or straight!' Jonathan remarked lightly, trying not to be irritated that Leon frequently defined himself by his sexuality. 'We could do a long weekend to the Big Apple sometime, even, and visit MoMA and the Met.'

'*That* would be a dream come true. I'd love to go to New York.' Leon's hazel eyes lit up, and Jonathan thought how beautiful they were and how handsome his companion was with his jet-black hair and tanned, rugged face.

'We can definitely do that too then,' Jonathan declared, thinking that he couldn't wait to visit all these cities that he loved with Leon at his side.

'Hmm, don't forget I'm not as free as you are. Billy's maintenance takes a whopping chunk out of my salary. Not that I mind,' Leon added hastily. 'My son is worth every penny.'

'Don't worry, we'll make it happen in time,' Jonathan assured him as they reached the top of the queue and he lifted his case onto the belt and presented his passport and flight confirmation to the girl at the desk. They had agreed to check in one piece of luggage between them to accommodate the shopping they proposed doing on their trip, as both of them intended to beef up their wardrobes with a shopping expedition to the King's Road.

Two hours later as they circled Stansted on their landing approach, Jonathan stared out at the verdant countryside beneath him and felt happier than he could remember feeling in a long, long time. The years of loneliness seemed a distant memory. The vague sadness that had been his burden for so long had been vanquished. Now he was starting a new chapter in his life. One where he was companioned as he'd always longed to be. Nancy's prayers had been answered. His mother had said goodbye to him on Easter Sunday with the fervent instruction, 'Have a wonderful trip with your friend and be very, *very* happy.'

It would be no hardship to follow Nancy's instructions, he thought, as Leon caught his gaze and said cheerily as the landing gear clunked down with a thud, 'London, are you ready for us? The boys are back in town!'

'That steak was to die for! That will set me up until dinner tomorrow night!' Leon patted his lean stomach, took a drink of his Châteauneuf-du-Pape and leaned back in the red bucket chair, enjoying the hum of chatter and laughter in the busy restaurant. He had gone for one of the restaurant's signature dishes, the steak *au poivre*. Jonathan had chosen the scallops that had oozed flavour.

'Could you manage a dessert?' Jonathan perused the menu.

'Could we share? I need to keep some energy for later!' Leon winked.

Jonathan laughed. 'Aahh we need a sugar rush,' he encouraged. 'What do you want? You choose.'

'Oooh it's hard to pick.' Leon studied the selection. 'OK, how about the *honey blancmange with champagne-poached rhubarb and pistachio madeleines*?'

'Perfect! And let's push out the boat and have a postprandial brandy, seeing as we *are* in a posh restaurant. Don't forget this meal's on me,' Jonathan reminded him lightly, not wanting Leon to be worrying about money.

'You certainly don't do things by halves, Jon. That hotel is something else. I've never stayed in a five-star before. And this place has been a real fine-dining experience.' Leon looked around at the iconic building with admiration.

'It's our first visit to London. I wanted it to be special.' Jonathan was about to reach over and squeeze Leon's hand but the waiter came to take their order.

It was almost 11.30 when they stepped outside onto the Fulham Road, and Jonathan yawned in spite of himself. The night air was just what he needed after the brandy, which had made him feel lethargic. 'Hey there, stop yawning, we've a full night ahead of us,' Leon giggled, stepping into the road and hailing a taxi.

'Sure we can walk back to the hotel? It will clear our heads,' Jonathan said, surprised, as a black cab drew to a halt beside them.

'The *hotel!* No, bro, *we're* goin' clubbin'.' Leon slid open the door and jumped into the cab.

Jonathan's heart sank. Clubbing had not been on his agenda.

'Heaven, Villiers Street, Charing Cross, please,' Leon

instructed the taxi driver. 'Or do you want to go to Trade or The Fridge?' he asked Jonathan as he climbed in beside him.

'Heaven's fine,' Jonathan said, trying to appear enthusiastic. He hadn't come to London to go to world-renowned gay nightclubs. Not this time. He wanted to spend time with Leon, to get to know him better, to become a real couple, not just a pair of gay men on a trip to a European capital. Leon held his hand and chatted animatedly as the cab pulled out into the traffic and Jonathan realized that the brandy had gone to his companion's head. He shouldn't have suggested it. They'd already had pre-dinner cocktails and a bottle of wine during their meal.

'I'd love to have seen Madge and Cyndi Lauper performing here,' Leon remarked a while later as they queued to gain entrance to the club. 'Let's see, tonight it's Rich B, and Miss Kimberly. It's Wednesday night, The Fruit Machine, Yay!' he exclaimed enthusiastically, kissing him as they waited in the snaking line of the queue. Eventually security people waved them in. 'Time for another drink. You grab us a seat and I'll get them.' Leon edged his way through the crowd at the bar and came back with four shots, two of which he gave to Jonathan. 'There ya go, dude, *slainte*!' He raised one of his glasses and knocked it back before plonking down on the sofa beside him. 'This is a beaut of a club,' he said happily, gazing around him.

'Bro, you can say that again,' a young American sitting beside him agreed. Without a moment's hesitation Leon leaned over and snogged him. Jonathan nearly fell off the sofa in shock. What the hell was going on? Was Leon behaving like this because he was plastered? Didn't he realize how disrespectful his behaviour was to Jonathan? 'I'm gonna hit the floor,' Leon grinned, winking at Jonathan. 'First score to me!' His eyes were bright with anticipation and alcohol and moments later he was swallowed into the heaving mass of bodies that were bopping in the dark psychedelic light to the loud thumping music.

If he had been in the form for it, Jonathan would have lost no time in following Leon onto the dance floor. He loved dancing but right now he felt gutted. He had hoped to be back in their beautifully appointed room with the big four-poster bed. Instead he was watching his companion kissing other men with not a care in the world, or a worry how Jonathan might feel.

He's younger than you. He doesn't get the chance to travel much. He doesn't get to be free to be gay. He hasn't come out at home yet! Jonathan silently made excuses for the other man as he finished his second shot, ignoring a come-hither look from a skinny, brown-eyed, sallow-skinned man who raised his glass at him. Jonathan nodded politely and turned away. He needed to go to the loo before he started dancing.

Finally Jonathan made his way onto the dance floor looking for Leon's distinctive silk purple shirt. He saw him bopping exuberantly in a group on the far side of the floor, and felt a wave of relief. Maybe kissing that guy on the sofa was a one-off! Spur of the moment stuff with the excitement of being in London in Heaven. Jonathan smiled at his friend's *joie de vivre* as he jived and shimmied uninhibitedly. *Stop acting like an auld fella*, he chided himself as a surge of sweaty, testosterone-filled bodies made him lose sight of Leon. He circled around the edge of the undulating multitude. And then, his stomach gave a sickening lurch as a gap in the swaying mass gave him a glimpse of Leon in a deep, lusty, open-mouthed kiss with a very camp blond young man whom Jonathan judged to be in his early twenties.

He felt as though he'd been punched in the gut, hard. He couldn't believe his eyes. His heart lurched before starting to race and a dreadful sense of apprehension enveloped him. Don't say he'd made the same mistake with Leon as he had with the others. Don't say he'd made a fool of himself again.

'Hey, what's going on?' He almost had to shout over the din as he reached the embracing couple.

'Meet Günter,' Leon yelled, dropping an arm around the young man and grinning broadly. 'I've pulled already. I *love* this place. Get out on the floor, dude, and shake your booty.'

'I don't *want* to pull.' Jonathan stood in front of Leon, shocked to his core.

'But that's what we came to London for, nothing else.' Leon couldn't meet his eye.

'I thought we came to be together.' Jonathan stared at him, hardly able to comprehend what Leon had just said.

'Aw come on, man, don't ruin my buzz. I thought we were just friends. I'm sorry if you're into me, but I just don't fancy you that way. You must know that. You're not my type.'

'But ... but ... you said it was fine to book a double room.' Jonathan was bewildered.

'Yeah because we wouldn't be in it much. You don't come to London to stay in a hotel room. You come to party! Look, Günter and I are gonna split later. I'm going back to his place. I'm sorry if you've got the wrong impression, Jon. I really like you as a friend. I think you're great, but I like my men small, slender, and youthful. Older queens don't float my boat. I'll see you back at the hotel tomorrow and we'll talk.' He shrugged, still unable to meet Jonathan's eyes.

Jonathan felt as though he was going to faint as he stared at the man he'd secretly hoped would become his life partner. He was in total shock. Leon had held hands with him in the taxi and kissed him in the queue and now he was telling him that he wasn't his type, and that he was practically a geriatric!

'You're here. Get in the groove, dude, you might meet someone tonight. A good shag will do you all the good in the world,' Leon said petulantly, wishing Jonathan and his long face would disappear and leave him to his dancing and Günter.

'You know, you're a real bollix, Leon,' Jonathan swore. Leon shrugged before turning away to begin dancing with Günter who simpered triumphantly, wrapping his arms around Leon.

Jonathan turned away, unable to watch them smooching, and made his way through the swarm of dancers towards the exit. The blood was roaring in his ears. He felt sick, shocked and utterly drained as he left the club and walked past groups of revellers under the arches beneath Charing Cross Station. He walked in a daze, stunned at the way things had turned out and Leon's cruel, almost calculated rejection of him, berating himself for being a romantic fool and wondering how he could have been such an idiot. *You did it again. You fool. You eejit! You sad bastard. Will you never learn? You are unlovable!* He was beyond gutted! He felt completely dead inside. *A good shag will do you all the good in the world.* Clearly Leon had come to London with that very agenda, and not to spend time with Jonathan.

It started to rain lightly, bringing him back to reality, and he hailed a taxi and gave the name and address of the hotel. *You're not my type. I don't fancy you.* Older *queens don't float my boa*t. The words clanged like clashing cymbals over and over in his head and he tried desperately not to cry as the elderly black taxi rattled and bumped down the Strand towards the Mall. Even the glory of the illuminated Admiralty Arch and the sight of Buckingham Palace, resplendent ahead, could not move him as it usually did and he barely glanced out the window as the taxi rounded the Victoria Memorial heading for Knightsbridge and the urgently needed sanctuary of his hotel room.

Ring when u can, I need to talk! Jxxx

Hilary gazed bleary-eyed at the text that had pinged on her phone, waking her up.

I need to talk!

Need! Was that good or bad? It certainly wasn't like the giddy texts Jonathan had been sending her yesterday, Hilary thought, yawning as she glanced at her bedside clock. Quarter to eight! He was up early after his night of unbridled passion.

The house was uncharacteristically silent for that hour of the morning. No one frantically running around, no rushing to shove breakfast down necks, no looking for school books, or keys and phones, just blissful peace. And then she remembered, the girls were on school holidays, Niall was in Dubai and she was only going to drop into the office for an hour or so later on. Hilary gave a luxurious stretch. She'd make herself a cuppa and a slice of toast and bring it back to bed and settle down for a gossip with Jonathan. Twenty minutes later, propped against the pillows, sipping her tea, she picked up her phone and dialled Jonathan's number.

'Hi,' came a muffled voice.

'What's up?' she asked, instantly alert to something being wrong.

'Leon went off with someone else last night. He told me that he didn't fancy me. He told me that he liked his men young, and slender, and that older queens didn't float his boat,' Jonathan said dolefully.

'What!' Hilary was stunned. 'He said *what*?'

Jonathan repeated Leon's words.

'Oh my God! I don't know what to say, Jonathan.' She couldn't believe her ears.

'What *is* there to say?' he said dully. 'I've made a complete, an absolute fool of myself, and kidded myself yet again that there's someone out there for me.'

'There *is* someone out there for you,' Hilary exclaimed, grieved at her friend's desolation and shocked at his totally unexpected news.

'I give up, I just give up.' Jonathan was near to tears.

'Where is he now?'

'Shagging young Günter somewhere, I suppose,' Jonathan said bitterly. 'I've spent a fortune to be treated like the biggest idiot going. I *am* the biggest idiot going.'

'Well you can't stay in the same room as him,' Hilary said decisively.

'I have to wait until he comes back – all his stuff is here.'

'Feck that for a lark! Pack it up and leave it in reception and check out! Let him go and bunk in with this Günter yoke!' Hilary was raging for her friend.

'I suppose I could do that and just get a flight home,' he said flatly. 'But I just don't think I can face an airport though. I'm afraid I'll start bawling and make a spectacle of myself in public.'

'I'm coming over,' she declared, surprising herself.

'You're going to come to *London*!' Jonathan exclaimed.

'Yes I am. I don't want you jumping into the Thames. It would be far too inconvenient right now,' she teased, and smiled when he managed a laugh. 'That's better. Let me come over and be with you. *A little help is better than a lot of sympathy*.' She reiterated her mother's oft-quoted saying.

'I'd love it if you did,' Jonathan said with heartfelt gratitude. 'Are you sure? Where will you stay?'

'Where will *we* stay,' she corrected him. 'Go book yourself into that hotel we stayed in when we went to that lighting exhibition a few years back. The one in Kensington near where Colette lived. It's lovely.'

'The Royal Garden?'

'That's the one! You go sort yourself and check out, and I'll go and see what's the story with flights. Talk to you in a while.'

'Are you *sure*, Hilary? I don't want to put you out,' Jonathan said, but she knew by his tone that he wanted her to come.

'Of course I'm sure. Unless you really want to come home immediately?'

He groaned. 'I really don't think I could stand in that ghastly queue in Stansted or even change my flight and fly out of Heathrow today,' he confessed. 'But honestly I don't expect you to fly over here.'

'You'd do the same for me. Wouldn't you?' she demanded.

'Of course I would. The next time a gay man breaks your heart I'll be there straight away.' He showed a glimmer of humour and she felt relief. She knew Jonathan occasionally suffered from bouts of depression and she was worried that in his current state of despair he might do something rash.

'Right, I'd better get up and at it, OK? I'll check out the flights. Stay calm, and get the hell out of that hotel. Love ya, Harpur!'

'I love you too, Hilary,' Jonathan said gratefully and she knew he was crying as she hung up.

She lay back against the pillows, thoroughly upset for her friend. She had met Leon several times and had liked him. Like Jonathan, she too had thought that he had finally met someone who, in time, might become his partner. She knew Leon hadn't come out to his family yet. That was a drawback to their relationship, but she'd hoped with Jonathan at his side he would have the courage to become the person he really was, and be true to himself.

And Jonathan had been so measured this time. He hadn't rushed in, like she'd seen him do before. He'd taken Hannah's advice and played it cool, for all the difference it had made. She hadn't planned on a trip to London, but she knew once she explained the reason to the girls and Niall they'd understand. A thought struck her and she flung back the duvet and jumped out of bed. She climbed the stairs to the attic conversion and knocked on each of their doors.

'Girls! Girls! Get up! How do you fancy a trip to London?'

'Whaaa!' Millie raised a sleepy tousled head from the pillow.

'Wow, Mam, what's going on?' Sophie bounded out of her room, liking the sound of what she'd just heard. Hilary went in and sat on the side of Millie's bed. Sophie sat on the other side expectantly, thrilled at the idea of going to London.

'Jonathan's had an upsetting experience. You know he was going to London with Leon for a few days and was hoping that this time he might have finally met the love of his life?' She gazed at her daughters who were suddenly all ears.

'Yeah,' Sophie said while Millie nodded.

'And?'

'Well it didn't work out as planned. Leon told Jonathan that he didn't fancy him and ditched him and went off with someone else,' Hilary explained ruefully.

Sophie's hand flew to her mouth in dismay and Millie sat bolt upright.

'Oh *no!*'

'That's *awful!*'

'Oh poor Jonathan! Of course we *have* to go to London to rescue him.'

'Let's get going!'

Hilary's heart lifted at her daughters' kind and heartfelt

responses. They were great girls, she thought proudly. They loved Jonathan dearly. He had been a big part of their lives and they were always eager to spend time with him. He was their confidant, their older brother, their fashion adviser, their cheerleader, and their relationship was one of mutual love, respect and great friendship.

'OK then, let's get the show on the road.' Hilary stood up. 'I'm going to see what flights are available, but we won't tell him you're coming. We'll give him a surprise!' She gave them the thumbs-up. 'Our boy needs us. Let's go.'

Sophie scrambled off the bed, aglow with excitement. 'The Hammond girls are off to London on a rescue mission. Tally HOOOOO!'

CHAPTER TWENTY-SIX

'What's going on? Everything's all packed up!' Leon gazed around the bedroom noting the two travel bags, and the case, side by side on the floor. There were none of his clothes draped on the chair where he had left them the previous evening, and nothing of Jonathan's on view. Jonathan had been sitting at the small coffee table flicking through a complimentary *Times*, staring out at the elegant, red-bricked, six-storeyed houses that lined the street, and the views of the Brompton Road, and the Oratory further down.

'I'm checking out,' Jonathan said quietly, noting Leon's bleary-eyed, dishevelled, unshaven appearance. 'There's an envelope in your bag with the money you paid for my fare. You can put it towards a room in Jurys.'

'Aw come on, Jon, there's no need for that! Look, I'm sorry if your feelings were hurt last night, but I never gave you any reason to think I was attracted to you,' Leon said defensively.

'We snogged, often,' Jonathan reminded him.

'We're gay! You're a good kisser. Look, if I fancied you I'd have jumped your bones long before now. I came to London to party and shag and I thought you did too.'

'Oh! Right. Excuse me for not thinking of you as the stereotypical gay cliché.'

'Listen, it's OK for you. I don't get the chance to express myself very often. I've a son to consider,' Leon said sullenly.

'Perhaps you should just grow up, Leon, and stop running away from it. You are what you are and there's nothing wrong with what you are. And you knew I was attracted to you. You're not thick! But despite the fact that you didn't feel the same, it didn't stop you from allowing me to spend a small fortune on you last night. You knew what you had planned. You knew all the while that you were going clubbing to pick someone up. Nice one!'

Leon flushed. 'Sorry! I suppose I deserved that,' he muttered. 'Now that we've sorted it, there's no need for you to go home. Can't we just stay and do our own thing and enjoy ourselves?' he urged. 'We could have a lot of fun.'

'Oh I *am* going to stay in London and have fun,' Jonathan said coolly. 'Just not with you. I'm going to meet up with a "real" friend.'

'Be like that then,' Leon said sulkily. 'I just want to shower and shave and change my clothes before I split.'

'Sorry, you should have done that in your little friend's gaff. I'm leaving now.'

'You go then! I'll freshen up and then leave.'

'I don't think so,' Jonathan said firmly. 'Time to go. Checkout is twelve and it's ten to. I want to settle my bill. They were very decent not charging me for the next two days.' He lifted Leon's bag and opened the door and deposited it in the hall. 'Your room card, please?' He held out his hand. Leon passed it to him with bad grace.

Jonathan ignored him and picked up his luggage. 'After you,' he said politely. Leon walked out the door and reached for his bag. Jonathan's heart twisted as he watched him lope down the corridor. He didn't feel they would ever meet again and it was painful in the extreme to acknowledge that. He stayed for a moment until the other man had rounded the corner to the lift before closing the door on his dream.

'That's rough. Poor Jonathan,' Niall said sympathetically. He sounded as though he was in the next room and not halfway across the world in Dubai. 'He never seems to get a break in his relationships.' Despite his accusation that Hilary spent too much time with the other man, Niall was fond of Jonathan.

She and Niall had been cool with each other for a few days after their tiff about Sue, but they were never able to hold on to a fight and he had agreed that Sue had to play her part. Music to his wife's ears. Besides, she would never have let him fly abroad without sorting out an argument and they had made love the night before he flew to the UAE.

'So you don't mind us going?' Hilary asked, tucking the phone under her ear and filling the kettle for a cuppa. 'I'll be spending even more time with Jonathan,' she reminded him sheepishly.

'Aahh he needs you. And it will be nice for you to have a jaunt with the girls. Perfect timing while they're on their holidays,' her husband said easily. 'Text me your room number when you get to the hotel and I'll ring you on the landline later, OK?'

'OK,' Hilary agreed. 'I'll just give Sue a call to let her know neither you nor I are around for the next few days.'

'Fine. Try and have some fun in London too. Talk to ya, love ya, babe!' Niall said before hanging up.

Hilary smiled. Niall was, for the most part, laid-back and easy-going, which was why he got antsy when he had to deal with family issues. She could stay the week in London with the girls, and spend a fortune, and he wouldn't say boo! She was lucky with her husband in that regard. Pity Sue didn't have his disposition. She didn't want to phone her sister-in-law, who had been extremely cool with her since their confrontation in Buswells. Margaret was recovering from another chest infection and was not up to doing her own shopping; she needed someone to keep an eye on her.

Hilary dialled Sue's number, but not surprisingly got no response. She left a message, and sent a text just to be sure. She wouldn't put it past Sue to say she'd got no voice message.

Hilary had booked an Aer Lingus flight leaving at 2 p.m. The girls were packed and all ready to go; she'd just pop over to the shops and get a few groceries for Margaret to keep her going, she decided. She could get the taxi to make a detour and drop them off on the way to the airport.

'It's a pity we're going to London because of something sad.' Sophie lifted the two bags of shopping from the checkout counter and followed Hilary to the exit.

'We'll try and make the most of it, and we'll do our best to cheer Jonathan up,' Hilary promised.

'It's *ages* since we had a girls' adventure!' Sophie observed.

Hilary felt a dart of guilt. Sophie was right. She needed to start spending more time with her daughters before they flew the nest. Millie would be going to college in the autumn. She could hardly believe how the years had flown by. 'Let's try and have a few jaunts this summer when Millie has finished her exams. How about a spa day sooner rather than later?'

'Nice,' Sophie approved and Hilary smiled. She would *definitely* organize that in the near future. There was a tangible air of excitement as they all piled into the taxi a while later. The unexpectedness of the trip added to the gaiety. This was what life was all about, Hilary thought as she listened to the girls discuss what they intended to buy in the duty free. Although it was far from trips to London and duty-free sprees she'd been brought up to, she thought in amusement. They took it all so much for granted.

'Hello, Gran,' she said cheerfully, when Margaret opened the door to her knock ten minutes later.

'Good gracious, I wasn't expecting visitors,' her mother-in-law said, flustered.

'We're not visitors, Gran,' Millie declared, bending down to give her grandmother a kiss.

'It's a flying visit, Gran, cos we're actually going to be flying in about an hour and a half,' Sophie grinned. 'We're going to London on a surprise visit. The taxi's waiting for us at the gate.'

'Oh that's exciting, Sophie,' Margaret said brightly, kissing them all.

'I just wanted to drop in a few bits and pieces to tide you over until we get back on Saturday, Mrs H. I'll pop them in the fridge.' Hilary took the bags from Sophie and walked into the kitchen and began to unpack the shopping.

'That's very kind of you, dear. Very kind. Now how much do I owe you?' Margaret followed Hilary into the kitchen.

'I'll put the receipt on the counter and you can give it to me on Saturday,' Hilary said, packing away the cartons of Ambrosia creamed rice that her mother-in-law was particularly partial to. Margaret was scrupulous about paying her bills and Hilary always took the money, not because she was mean about money but to respect her mother-in-law's dignity and independence.

'I'm very grateful for all you do for me, Hilary. You're so thoughtful. I know you're so busy and I take up so much of your time,' Margaret said and Hilary turned to look at her and saw that her lip was trembling.

'Mrs H! What's wrong?' she exclaimed in dismay, putting her arms around the elderly lady as Sophie and Millie looked at their grandmother in alarm.

'Nothing, dear. I'm just a terrible old nuisance and it bothers me that you have to do so much for me when you're so busy yourself,' Margaret said tremulously. 'And I know Niall and Sue are very busy too—'

'Now, Mrs H, you listen to me, we are *never* too busy for you,' Hilary said firmly.

'But you can't all be taking time off to bring me to appointments and the like. I'm going to start going by myself from now on. Other people have to, so can I,' Margaret said shakily. Hilary's lips tightened. *Sue*! She must have said something to her mother about bringing her to the warfarin clinic.

She could have kicked herself. She should have known that Sue would pull a stunt like this. The selfish madam.

When she got back from London she was going to give that one a piece of her mind, she vowed furiously, trying to hide her anger from Margaret.

'Don't be worrying about your appointments; we'll sort something out,' she said kindly. 'Now why don't I make you a quick cuppa to have with one of the scones I got for you, and I bought you the latest *Hello*! You can keep it for me and I'll get it off you when I get back.' She gave her mother-in-law another hug. She knew the meter was running in the taxi but to hell with it. She wanted to make sure Margaret felt cherished and reassured before she left. 'Millie, butter a scone for your gran while I make the tea,' she instructed.

'Gran, you are never to call yourself a nuisance again,' Sophie said sternly. 'You're our gran and we love you *very* much.'

'We certainly do, Gran,' Millie assured her, adding an extra-large spoon of strawberry jam to the scone, just the way Margaret liked it. 'And I'm going to get you something nice from London.'

'Now don't go spending your money on me,' warned her grandmother, recovering her composure and enjoying the cuddle Sophie gave her. 'Thank you, dear, that was just what I needed.'

'We'll be home Saturday and we'd love you to come to lunch on Sunday to tell you all about our trip. I'll come and collect you,' Hilary invited, carrying the tray into Margaret's sitting room and placing it on the side table beside her armchair. She waited until Margaret was settled with her magazine and bent down and kissed her. 'You are very, very dear to us. Don't forget that now. I'll ring you tonight,' she said.

'I'll look forward to it, Hilary.' Margaret patted her cheek and Hilary thought how sad it was that she didn't have a warm relationship with her only daughter.

'It's horrible being old, isn't it?' Millie reflected as they drove away from her grandmother's house.

'Some people have better experiences of old age than others,' Hilary said grimly, wishing she could have ten minutes alone with Sue. 'Anyway forget about being old for the time being. We're on a girls' jolly, so let's have fun. We'll have to lift Jonathan's spirits for sure, so we need to be in tiptop form.' She smiled at her daughters and put thoughts of Sue aside. She would deal with her when she got home.

Jonathan gazed out the window of his fifth-floor hotel room at the green, almost rural vista spread out before him. It was hard to believe he was in the middle of a bustling metropolis. The gilt-edged gates of Kensington Palace bathed in the midday sun brought back memories of massed banks of flowers laid in tribute to the beautiful, tragic princess who had lived there. The blue of the Round Pond between blossom-sprigged branches giving a vivid splash of colour to the green palette of the park. The elegance of the dome of the Albert Hall and the skyline of south London in the distance a reminder that he was in one of the world's greatest cities.

Below him, Londoners and tourists strolled, skated, jogged and strode along the pathways, or sat and relaxed under the warming sun on the grassy emerald swards of the spring-dressed park. They all seemed so carefree, untroubled even.

Not like him: sad, dispirited, and entirely disenchanted with life.

He could pull the heavy drapes on the sunlight, whose bright gaiety seemed like an affront to his desolation, and go for a snooze on the inviting bed, he supposed. He hadn't slept the previous night and Hilary wouldn't arrive until late afternoon. He had a sinus headache to boot and his eyes and cheeks ached. He needed to take something for it or it would only get worse. He remembered going to a Boots beside M&S the last time he had stayed in the Royal Garden; he might as well go and stock up on his meds, he decided, and then go for a nap.

The noise of the High Street jarred as he emerged through the revolving doors in the foyer, and was asked by a courteous doorman if he required a taxi. He decline politely and walked down the marble steps and turned right, wincing at the roar of the heavy traffic and the fast-paced gaits of the other pedestrians. His head throbbed. He wanted to get back to the peace of his room fast.

I just don't fancy you that way. It was the casual utterance of those heart-piercing words, in so public an arena, that seemed so cruel. Leon had given no thought to the effect his admission might have on Jonathan, and that hurt almost as much as the words themselves. He must have known Jonathan had feelings for him despite his protestations that he thought they were just friends. It was painfully obvious now that Leon had used Jonathan, enjoying the meals out, the visits to the cinema and theatre that Jonathan had, more often than not, paid for when Leon would admit that he was broke because of his maintenance and mortgage expenses.

Jonathan crossed Kensington Church Street, and in spite of his misery, the sight of the flamboyant array of multihued blooms at the flower stall beside the impressive architectural elegance of St Mary Abbots momentarily banished his misery. He loved tulips and he decided to buy Hilary a bunch as a little token of his deep gratitude that she would fly to London to support him in his hour of need.

The arcade housing Boots was thronged with commuters heading in and out of the tube station and as he passed Marks' Food Hall and Pret A Manger, he realized that he was actually a touch peckish. That was perhaps why his headache was worse than normal. He hadn't eaten, apart from a cup of coffee in the Franklin. He bought Sinutabs and a packet of Nytol and some Rescue Remedy and crossed over to Pret. He grabbed a BLT and a Coke and paid for it and had his snack and a Sinutab sitting at one of the window seats staring unseeingly out at the busy concourse.

Nancy would be disappointed for him when he told her that Leon was not 'the one'. He wondered what Hannah would say. One of the sayings of Florence Scovel Shinn, a teacher of metaphysics, came to mind. *No man is my friend. No man is my enemy. Every man is my teacher. The Game of Life and How to Play It*, the book she had written, had given him much food for thought over the years since Hannah had gifted it to him.

What was Leon's rejection of him teaching him? he wondered miserably. He had to raise this incident to a higher level; otherwise he would wallow and drown in self-pity and sorrow. But he was only human – he wanted to wallow. All these spiritual teachers like Hannah were much more evolved and adept at dealing with life's disasters than he was. He was still mired in the lower energy of life. He scowled as he made his way back through the arcade to Kensington High Street. Of course Hannah wouldn't call this latest episode a disaster, he thought crossly. She'd call it 'a growth opportunity'. Well he was fed up with having 'growth opportunities' through woe. He wanted his opportunities to come through joy. He was sick of all this rubbish that Hannah spouted every time he visited her. It was getting him nowhere, he raged, consumed with anger at his counsellor and her unpalatable take on things. He trudged along, heavy-hearted, until he got to the florist's stall. He chose two bunches of glorious purple and yellow tulips and paid for them. Leon had bought him tulips the previous week when Jonathan had invited him to his apartment for a home-cooked dinner. How vibrant they had looked in the John Rocca vase on the table and how happy they had made him. Tears blurred his eyes and desperate not to be seen crying in the middle of a London high street he slipped through a side entrance to the high-spired church and wandered into the very small peaceful garden so many passed by without seeing. Clumps of snowdrops, tulips, daffodils and bluebells grew wild in the grass, under the shade of freshly budding trees. Outside the iron railings life surged on, but he felt protected and distanced from it all as the tears streamed silently down his cheeks and he leaned against a buttress that was hidden from view and cried his eyes out as though his heart would break. Waves of grief engulfed him. *Why?* he shouted silently. *Why?*

No answer came but a bird sang on a blossoming green branch that reached towards the high spire that pierced the blue Kensington sky. A measure of peace descended on Jonathan's troubled spirit as he sat on a ledge and composed himself, oblivious to the noise and flurry that carried on relentlessly, just metres away.

'I'm so excited. I can't believe I'm in London,' Sophie bubbled as they hurried along the narrow, grey, tubed structure that led from arrivals to the exit at Heathrow.

'It's lovely out too,' Millie exclaimed as they emerged into the rounded glassed area and the sun gave hint to the welcome balminess that often occurred during springtime in London. Ten minutes later they were sitting on the Heathrow Express, delighted with themselves that they had made the departing train by the skin of their teeth, and would soon be winging their way to Paddington.

'I'll ring Jonathan when we're in our taxi to the hotel,' Hilary decided, rooting in her bag to turn on her phone.

'Don't forget to say *I'm* here, not *we're* here!' Millie reminded her.

'Good thinking, wonder girl.' Hilary grinned at her daughter.

'Can we go to the London Eye?' Sophie asked eagerly.

'I don't see why not,' Hilary agreed as the whistle blew and the train chugged out of the station.

'It's nice being on a girls' trip, all of us together.' Sophie snuggled in affectionately against her mother.

'It's a real treat being with my two gorgeous daughters. I was just thinking that when you've finished the Leaving

Cert, Millie, we'll definitely go to Powerscourt Springs for an overnighter and some beauty treatments, the three of us.'

'Cool.' Millie's eyes lit up.

'I'm going to spend *all* my time in the pool and jacuzzi,' Sophie declared, 'and eating that scrumptious walnut bread you brought home the last time you were there.' They laughed, and Hilary thought how blessed and lucky she was and hoped that she would always be as close to her daughters. Sue was missing out so much in her relationship with Margaret. It was a shame for both of them. Families were so different, she reflected. Hers wasn't perfect but she was very thankful for a reasonably good relationship with her daughters and her own mother and sister.

'Gosh I'd hate to live in a high-rise,' Millie remarked after they had emerged from the tunnel and had sped through Southall and West Ealing.

'It's nice to have a garden,' Sophie observed.

'Yes, and one that's so private. We're very privileged and lucky,' Hilary reminded them.

'You know I don't think you should ring Jonathan from Paddington,' Millie said thoughtfully. 'I think we should check in and you tell him to come up to the room and we can hide in the loo and surprise him.'

'Yes,' agreed her sister. 'And I think we should buy a bottle of something to clink glasses, seeing as it's our first time in London with him!'

'Champagne!' exclaimed Millie in anticipation.

'Well perhaps not champagne,' Hilary demurred. 'Remember he's very upset. Maybe a bottle of Prosecco.'

'But can't I have some too? I don't want to be drinking 7 Up like a child!' Sophie insisted.

'Yes, seeing as it is a special occasion. But just the one glass,' Hilary agreed.

'Yaayyy!' Sophie punched the air as the train drew to a halt at Platform 7.

'You're in your *room*! Brilliant, I'll be there in five minutes. I just need to wash my face and wake myself up. I fell asleep on the bed,' Jonathan said, yawning. 'What number?'

'346,' Hilary said, grinning at her daughters who were exploring the contents of their mini bar.

'Can't wait to see you. I can't believe this time yesterday I was deliriously happy. I feel like I'm in some sort of weird dream.' He sighed deeply.

'Let's have a cuppa and a chat while I'm settling in, and decide what we're going to do for the rest of the day. I'll boil the kettle.'

'Won't be long,' he assured her, flinging the throw off and padding into the bathroom to freshen up. At least he wasn't on his own now. He could pour his heart out to Hilary, say what he liked about Leon and his own stupidity and know that she would provide a listening ear and a shoulder to cry on.

CHAPTER TWENTY-SEVEN

'Why didn't you get a double?' Jonathan asked when he followed Hilary into the room after giving her the tulips and hugging the daylights out of her.

'I did,' she told him, leading him to the seating area.

'Did they make a mistake?'

'Nope,' Hilary grinned as the girls burst out of the bathroom yelling 'Surprise! Surprise!'.

'What are you two doing here?' He was flabbergasted.

'We are the Jonathan Harpur Rescue Society,' giggled Sophie, barrelling across the room to throw her arms around him. 'That Leon fella is a prize dodo!'

'Yeah, a real loser.' Millie added her tuppence worth, planting a kiss on his cheek and squeezing his hand.

'Oh girls!' gulped Jonathan. 'I don't know what to say!' He burst into tears, much to Sophie's horror.

'Don't cry, Jonathan. *We* love you,' she said fiercely, holding him tight.

'Sorry! Sorry! I feel a right eejit!' He tried to compose himself.

'You're not an eejit,' Millie assured him earnestly. 'It's *horrible* when a boy breaks your heart!'

'You can say that again,' Jonathan agreed with heartfelt emotion and they looked at each other and cracked up. Their laughter echoed around the room as they chortled and guffawed, Jonathan more loudly than any of them, his natural humour reasserting itself, and the release of pent-up tension a welcome relief.

'Aw girls, you're a tonic,' he said, wiping his eyes, grinning at Hilary.

'Time for a drop of sparkly to start the evening,' she said, waving the bottle of Prosecco. 'We thought champagne might be somewhat inappropriate but this will do the job.' She rooted in the mini bar for glasses and asked Sophie to get the two out of the bathroom. She took some packets of nuts and snacks out of the bar and opened them, cracked open the Prosecco, poured the sparkling golden liquid into the glasses and handed one to Jonathan. 'To a lucky escape, I'd say!' She raised her glass.

'For you're a jolly good fellow!' Sophie clinked hers with Jonathan, and took a long glug.

'Go easy, you, miss! One glass, remember!' Hilary cautioned.

'OK! Can I have glass of wine at dinner?' she asked brightly.

'Two chances: slim and none,' her mother assured her.

'I'm starving,' Millie announced. 'What *are* we doing for dinner? Can we have something to eat soon?'

'How's your appetite?' Hilary eyed Jonathan over the rim of her glass.

'I could manage a bite or two. I only had a BLT at lunchtime.' He took a drink of his Prosecco and felt himself begin to relax for the first time since Leon had dropped his bombshell.

'OK, where do you want to go? Any preferences? Fancy or casual?' Hilary asked.

'If we want to eat straight away, timing's not great. It's between lunch and dinner.' Jonathan glanced at his watch and drained his glass. 'So I'd suggest casual.'

'Anywhere as long as there's food,' Millie urged, gobbling some nuts.

'I remember Colette telling me that she took Jazzy to Sticky Fingers, you know, Bill Wyman's restaurant, and it's just up the road. We could give that a bash,' Hilary suggested. 'Or there's that lovely Italian place just off the High Street that you and I went to when we stayed here.'

'You pick, girls,' Jonathan said graciously.

'Sticky Fingers!' they exclaimed simultaneously and Hilary threw her eyes up to heaven. 'Tomorrow then it's posh! I want a proper dressy-up night out!'

'OK', they agreed, beginning to retouch their make-up, eager to get going.

'Come next door to my room, Jonathan. I just want to change my top and I'll ask housekeeping for a vase for the tulips,' Hilary suggested lightly. There were some conversations she wouldn't have with him in front of the girls. 'He didn't take money from you or anything like that, did he?' she asked bluntly the minute they were out on the corridor.

'No, nothing like that. We had a great trip over, and a fantastic meal in Bibendum – I spared no expense,' he added drolly. 'In my head we were going back to the hotel. In his head we were going clubbing, and worse, going clubbing to score other people. He's obviously come over to London before. He knew all the clubs, where they were. Knew who was DJ-ing. He's no novice! I'd say he comes once or twice a year, parties, scores, shags a few people and then comes home to be "normal". He doesn't want to come out, he's perfectly happy the way he is. Just my luck to be taken in and fall for him. I was the perfect patsy for him.'

'Well he's the loser, big time. You're better off without him if that's the case,' Hilary declared, opening the door of her room. She laid the tulips on the table and rang house-keeping for the vase, while Jonathan meandered over to the window to have a look out.

'We're on the same side, I'm on the floor above you,' he said, watching a personal trainer do press-ups with a client on the grass below.

'I asked to be close to you when I was booking.' She pulled her T-shirt over her head.

'I honestly can't believe it, Hilary. I was so sure it was different this time.' Jonathan came and sat on her bed forlornly, while Hilary took a pale aqua top out of her case that was cooler than the one she had travelled in.

'I don't know what to say, Jonathan. Platitudes won't help. It just stinks!'

'Look, the fact that you and the girls came over helps more than you'll ever know. I feel such a part of your family, Hil. And I know Millie is supposed to be revising for her Leaving Cert so I really appreciate her travelling.'

'Well believe me it was no hardship for her to stop revising for a few days. She jumped at the opportunity to come with us,' Hilary assured him. 'And don't forget we think of you as family, always,' she said, pulling on the aqua top and running her fingers through her hair. 'And talking of our family, guess what Sue did?'

'Nothing good, I'd say, knowing The Secretary,' he said caustically. 'Don't tell me she invited Margaret to stay and she's looking after her while you're away?'

'Are you for real?' Hilary scoffed and proceeded to tell him of her sister-in-law's latest stunt, knowing it would take his mind off himself for a while.

A young housemaid knocked to deliver the vase and Hilary watched Jonathan artistically arranging the flowers and hoped against hope that he wouldn't let Leon's rejection of him lead him into a downward spiral. Life was so strange and cruel sometimes. He'd had his hard times; surely it was time for her beloved pal to get some sort of a break.

'Hello?' Colette saw a London number come up on her caller ID but didn't recognize it.

'Guess where I am?' Hilary's voice came clear as a bell down the line.

'Well London, obviously. I recognize the prefix number. What are you doing there?'

'Umm, I'm over with the girls for a little jaunt, and I'm in one of our favourite haunts.'

'Why didn't you tell me you were going?' Colette demanded. 'I could have taken a few days and flown over.'

'It was kind of spur of the moment, and that's what you get for not keeping in touch more often,' Hilary said acerbically.

'Oh OK.' Colette backed down. 'Where are you?' she

asked wistfully. How she would love to be in London in spring with Hilary.

'The Royal Garden. I'm looking out over the Palace and the park, it's a fabulous day here.'

'Stop! I can't bear it,' Colette sighed. 'Are the trees gorgeous? And are the bluebells out? Is the sun shining on the Pond?'

'Yeah, I shouldn't have phoned and made you homesick. I was just remembering some of the giddy times we had here when you came over first,' Hilary said apologetically.

Colette giggled. 'Remember the time we went to visit the National Gallery, and the security guard held out his hand to check your bag and you thought he wanted to shake hands?'

'And then when he opened it, I'd shoved my socks into it because my feet were killing me after all the walking and because it was so warm, and they were pongy to say the least!' Hilary chortled.

'And remember the time we went into the sex shop in Soho, my first time *ever* in such an establishment, and we fell around the place laughing at some of the stuff and the male customers were *not* impressed, and then you treated me to lunch in that posh restaurant in Mayfair – I can't remember the name – and we saw Kenneth Branagh and Emma Thompson? The first time I ever saw someone famous.'

'I still have the dent in my ribs where you nudged me,' Colette laughed. 'I'd forgotten what good times we had. It all seems so long ago now, doesn't it?'

'I know, and look at us with our daughters practically

grown up. I'm beginning to feel a bit ancient and decrepit.' Hilary stretched luxuriously on the bed. 'Anyway I'd better go, we're heading to Sticky Fingers. I just wanted to give you a call and tell you I was thinking of you.'

'Sticky Fingers! Jazzy's favourite place to eat in London. Tell the girls to enjoy it. Listen, thanks for ringing, sweetie. How about I call you next week when you're home and we'll have a natter and a catch-up,' Colette suggested.

'Perfect! Take care.'

'You too,' Colette said, feeling surprisingly lonely when the phone went dead. It would have been such fun to be in London with the girls. Hilary was right, she *should* keep in touch more. If it wasn't for her friend ringing every so often their friendship would be practically non-existent, she conceded. It wasn't that she meant to not keep in touch, it was just that out of sight was out of mind, and her life was so busy time just seemed to pass. And then when she did speak to Hilary, she'd get lonely and want to be at home or in London and she'd feel down after the call, like she did now.

She'd pull her socks up regarding their friendship, she promised herself, as the phone rang again and the chair of one of her charity boards came on the line to tell Colette that the CEO had been caught fiddling the funds and it was going to be on the news that very day, and the backlash was going to be awesome, and she was thinking of resigning. ' . . . and if I were you I'd do the same. No one wants to be tainted with that sort of failure.'

Thoughts of Hilary and London flew out of Colette's head while she wrestled with this new dilemma and wondered should she, instead of resigning, go after the plum position of chair – if Dana Sinclair was sincere about jumping ship – and bring the charity back from the brink?

Hilary smiled, glad she had acted on her spur of the moment impulse to ring Colette. She touched up her make-up and spritzed some 212 on her wrists. It seemed like another life-time ago when she and Colette had gadded around London with not a care in the world. She had omitted to tell Colette the real reason she was in London. Jonathan's break-up was his business. There was little love lost between them: there was no need for her to know. She wouldn't mention to Jonathan either that she had made the call. He'd only say something bitchy about the other woman, as he usually did, so there was no point.

It had been nice to hear her friend's voice after so long. There was never any awkwardness when they spoke, no matter how long they hadn't heard from each other, but Colette was the world's worst for keeping in touch and sometimes Hilary wondered if she didn't make the effort would their friendship evaporate into the ether as friend-ships often did.

'Mum, are you ready?' Millie knocked on the door and Hilary went to let her daughters in, determined to enjoy this unexpected break with them, evaporating friendships or no.

'This place is deadly.' Sophie gazed around at the rock and roll memorabilia that hung on the walls of the glitzy American-themed café.

'I have to say, Mick Jagger never did it for me,' Jonathan

admitted as the music of The Rolling Stones blasted through the restaurant.

'Me neither, those loose lips and the skinny, knitting-needle legs ... no thanks! Same with Paul McCartney. Give me a hard muscular thigh any time,' Hilary announced, sipping her pre-dinner Brandy Alexander.

'Leon might have liked *him* years ago. He likes his men young, and slender, he informed me!' Jonathan necked a bottle of beer.

'You're young and slenderish!' Sophie said loyally.

'Not young enough, too lanky, not small and perfectly formed, unfortunately. But thank you, dear heart, for your kindness,' he said affectionately.

'And did he drop you like a hot potato, just like that, as soon as you got here?' Millie asked, stirring the ice in her Coke.

'Well he had a good feed in – as your mother would call it – a posh restaurant, with expensive cocktails beforehand, the best of wine during the meal, and a brandy to finish off, and *then* he ditched me, right in the middle of a nightclub.' Jonathan couldn't hide his bitterness.

'I think he's a bit sad, if you ask me,' Sophie declared.

'Why so?' He looked at her, surprised.

'Well he's in his thirties, and he does the kind of thing teenagers do. You know, dropping people after using them, often in nightclubs. He doesn't sound very mature to me.'

'Oh! I suppose you have a point.'

'And he hasn't even come out properly. He's a coward as well, running away to London for a gay weekend and going home and pretending he's straight,' Millie said derisively.

'You know who you are and you aren't ashamed of it. Sophie's right, he's sad.'

'So am I sad, even though everything you said is right.' Jonathan sighed a gusty sigh.

'Is this the worst thing that's ever happened to you?' Sophie asked sympathetically, reaching across the table to give his hand a squeeze.

'No, I don't suppose it is,' he said slowly.

'That's good, and at least you have us to mind you.'

'Indeed I do, how lucky am I?' He smiled at her and squeezed her hand back just as the waitress arrived with platters of ribs, buffalo wings, pulled pork, corn-bread muffins, jalapeño peppers stuffed with cream cheese, and fries.

'Yum! Yum!' Sophie approved, diving on the wings.

'I needed this badly. I just wish it wasn't such a sad occasion for you, Jonathan.' Millie selected a sticky rib.

'I'll get over it,' he assured her and right there and right then he felt he would and that was enough for now.

Margaret sat at her table as the sun spilled its rays into her small kitchen and stared at the array of tablets in their blue containers. How many days had she sat here every morning going through the same routine before breakfast? Her phone rang and she saw Hilary's number displayed. 'Hello, dear? How is London going? Are you and the girls having a good time?'

'We're having a wonderful time, Gran.' Her daughter-in-law's clear tones came down the line as though she was next door and not in another country. 'We're meeting Jonathan for breakfast in the dining room and then we're heading off to take a trip on the Eye. I'm taking lots of photos. You'll love the ones of Kensington Palace from my room. I've a terrific view of it and the park. How are you feeling today?'

'Great, pet, great,' Margaret lied. 'Delighted to hear from you.'

'Are you taking your tablets?'

'I am.'

'Well we'll see you tomorrow evening and don't forget to keep Sunday free to have dinner with us,' Hilary reminded her.

'I look forward to it, dear. Enjoy the rest of your day and love to everyone.' Hilary was such a good person, ringing to see if she was OK. Sue wouldn't bother her skinny backside. Her daughter was so resentful at having to bring her to the medical appointments. *And* she'd tried to blacken Hilary by saying that Hilary had being moaning about being too busy to be taking time off. There had been no need for Sue to tell Margaret that, even if it was true. Now she felt a real and proper nuisance and she knew the way her body was failing it was only going to get worse. Sue would have her in a nursing home if it were left to her.

Margaret gave a deep sigh and poured herself another cup of tea from the china pot she favoured. It was heavy and her hand trembled with the effort. Imagine, she thought in disgust, not even being able to hold a teapot without shaking. What was to become of her?

She could get some home help, she supposed. And in that she could be lucky or unlucky, listening to her friends and the experiences they had. One friend had a home help who even baked bread for her and was extremely kind; another had been robbed blind and lost several hundred euros and some sentimental jewellery.

Margaret buttered her toast and spread it with marmalade and bit into it. Was it that her taste buds had faded, too? Food never seemed as flavorsome any more, and truth be told, she had gone off quite a few foods that she'd liked, and her appetite was getting smaller and smaller.

Old age, all down to old age, she fretted, hardly able to see the writing on the Old Time Irish marmalade jar without her glasses. Her sister-in-law had ended up in a nursing home, nearly blind and shaking with Parkinson's. Margaret had visited her a few times, her heart sinking at the sight of the once glamorous and proud woman slumped in a wheelchair, hands shaking as she stared unseeingly out at the rose garden beyond.

That might very well be her in a couple of years. Margaret felt the familiar flutter of apprehension envelop her when she contemplated the future.

The warfarin, red, yellow and brown today, lay waiting to be swallowed along with Liposol, and a water tablet. She shook the tablets into her hand and gazed at them. She was being kept alive by tablets, of that there was no doubt. But the more tablets she was prescribed the more they interacted, causing complications. The last antibiotic had given her a most excruciating pain in the tendon in her ankle and calf and the GP had taken her off it immediately and told her to say she was allergic to it if she was ever offered it again. Another friend, Esther, had gone into anaphylactic shock after taking penicillin that she had taken all her life. Esther had spent a night on a trolley in the Mater and had to be resuscitated. She had never got over the episode, which had weakened her considerably, and she had confided to Margaret that she wished she had gone to the lovely peaceful energy that was inviting her to become one with it.

Margaret studied her tablets. Decisions had to be made. Either she could make them or they would be made for her. And having people make decisions for her was the vexing position she just did not want to be in.

'You've raised two great girls,' Jonathan complimented Hilary as they strolled towards Tate Modern along the South Bank, having had an exhilarating half-hour on the London Eye. The sun was warm on their faces, dazzling on the grey-green waters of the Thames, and a soft breeze rustled gently through the trees.

'Thanks.' She tucked her arm in his.

'They're so non-judgemental! They're completely accepting of me.'

'Why wouldn't they be?' She looked at him quizzically.

'Well you know ... being gay.'

'But, Jonathan, they've known you since they were kids, they *love* you, and besides their generation don't put any pass on whether you're gay, straight, bi or whatever. Thank God they have the wisdom to see that it's no big deal,' Hilary said matter-of-factly. 'And I'm surprised that you even felt the need to say that.'

'It's probably after being with Leon,' he sighed. 'He really is tormented about his sexuality and I guess it's washed off on me.'

'Well that's his problem, not yours. And to be honest with you, I don't think it would have worked with you two if he was keeping his relationship with you a secret. It would have caused *huge* problems for you.'

'I was hoping he would have felt brave enough to come out eventually, if we were together.'

'Umm ...' Hilary was skeptical.

'Maybe you're right but it doesn't make it any easier. I feel ugly and unlovable and unattractive and that's Leon's legacy to me,' Jonathan said dourly.

'Jonathan Harpur, don't you *ever* let me hear you saying anything like that again, and don't you *dare* start feeling sorry for yourself. He's the loser, not you, now stop it!' Hilary ordered as the girls caught up with them.

'Mum, could we go and see where Princess Diana lived? It looks so pretty from our hotel window,' Sophie asked. 'We don't *really* want to go to art galleries and theatres.'

'I hate abstract art, Mum, I hate all those angles and distorted faces and bodies, they do my head in.' Millie made a face. 'I just don't like Picasso and Dali and Bacon. I much prefer the Impressionists.'

'There are some Monets and Turners too,' Hilary pointed out.

'Mum, I don't like those squiggly weird sort of paintings either,' Sophie grimaced.

'Jonathan and I might like to see them. He's an interior designer, don't forget. He draws inspiration from paintings. A bit of culture is good for you,' her mother pointed out.

'Oh!' Sophie was crestfallen. 'OK.'

'Nah, let's go visit the Palace. It was Princess Victoria's

home until she became Queen at the age of eighteen. We can have a cultural history lesson.' Jonathan winked at Sophie. 'There's a gorgeous garden, and a restaurant called the Orangery. It's so fine today we could have lunch outside on the terrace if you like,' he suggested affably.

'Oh cool,' enthused Millie. 'I love being a tourist and eating outside.'

'A tourist you will be, then,' Jonathan said. 'Let's get a black cab.'

'This is a really wide river. I remember being in London when I was small once and we went to Madame Tussaud's,' Sophie remarked as the taxi crossed Blackfriars Bridge and turned left along the Embankment.

'That was a long time ago. You and Jazzy were only toddlers,' Hilary smiled.

'Sometime I'd like to do a river tour past Big Ben and the Houses of Parliament – I love those buildings.' Millie stared out at the ships and barges moored along the riverbank.

'We'll come back for a longer stay another time,' Hilary promised. 'Don't forget this was a spur of the moment trip.'

'Well I'm having fun,' Sophie said happily, exceedingly relieved to have got out of visiting Tate Modern.

Jonathan stared out of the car window experiencing a sense of déjà vu, as for the second time in twenty-four hours he sat in the back of a taxi, driving down the Mall and around by Buckingham Palace, and wished with all his heart that Leon was by his side sharing the delights of the city with him. *Don't think about it now. Enjoy your time with the girls,* he told himself as they motored past Hyde Park towards Kensington Palace.

The afternoon flew by. After a tasty lunch in Queen Anne's delightful Orangery, they sipped their coffee served in exquisite china cups and looked out over the immaculately maintained gardens. They took photos for Margaret, particularly of the Sunken Garden, Hilary marvelling at the lavish regimental displays of tulips, wallflowers and pansies. They spent three hours exploring the magnificent state rooms and gallery of the impressive palace, listening to the guided tour through their headphones. Jonathan, setting his woes aside, was as engrossed as the others.

'That was a very, very interesting afternoon. Thanks so much for bringing us,' Sophie said as they stood at the bank of lifts in the foyer of the hotel waiting to go to their rooms to shower and change for dinner. They had decided to eat in the tenth-floor restaurant, with its spectacular views over London; starting with pre-dinner drinks in the adjoining bar. That evening, dressed to the nines, they sat sipping their cocktails, watching the sun begin to set, silhouetting the Palace and Gardens against the sky. It was an eye-catching tapestry of peach and gold, as dusk began to deepen and the lights of the city to sparkle in the night sky. The London Eye, to the south, dominated the skyline once the city lights came fully into their glory and they reminisced about their morning on the South Bank. After a while they moved to their window table in the restaurant and ordered their meal, enjoying the soothing ambience, low lights and soft music while the waiters glided between tables, discreet and watchful of their every need. Millie and Sophie bantered back and forth across the table as they ate the delicious food that was perfectly cooked and presented and all of them agreed it had been a spectacular meal as they managed to finish the lightest chocolate mousse and French silk pie between them.

'You and the girls have been balm to my spirit,' Jonathan said gratefully as he sprawled in one of the chairs in Hilary's room, having a nightcap after Millie and Sophie had gone to bed. Hilary had undressed and changed into her towelling robe and slippers and was cleansing her face, sitting on the side of her big double bed.

'Are you sure you won't get a flight home with us tomorrow? You don't really want to fly Ryanair and meet Leon, do you?' She turned round to face him.

'No to Ryanair and Leon. And believe me I've given this some thought,' he said grimly. 'But I'm not going to give him the satisfaction of thinking I'm a chicken. I'm going to look him in the eye, Hilary, because I know he won't be able to look *me* straight in the eye. He couldn't do it the night before last and he won't be able to do it now. I want that little user to see that I'*m just fine, thank you very much!*'

'We get in twenty minutes before you do if that's the case, so we'll wait for you to make sure everything's OK,' she insisted. 'Come home with us and have a bite to eat and I'll drive you home.'

'What would I do without you?' He smiled across at her and raised his glass.

'You would do the same for me.' She raised her glass back at him and felt so sorry for him when she saw the sadness in his eyes and the air of desolation that was once again enshrouding him.

*

'Safe journey, see you later,' Hilary said when they had all hugged Jonathan before escorting him to the foyer to check out. Hilary too was settling her bill and they stood side by side while the attentive receptionists, Ailine and Tyrone, settled their accounts and asked had their stay been satisfactory.

'As ever,' said Jonathan warmly. 'It's a superb hotel.'

'Ditto,' said Hilary. 'My girls loved it. We'll be back.'

'Very friendly staff,' Jonathan remarked, walking over to the couches where the two girls were sitting waiting for them with the luggage. They had got up early and gone clothes and make-up shopping and all the cases were bulging.

'Time to go our separate ways. See you at Dublin Airport. Wish me luck. Do I look OK?' he asked anxiously.

'Ammaaazzing! That leather jacket is dead cool and those winkle-picker shoes, way to go, JH,' Millie approved.

'And I love the D&G shirt,' Sophie declared. 'Weep into your cornflakes, Leon, you idiot,' she added, knowing how Jonathan was feeling about seeing his erstwhile friend at Stansted.

Jonathan laughed and turned to Hilary. 'See ya soon. Thanks for everything. I love ya!'

'I love you too, now go and swan through Stansted as though you hadn't a care in the world and we'll meet you at the other end.'

'Will do!' he promised, taking heart from her words as the doorman hailed his taxi. As they detoured past the elegant mansions of Belgravia, because there was a delay at Hyde Park, his courage began to fail and a terrible sadness seeped into Jonathan's bones. He should have ignored his pride and booked a flight home with Hilary and the girls. By the time they drove along the Embankment he had almost persuaded himself to tell the driver to drop him at the nearest tube so he could make his own way to Paddington and get the Heathrow Express and try and book a flight with Hilary. When he saw the pale-brick, glass-canopied building of Liverpool Street Station loom into view and the driver pulled up to the rank beside Platform 10, he was ready to puke. With shaking hands he paid his fare, grabbed his luggage, plonked it on the ground and stood in the fresh air gulping deep panicky breaths.

Do not have a panic attack here. DO NOT HAVE A PANIC ATTACK HERE! he ordered silently. He stood gathering his composure and decided to buy a bottle of water and some sucky sweets because his mouth was so dry. Resolutely he set off to WH Smith where he added a copy of *Homes & Gardens* to his purchases. There was a train waiting at Platform 10 although it wasn't scheduled to depart for another ten minutes. He wondered was Leon already on it. He stared straight ahead and walked down towards the middle carriages, stowed his luggage in the baggage rack, got a seat at a window and heaved a sigh of relief as a young woman came and sat beside him. Even if Leon did see him, the carriage was fairly full. When the train pulled out, Jonathan didn't know whether Leon was on it or not.

He saw his former friend before the other man saw him. Jonathan was heading airside after checking in his luggage, and he saw Leon strolling across the concourse. Jonathan quickened his step. He had no desire to spend any time with the man and he hurried onto the transit train to get to departures and find a quiet spot in a bar to wait until his flight was called.

He ordered a beer, opened his magazine and forced himself to concentrate on what he was reading. He left it to the last minute to join the queue for boarding and he could see Leon up ahead scanning for him. Leon saw him and waved for him to go up to him but he stayed put. He wasn't going running just because Leon waved at him.

As the usual mad scramble began, Leon shouted to him, 'I'll get two seats.'

Don't bother, Jonathan thought, annoyed that Leon would even think Jonathan would want to sit beside him.

Making his way down the plane he could see Leon midway along standing up and stowing his bag. Jonathan saw an empty seat in row five, between a man and a woman, and he stopped and hefted his carry-on bag into the baggage bin overhead and excused himself and sat in between them. He hated sitting in the middle seat normally but he was damned if he was going to make polite conversation with Leon for the duration of the flight. And he'd be off the plane before him too.

One thing he had to say about Ryanair, they were generally on time if not early, he thought gratefully when the Boeing thumped down onto the runway at Dublin and taxied to the gate. Without a backward glance Jonathan stood up, got his bag and was ready to move as soon as the doors opened. He raced across to the terminal building, and then remembered he had checked in a case. Damn. Leon would see him at the baggage hold if he'd checked in luggage too. Maybe it was just as well, he mused as he slowed down a little. He didn't want to give the impression that he was running away from him, too upset to talk. That would give him the upper hand.

'Hey, bro, I'd kept you a seat,' Leon said, all hail-fellow-well-met a few minutes later coming to stand beside Jonathan as he waited for his luggage.

'Oh did you?' Jonathan was proud of his faux nonchalant air. 'Sorry, I just sat in the first seat that was free.'

'I knew you had to collect luggage so I came to see if you wanted to share a taxi. We could have a drink and a chat?' Leon suggested casually.

'Thanks but I've got plans.' Jonathan kept his eyes focused on the bags dropping onto the belt.

'Nice jacket, is it new?' Leon fingered the soft leather jacket Jonathan was wearing.

'Yep, and most of what's in this case. Had a ball shopping.' Jonathan grabbed his case off the carousel.

'Where'd you go?' Leon asked eagerly as Jonathan plonked his hand luggage on top of the case and began to walk away.

'King's Road, Bond Street.'

'Ohhh expensive clothes there!'

'Indeed,' said Jonathan, politely smiling as though he hadn't a care in the world.

'So listen, I know things didn't go exactly as planned; perhaps we could meet and have a drink and a chat about it next week seeing as you're tied up now?' Leon persisted, falling into step beside him.

'Sure, if I'm free, that sounds fine,' Jonathan said casually, knowing Leon had a snowball's chance in hell of that happening.

'So did you have a good time after all then?' Leon probed as they approached the Blue Channel and the exit.

'I did, had a great time actually. I was disappointed that you weren't more honest with me before we planned the trip. I thought you had more integrity than what you showed, but hey, it happens. Sometimes people aren't who you think they are. Have to leave you now,' he said as the big doors to arrivals slid open. 'I have friends waiting outside so I'll say goodbye.' Jonathan looked around at the people waiting at the barrier, saw Sophie waving madly and broke into a smile. Real friends were worth more than gold, and he had the best.

It was hard; he knew he was going to have some tough times because Leon's rejection had cut deep. He'd been in this dark place before but he'd climbed out of it. It was something he had to face. The sooner he dealt with it the better. 'See ya around,' he said to Leon, proud of his acting and his blasé approach to their final encounter.

'Absolutely. I'll phone you about that drink,' Leon said, but his words were left floating in the empty space between them as Jonathan hurried to the shelter and welcoming arms of the Jonathan Harpur Rescue Society.

Chapter Twenty-Eight

'Sue, we need to talk. I want to know why would you say what you said to your mother about me being too busy to bring her to the clinics?' Hilary asked, determined not to lose her cool but equally determined to let the other woman know that her behaviour was unacceptable.

Sue glared at her. She did not appreciate being doorstepped on a Monday evening after her aerobics class, when she was red-faced and sweaty, and looking less than her groomed self. She did not relish this encounter with her sister-in-law because Sue knew she had overstepped the mark. 'For goodness' sake come in and don't start arguing with me at the front door,' she snapped, inserting her key in the lock.

'Fine, I just want to sort this and then I'll be off,' Hilary said coolly. She followed Sue into the magenta-painted hall and pristine white lounge with an aubergine sofa and one glass coffee table the only furniture. A spray of lights in the corner and a large abstract painting on the wall softened the stark white of the room but Hilary felt it was cold and sterile, a bit like Sue herself, she couldn't help thinking.

'Now, what's your problem, Hilary?' Sue went on the attack immediately.

'My problem is that you said something to your mother that made Margaret feel under pressure, hurt and upset about me bringing her to her clinics. Something I *never* did. Why, Sue? She's elderly. There was no need for it. All I did was ask you to help your own mother.'

'No! What *you* did was try and make *me* feel guilty and under pressure,' Sue retorted.

'That's not fair, Sue,' Hilary said tightly, determined not to lose her temper.

'Life's not fair, Hilary, deal with it,' Sue retorted.

'What exactly is your problem? I don't understand your attitude.' Hilary stared at her.

'Oh for God's sake, my problem is having to listen to how "wonderful" Hilary is, and how great those girls of hers are and what a pity I never had children, blaa de blaa de blaa!' Sue snapped. 'It gets wearing when you're constantly listening to it, believe me. Not every woman wants to have children. We're not all earth mothers. I don't see why my wishes couldn't be respected without having to endure my own family constantly trying to guilt-trip me. I live the life I want to live and if people don't like it they can lump it.' Sue's eyes flashed with frustration and temper.

'Well I'm sorry about that,' Hilary said, taken aback by the venom in her sister-in-law's tone. 'And I'm sorry for you and Margaret that your relationship is so . . . so . . . fractured. But please in future don't use me as a weapon to inflict discomfort on your mother. She's not going to be around forever, and she deserves as worry-free an old age as we can all possibly give her. It's the least we can do for her. I'll see you.'

Hilary turned and walked out to the front door, relieved that her sister-in-law didn't follow her. She was glad she had kept her temper. It was clear Sue felt very irked with Margaret. Their issues were between them and something she didn't want to get involved in.

Hilary got into her car and turned on the ignition as she mulled over their conversation. At one level she could understand her sister-in-law's exasperation. Not having children was her choice, even if Margaret and others didn't approve. And it must be grating for Sue, she conceded, having Hilary and the girls shoved down her neck, but still, there was no need for the other woman to have dragged Hilary into her problems with her mother. Families could have such lethal undercurrents. You could choose your spouse, but the in-laws that came with them could be a blessing or a bane.

Her trip to London with her daughters had given Hilary food for thought. She had come to a decision that would impact on all their lives. She was going to cut back on her work and employ someone, part-time, to work on the lighting design aspect of the business. She would finish up the projects she had ongoing with Jonathan but after they were done and dusted she would be more picky.

Hilary felt a burden lift from her shoulders as she drove away from Sue's elegant townhouse. For the last few years she'd felt pulled in all directions. Now it was time to step back. Business was booming, she could offer employment to someone else and still be involved, have time for her family, Margaret, and most importantly, *herself*. She had thoroughly enjoyed the few days in London with the girls. It was time to get off the hamster wheel for a while and start living again. Feminists would probably accuse her of wimping out. Sue certainly would, Hilary thought ruefully, driving along Wellington Road and admiring the large, stylish houses that lined the street. Other women might be adept at constantly juggling all the facets of their busy lives. She had reached her limit and if that made her a failure in other women's eyes so be it, she could live with it. The Celtic Tiger could roar away; she was getting off its back for a while and having made her decision all she felt was relief.

The traffic lights turned red at Haddington Road and she scrolled for Jonathan's number on her hands-free. She wanted to tell him of her showdown with Sue and of the decision she'd made. It rang out and went into his message minder and she left him a brief message. Jonathan would support her whatever she did, she knew with certainty, and she knew Niall would be more than pleased.

Was cutting back on work a sacrifice on her part? Hilary pondered, watching two women jog effortlessly along the tree-lined street. At least she was lucky enough to have the choice. Plenty of women had no choice. With the massive size of mortgage repayments many women would be working for a long time, whether they wanted to work outside the home or not. Thank God she'd insisted on paying off their mortgage when the money had started rolling in. The investment adviser in the bank had not been in favour of that step, wanting instead for Hilary to keep paying off the mortgage and use her new income to invest in stocks and shares. She had declined. She was 'too cautious', he'd said pompously. Cautious and a failure as a career woman, that was her!

Hilary grinned, whizzing down Bath Avenue. She could live with that.

'Get dressed, we're going out. You know we have an important consult today.' Hilary stood at Jonathan's bedroom door scowling.

'I don't want to go,' he groaned. 'Make an excuse for me.' He was lounging against his pillows watching morning TV.

'I will *not!*' she retorted, pulling open the long drapes that covered the sliding doors to the wraparound deck outside Jonathan's bedroom. 'What are you watching that horrible little Gollum for? He's obnoxious, stirring up shit between people.' She stood with her hands on her hips at the end of his bed, glaring at the TV screen where a presenter was shouting at a woman for sleeping with her neighbour, while the downtrodden husband looked mortified.

'I don't usually watch him. I don't even like him,' Jonathan said, shamefaced, switching off the TV with the remote. 'It just shows how low I am at the moment.'

'Sinking to a new low, you mean.' Hilary showed no mercy. 'And you pong. Go have a shower while I air this bedroom and tidy up the sitting room. You're a disgrace, Harpur, and I'm not standing for it any more. You've had three weeks to have your nervous breakdown. Now go and see Hannah and deal with it because I'm sick of it.'

'No one asked you to come, ' he said sulkily.

'Eh ... we have a business, remember? We have an appointment with Gina Grant in an hour and a half, buster, so get UP!'

'Oh crap! Is that today?' Jonathan exclaimed in dismay.

'Yes!'

'Sorry, Hil, it went out of my head. I won't be long.' He leapt out of the bed and hurried into the wet room adjoining his bedroom. Hilary was relieved when she heard the sound of the power shower gushing water. She threw empty cereal and yogurt cartons into a waste bin, pulled the sheets and pillowcases off the bed and rolled them into a ball for washing. A salty breeze blew in through the sliding doors. An easterly was blowing in from the Irish Sea along the Liffey below. The never-ending traffic on the quays rolled along steadily, brakes squealing at the lights. Pedestrians hurried along the pavements, occasionally jaywalking across the quays, non-stop frenetic movement adding to the fast pace of city life, and still the seagulls swooped and dived along the river in graceful symmetry, a peaceful contrast. No wonder Jonathan liked sitting out on his deck in his penthouse eyrie over the city.

She hadn't seen him since he had returned from his ill-fated trip to London. He had shut himself up in his apartment and taken to his bed. When she'd phoned him he'd given monosyllabic answers, when he'd actually bothered to answer his phone, that was.

She had been as sympathetic as she could and tried to persuade him to go to his counsellor when she sensed depression was taking hold but he wouldn't listen to her and told her he'd deal with it in his own way. She knew he was utterly devastated by the episode with Leon and she grieved for him, but hiding in his bedroom eating cereals and watching trashy daytime TV programmes was not going to mend his broken heart or his shattered equilibrium.

Now Hilary's patience was at an end. Jonathan was the one who had sourced the Grants as clients. He could either tell them he was pulling out or get up off his ass and get back to work. She had phoned him three times the previous day and he hadn't taken her calls and that was when she had made up her mind to confront him. She'd taken the spare set of his keys that he always left in her house and driven over to tackle him.

She saw his mobile phone on the coffee table in the sitting room and realized it was flat. He probably hadn't even got her messages. The charger was on his desk in his office so she plugged it in and went into the kitchen and brewed up a pot of fresh coffee. God only knew how many of his own clients he'd let down in the past three weeks. He'd need to pull his socks up and make a grovelling apology to them if he wanted to keep them, she thought crossly, flinging dirty dishes into the dishwasher and wiping down his counter-tops.

'Leave that. I'll give Svetlana a call and get her to come and blitz the place.' Jonathan came into the kitchen in a towelling robe, drying his hair.

'It needs it,' Hilary said shortly. 'Jonathan, we've been friends and business partners for a long time and I don't appreciate you not taking my calls ... on both a friendship and a business level.' She glared at him.

'Don't be crotchety. I just didn't want to talk to *anyone*,' he moaned. 'I was so shattered I just wanted to curl up in a ball and escape the world. I've had Mam on my back for a week.'

'That's not good enough, Harpur. You've built up a first-class business. You should be ashamed for allowing it to start sliding down the tubes all because a little creep did the dirty on you and turned you down. It happens to us all and we have to get over it.'

'It's OK for you!' he burst out heatedly. 'You don't have a *clue* what it's like! You have Niall and the girls. You don't come home to an empty house every night. You have someone to put their arms around you. I don't! I'm lonely, Hilary. *LONELY!* Every time I think I've found someone I get dumped and I feel totally rejected and that there's something wrong with me.'

'That's because you're too needy, Jonathan. And that's not easy to say because I love you and you're my friend,' Hilary said quietly.

'*Needy?* Me?' He was shocked.

'There are worse things than coming home to an empty house,' she said firmly. 'Coming home to someone who isn't right for you. Coming home to someone who doesn't want to be with you, and who stays with you because they feel they have to! Coming home to someone who's with you because you keep them, and provide very well for them, and if you didn't, they wouldn't stay. Do you *really* want a relationship like that? The grass is not always greener on the other side of the fence,' she pointed out.

'I know all these things. I tell myself them, but, Hilary, what's so wrong with wanting to share my life with someone?' he demanded.

'Nothing, nothing at all.' She slipped an arm around his shoulder. 'Just be patient and the right one will come eventually, but don't throw away everything you've built up because of someone who's completely unworthy of you.'

Tears filled his eyes. 'I won't, Hilary. Thank you so much for saying that.'

'I said a lot, what in particular?' She smiled at him and gave him a comforting pat on the back.

'That Leon was unworthy of me,' Jonathan gulped.

'Well he was, totally, and he was a fool to throw away a relationship with you. So don't ruin it all because of him.'

'OK, I won't,' he declared shakily.

'Good, and do yourself a favour.'

'What's that?' He smoothed some gel into his hair.

'Make an appointment to see Hannah. She always gives you a great perspective on things and you know you always feel better having talked to her.'

'I suppose,' he said dubiously. 'She'll only repeat what you've just said.'

'Excellent,' said Hilary briskly. 'Then it might just sink in.'

Jonathan flicked his towel at her ass. 'Ha ha!' he said, but he was smiling.

'Oh look, it's the Parthenon!' Jonathan exclaimed as they drove up a ruler-straight drive lined with cypress trees and surrounded by immaculate manicured lawns.

'Stop it! Don't make me laugh when we're inside,' Hilary warned him.

'Good God, is that a turret?' he exclaimed. 'And look at the circular glass window! Windsor Castle with a touch of Notre-Dame. Hard to know exactly *what* era this is from. Hollywood *circa* Cecil B. DeMille, if you ask me.'

'Jonathan, please stop,' chuckled Hilary.

'You could have Ben-Hur doing chariot races up and

down those lawns. Look at the Bentley and the Rolls.' He gave a low whistle as they slowed to a halt at the front of the house. A uniformed houseman opened the door and led them across a massive circular entrance hall with a double staircase and the biggest glass chandelier hanging from the dome ceiling that either of them had ever seen. He opened the door to a very grand reception room. 'Please make yourselves comfortable,' he said politely.

Hilary straightened her jacket, glad that she had put on a simple string of pearls to add a touch of class. Her grey suit was pressed; she was wearing heels and carrying a smart briefcase, so she felt she looked the part. Jonathan had on the light brown leather jacket that he'd bought in London, over a white Armani silk shirt and D&G jeans. An orange tie-dye scarf was looped around his neck, and his gelled hair gave him a faintly exotic air. He wouldn't go too far wrong in Hollywood, as well as this pad, Hilary thought, amused by his description of Bramblewood Manor.

'It's like a film set, very Louis XIV. A touch of the Charles Le Bruns in the silverwork. This room alone has cost a small fortune,' Jonathan whispered when the young man went to tell the Grants that they'd arrived. 'I hate sitting on this kind of chair and sofa. I always think they're going to collapse!' He perched gingerly on a narrow gilt-edged sofa.

'I hate walking on Aubusson carpets in heels.' Hilary gazed down at the hand-woven pastel-green-and-ivory-pink rug under her feet. The clickity-clack of high heels and the firm thud of a man's footsteps echoed across the hall and

Jonathan stood up as a tall, elegant couple walked into the room. Gina Grant strode towards Jonathan, arm outstretched to shake hands.

'Jonathan, so nice to finally meet after speaking to you on the phone. And you must be Mrs Hammond.' She turned to Hilary and gave her a limp handshake. Gina Grant could have been any age from thirty-five to sixty. Her ash-blonde hair was perfectly coiffed, no lines troubled her face, her green eyes had that faintly pulled, tell-tale slant that hinted at cosmetic surgery. A golden, even tan and the jangle of gold at her wrist gave Gina an air of affluent sophistication that only money could buy.

'Hello, I'm Shaun Grant.' The tanned, grey-haired man introduced himself in a polite but uninterested voice. Shaun Grant, one of the country's wealthiest businessmen, was clearly not one for small talk. 'I'm going to leave you in my wife's hands. All I'm saying is, for myself I don't want pink anything, in any way, shape or form. Keep it masculine, and don't damage the lawns when the builders come. Use the best of materials but don't rip me off. Nice meeting you.' He turned to Gina. 'Vyacheslav Fyodorov and Makar Polzin and their wives are coming from Moscow next week. Tell Chef to practise his Russian cooking. I'll see you tonight.' He gave her a perfunctory kiss on the cheek before striding out to the entrance where a chauffeur-driven Merc was waiting for him.

'So, Mrs Grant, are you considering having a His and Hers treatment room, then?' Jonathan asked casually. 'I thought from our conversation that you wanted a relaxing space.'

'I do,' she exclaimed, sinking gracefully onto the sofa he'd been sitting on. 'I'm exhausted running around, entertaining morning, noon and night. Going to this gala event or gold classic or race meet. I have to run this house and cater for Shaun's needs and entertain his business associates and clients. You've just heard him, the Russians are coming and I'll have to make sure Antoine can cook some Russian food for them. I meet myself coming back, Jonathan, I don't have a minute *and* I'm in the middle of the menopause! I *need* a relaxing space.' Unexpectedly the sophisticated woman in front of them crumpled and burst into tears.

'Aah you poor love!' Jonathan said soothingly, sitting beside her and taking her hand in his. 'Now it's imperative, Gina, if I may call you Gina, that you have your *own* treatment room. As your interior designer I *forbid* you to install a His and Hers. Why would you want to listen to a stressed husband venting when you're having a massage? I don't think so. That would defeat the whole purpose entirely.' He smiled at her. 'Let's design a most relaxing, serene, peaceful place just for *you* to run away to. As pink as you wish. And we can give the man of the house his own masculine space. What do you say?'

Gina gave him a watery smile. 'That sounds wonderful,' she sniffed.

'And it will be,' he assured her. 'Now let's go and see where you want to have your spa installed. Near the pool, I think you said. Hilary and I can get to work immediately on the design, so you can have it as soon as possible. You clearly need a place of your own to escape from the world.'

'*Exactly!*' Gina said with heartfelt emotion. 'Jonathan, you understand perfectly.'

'We'll install very soothing lighting that you can control with dimmer switches, little pools of illumination fading into shadow, very balming to the eyes and spirit.' Hilary sat on the other side of her and slid a glossy brochure of their previous work over to her.

'Oh, I *like* this.' Gina wiped her eyes, pointing to a sunken bath surrounded by flickering candles and diffused opaque lighting.

'And this is a floatation-therapy room we did in a spa hotel.' Hilary turned a page and gave Jonathan the tiniest wink as their new client forgot her distress and turned her attention to the goodies that would soon be coming her way.

'You smooth charmer, Harpur,' Hilary slagged an hour later as they drove away from Bramblewood Manor with a preliminary design for Gina and Shaun's spa ready to work on. 'You had her eating out of the palm of your hand.'

'Indeed, as did you, missus, showing her the sunken bath and the floatation-therapy room. What a team we are,' Jonathan said smugly. '*And* we're building two treatment rooms instead of one, *and* installing a new steam room and sauna! *Plus* a relaxation room complete with fish tank. I hadn't expected the half of it, to be honest.'

'Imagine being wealthy enough to employ your own beauty therapist, and having the space for all of that. I'd spend my whole day in it,' Hilary sighed.

'Me too,' Jonathan agreed. 'We did a good day's work today, Hammond. Thank you for dragging me kicking and screaming from my bed.'

'We did, Harpur, and you're welcome. Glad to see you back in the saddle.' Hilary smiled at him.

'I sent a text to make an appointment with Hannah,' he said.

'You took your time about it. No better woman to sort you out,' Hilary declared. 'Any word from his nibs?'

'Yeah, I spoke to him on Sunday. He asked me did I want to go for a drink but I told him I was busy.'

'And will you ever go for a drink with him again?' She cocked an eye at him.

'I might, just to show him I'm not as upset as he thinks I am, even though I *am*.' Jonathan shrugged.

'You do that. Nothing like a show of nonchalance to prick Master Leon's conceit.'

'A prick for a prick,' Jonathan wisecracked and Hilary laughed, most relieved that glimpses of the old Jonathan were making their welcome appearance.

'And what did you learn from this encounter with Leon?' Hannah sat with her hands in her lap, studying Jonathan as he sprawled in the easy chair opposite her.

'That I'm a fool. That I'm not a good judge of character. That I only saw what I wanted to see?' Jonathan didn't spare himself.

'You're very hard on yourself, Jonathan,' Hannah said mildly. 'Let me put it another way: you saw what you *didn't* want in a relationship. Would I be right?'

'I suppose so,' he said slowly.

'And what *do* you want in a relationship?' she probed.

'I want someone to love me and respect me as much as I love and respect them,' he sighed.

'Now you've said it, Jonathan,' Hannah exclaimed in satisfaction. 'Do you realize this is the first time that you've ever said that to me? The episode with Leon might have been very painful but it was your wake-up call. You will never let anything like that happen to you again.'

'You're right,' Jonathan agreed. 'I won't.'

'You've seen what you don't want in a relationship. You've acknowledged that you want to be loved and respected. Remember we are *all* equal.'

'You always make me feel I'm so worthy, Hannah, and I wish I could feel like that all the time.' He shook his head.

'Why do you think you're not worthy?' Hannah gazed steadily at him.

'Umm ... I don't know ... I suppose ... probably because I'm gay!' he blurted.

'Aahhh, now we're getting to the root of things,' Hannah approved.

'I don't know why I said that. I thought I'd come to terms with who I am.' Jonathan frowned.

'Perhaps it's just a final clearing for you, Jonathan, and that's why you experienced what you did with Leon. Because at another level you know that you *are* worthy, and that it is an insult to think otherwise.'

'I know, but the Church says being gay is wrong and a sin.'

'The Church says many things, Jonathan,' Hannah smiled. 'What do *you*, the Divine Creation, say?'

'I say I'm worthy!' Jonathan smiled back at her. '*Very* worthy.'

'*Now* you're in tune with the Universal Language of Love.

Remember you must first love yourself before you can love another.'

'I am worthy. I am worthy!' he repeated, walking to his car after the session. 'I am Jonathan Harpur, the Divine Creation, and I am worthy of love!'

CHAPTER TWENTY-NINE

'Look, why don't you come for a week even, we'd love it, spend two days in the city and then we could go to Nantucket for the other five days. It would be fabulous. We could catch up and have fun just like the old days. Come after Millie's exams,' Colette urged as they sat on the Hammonds' candlelit patio eating dinner on a warm Friday night in late May. Des and Colette were on a rare visit, having spent a few days in London. Colette had phoned Hilary to let her know that she was coming home and had inveigled an invite to dinner. 'It's been so long, and we've soooo much to catch up on,' she'd said eagerly, looking forward to seeing her old friend more than she'd imagined. And it had been a fun reunion, hence the spur of the moment invite to visit them in the States.

'Come on, bud, we've been asking you for years,' Des exclaimed expansively, eyeballing Niall while he scoffed the organic fillet steak Hilary had cooked. 'The girls would love it.'

'We'll think about it,' Hilary interjected smoothly, offering Des another helping of fried onions and creamy mash.

'Well it's just we need to know a little in advance, that's

the only thing. We do a lot of entertaining.' Colette helped herself to a small portion of baby carrots and petits pois. Hilary eyed the creamed mash longingly but decided not to have seconds. She felt like a horse beside Colette who was looking stunning in a pair of tight white jeans and a red Moschino body-hugging top that clung to her petite curves. Her tan was deep and golden, her blonde hair expertly highlighted, worn in a topknot with tendrils curling artfully to frame her smooth, unlined face.

Hilary was glad she was wearing a loose, floaty, midnight-blue top, which covered a multitude, including the love handles that even the elasticated waist on her white M&S tailored trousers could not hide.

Des had not aged as well as his wife, she observed, noticing the hint of floridity, the bags under his eyes, and the thickening waistline. But the boastful patronizing bombast was as pronounced as ever and she had caught Niall's glazed-eyed look of utter boredom after a twenty-minute dissertation on the American educational system, and all because Hilary had asked if Jasmine liked her boarding school.

'I suppose entertaining is part and parcel of your job, Des. Thankfully most of Niall's is done abroad and doesn't impact on me or our home life too much.' Hilary poured a small amount of pepper sauce onto the last piece of her steak.

'I'm used to it at this stage,' Colette pouted. 'We've always had to do it, even when we were living in London. We hired a jet and took some guests down to Turks and Caicos in the spring. Of course it's high season there then. The hurricane

season hits around August, September even though techni-
cally in the Caribbean it's June to November. Don't make the
mistake one of Mum's friends made and go down there in
the summer and have a washout for a holiday,' Colette said
brightly.

'Private jet, wow!' Hilary exclaimed, knowing that Colette
was clearly expecting a response.

'We're certainly not in that league, are we, Hil?' Niall
grinned. 'Although I did once bring a client on a flight simulator.'

Hilary laughed, she couldn't help it.

'*Funeee*,' Colette drawled, miffed that he was mocking her.

'How's the shop?' She changed the subject and switched
her attention back to Hilary.

'Booming, we've more work than we can handle, working
flat out actually.'

'And how's the decorating going?'

The way she said it, Hilary had an image of herself and
Jonathan out with their wallpaper stripper and paintbrushes.
'Well I've taken a step back and employed an assistant but
we're busy, busy, busy. We're up to our eyes lighting and
decorating beauty spas, and revamping hotels, which is how
the business has taken off, but we do private clients too. We
did a spa for the Grants recently—'

'Gina Grant?' Colette's eyes widened.

'As in Shaun Grant?' Des was all ears.

'Yep.' Hilary speared a baby carrot and covered it with
mash before forking it into her mouth, secretly pleased with
the other couple's reaction. *Decorating indeed! Put that in you
pipe and smoke it, you pair of posers.*

'So you're *really* going places?' Colette raised an eyebrow.

'Indeed,' Hilary said a touch drily.

'Do you have live-in help?

Niall raised his hand. 'Me,' he supplied laconically. 'Hilary spends more time with Jonathan than she does with me.'

'Why doesn't that surprise me? Jonathan likes to have Hilary's undivided attention,' Colette remarked acidly. 'I remember that from the very first time I met him.'

'You should have warned me, Colette. I wouldn't have let him get his feet as far under the table as he has.' Niall flashed a grin at her and she was reminded again of how dishy he was still.

'Hmm, he's a pushy boy all right.' Colette slanted a flirty glance at Niall. 'Just as well he plays for the other side or you might have something to worry about.'

'Would the pair of you give over. I could say that your secretary sees more of you than I do, Niall, if it comes to that.' Hilary suppressed a surge of irritation at them. What did Niall have to go and say a thing like that for, and to Colette of all people who had never liked Jonathan?

'Listen, Hilary, any chance you could set up a game of golf with Shaun Grant for me?' Des interjected. 'I could put him in touch with some of the best in Wall Street and make a fine fat profit for myself. He'd be a five-star client to have. I'd make it worth your while, Hilary,' he added condescendingly.

'Thanks, Des, I *really* appreciate that.' Hilary tried to keep the sarcasm from her voice but her friend's husband was so keen on snaring another billionaire for his portfolio he didn't even notice. 'However, you more than anyone will understand how important it is to respect a client's privacy and that's a boundary I couldn't possibly cross. Gina's already put several new private clients our way.'

'Oh! Well if the opportunity ever arises see what you can do,' he said, peeved.

'Sure,' she said airily.

'Did you ever think we'd have billionaires in Ireland?' Colette remarked. 'The Celtic Tiger's something else, isn't it? All the new development. The quays and docklands are really getting a makeover.'

'The economy's expanded at an average rate of 9.4 per cent since 1995.' Niall topped up their glasses.

'Where are you stashing your loot?' Des asked bluntly. 'Property? Stocks and shares?'

'We've a fairly wide spread,' Niall said non-committally. 'Eggs in a few baskets.'

'This Anglo Irish Bank seems to be the leader of the pack. Grant is fairly deep in there.'

'Everyone's in Anglo!' Colette yawned. 'It's all Mum and Dad's crowd talk about. Seánie this, and Tiernan that. Quite the men to play golf with, it seems.'

'And how are your parents?' Hilary asked, not because she was particularly interested in Jacqueline and Frank's welfare, but because she wanted to change the topic of conversation. The cheek of Des asking where their 'loot' was stashed. He was as brash and nosy as ever. She'd forgotten how insufferable he could be sometimes.

Hilary was disgusted with Jacqueline and Frank. Hilary and Dee had organized a surprise birthday party for their mother. Jacqueline had accepted the invitation but, on the night, had dropped in for half an hour saying that Frank was tied up because of tribunal work and she was heading off to another event. Jacqueline hadn't invited Sally and Mick to her big birthday bash two months later, and Sally had been hurt.

'They're working all hours.' Colette shrugged. 'Dad's working on the planning tribunal and Mummy's up to her neck in Moriarty. Couldn't have chosen a better way to end their legal careers. They're more than set up for retirement. They're earning an *absolute* fortune!'

'Indeed ... of taxpayers' money!' Niall drawled.

'*Niall*!' hissed Hilary.

'Sorry!' he said, totally unabashed, ignoring the glare Hilary gave him. 'I always felt those outrageous salaries should have been capped.'

Hilary's mobile vibrated. She had it on silent, but she always kept it close in case her mother-in-law rang. Margaret was recovering from a kidney infection and was finding it hard to tolerate the antibiotics.

She was surprised to see Sophie's number come up. 'Excuse me, I need to take this, it's Sophie. I just want to make sure everything's OK.' Sophie had taken Jasmine to her youth club's disco and Hilary was collecting them at 12.30 p.m. 'Hi, is everything OK?' she murmured, walking down the garden.

'Mam, Jazzy's smashed! She had a bottle of vodka in her bag and she drank it real fast. She's pukin' all over the place and she's being really aggressive to the bouncers. You've got to come and get her. I don't know what to do with her.' Her daughter was nearly in tears.

'For God's sake! OK, stay calm. I'll be there shortly. Is Leanne with you?' Hilary tried to keep the exasperation out of her voice.

'Yep, she's holding her head while I'm ringing. It's gross, Mam! Gross!'

'Right, I'm on my way.' Hilary hung up, irritated that she was going to have to drive because she was the only one not drinking and wishing she could get her hands on Jazzy and wring her neck.

'What's up?' Niall cocked an eyebrow.

'Sorry to have to tell you this, you guys. Jazzy had a bottle of vodka in her bag and she drank it very fast and she's pissed and puking and being aggressive. We'd better go and get her,' she said crossly.

'Aw the little bitch,' Colette exclaimed.

'For Chrissake, what is it with her?' Des exploded. 'Can't you get her to behave? First the weed affair and now this!' He glared at his wife.

'Excuse *me*?' Colette said icily. 'Might I remind you that *you* are her father!' She was furious with him for mentioning the marijuana episode that had nearly got their daughter expelled from boarding school recently. Only a hefty donation towards upgrading the science lab had sorted that hiccup.

'Well you'd better go and get her,' Des snapped.

'And you'd better come with me,' she snapped back. 'Sorry about this, Hilary, can you give us a lift?'

'Of course, I'll just get the car keys and a couple of plastic bags.'

'That's unfortunate.' Niall stood up and followed them into the kitchen.

'Kids, who'd have 'em!' Des growled, draining his glass and leaving it on the kitchen counter.

'I'll murder her,' Colette fumed as Hilary grabbed some plastic freezer bags. She didn't want her car covered in puke.

'Look, these things happen. I'm never, ever smug about Millie or Sophie, believe me. The things you hear about teenage behaviour would make your hair curl. Come on, at least it's not in town, we'll be there in ten minutes.'

There was no chit-chat in the car. Colette stared out of the passenger window and Des glowered in the back seat, scrolling down through his text messages as Hilary sped towards Raheny along the Howth Road.

'You go and get her,' Colette said tightly to Des when Hilary pulled up outside the youth club. Hilary could see Sophie and Leanne bending over Jazzy who was slumped in a half-sitting position against a wall. One of the bouncers was standing with them. 'I'll come with you,' she offered. She wanted to make sure Sophie and Leanne were OK.

'Thank goodness, Mam. She's not puking any more but she's passed out.' Sophie ran towards her.

'It's OK.' Hilary gave her daughter a comforting hug.

'She just needs to sleep it off. I'll give you a hand to get her to the car,' the bouncer said matter-of-factly to Des, who bent down and gave his daughter a rough shake.

Jazzy opened a bleary eye. 'Uuhhh ... Hi, Dad,' she slurred and closed her eyes again.

'Get her under the arms,' the bouncer instructed, taking up position on one side. Des took the other and between them they dragged the comatose teenager to the car.

'I'll drop them home to Sutton and come back and collect

you. Is that OK?' Hilary asked the two riled teenagers standing in front of her.

'But you said we could stay until half twelve!' Sophie exclaimed.

'I know, I just didn't want to have to come out again,' Hilary sighed.

'I can ask my mam to come and collect us,' Leanne said helpfully. 'I'll ring her.'

'It's OK, I'll come back,' Hilary said. They had a rota going with other parents and it was her turn to collect the girls and it was just her tough luck that Jazzy had mucked up her night. 'See you later, enjoy yourselves, and no drinking!' she warned. She certainly wasn't a hundred per cent sure that the pair in front of her hadn't had a nip out of Jazzy's bottle but they were absolutely in control of themselves, and she remembered how when she was in her teens she and her friends had swigged out of a bottle on a few occasions, in the toilets at the Grove.

Colette looked pinched and miserable and Hilary's heart went out to her as she got into the car. 'Chin up, it goes with the territory.' She reached over and squeezed her friend's hand. 'We had the odd hairy moment ourselves.'

Colette gave her a weak smile. 'Yeah, we did, I suppose.'

'No supposing about it – remember the night you barfed into Darina Ryan's handbag because you didn't want to ruin the new Calvin Klein one your mother had bought from New York? Darina was fit to be tied.'

'Shush, don't let Jazzy hear you saying that,' Colette hissed.

'She's snoring.' Hilary glanced over her shoulder to see

the unkempt teen lying against the seat, eyes closed, mouth open, out for the count.

'Thank God the parents are dining out in the Windmill in Skerries. Could you imagine what they'd have to say if they saw this,' Colette groaned as Hilary reversed out of her parking space and headed for Sutton.

'Well that's a bit of luck. Be thankful for small mercies,' Hilary soothed, relieved that the traffic was relatively light. The sooner she got Jazzy out of her car the better.

'Thanks so much, Hil, and sorry for the way the evening ended. Let's try and meet up for lunch before I go back to London next week,' Colette said gratefully when Hilary pulled up outside the O'Mahonys' front door.

'I'll do my best. I'll need to check my diary. I'll call you tomorrow and see how the Sleeping Beauty is. Let me help you get her out. You open the front door.'

'Right,' Colette agreed. 'The sooner she's in bed the better.' Between them they managed to get Jazzy upstairs to bed and as she made her way downstairs, Hilary heard the unmistakable sound of noisy retching and Colette yelling at Des, 'Get a towel or a basin quick! Mum's Frette sheets will be ruined.'

And that would be a tragedy! thought Hilary sarcastically as she pulled the heavy mahogany front door with the two intricate stained-glass side panels closed behind her.

'What did you make that daft remark about Jonathan to Colette for?' Hilary said crossly as she and Niall finished stacking the dishwasher and clearing up after their dinner party. Sophie and Leanne were safely collected from the disco and were upstairs giggling and gossiping over the night they had spent. Millie was staying at a friend's house, and Hilary was tired and disgruntled.

'It was a joke,' he sighed in exasperation.

'Yeah, well it was a crap joke and I didn't appreciate you talking about Jonathan like that, and to her of all people. She never has a good word to say about him and I can tell you one thing, Niall, Jonathan's been a better friend to me in the ten years I've known him than Colette has been for most of our lives, and you know that,' Hilary scowled, collapsing onto the sofa.

'OK, give it a rest. You're not serious about going to visit them in New York, are you?' he said, changing the subject and handing her a glass of red wine.

'I wouldn't mind going to Nantucket for a week and staying in a house on the beach with a swimming pool.' Hilary yawned.

'Yeah but remember when Rowena and Pete were invited over and because some of Des's clients flew in from Hong Kong he made Colette bump them out of the house to stay in a hotel? Trust me, they'd do that to us and it wouldn't cost them a thought. If you want to go to Nantucket, I'll bring you to a hotel,' Niall said firmly. 'Or we could rent a place ourselves.'

'Ha! Don't be daft. You wouldn't get a place to rent in Nantucket during the summer, not unless you paid out a lot of lolly, and I'd say we'd want to have booked it before now.' Hilary kicked her shoes off and lay back against the cushions.

'I don't think I could spend a holiday listening to them

boasting and bragging, and being told where to invest our "loot",' Niall said emphatically. 'Not that he'd be on the island for a week. He's so important, JPMorgan can't function without him; he'd be in his corner office on Wall Street dealing with his billionaires.'

Hilary laughed and began to relax. 'He's the pits, isn't he? He's got even worse than what he used to be. I'd go mental if I was married to him.'

Niall put an arm around her shoulder. Hilary stiffened for a moment. She was still annoyed at Niall for his smart remark, but at least she'd aired her displeasure and she was too tired to stay in a snit. 'Colette couldn't wait to let us know about hiring the private jet.' She leaned in against him and took a sip of wine.

'They're way out of our league now.' Niall smiled down at her, relieved that their spat hadn't developed into a row.

'You were *bad* when you said about the simulator,' Hilary grinned.

'Not half as bad as I'm going to be now,' Niall murmured, sliding his hand under her floaty top and cupping one of her breasts.

'Stop! The girls might come down.'

'No they won't.' He nuzzled her ear.

'No, stop, Niall, I'm tired.' Hilary sat up. 'I'm going to bed.'

'You're always tired these days,' he said irritably, taking a slug of wine and switching on the TV. He grunted 'Goodnight' when she gave him a chaste kiss on the cheek.

As she lay in bed listening to the girls giggling upstairs, Hilary felt weary to her bones. It had been a long day and

Jazzy's episode hadn't helped. There was a time when she would have enjoyed having some nookie on the sofa, but tonight she wasn't in the mood for sex and she wasn't sure if it was because she was annoyed with Niall, or because she was whacked from work and having to entertain Colette and Des to boot. It was probably a combination of all of them, she sighed. She might have put on an airy façade for Colette about work but the truth was, even after employing extra staff, she and Jonathan were snowed under with work and she was finding it hard-going. She had tried to ease off after she'd gone to London with the girls but despite her best intentions and her new assistant, the firm had never been busier and neither had she. She was a successful career woman, certainly, thanks to the Celtic Tiger, but her marriage was wilting under the pressure. Niall just didn't seem to get it that she was the one keeping all the balls in the air, the girls, the household stuff, the responsibility for elderly parents, Hilary thought resentfully, yawning her head off. She was asleep before he came to bed.

Niall poured himself another glass of wine. He was nicely woozy. Unlike Hilary, he'd been able to have a few drinks at dinner and this little nightcap was tipping him over the edge. Just where he wanted to be right now, he thought gloomily. There was a time when Hilary would have welcomed his advances with a passion that matched his own. But these days she was too tired, or had too much on the go, and their sex life was suffering. It wasn't just the sex, it was the intimacy, the cuddles and snuggling, that he was missing.

This was the kind of thing that drove men to having affairs. Colette had been giving him the eye tonight, flirting with him. If he'd made a pass at her he was damn sure he wouldn't have been rejected and pushed away like he'd just been by Hilary, Niall thought drunkenly, feeling very sorry for himself while he channel-surfed and polished off the remainder of the wine.

'What did you have to mention the weed episode in front of them for?' Colette glowered at her husband as they undressed for bed in her parents' guest room.

'I was pissed off with Jazzy. I was *enjoying* that meal. Best steak I've had in ages and she goes off and pulls one of her stunts! We've given her everything, the best education, homes you or I never dreamed of having, a lifestyle fit for a princess, and she goes and gets tanked and makes a show of us. Thank God it was in some hick little disco and not in front of any of the City crowd back home. She's so grounded!' Des was not in the mood for recriminations from his wife.

'There was still no need to mention that weed episode,' Colette snapped, sliding a silk nightdress over her head and shoulders. 'I was mortified.'

'Who cares about what they think – we won't see them again for years,' Des said dismissively.

'We invited them to come and stay with us,' she reminded him irritably.

'*You* invited them,' he corrected her. 'Make sure they don't come when we're entertaining. You should have told them to come after Labor Day. Tell them we're booked up until then,' he carped, climbing into bed and pulling the duvet over his shoulder as he turned his back on her.

'They can't come in September. Sophie will be back at school,' Colette pointed out as she cold-creamed her face.

'Tough, not our problem. Don't read for long, I'm beat.'

Colette didn't answer. She had just heard her parents' taxi pull up. She hoped fervently that Jazzy would stay sleeping. She was snoring her head off in her drunken stupor, but at least she'd stopped being sick. Colette got into bed and switched off her bedside light. She was beyond stressed. Jazzy's behaviour was unacceptable, but no matter how much she was grounded or chastised, it was making no difference. She wasn't alone in worrying about her child. Several mothers in her set had behavioural problems with their children. Not that they alluded to it directly. Colette heard these snippets on the grapevine. No doubt the other mothers heard nuggets about Colette on the very same grapevine. There was no one back in New York that she could confide her worries to. There was no one here either, apart from Hilary, she thought glumly as Des began a crescendo of snores that could be heard in Howth.

She couldn't bring herself to say it to Jacqueline. She didn't want a lecture on her parenting skills or lack of them. Hilary had been kind earlier when they'd gone to pick Jazzy up. But then it was easy for her to be kind. Her kids were Little Misses Goody Two Shoes compared to Jazzy, and always had been. It had been utterly humiliating when they were children and Jazzy would throw a strop, and screech and stamp her foot in front of Millie and Sophie. She was still doing it, albeit in a different manner. Still looking for attention and getting it, still showing Colette up in front of the Hammonds.

Was she mad to have invited them to the States? They really had nothing in common any more; that had been more than evident this evening. Niall had not been in awe when she'd told him about hiring the jet. He'd made a derisory joke at their expense. He was still handsome, the touch of grey at his temples doing nothing to take away from his rugged good looks. And still as laid-back and cool as ever, and not at all impressed by their success. Yes, Niall was still a dish, but Hilary had let herself go somewhat. She was carrying extra weight and the lines around her eyes and lips had deepened. Her nails needed a good manicure, and there were grey hairs in her luxuriant chestnut locks, which needed styling. Colette could give her twenty years in looks, she thought smugly. If the Hammonds came at holiday-time, she'd be able to swan around in her bikini on the beach. Hilary would surely have to wear a one-piece. Niall would still look good bare-chested, she imagined. And in spite of himself he'd have to be impressed with their Upper East Side apartment and the house on the island. She would very much enjoy being the hostess with the mostest, should they come to visit. There had been an uncharacteristic edge between her host and hostess tonight. Niall and Hilary had sniped at each other about Jonathan, much to her surprise. And Niall had given her the eye once or twice. Colette was sure of it. *Interesting!* she thought, remembering the glint in his eye when he'd smiled at her.

Colette wrinkled her pert little nose when Des let off a rasper in his sleep. Nothing dishy about her husband right now, she thought grumpily, turning on her side, wishing she could go and sleep in her own luxuriously appointed guest room, which she often did when she was at home in Manhattan. Why was it that she always looked forward to coming back to Ireland, but when she actually got here, it was never as good as anticipated and often, indeed, she couldn't wait to be gone.

CHAPTER THIRTY

'You should give Jazzy a call and see if she's OK,' Hilary suggested over breakfast the following morning.

'What? Why should I ring her? She should ring *me* and apologize,' Sophie exclaimed indignantly. Leanne prudently said nothing and demolished another mouthful of crispy bacon topped with fried potato and dipped in egg yolk.

'I know that. You know that. But still I'm sure she's embarrassed and after all she *is* in a strange country and doesn't know many people here. It would be a kindness,' Hilary said lightly.

'Yeah well I don't feel kind,' Sophie retorted, spearing a piece of sausage.

'It's up to you, of course.' Hilary smiled, offering her daughter a slice of buttered toast.

'Uuhhh,' muttered Sophie, wishing her mother wouldn't do the emotional blackmail stuff on her.

'I suppose I'd better ring the little skanger,' Sophie moaned to Leanne later that morning as they warmed up for a basketball match against a rival school's team. She dribbled the ball along the court at a run, segued into a lay up and felt a ripple of satisfaction as the orange ball sliced through the net cleanly, giving a satisfying thud as it bounced on the wooden floor.

'We'll do it when we're finished here. ' Leanne shrugged. 'It's no big deal and it will get your mother off your back. You only need to say hello and goodbye.'

'OK,' Sophie agreed, catching a rebound from the board from a shot missed by another girl. She aimed and scored again. If she could do the same when they were playing the match she'd be more than happy.

'That's unfortunate, darling, that you are off colour. You were fine when you were going out last evening.' Jacqueline gazed at her granddaughter, noting her pallor and the way she winced every so often as if the light hurt her eyes. 'What would you like for lunch, seeing as you had no breakfast? We've had ours but there are cold cuts and salad, or prawns and crab—'

'Umm ... just coffee and toast, Gran, please,' Jasmine interjected hastily, afraid if she heard any more about food her stomach would erupt again. She felt truly horrendous, but at least the hellacious headache she'd woken up with had eased. Her parents had gone apeshit this morning before they had gone out and demanded her credit card back and told her that she was, like, so grounded. It was a real bummer.

'Well the dead arose and appeared to many. You're up at last,' Frank exclaimed jovially, strolling into the breakfast room with his *Irish Times* under his arm. 'As soon as you've had something to eat I'm going to take you into the Law

Library with me. If you decide to study law, and I really hope you do, you'll find no better place of learning than the King's Inns Law Library. It will rival the best of anything you have in the US, I can tell you,' he declared proudly. Jasmine's heart sank. Her grandfather really wanted her to be a lawyer and was always going on about the King's Inns. The last place she wanted to go to today was a stuffy old library.

'Em ... the thing is—' Her cell phone rang and she slid it out of her jeans pocket and flipped it open. 'Excuse me a sec, Granddad,' she said politely, and opened the French door and sauntered into the sun-drenched garden. She had thought it might be her mum but the number that flashed up on her screen was an Irish number and she saw Sophie's name. She cringed. She had made such a jackass of herself last night, much of which she couldn't remember. The last person she wanted to talk to was Sophie.

'Hello,' she said cautiously, expecting a barrage of abuse.

'Hi, Jazzy, how are you feeling?' Sophie asked politely.

'Umm, not so good,' she confessed.

'OK ... Well I just rang to see if you were OK,' Sophie said awkwardly and Jasmine guessed her mother had pressurized her to make the call.

'Look, sorry if I ... er ... messed up your night.'

'No probs, enjoy the rest of your holiday.'

'Listen ... em ... could I hang out with you for an hour or two? Could I take you for a pizza or McDonald's or latte or something to make up for last night?' Jasmine saw a potential escape from the trip to the dreaded Law Library.

'It's fine, honestly, no worries,' Sophie said hastily.

'*Pleeease*, Soph! My granddad wants to bring me to the Law Library and I have the hangover from hell and I can't tell him that,' Jasmine blurted.

'Oh! Well, Leanne and I have sort of made plans,' Sophie said crossly.

'Please, Sophie, cut me a break here,' Jasmine pleaded. 'I swear to God, it's just for an hour then you can split and I can do my own thing.'

'Hold on, I need to check it out with Leanne.' Jasmine could hear a muffled whispered conversation, and Leanne saying, 'Do we have to?'

Jasmine felt like telling them to get lost, but if she could say she was meeting them, even for a short while, it would get her out of spending the afternoon with her granddad and his beloved legal tomes.

'OK, then. Meet us in an hour at the DART station in Clontarf and we'll go to Barcode for pizza. Text me when you're on the train in Sutton and we'll get on the same one in Killester,' Sophie said crisply. 'See ya!'

Jasmine slipped her phone into her pocket and walked back into the breakfast room. Her grandmother had just placed a basket of toast on the table, and a mug of steaming coffee. Coffee, just what she needed. 'Thanks, Gran,' she said gratefully, inhaling the rich aroma.

'Eh ... Granddad,' she said to her grandfather who was immersed in his crossword. 'That was Sophie on the phone and we had sort of made a loose arrangement to meet up and she was just ringing to confirm,' she fibbed.

'Oh!' He looked disappointed. 'Ah well, another time, perhaps,' he sighed, lowering his head to his paper.

'That's nice that you're meeting Sophie. Did you have a good time last night?' Jacqueline asked, sitting down beside her at the table.

'Yep, it was cool,' Jasmine lied. 'Gran, can you give me a lift to the DART station in a while? I don't think Mom and Dad will be back in time.' She nibbled on the toast and found it surprisingly tasty.

'Of course, dear.' Jacqueline smiled fondly and Jasmine leaned over and kissed her on the cheek. 'You are so kind to me, Gran. When I get back we could go for a walk on the beach with Nomos.'

'Lovely, Nomos will enjoy that.' Her grandmother's eyes lit up. Nomos, hearing his name mentioned, uncurled himself from the sunspot on the floorboards by the windows and padded over to them. Privately Jasmine thought Nomos was a silly sort of name for a dog, and a big golden Labrador at that, but her grandfather had called him after the god of law in Greek mythology. Jasmine had heard her dad say once to her mom, 'Frank is so pretentious, he thinks he impresses people calling his dog that ridiculous name.'

'You are just as bad as he is sometimes,' her mom had retorted, annoyed that Des should criticize her father.

'Hi, Nomos, walkies later,' she said, surreptitiously feeding him a piece of toast, loving how he lapped her fingers with his tongue, his tail wagging like crazy. She would adore to have a dog but her parents wouldn't allow it. 'A city apartment is no place for a dog,' her father said firmly and no amount of begging or pleading could change that. Being with Nomos was what she loved most about coming to visit her grandparents. Nomus loved her like no one else did. There was no need to demand love or attention from him. It was willingly given and returned in equal measure.

'I'd better go and put on my make-up and put my hair up.' She swallowed the last of her toast, gulped her coffee and smiled at her grandmother.

'Breakfast dishes in the dishwasher, dear,' Jacqueline said firmly.

'Yes, Gran,' she said meekly, doing as she was bid.

Three quarters of an hour later she sent a text to Sophie. On the subway. C u in a while. A woman with a toddler squirming in her arms, sitting opposite, smiled at her. 'Lovely day, isn't it? This one's a handful – she wants to be walking,' she said, jigging the little girl on her knee.

It astonished Jasmine how complete strangers in Ireland would strike up conversations, mostly about the weather, it seemed. She had never known people to be so obsessed with weather and weather-related matters. At home, people didn't make eye contact and kept to themselves on public transport.

Some Spanish students chattered away gaily in the seats on the other side of her aisle. Vociferous and expressive and full of self-assurance, they seemed so vibrant and cool, she thought enviously. She would love to be that self-possessed. Although she gave the appearance of confidence she wasn't really a confident girl. Deep down she was unsure of her place in life and the world. Unsure of her looks, her academic capability, her ability to attract boys. She had been really nervous going out with Leanne and Sophie last night and that was why she had drunk the vodka so quickly. Leanne and Sophie seemed so sure of themselves. And they were such good friends. She envied them. She had friends of course, but none that she could truly be herself with. Her set was riven with jealousy, competitiveness and spiteful back-biting. Just the way their mothers behaved, she supposed, Jasmine thought glumly as the suburbs flashed by inter-spersed with verdant green hedgerows and a view of the sea sparkling in the sun before it disappeared. The little girl was on the floor now, between the woman and Jasmine. The train gave a slight lurch and the toddler grabbed Jasmine's knees and flashed her a gummy smile. She just had two front baby teeth and her eyes were the bluest Jasmine had ever seen. Her heart melted and she smiled broadly as she reached out to steady the child. 'Say ta ta,' said the woman.

'Ta ta,' the little girl said obediently, beaming at Jasmine.

'She's lovely,' Jasmine astonished herself by saying, enjoy-ing the feel of the pudgy little hands placed so trustingly on her knees.

'It's time for us to get off now. Say day, day,' the woman said, standing up and taking the little girl's hand.

'Day, day,' said the infant, blowing a kiss as her mother led her to the door.

'Day day,' Jasmine echoed, feeling a bit silly. This was so not her. If any of her friends back home saw her they would think she had lost it big time, speaking baby talk to strangers on a train. She watched the mother and daughter walk along the platform and wondered would she ever have children of her own. Most of her friends, like her, had been raised by nannies and au pairs, and then sent to boarding school.

Sophie was so lucky to live at home and have a sister for company *and* her own space upstairs to entertain her friends. Hilary was not a strict mother that Jasmine had noticed. The only thing was the Hammonds were not at all wealthy, not like her parents were anyway. She would be getting a car when she was sixteen – her next birthday. She would be travelling to Europe; she would be skiing in Aspen. She had a better life, she assured herself as she heard the announcement that Killester was the next station.

She saw Sophie and Leanne on the platform as the train drew to a halt. She wondered should she wave to attract their attention, but they had stepped into a carriage further along so she sat back in her seat and glanced in her bag just to make sure she had her wallet with the crisp fifty-euro note her grandmother had given her. She had another forty euros; surely pizza wouldn't cost that much for three in this Barcode restaurant. She felt bereft without her credit card. As if her security had been taken away.

The train crossed a bridge and the vista of Dublin Bay opened out before her on her left, the square tower of a church on her right, before they crossed over a main road. She saw a grey building with a car park and a sign for Barcode and was relieved it wasn't too far to walk. She could spend half an hour with the girls and then go and have a stroll around before getting the train back to Sutton, she decided as they trundled into the station. Dublin was a picturesque city, she acknowledged, looking at the small flotilla of boats sailing in Dublin Bay. She especially loved that you could see the mountains in the distance. In New York all you could see was buildings.

She pressed the red button to open the carriage door and took a deep breath. She had made a fool of herself last night. These two girls didn't particularly want to be with her. This would not be easy. They were walking down the platform towards her, deep in conversation. Jasmine took a long breath and hung her thumbs in her jeans pockets.

'Hi, guys,' she said with pretended airiness.

'Oh ... hi, Jazzy,' Sophie said politely. Leanne merely nodded sullenly. Jasmine's heart sank.

'I guess that's Barcode where we're going.' She jerked her thumb to the left.

'Yep,' Sophie said succinctly.

'It looks cool,' she said flatly. Perhaps she would have been better off going to the Law Library with her granddad. At least he would have talked to her.

'It is quite cool actually. It's got a brilliant disco,' Sophie volunteered as they clattered down the steps to the exit barrier.

'Oh ... really? Why didn't you go there last night then?' Jasmine asked as they fell into step and walked out into the sunshine and sea air that ruffled her hair and made her breathe deeply, enjoying the salty tang that reminded her of Nantucket.

'Not allowed. Mam says I'm too young. Millie goes. It's deadly; people come from all over the city to go to it. I can't wait until I'm allowed.' Sophie shrugged. 'But the bouncers are quite strict about being drunk,' she added pointedly.

Jasmine was mortified. *Bitch*, she thought. There was no need for that.

'Oh well, they won't have to worry about you then,' she

drawled sarcastically. 'Look, I guess you and Leanne don't particularly want to be here. I thought I'd try and make amends for last night but I'm not going to spend the next hour trying to make polite conversation with you guys. Let's split now if you like.' She wasn't going to prostrate herself at their feet for another minute. She could be as rude and off-hand as they were.

'What about our pizza? I'm starving,' grumbled Leanne. 'We played a basketball match this morning already and we delayed our lunch to meet up, and now you're going to brush us off just like that?' Her voice rose in an indignant squeak. 'We can sit at separate tables and—'

'Stop, Leanne,' Sophie remonstrated. 'Look, we were mad about last night and that's a fact but let's forget it and go and share a pizza like we said.'

'Yeah well, it's not easy for me, and I have apologized,' Jasmine said sulkily.

'OK, apology accepted. Come on, let's go and eat,' Sophie grinned. 'And you can tell us if Irish pizzas are as good as Yankee ones.'

Jasmine felt some of the tension evaporate. Sophie was a kind girl. If the tables were turned and they were in New York she might not have been so forgiving, she conceded.

'Er ... thanks for meeting up with me.' She caught Sophie's steady gaze.

'Well we couldn't let you spend an afternoon in a library. That would be enough to turn anyone to drink,' the other girl teased and even Leanne laughed. An hour later, sitting on a banquette, in the trendy eatery, eating a *margherita* with fries and coleslaw on the side, and sipping a glass of the house red, they were thoroughly relaxed and enjoying themselves. The waitress clearly had thought they were old enough to be served drink, and certainly Jazzy, who had ordered the wine, looked much older than her years.

'I can't believe you have your own credit card,' Sophie remarked enviously after Jasmine had told them her parents had taken her card back as a punishment.

'Like, we all have, in my group, and I have a charge account in all the big stores. It's no big deal,' she said matter-of-factly.

'That's a gorgeous top,' Leanne complimented.

'It's A&F. And the jeans are Calvin Klein.' She stretched out her long legs encased in the designer jeans. 'They are pretty awesome. I love them.'

'We don't have A&F here,' Sophie shrugged. 'If we ever come to visit you in New York I am going to spend all day, every day, shopping.'

'And do you just ask your parents for money or do you have an allowance?' Jasmine asked, unable to grasp what life would be like without charge accounts and a credit card.

'I get twenty-five euros and I have to work in Mam's showrooms some Saturdays and during the holidays,' Sophie explained.

'Jeez, you have to *work*!' Jasmine was aghast.

'I work in the local coffee shop on Sundays.' Leanne took another sip of wine.

Jasmine's phone rang. It was her mother. 'I'm on my way back from town and I want to call into Diffusion, that boutique in Clontarf. Cross over and walk up to the shops beside the Garda station and meet me there and I'll drive you back home. Gran said you were meeting Sophie for pizza.'

'Aw Mom, can't I get the DART to Sutton! I'm with the girls,' she protested.

'No! You're supposed to be grounded and I'm not driving back over to Sutton DART station,' Colette said crossly. 'I'll be there in twenty. Be there.' The phone went dead.

'That was Mom. She's like so mad with me, she says I've to meet her in some boutique called Diffusion, in twenty,' Jasmine said dolefully.

'Aww, just when we were having fun and getting to know each other,' Sophie exclaimed. 'Look, why don't I ring my mam and ask her to ring yours and ask can you stay over. I can give you PJs and we could get a few films in and watch them and we could sneak up another bottle of wine, but we won't get smashed because my parents would go bananas if they caught me drinking. But Leanne and I do sometimes, when we're having sleepovers, don't we, Leanne?'

'Yeah, sounds good to me,' Leanne agreed. 'Ring Mrs Hammond and see what she says.'

Sophie crossed her fingers when she had dialled Hilary's number. 'We're having a really nice time catching up cos it's been *ages* since we've seen each other. So please ask Jasmine's mam to let her stay over,' Sophie said earnestly.

'Well I'll do my best but I can't interfere if they really want to ground Jasmine,' Hilary said firmly. 'I'll ring you back.'

'She's ringing back.' Sophie took a glug of her wine.

'Fingers crossed.' She waved her fingers in the air and giggled.

'I bet she won't agree,' Jasmine said gloomily, completely forgetting she had promised to go for a walk on the beach with her grandmother and Nomos. 'She is like so pissed at me for last night. I haven't a hope.'

'It's nice that they're bonding, Colette, and it must be boring for her not having any friends to hang out with in Ireland. I'm fine with it if you are,' Hilary said matter-of-factly. It was no trouble having the teen to stay. Sophie's room was big enough for the two girls to sleep over. They wouldn't be in her way.

'Well we took her credit card off her so that's a fairly stiff punishment in itself, so OK then, if you're sure.'

'We were teens together; it's nice that our children have a bond too,' Hilary said cheerfully. 'I'll ring them back and let them know.'

'You *are* a good friend, Hilary, thanks,' Colette said gratefully.

'I know I am,' Hilary said sardonically but Colette knew she was smiling.

'She said yes,' Sophie grinned, conveying Hilary's message. 'Let's go into town for a couple of hours, and then we can stop off at Xtra Vision and rent out a couple of films and stock up on goodies.'

'Good plan,' agreed Leanne, finishing off the coleslaw.

For a day that had started off so badly, this was turning out to be a truly awesome one, Jasmine thought happily.

After their initial rocky start, and once the awkwardness of the previous night's episode had been dealt with, she'd found it surprisingly easy to talk to the two Irish girls. In fact she felt very, very comfortable with them. It was amazing. Their lives were so different she felt no need to try and impress them in the slightest. It was very liberating. She actually felt Sophie and Leanne could become 'real' friends. Jasmine felt an uncharacteristic frisson of happiness. This was just so cool.

'Oh ... well that's nice for her. It's good that she's making friends here. And especially nice that it's Hilary's daughter,' Jacqueline remarked when Colette informed her that Jazzy would not be home that night. She tried to ignore the pangs of disappointment. She had been looking forward to the walk on the beach with her granddaughter.

'I'm going to bring Nomos for a walk on the strand. Fancy coming?' she asked Colette, who was sipping coffee and flicking through *Hello!*

'Mum, I'm pooped, I think I'll have a nap. We're meeting the Osmonds for cocktails in a couple of hours, when Des has finished his round of golf. Do you mind if I skip it?'

'Not at all,' said Jacqueline brightly. 'Nomos and I will entertain each other. Come on, boy, let's go for a walk.'

It was an irony, thought Jacqueline twenty minutes later, as she flung a stick along a stretch of white sand for her dog to catch, that all those years ago when Colette wanted her company she was too busy to devote a lot of time to her daughter. And now when she had more time to spend with her family, the only one who had time to give her was

Nomos. Jacqueline sighed as her dog yelped with pleasure, panting and wagging a sandy tail at her, proud to return the stick and have it thrown again for him to chase.

'Good God, is that Frances Collins? Look at the size of her! She has an arse like the back of a bus. She's really let herself go. She needs to get herself a good trainer or go to the gym.' Colette stared with distaste at a woman walking through the foyer of Clontarf Castle with an elderly couple as she and Hilary sat having coffee at one of the small tables near reception.

'Colette, don't be so pass-remarkable. Frances is recovering from cancer, she's on steroids, and she's minding her elderly parents as well,' Hilary remonstrated, irritated at how superficial and judgemental Colette could be. If you weren't thin you were a failure in her eyes.

'Oh! Well I didn't know that.'

'Yet you felt free to make a judgement about her weight nevertheless. You should stop it. You do it all the time and it's not nice.'

'Oh shut up,' Colette snapped. 'I suppose you never make bitchy comments when you're with your little queen friend.'

'There you go again,' Hilary retorted.

'Well he is a little queen with those scarves and pointy winkle-pickers,' Colette said sulkily.

'Jonathan is the best friend anyone could have. You'd be lucky to have a friend like him.' Hilary decided against having the little ginger biscuit served with her coffee in case Colette made some remark about *her* weight.

'I have you,' Colette grinned, and Hilary laughed.

'It's good to see our girls becoming close.' Colette sat back in her chair displaying her tanned legs to the best advantage.

'They had a great time the other night. There was lots of giggling and laughing.'

'That's probably the bottle of wine they smuggled upstairs. Jazzy told me that Sophie is quite the little plonkie behind that innocent façade.'

What a bitch you are, Hilary thought in disgust. *You could have kept that to yourself.*

'I did tell you that night we had to collect Jazzy when she was pissed that I have no doubts that Millie and Sophie drink behind my back. We did it, Colette. Why would our daughters be any different? It's a rite of passage.' *But at least I've never had to collect my daughter from a disco because she was falling down drunk,* she wanted to add, but she refrained. She wasn't going to sink to Colette's level of bitchiness.

She drained her coffee cup. 'I have to go. I have to inspect a building and make sure everything's being done as per the plans,' she said.

'Aw no, I thought we were going to have a good gossip. We never got a chance to the other night,' Colette protested.

'Sorry, I'm not on my hols like you are,' Hilary said lightly, standing up.

'But I won't get to see you again,' Colette pouted. 'Do come out, we'd love to have you visit.'

Not in a million years, thought Hilary, picking up the bill. 'I'll get this,' she said briskly. 'Take care, Colette.'

'OK, see you.' Colette stood up and gave her an air kiss. 'Keep in touch.'

'Sure,' Hilary threw over her shoulder as she walked to

reception to pay their coffee bill. Was this the way a friend-ship ended? she wondered. Over coffee, with promises to keep in touch? For the first time ever she couldn't give Colette any leeway or make excuses. She was just not a nice person and that was it. She couldn't *wait* to let Hilary know that Sophie had smuggled a bottle of wine in for their sleep-over.

She'd have to deal with that later, she thought grimly. Or would she? Hilary and Colette and all their friends had drunk alcohol behind their parents' backs at Sophie's age. She just might subtly let her daughter know that she was keeping an eye on her.

When she got home, she went into the garage and rum-maged through the bag of empties that would be going for recycling. Blossom Hill, there it was. She and Niall hadn't drunk that. She took the bottle out and brought it in and placed it on the kitchen counter.

She was chopping onions for the spaghetti bolognese when Sophie bounced into the kitchen. 'Hi, Mam, what's for dinner? I'm starving!'

'Your favourite,' Hilary said affably. 'Will you be having wine with it?'

She stared at the empty bottle on the counter.

Sophie blushed to her roots. 'Oh!' she exclaimed, morti-fied.

'Just be careful, Sophie. That's all I'm asking you. Drink can be a very dangerous thing. You saw what happened to Jazzy.'

'Sorry, Mam,' she said guiltily. 'We were just having fun.'

'I know. But you're still very young so just be careful.'

'I love you, Mam.' Sophie flung her arms around her.

'And I love you,' Hilary said, hugging her daughter tightly. Maybe Colette had done them a favour in spite of herself, Hilary thought, relishing the closeness she had with Sophie and the loving affection behind her daughter's embrace.

CHAPTER THIRTY-ONE

'Niall, were you talking to your mam today?' Hilary asked, trying to keep the note of concern out of her voice.

'Er ... not yet, no,' her husband admitted. 'I was in meetings all morning. Why?'

'She's not answering her landline or her mobile,' Hilary said, trying to quell the feeling of dread that was rising in her. 'I'd better drive over and make sure she's OK.'

'You have the key, don't you?'

'Yeah.'

'Any of the girls around?'

'No, Sophie's gone into town with her gang and Millie's minding Gillian Nolan's kids for an hour or two. I'd better go. I'll ring you from Gran's. Bye.'

'Bye,' he said. 'Thanks, Hilary.'

Hilary dialled Margaret's phone once more, almost holding her breath, hoping against hope to hear the familiar, if slightly breathless, tones of her mother-in-law with her usual cheery greeting. The phone continued to ring, unanswered. She would have been very surprised if Margaret had gone somewhere and forgotten her phone. She had been very wheezy the past month and had been on steroids again. She was in no fit state to be going any-where.

Hilary grabbed her bag and keys and hurried out to the car. It was very unlike Margaret not to answer her phone. Once or twice before, Hilary had phoned and Margaret had been in the toilet or out at the bin and she had phoned back, but there was no call back this morning, despite several attempts to contact her, and Hilary was worried. At that age and with her dodgy heart, it was inevitable that someday something would go wrong. The last year had been particu-larly hard for Margaret. She had become more chronically ill, less able to enjoy her life. It was one medical drama after another, Hilary acknowledged, reversing out of her drive. Difficult for her and Niall too. There was always that vague sense of dread, knowing that the day would come when Margaret would not recover. And even worse, thought Hilary with a sickening clenching of her stomach. What would she find when she got to her mother-in-law's? No matter how much death was expected, it was still a life-changing shock for those left behind. 'Let her be OK,' Hilary prayed, almost dizzy with fear and apprehension.

Margaret could hear the phone ringing as if from some far-distant place. She knew it was Hilary. Hilary was the only one who rang her in the mornings. She closed her eyes again and felt herself drifting off. She was in such a peaceful place. Even her breathing was easier. If she had known it would be like this she would have stopped taking the tablets long ago.

The fear of anticipation she'd endured these past few days was no more. In fact she'd never felt more empowered,

Margaret realized, pleasantly surprised. She had made the choice. Not some anonymous medic, or her children. She gave a little sigh. That last time in A&E had been the turning point. How she had cried when the ambulance crew had placed her gently on the trolley, when she had collapsed at Sunday evening Mass in January. 'I don't want to go there, just bring me home,' she'd pleaded. The men were kind to her. Very kind. She could not fault them. She had been in the care of Dublin Fire Brigade and Ambulance crews so many times in the past years. And always the kindness. But not even kindness could erase the dread of what awaited her beyond the doors of hell as Margaret had come to think of A&E.

This time had been even worse. There were no beds, no cubicles. The entrance hall was lined with patients on trolleys and ambulance crews waiting for their trolleys to go back out on the road.

'Been here three hours,' Margaret heard one crewman tell her minder. 'That man over there has MRSA, post surgery open wound, should be in isolation. He's been attended to behind a screen. It's crazy!'

Crazy it was. She had eventually been transferred to a bed in a cubicle, with a drunk, yelling and puking, in the adjoining cubicle. The nurse and doctor were trying to calm him down, pacifying him with enormous patience. How she had longed to get out of her bed and go over to him and smack him hard and tell him to behave himself and leave beds for people who were ill through no fault of their own.

And then the pain of the cannula being inserted into her frail hands. It had made her cry. And the blood tests, the interminable blood tests. She was black and blue after it, her arms like pincushions from the nurses trying to find veins that would give up their red bounty.

Two days and nights she had lain in that nightmarish place, unable to sleep, or eat the slop they called food. Niall, Sue and Hilary had taken turns to be with her and she had fretted at the amount of time they had to waste, standing, without even a chair to sit on, when their own lives were so busy. Never again, Margaret had sworn when she was finally wheeled away to a hospital ward.

She had felt the effects of that last hospital stay much more than previous ones. All she was able to do on her return home was potter around, from her sitting room to her kitchen, and watch TV. Her sight was fading, even with her glasses. She could no longer see the birds feeding out in the garden. Reading was difficult. All she was doing was waiting for the inevitable. What was the point of delaying it? New medical discoveries and medications were prolonging life, but at what cost when you were existing as opposed to living? In her day pneumonia was known as the old people's friend. Now it was treated with antibiotics and steroids. Until another dose came and the whole palaver started again. What was the point of keeping her alive with her ageing heart and aching body, when she had come to know that death was preferable? Why did she have to do this alone? Could hospice care not be extended to all? In a hospice death was given the respect it deserved. In hospital you were made well enough to be discharged. And then they were finished with you and you had to get on with it until the next time. Margaret had spent many hours pondering the ethical questions. The spiritual questions. The practical questions. Until she had made peace with her decision. It didn't matter what anyone else thought, she decided. If she was at peace with it, and she was, then that was all that mattered. That knowledge gave her comfort and courage.

When the time came to make the decision to stop taking her tablets, she was well prepared. She had spent a delightful Sunday with Niall, Hilary and her beloved granddaughters, making the very most of it, knowing that it was her last one with them. She would miss them dreadfully, especially Millie, her favourite. Sadness crept around her weary heart. Millie and she had always been extra close. But her grandchildren were young and, though they would grieve for her, their lives were so fast-paced now that she would become but a faded memory that would bring a smile in years to come. That was the way of it.

Margaret felt a shudder ripple through her body, not an unpleasant sensation, just like a slight shiver. She was tired now, very tired; she'd close her eyes for a while. She'd say a Hail Mary and then let go. '*Hail Mary, full of grace, the Lord is with thee,*' she managed, before a beautiful all-encompassing light of love and peace enveloped her and she slipped gently back to the place that had always been home.

'Aw, Gran H.' Hilary ran to her mother-in-law, who was slumped against the cushions on the sofa, and knelt beside her. She knew instinctively before she searched for a pulse that Margaret was gone. Her body was still warm. If she'd come even fifteen minutes earlier she might have been able to save her, Hilary thought, heartsick, tears spilling down her cheeks as she cradled the frail body of the elderly woman in her arms. She whispered an act of contrition, and laid Margaret back against the cushions, glad that her eyes and mouth were closed and she wouldn't have to force them. She put the soft angora throw over her, knowing it was irrational to think that Margaret would feel cold. She was just about to phone the doctor when the doorbell rang. She could see a man's silhouette against the frosted glass. Bad timing, whoever he was, she thought, trying to compose herself before opening the door. 'Niall!' Hilary exclaimed when she saw her husband standing on the step. 'Oh Niall, I'm so sorry.'

'Oh God, is she gone?' Her husband turned ashen and brushed past her. 'Where?'

'The sitting room,' she said, before bursting into sobs. It broke her heart to see Niall on his knees cradling his mother, whispering endearments into her hair, telling her that he loved her.

'I knew something was up. I didn't want you to find her on your own. I came as quickly as I could.' He raised a tear-streaked face to her.

'We're with her now, Niall. She's not alone, and she looks so peaceful. I'm glad it was in her own home and not in hospital.' Hilary knelt beside him and put her arms around him and they stayed like that awhile, reluctant to give Margaret to the doctors, undertakers and priests, who would do what they had to do to prepare her body for its final journey.

Sue's heart sank and apprehension swamped her when she saw Niall and Hilary in the foyer. The receptionist had told her two people wished to see her. Both had been crying. She could see the puffiness of their eyes and the grief etched on their faces and she knew instantly that her mother had died.

'Come into my office,' she said calmly, determined that she would keep her composure. 'It's Mam, isn't it?' she said, closing the door.

'Yes.' Niall walked over to the window.

'How?'

'A heart attack, her doctor said.' Hilary marvelled at the other woman's self-possession.

'Where?' Sue faltered a little.

'At home. She never answered the phone this morning so I drove over and found her. Niall and I wanted to tell you in person. We didn't want you to find out in a phone call,' Hilary explained.

'Thanks. I appreciate it. We'd better make funeral arrangements.' Sue glanced over at her brother.

'Yes, we wanted to discuss it with you. Although Mam's wishes were very clear – she wanted to be waked at home before being brought to the church—'

'Oh no! I hate all that stuff with the neighbours coming in and peering into the coffin, and looking around the house,' Sue exclaimed. 'Could we not at least wake her in a funeral parlour?'

Hilary looked at Niall feeling it wasn't up to her to respond. She was horrified that even in death Sue couldn't respect her mother's wishes.

'No, Sue, we'll do it the way Mam wanted, if you don't mind,' he said quietly.

'Well then, what's the point of asking me to get involved?

You and Hilary have clearly decided what's to be done,' she said huffily.

'No, we just want what Mam wanted. What Hilary and I want is irrelevant,' Niall said with an edge to his voice.

'Well let me know where I've to be and when,' Sue said frostily.

'The doctor has said there's no need for a post mortem. She says the steroids Mrs H was on affected the warfarin, and weakened your mother's heart even more, so she can sign the death certificate. The undertaker said she could be with us this evening. Niall and I and the girls will stay the night with her. The removal will be tomorrow and the burial on Thursday. It's up to you whatever you wish to do,' Hilary said coolly.

'Very well. I need to speak to my boss and sort things out here. I'll see you at the house tonight,' Sue said without a hint of emotion.

'OK, see you then.' Niall glanced at Hilary, clearly baffled by his sister's reaction.

'I'm very sorry for your loss, Sue. Your mother was a lovely woman.' Hilary offered her condolences. She was shocked that Sue didn't want to engage in any of the arrangements. She had been about to ask her was there any outfit that Sue wanted to suggest for Margaret to be buried in. Hilary felt, as a daughter, that call was Sue's to make, but clearly her sister-in-law had no intention of being involved.

Sue bent her head. 'Thank you,' she murmured. 'And thank you for telling me in person. I'll see you tonight. Bye.' She turned away and punched in a number on the phone.

Dismissed, Niall and Hilary walked out of Sue's office.

'Why am I surprised?' Niall muttered as they waited for the lift in the foyer.

Hilary said nothing. She was not going to diss her sister-in-law to Niall. The sooner Margaret's funeral was over the better and if they could get the poor woman buried without a family row they would be doing very well indeed, she thought, heavy-hearted, stepping into the lift with her husband.

Sue's heart was thumping so loudly she was sure Tina could hear it in reception. Mam was dead. Gone! In an instant. She couldn't quite believe it. The memory of her father's death came roaring back in a tidal wave of memories. Her mother weeping. Telling them that her husband had died at his desk at work, from what turned out to be an aneurysm. The terror of seeing her dad in his coffin, pale and waxy-looking. Feeling his marble coldness. Knowing he was gone from her life, never to speak to, or hug, or laugh with again. Her champion, her mentor, cleaved away from her without even a last farewell. Watching their mother turn to Niall for comfort and advice, sidelining Sue as though she hadn't a thought or contribution to make, had made it all so much more difficult to bear. She was only a woman after all: what would she know about wills and probate and the like?

Bitterness rose in Sue at the memory. Girls should marry and have children. That was the way of it, her mother had told her once, when news of Hilary's first pregnancy had broken. 'You should be thinking of marrying and settling down.' And then, she had finally married, a divorced man, in a small private civil ceremony, 'Because you were too mean to invite your relations and it's not a proper wedding,'

Margaret had accused crossly, annoyed that it hadn't been done 'properly' and she'd have to explain to family and neighbours that Cormac was divorced, and in her eyes, therefore, not free to marry at all.

Time had softened Margaret regarding the lack of a 'proper' wedding or marriage and her mother had pressed her constantly for news of a pregnancy. One day Sue had told her straight out. 'I don't like children and babies. I wouldn't be a good mother so I'm not going to have any.'

'And what does Cormac think of that? Does he not want children with you?' her mother asked, taken aback by her daughter's vehemence on the subject.

'He agrees with me,' Sue retorted. She hadn't told her mother that Cormac already had children from his previous marriage. That would have caused consternation.

'Well the pair of you are well suited so,' Margaret sniffed condescendingly. She had never really taken to Cormac and his dry sarcastic humour and his highbrow ways. Sue knew her mother put on a façade of acceptance of their union but in reality Margaret felt that Sue had let down the family yet again by marrying a divorced man who had failed another woman. Cormac was a freelance proofreader and it was Sue who made the money in their marriage, another no-no for Margaret. 'A man should keep a woman, not the other way round,' she'd jibed once, after they'd had one of their periodic spats. Hilary might think that Margaret was all sweetness and light: Sue was the one that got the sharp end of her tongue more often than not.

And now her mother was dead. Each of them had disappointed the other, and it was too late to resolve their differences. And that she would have to live with, Sue thought forlornly, dreading the thought of the next few days.

In Margaret's small kitchen Millie and Sophie buttered slices of bread and placed ham, tomatoes and lettuce on them. Their grandmother was lying in a coffin in the sitting room, and the neighbours were in paying their respects, then chatting, and having tea and sandwiches in the dining room. Niall and Hilary took turns to sit with Margaret, and later, when everyone was gone, Millie and Sophie would share the intimate vigil with their parents.

'It's just so hard to believe that one minute you're breathing and everything is normal, and the next minute you're dead,' Millie murmured as she cut the sandwiches diagonally in dainty triangles.

'It's scary!' Sophie declared, nibbling at a cut of ham. 'I just can't believe we'll never see Gran again. I feel like my heart is like lead in my chest.' She started to cry.

Millie put her arms around her younger sister. 'It's a horrible feeling. I've been sad before but never like this. I know this is an awful thing to say, but I'm glad I got my Leaving Cert done; I'd never have been able to concentrate if Gran had died before it. I keep trying to think what were her last words to me. And I didn't even know they *were* her last words, whatever they were . . .' She trailed off.

'Me too. I *think* we talked about when Gran was young and she lived near the railway line and they used to walk along it to the dance hall when they were young, and how Granddad used to bring her a bunch of roses every time they went to a dance.'

'It was real old-fashioned then, wasn't it? Like in those old films,' Millie remarked. 'If you walked along a railway line to a dance now you'd be brown bread.'

Sophie giggled. 'Fried! What a sight that would be. Your hair in a frizz and your eyes bulging. Imagine looking like that in your coffin! They'd all be screaming.'

'Stop,' Millie grinned, giving her sister a poke. 'Get buttering – here's another lot,' she sighed as the doorbell rang and more neighbours and relatives came to say their farewells to their grandmother.

'She looks peaceful,' Sue said, gazing down at her mother's serene expression. 'They did a good job at the undertakers'.'

'Yes, they were very kind and helpful,' Hilary said, standing up. 'Here, take the chair and I'll leave you with her for a while so you can be alone. I'll keep everyone out until you're done,' she offered kindly.

'Thanks, I'd appreciate that. I hate having to do small talk. Mam loved you. You know that though,' Sue said matter-of-factly. 'I was a big disappointment to her. You and Niall were the perfect ones. Cormac and I were the failures. He couldn't come by the way, he has a strep throat.'

'I'm sorry to hear that,' Hilary said uncomfortably. Surely with your mother lying in her coffin you would try and make some effort to put bitterness aside, she thought.

'Mam won't mind – she didn't really like him. She pretended to and was civil to him but she didn't. I knew.' Sue sighed. 'I can almost hear her saying, "I wouldn't want him gawking at me in my coffin!"' She caught Hilary's eye.

Hilary laughed, in spite of herself, and Sue gave a small chuckle. 'Isn't that what she'd be saying?'

'She would say something like that all right,' Hilary agreed.

'I know you'll be shocked by this, but I won't be staying long. We didn't have a lot to say to each other in life. I don't really have anything much to say to her in death. That's the way of it,' Sue shrugged. 'You think I'm hard, and maybe I am. But I am what I am and she could never see that and accept it.'

'Sue, you had your relationship with Margaret and I had mine. It wasn't a competition. I know being a daughter can be hard sometimes. I resented things my mother expected of me when I was younger, and things she expects of me now, so don't think I don't understand that. Don't be hard on yourself – it's a difficult enough time as it is. I'll leave you in peace to say your goodbyes, and, when this is over and things have settled, you know where Niall and I are if you need us,' Hilary said generously. 'We *are* family when all is said and done.'

'Thank you,' Sue murmured, touched in spite of herself. Hilary closed the door and Sue was alone with her mother. 'What do you think of that, Mam?' she said wryly. 'You were right all along. Hilary *is* a feckin' saint. No wonder you loved her. I could never in a million years be that good-natured if I tried.'

The poignant strains of 'Nearer My God To Thee' drifted down from the gallery while the mourners sat after communion at Margaret's funeral before the final blessing. Out of the corner of her eye, Hilary saw Sue reach down to her handbag and then she was dabbing a tissue at her eyes, and the sound of an unmistakable sob broke the silence.

Thank God, Hilary thought with relief. *Thank God there's grief because where there's grief there's love and someday she'll realize that.* Beside her, Millie and Sophie cried quietly, and Niall had tears streaming down his face. She squeezed his hand in silent comfort and he squeezed back. Hilary raised her face to the sun pouring through the stained-glass window behind the altar. The rays bathing the coffin in ethereal red and blue and green.

Margaret's fears and worries about her future were all behind her now, and she'd been lucky the way she'd passed. *And* she'd orchestrated it.

Hilary had noticed that all her mother-in-law's tablets for the previous five days had been untouched in the blue receptacles. Hilary always did the weekly tablets with Margaret, popping them into the receptacles for her, because she found it difficult to do with her arthritic fingers. Hilary knew what she was taking and what dosage she was on.

She'd been shocked at the discovery! Could it be said that Margaret had committed suicide? Could not taking tablets that kept you alive be considered in the same way as taking an overdose? Hilary agonized. Should she tell the doctor and Niall? But what difference would it make now, she argued with herself. It was very clear that Margaret had made a decision to stop taking her medication. She'd had a few days to reverse the decision. She hadn't. Death was the required goal. Death was the result. Margaret had chosen her way to go. If Hilary hadn't known anything about her mother-in-law's medication she would have been none the wiser.

Hilary kept the knowledge to herself. Niall did not need to be troubled by it, or indeed Sue. Because troubled they would be. Guilt would come knocking on their door. Margaret would not have wanted that. There was nothing they could do now to change the way of their mother's passing.

You did it your way, Margaret. That's all that matters, and I respect your wishes, she silently saluted her mother-in-law, and it seemed that the beams of light shone even brighter as the music faded and the priest stood up and bowed over the coffin and called them all to prayer.

Sue read the letter a second time.

My Dear Daughter

If you are reading this, then I have gone to my maker and my will is being read. You will know that I have left everything to be equally divided between you and your brother, with a bequest for Hilary and the girls.

Dear Sue, I want you to have my wedding and engagement ring, and the gold bracelet and chain that your father bought for me. I know you loved your father dearly so it is fitting that you should have these.

I know you always felt I favoured your brother and perhaps I did, because I was always content in the knowledge that you were your daddy's pride and joy. The reason Niall was so precious to me was because before I had him I had endured three miscarriages, quite late in my pregnancy each time, and I was broken-hearted and would sink into despair. I would so much have loved a sister for you, close in age. When Niall was born I couldn't believe I had carried him full term. I knew you were jealous of him as a child. I should have been more careful with you and I wasn't. For this I ask your forgiveness and your understanding.

I suppose because I lost three much wanted children I could never understand your desire not to have any. If my lack of understanding has hurt you in any way, my dear daughter, I ask your forgiveness.

Do whatever makes you happy in life and enjoy it to the full (but try and give up the cigarettes). I'm glad that Cormac makes you happy.

Know that, despite the fact that we sometimes had sharp words (we are more alike than you might think), I love you, and am grateful for all you did for me.

Love
Mam XXX

'Ah Mam! If only we'd had this conversation before you died, how different it might have been,' Sue murmured, holding the letter to her heart. She'd never known about her mother's miscarriages, or the grief they had caused Margaret. No wonder Niall had been the apple of her eye when he'd been born. No wonder Margaret felt that children were a blessing, having lost her own much longed for babies.

She slid her mother's wedding ring onto the fourth finger of her right hand and saw how snugly it fitted. She rubbed it gently with her thumb. 'Always with me now, Mam, always with me,' she said, folding the letter carefully and putting it back in the envelope with the other items of jewellery Margaret had left her. She would go to the grave with forget-me-nots, her mother's favourite flower, when all the fuss was over, Sue decided. And there she would try and reconcile the past and make her peace with her mother.

'She went the way she wanted, Niall. She didn't end up in a nursing home or hospital; she went gently in her own home. Take comfort from that,' Hilary said consolingly as she and her husband sat drinking mugs of tea in the quiet of their kitchen that evening.

'I know. And I'm grateful, and Hilary ...' He reached across the table and took her hand. 'I can't thank you enough for your goodness to Mam. I'm really sorry I took advantage of you and your good nature and didn't pull my weight – either with her or in the house.' He choked up, tears glistening in his eyes.

'Well there were times when it was difficult and I was fraught, I won't deny it, Niall, but I loved Margaret like my own mother. We were lucky, she and I, that we got on very well. In-law relationships can be hell sometimes,' Hilary said quietly.

'I know that. And I know that I expected far too much of you regarding Mam ... and everything else.' He cleared his throat. 'Look, I'm sorry that I was an idiot and I know I often made you feel that my job was more important than yours.' He shook his head. 'Mam used to give out to me about it. But I didn't want to hear,' he admitted, shamefaced. 'I'm sorry, Hilary. Can we start over and stop rowing, and be like we used to be?'

'Oh Niall, I'd love that,' Hilary said vehemently. 'I hate all this sniping that goes on between us. I hate resenting you and feeling that you aren't supporting me—'

'I'm sorry, Hil. I never meant you to feel like that.'

'Well you did, Niall. And I turned into a nag and I hated that, and you wouldn't speak to Sue about Margaret, and I was really stressed sometimes.' She didn't hold back.

'I just missed the way things used to be before you set up the company with Jonathan. I missed having you around. Selfish, I guess,' he said sheepishly.

'Yeah, I won't argue with that. But now you've admitted it, and you're turning over a new leaf, we'll put it behind us and you can wait on me hand and foot,' Hilary joked, reminding herself that Niall had buried his mother only hours ago and that it wasn't really the time to have a go at him.

'I'll bring you tea in bed in the morning,' he smiled at her. 'And I just want you to know that I think you've done a fantastic job of the company. You should be really proud.'

'Thanks, I am, actually, and I've enjoyed it very much.' She smiled back at him. 'But the truth is, I know many women working outside the home are pulled from every angle, and depleted most of the time. I know I got roped in to doing more projects, but look, we've bought the apartment on the seafront for the girls—'

'And spent a fortune on it. Imagine, it cost five times as much as this house did when we bought it,' he interjected, grimacing.

'I know but at least they have a place because they'll never be able to afford to get on the property ladder with the prices here.' Hilary sighed. 'So now that we have it rented to pay the mortgage, I really am going to cut back at work.'

'You don't have to. I'll muck in a lot more,' Niall said earnestly. 'Honestly.'

'I *want* to. Life's too short to be killing myself trying to juggle all the balls in the air. I want to enjoy my life, my family ... my marriage.' She squeezed his hand, so relieved that they were finally discussing their problems.

'I love you,' Niall said. 'Very much,' he added, entwining his fingers with hers.

'I love you, too,' she echoed.

At the kitchen table, in the soft opaque light of the setting sun, they smiled at each other over their mugs of tea, comforted by their rapprochement.

PART THREE

2008
BUST

CHAPTER THIRTY-TWO

September 2008

He should have sold those bloody shares when the Koreans had shown interest in buying the bank. The shares went up 5 per cent. He would have taken a massive hit certainly, but not the decimation he was facing now. Des felt himself break out in a cold sweat, as Colette lay asleep beside him blissfully unaware of what was coming down the tracks. The Dow nearly 300 down, S&P down 500 – the figures rolled around in his head, his thoughts like a washing machine on spin. Geithner and Bush were letting Lehman Brothers slide down the tubes. Clinton's massive surplus was only a memory. The current deficit – in the trillions – meant the good times were well and truly over and all that he had worked so hard for was turning to dust.

He should have known it was time to get out when Lehman Brothers closed its sub-prime lender the previous year. Should have known it, he silently upbraided himself. But still, it seemed unthinkable that a bank that size would be allowed to fail. Commentators were talking about the Great Depression. Joe Kennedy had quit the stock market and kept his wealth when a shoeshine boy had given him stock tips. Des should have known the jig was up when their own housekeeper talked about her Fidelity blue-chip fund, and her Citicorp, IBM and US Steel portfolio. Only the ones who had learned the lessons from history would make it, not nouveau riche players like him.

He should have flogged the Florida properties, and his stock, instead of waiting for a last rally. For all his financial knowledge he was no better than a race punter, he thought, disgusted with himself. And wouldn't old man O'Mahony crow when he found out. Frank would rub his nose in it. Time had not endeared his father-in-law to him, and vice versa, and now he'd have to listen to his bullshit about 'wise investment'.

Des twisted and turned in the bed, desperate for sleep. He needed his wits about him more now than ever. Decisions had to be made that would salvage something and keep the show on the road.

'Turn off that Joe Duffy fella – he's going to cause a panic about the banks. There'll be a run on them the way he's going on,' Hilary urged Jonathan as they sped back to Dublin along the M1 after doing a final inspection on a hotel they had revamped in Newry.

'I think we're up shit creek,' Jonathan said, switching the stations over to Lyric, filling the car with the soaring tones of Cecilia Bartoli.

'But the regulator has said the banks are fine. The rating agencies gave Anglo Irish A ratings, so what's going on?' Hilary proffered a Murray Mint.

'That regulator guy wouldn't inspire me with confidence.

I don't think he's able for the job at all, and Moody's and S&P and the rest of them are only a shower of chancers,' Jonathan scoffed. 'Thank God I sold the apartment last year! They're talking about soft landings for the economy and the property market. Ha! We're for it, there's not going to be anything soft about it, and you just watch out, all the rats are going to desert the sinking ship. And we won't be doing too many spa hotels any more, either,' he added glumly. 'There are too many new hotels out there as it is for an economy that's on the slide.'

'Yeah, I think you're right. Business had certainly tailed off in the last year,' sighed Hilary. 'You did well to sell up when you did. We're going to take a hit on the apartment we bought on the seafront in Clontarf. We just wanted to make sure to have somewhere for the girls in years to come. I don't think they're ever going to be able to afford to get on the property ladder.'

'At least we own our own homes,' Jonathan comforted her. 'We can chop firewood and huddle around our log-burning stoves if we can't afford to pay the heating bills.' He grinned at her. 'I've got a hotplate on mine too. I can cook a stew on it if needs must, so we won't starve!'

'It's not funny, Jonathan! We've a hell of a lot of money in bank shares, especially in Anglo. They were our pensions. We put them in what we thought was the safest possible place. We didn't friggin' gamble on high-risk stuff. Do you think we should stop at a bank link and withdraw some cash in case there *is* a run on the banks? Remember that bank in England that went belly-up a while back?'

'OK, we can go to one when we hit Dundalk. You can

only withdraw six hundred euros in a day though,' he pointed out.

'I think I'll transfer a couple of thousand to the girls' Post Office or Credit Union accounts when I get home. Just to be sure they have money, in case the banks fail,' Hilary fretted. The *Liveline* programme about an imminent banking crisis was scaring her. Millie was working as a chartered accountant in Manchester and Sophie was teaching French and English at the DIT school of languages in Kevin Street, and sharing a house in Portobello. They were happy and independent and she couldn't wish for more for her daughters. Nevertheless if things were getting rough she wanted to make sure they had money at their back.

'Imagine, you have a twenty-six-year-old and a twenty-three-year-old,' Jonathan remarked, switching to cruise control as they drove south across the border, and the standard of the road improved considerably.

'No need to remind me.' Hilary threw her eyes up to heaven. 'Imagine, I'm over fifty! I'm well and truly middle-aged and I have the grey hairs to prove it, and so have you!'

'Well you disguise them pretty well. You look good for an ould wan, deah!' Jonathan grinned over at her. 'That ash-blonde colour suits you.'

'I had to do something, deah! I was only getting six weeks out of a colour, and my roots were as grey as a badger,' she moaned.

'I know, I've more grey than blond. I'll have to start using Grecian 2000.' Jonathan made a face.

'You don't look bad for an ould fella! Even if you have a touch of a jowl.'

'I know, it's horrific. My chiselled good looks are gone! I may have to go under the knife!' Jonathan grimaced, patting the loose flesh under his jawline. 'Where did those years go?'

'It's a blur! One minute I had teenagers, then I had college students, and now I have grown-up daughters. I'm so glad I took time out after Margaret passed away. I was able to spend time and do things with the girls and with my parents, before Dad died.'

'Yeah, that was a good call. You were much happier, much more relaxed. You did the right thing.'

'And what was all that hard work for anyway? So Bertie, McCreevy and that shower in Fianna Fáil could bankrupt us,' Hilary said bitterly. 'I could have spent my time at home with my kids when they were in primary school and still be as well off. And what sort of a future are they going to have, Jonathan? I remember the recession in the eighties; I think what's ahead of us is going to be far tougher.'

'If I promise to stop and treat you to a cream cake and coffee in Dundalk will you stop talking like that? You're depressing me,' Jonathan groaned.

'Sorry! Sorry!' Hilary apologized. 'Cream cake might just do the job.'

The tinny sounds of 'Goldfinger' cut off Cecilia's aria and Jonathan saw Nancy's name flash up on his Bluetooth. 'Hello, Mam,' he said cheerfully.

'Jonathan, I'm listening to Joe Duffy and I think you should take your money out of the bank. I'm getting Rachel to bring me to withdraw my money this very minute. I'm going to put it in the Post Office and if I were you I'd buy some gold – it always increases in value when times are bad.'

'That's good thinking, Mam. Hilary and I are here in the car heading for Dundalk, so we're going to withdraw some cash ourselves.'

'Honest to God, when you think of that other clown up in the Dáil before he was given the heave-ho, spending a fortune of *our* money on his make-up, preening and pontificating and telling us there was nothing to worry about in the economy, when the dogs in the street knew that the property boom wasn't sustainable. I *never* voted for that crowd, and the people who did only have themselves to blame for getting us into this mess. And as for that Cork fella on the *Late Late*, with his brownnosing and lick-arsing. I'm telling you, he swung that election, Jonathan, and he got his payback for it with a cushy job in the Senate and his fine fat salary and pension. So it's as much his fault as anyone's but no one has anything to say about *that!*' Nancy vented her spleen against the individuals who had steered the country so disastrously down the tubes. Jonathan glanced over at Hilary and shook his head. When Nancy got going there was no stopping her. She was still as sharp as a tack, still living an independent life, and had plenty to say about everything.

'Hello, Hilary, how are you?' Nancy enquired, having got her displeasure off her chest.

'I'm well thanks, Mrs Harpur. Good to hear you in fine fettle.'

'Well wouldn't that lot of goms drive you to drink, if you were so inclined,' Nancy retorted. 'How is your mother keeping? It's hard on her, I'm sure, since your daddy passed away. It takes a long time to get over it.'

'I know. Hard to believe it's five years now. But she's not too bad. Like yourself, she keeps herself busy,' Hilary said. 'Dad's passing was a blessing really. She wasn't able to look after him, even with our help, and he would have ended up in a nursing home and he would have hated that.'

'Yes, God can be merciful sometimes and death can be a happy release. Well give her my best wishes, pet, and, Jonathan, drive carefully. No speeding now and invest in some gold,' Nancy cautioned.

'Yes, Mammy,' Jonathan said meekly, and Nancy laughed.

'God bless, son, take care of yourself. Here's Rachel so I must be off. I'll see you on Saturday. I'll make a biscuit cake for you.'

'Can't wait. Love you, Mam.'

'And I love you too, son. Bye, Hilary.'

'Bye, Mrs H.'

'She's great, isn't she?' Hilary said when the phone went dead and Cecilia's golden tones rang out again. 'So vibrant still, despite her age. And so on the ball! She's right about buying gold. That generation is a hardy lot. We'll be lucky to do as well as them when we get to their age.'

'I know. I *feel* their feckin' age,' Jonathan retorted, indicating to take the slip road off the motorway to get to the nearest bank and then to bring Hilary for the cream cake and coffee he'd promised her as soon as they reached Dundalk.

Shaun Grant shook hands with his solicitor. 'Thank you, Edward. Glad we've got everything sorted. Best for everyone all round.'

'Indeed,' Edward Delahunty said suavely. 'Good luck, Shaun, Gina, safe journey.'

'Thank you, Edward, for all your help and advice,' Gina said graciously. She looked tired and strained, but as elegant as ever in a beautifully cut raspberry-pink designer suit and high-heeled Louboutins.

He walked his high-profile clients to the door of his Morehampton Road mansion. He had chosen to see them at home, discreetly, rather than at his Merrion Square office. The papers were doing all kinds of articles on property developers and high-profile businessmen. The Grants were on their hit list. But now they'd have to follow them to the States. The Grants had a private jet waiting for them at Dublin Airport and they were leaving the country. Their mansion with its designer spa, heli pad and cinema was up for sale. Edward gave a polite wave as he watched them walk down the marble steps to their navy Merc. Shaun Grant to all intents and purposes would soon be a bankrupt, golf-playing OAP, with a very rich wife and a family of sons and daughters who were nicely provided for with a substantial trust fund. All eventually paid for by the ordinary folk who had done nothing wrong but who would be ground down with even more taxes to pay for the reckless, immoral gambles the Grants and their ilk had ruined the country with. It fascinated him how so many of them felt that a 'personal guarantee' didn't apply to them the way it did to the hoi polloi who defaulted on their bank loans and mortgages. It truly was one law for the rich and another for the poor.

And he, Edward Delahunty, had enabled many of his

clients – for a very fat paycheque, it had to be said – to get away with it. He was as culpable as they were, at one level, he reflected, going back into his impressive book-lined library and pouring himself a double measure of whisky.

'Sell everything except the commodities. We can buy again when they're on the floor. Buy gold and water and keep me updated,' Des ordered his stockbroker, marching up and down the kitchen.

Colette felt tentacles of fear coil themselves around her gut. She had never seen her husband so agitated. She poured herself a cup of coffee waiting for him to hang up. 'How bad is it?' she asked as he flipped his cell closed.

'Let's say we won't be hosting our Christmas bash in Aspen this year,' he said grimly. 'Get a rental agency on the phone and rent it out. It's going to have to pay its way. We're going to London for Christmas. That will get us out of entertaining or being entertained. We'll have to offload the Florida properties. We'll sell them through London. We shouldn't take too much of a hit on them.'

'How has it come to this?' Colette was aghast.

'Scrapping the net capital rule, George W and his crony Henry Paulson, deregulation, capitalism, greed. Take your pick.' Des gulped his coffee, and gave her a peck on the cheek. 'It's gonna be a late one. I'll see ya.'

'OK,' she said. 'I'm meeting Jazzy for lunch at the Met and then I've a meeting with the directors of Dickon and Austen's UK, and dinner later with them tonight.'

'Tell Jazzy she might have to sublet and move back home if things don't improve,' her husband said gloomily, grabbing his briefcase and taking one last swig of coffee before striding out to the elevator.

Surely it wouldn't come to that, Colette thought, horrified. Jazzy would hate to move back home. She was having the time of her life in her small, one-bed apartment in Turtle Bay, between Lexington and Third.

She was doing a three-day-a-week digital internship in a big advertising company specializing in billboard and digital advertising and she was loving it, having majored in advertising and marketing at Cornell. She had a part-time job developing social networking sites for a quirky, independent publishing group, and she was dating a Boston lawyer. Jazzy's life was sweet right now. Colette intended to keep it like that. If needs must she would work an extra day instead of the two days a week she worked at the small, exclusive fine art gallery she had set up for Dickon and Austen's in New York five years ago.

Des was a terrible worrier and always had been. One of these days she would spend an afternoon with their wealth manager and find out exactly what assets they had. At least she had the Holland Park property at her back, and whatever her parents left her when they shuffled off their mortal coil, and Jazzy would be a very well-off young lady indeed so she wasn't going to get *too* perturbed, Colette decided, strolling into her walk-in closet to select her outfits for lunch, business meetings and dinner.

Chapter Thirty-Three

'Jonathan, they're beautiful. You always bring down such lovely pots of flowers for the grave,' Nancy approved when he showed her the vibrant tub of autumn heather, and the yellow, red and purple chrysanthemums that filled the second one. 'Will we go and put them on the grave after you've had a cup of tea?' she asked eagerly.

'If you'd like to,' Jonathan agreed.

'I would. Then they'd be on it for Sunday,' his mother declared.

The biscuit cake was scrumptious and he was on his second slice when the phone rang. 'I'll get it. Stay where you are,' Nancy instructed. Jonathan watched her walk to the phone on the kitchen wall, noting that she was a lot slower and stiffer than she used to be. He hated seeing his mam ageing. He knew they were so lucky to have had her with them for so long and for her to be in relative good health, but as she often said to him, only half joking, 'I'm in the departure lounge now. I've had a good innings, so when my flight takes off, don't you be wailing and bawling. There'll be no need for it.'

'Well do you know, I clean forgot, Kitty,' he heard her

exclaim. 'I'll get Jonathan to run me up. He's just arrived. I'll see you soon.

'Jonathan! My memory's gone to the divil. I was so busy getting ready for your arrival I forgot I'd told Kitty Welsh that I'd do an hour's vigil in the church. They're holding the Forty Hours Adoration in St Anthony's. Will you drop me over as soon as I get myself ready? I'm on the half twelve to half one shift.'

'Of course I will. I can bring the pots over to the grave and give the headstone a clean while you're praying,' he said obligingly.

'Grand. I'll go and put on my face then.' She smiled at him, and he thought how cool she was to still insist on putting on her Max Factor powder and lipstick before going anywhere.

The small country church was sombrely shadowy, illuminated only by banks of glowing, flickering candles burning in the shrines in front of the altar and at the sides. A couple of people knelt beside the old-fashioned box waiting for confession, and a few elderly parishioners knelt in the front pew reciting the Rosary. Jonathan escorted Nancy up the aisle and heard her give a little gasp as she genuflected. Her arthritis was troubling her but she wouldn't give in to it. She was a real trouper, he thought proudly as she moved along the seat to join the others, some of whom he recognized.

'Hello, Jonathan,' came the murmured greetings and he saluted the ones he knew before they resumed the prayers that Nancy's arrival had interrupted.

He sat for a while letting the peace of his surroundings envelop him. He had always liked the Forty Hours as a child. The altar would be beautifully dressed, with splendid arrangements of flowers, and the candelabra that were only used for special ceremonies ablaze with long tapers, spilling illumination on the ornate golden monstrance, which had always reminded him of a rising sun.

The faint scent of incense mixed with candlewax wafted down from the altar and Jonathan inhaled it, remembering how much he had enjoyed being an altar boy, especially if he was given the responsibility of swinging the thurible. The first time he had been on censing duty Father Deasy had had to admonish him for swinging the gleaming brass censer too enthusiastically, a voluminous cloud of charcoal smoke and incense enveloping them on the altar.

He smiled at the recollection. Today would have been a day for three double swings, if memory served, as it was a day of public veneration, but there were no more young altar servers to swing thuribles. All the clerical child-abuse scandals had put paid to that.

An elderly priest made his way to the sacristy. Jonathan didn't recognize him. He must have been a visiting priest hearing confessions. He wore a cassock. It was a long time since he'd seen a priest in a cassock. Jonathan had rather fancied himself in his own one. He loved the swish of it around his ankles. Always the little queen, he smiled, remembering how much he'd loved his robes.

He genuflected and made his way out to the blustery September sunshine and walked over to where he'd parked. He'd brought a bucket, some cloths, a scrubbing brush and Flash spray and he shoved them all in the bucket, hung it on his arm and lifted out the two flowerpots from the boot.

'Lazy man's load,' Nancy would have scolded if she'd seen him manoeuvring through the red swing gates that led to a side path in the graveyard. His father's plot was neat and well tended as always. His sisters took Nancy to visit every week. Even after all these years she still took solace from the time she spent at her husband's grave.

The tubs of pansies and geraniums already there were still blooming and fresh-looking, if in need of watering, so he laid his two pots beside them. 'There you go, Dad,' he said cheerfully, taking out his cleaning spray and squirting some over the marble headstone. He cleaned and polished, enjoying the sound of birdsong, and the somnolent buzzing of a fat stripy bumblebee that feasted on the blooms that adorned his father's grave. He took the bucket and walked down to the tap at the side of the big iron gates and filled it. He'd give his own pots a drenching too. He noticed the priest who had been hearing confessions walking slowly along the pathway reading his breviary. He must be praying his office, he mused, remembering how Father Deasy also used to walk around the graveyard to say his daily prayers. He used to say that the dead always gave him peace while the living pestered him.

Careful not to spill the water, Jonathan walked back towards the grave and he couldn't help noticing how neglected Gus Higgins's plot was. He paused and shifted the bucket of water to his left hand. His right one ached from where he had hit one of his knuckles with a hammer when upholstering a chair for Orla, his old friend and former flatmate.

There were weeds thrusting up through the cracked

cement of the unkempt plot. It reminded Jonathan of that dreadful cracked weedy garden path he'd walked along, many times, to the Higginses' front door.

'Hope you're screaming in hell,' he muttered, thinking that if Hannah heard him she would despair of his progress towards forgiveness. That wasn't really fair! *Sorry, Hannah,* he silently apologized. His counsellor never despaired of him or judged him.

'Nice to see the younger generation honouring the dead.' The priest came abreast of him and lowered his breviary.

'Not that young, unfortunately,' sighed Jonathan. 'And I'm certainly not honouring this creep,' he added a touch bitterly.

'Oh dear! And why would you malign the dead so?' The priest raised a bushy eyebrow, staring at Jonathan disapprovingly.

'Because he was very malign to me, actually, if you must know,' Jonathan retorted rudely, highly annoyed at the unexpected interrogation.

'How so?' came the next imperious question.

'He abused me when I was a child.' Jonathan glowered at the cleric.

'Tsk, tsk,' the old man tutted, shaking his head. 'I'm sorry to hear that.'

'Oh, OK,' Jonathan replied, slightly mollified.

'And have you spoken to your confessor? I'm sure you have after all this time.' The priest eyed him keenly.

'Why would I do that?' Jonathan asked, mystified.

'For forgiveness, my son.'

'Forgiveness for whom? Surely it was up to Higgins to speak to his confessor?'

'Indeed, indeed,' the old man nodded earnestly. 'And let us pray that he did seek forgiveness and absolution, but you too must be absolved.'

'Of what?' Jonathan began to wonder if the elderly priest was the full shilling.

'Haven't you asked what part you played in this heinous sin?'

The world seemed to stop, the sounds of nature vanished. All Jonathan could hear was the roaring of his own heart in his ears as the words echoed in his head.

Haven't you asked what part you played in this heinous sin?
HAVEN'T YOU ASKED WHAT PART YOU PLAYED IN THIS HEINOUS SIN?

A powerful anger surged through Jonathan, a rage so ferocious he had to restrain himself from grabbing the other man by the throat and throttling him. 'I was a child,' he shouted. 'A CHILD! What sort of a human being are you? You disgrace the name of Christ. That man' – he pointed a shaking finger at his former neighbour's grave – 'he was an adult and I was a child and he abused me. How can you possibly think I had a part to play in that?'

'Calm down, my son,' the priest said hastily, a glimmer of apprehension in his eyes as he stepped back from Jonathan's towering rage.

'I am not your son, you excuse for a Christian. You apologize to *me*, this minute, or I will drag you through the courts for slander.'

The priest shook his head. 'I never understand why they get so angry,' he said almost as though he was talking to himself. 'It's what my own confessor said to me.'

'A priest said this to *you*?' Jonathan demanded. 'Why? Were you abused?'

It seemed as though the old man sagged, his air of authority crumbling. 'Yes. A long time ago,' he muttered.

'What age were you? Not that that makes any difference: abuse is abuse.' Jonathan spoke more gently this time.

'I was seven or thereabouts. My uncle ...' He spoke so low Jonathan could hardly hear him.

'And a priest said that to you.'

'Yes.' His tired, watery old eyes were sad as he looked up at Jonathan.

'But you were a *child*! Don't you understand that? An innocent child!' Jonathan exclaimed. 'You probably didn't even understand what was happening.'

The priest bowed his head, his shoulders hunched. 'It was a long time ago,' he mumbled. 'I should go. I'm sorry if I offended you.' He turned to walk away.

'No! Wait, Father! Have you ever spoken to a counsellor?' Jonathan's anger evaporated.

'No, we didn't have them in our day. That's all newfangled stuff. We just went to confession,' the priest said heavily.

'I just need to know one thing,' Jonathan said grimly.

'And what's that?'

'Did you ever abuse a child?'

'I did not! I would not, *ever*!' the priest said, affronted.

'You see how horrified you were when I asked you that? If you had a seven-year-old boy here and you molested or raped him would you think it was his fault?' Jonathan probed.

The priest looked stunned as he stared back at Jonathan.
'Well?' Jonathan pushed.

He shook his head. 'No, no, of course not.'

'Well then, how can you ask that question of anyone who has been abused?'

The old man's face creased and he gave a strangled sob. 'My mother said I was a dirty little liar when I told her, after two years, of his filthy carry-on.' He wept brokenly. 'She told me to go straight to confession. And that's what the priest asked me. I have been in hell ever since. I became a priest to try and make reparation and absolve myself of my sins.'

'That's terrible!' Tears came to Jonathan's eyes as he put his arms around the distraught old man and held him gently while he cried great gasping, heaving sobs, as years of repressed feelings were released in a torrent of grief.

'I apologize for losing control of my emotions,' he said wheezily, his nose running and tears still blinding him as he fumbled in his soutane pocket for a handkerchief.

'That's quite all right. You've nothing to apologize for. I've done that many times myself,' Jonathan said kindly. 'I'm Jonathan Harpur.' He held out his hand.

'Derek McDaid,' the priest said shakily.

'Father McDaid, would you go and see a wonderful person, who would say our meeting wasn't an accident or coincidence. She would say we were meant to meet. You need to talk about what happened to you.'

'Ah sure I've lived this long without talking about it. I have the good Lord to talk to,' he said wearily.

'You carry a very heavy burden. And if you spoke to my

counsellor you might be able to help other priests of your generation who suffered abuse and haven't been able to talk about it. Or priests like you, who have been made to feel guilty because of questions such as the one you were asked. Judgements like that can do such damage. As you *have* been damaged,' he reminded him.

'That's true, I suppose,' the priest said slowly.

'The Lord works in strange ways.' Jonathan gave a tentative smile.

'I can't argue with that,' Father McDaid agreed, taking several deep breaths.

'Let me go to the car and get a pen and paper and I will give you Hannah's phone number and address,' Jonathan offered.

'I'm not promising anything now,' the old man said crabbily.

'That's all right. If you are meant to go you will go,' Jonathan assured him. 'And do it for yourself, not for anyone else.'

What a weird day, Jonathan thought, somewhat shaken, rooting in his dashboard for a pen and paper to write down his counsellor's contact details. Hannah would surely say something like 'When the pupil is ready the teacher will come' about his encounter with the tormented priest. 'I've put my phone number on this page as well in case you'd ever like to get in contact or talk about what happened to you,' Jonathan said helpfully, handing him the page.

'Very kind of you,' Father McDaid said gruffly, and Jonathan could see that he was now highly embarrassed. He picked up his bucket of water.

'I'll leave you in peace to say your Office,' he said matter-of-factly.

'Oh! You know about the Office. Not many do now.' Father McDaid looked surprised.

'I was an altar boy once. Take care of yourself, Father.'

'Thank you ... and eh ... again my apologies for upsetting you.'

'And if I upset you, I too apologize,' Jonathan said gravely.

'Good afternoon, my son.' The priest gave a slight bow and resumed his walk along the pathway, shoulders bowed. Jonathan watched as he walked out of the iron gates and down the narrow country road. A life ruined by abuse and religion, and a mother whose cruelty was as abusive in the damage it caused as was his uncle's, Jonathan reflected, walking back to water the flowerpots on his father's grave.

'Jonathan,' he heard Nancy call him as she made her way through the swing gate. His heart lifted at the sight of her tip-tapping her way along the stone-edged path with her elegant silver-topped walking stick.

'Did I tell you today that you are the best mother in the whole wide world?' He hugged her.

'You didn't,' said Nancy spiritedly. ' You'd better tell me.'

'Well you are,' he said. 'Not only in the world, but in the entire universe.'

'That's more like it,' Nancy said smugly, patting her husband's headstone.

'Yes, Mother!' Jonathan grinned.

'And of course you know you're the best son.'

'I know that but you can tell me again,' Jonathan teased.

A Time for Friends

And their laughter was an added blessing as the sun shone on Rosslara's tranquil graveyard.

'I wonder will he come to you, Hannah? Was that the reason I met him in the graveyard at Gus Higgins's grave?' Jonathan remarked to his counsellor the next time he had an appointment with her.

'He hasn't made contact yet. But that's neither here nor there. It's all about Divine Timing, isn't it?' Hannah lit a candle before they began their session.

'It was the weirdest thing, though. Right at that grave, of all the graves in the graveyard. It still gives me the shivers thinking about it.' Jonathan shook his head.

'Perhaps Gus was trying to make amends from beyond the vale of forgetting,' Hannah suggested with a smile.

'Hannah, once I would have argued with you,' Jonathan said sombrely, 'but the longer I live, and the more I see the synchronicities you talk about, the more I believe there is a much bigger picture to our lives that we just cannot see or fathom. But the next time I come back, *if* I come back, I'm taking a much easier path, I can tell you.'

'And I'm coming back as Hugh Jackman's wife,' Hannah said with a wicked glint in her vivid blue eyes, chuckling at Jonathan's hearty guffaws.

465

CHAPTER THIRTY-FOUR

December 2008

'It has been alleged that Madoff was operating a giant Ponzi scheme, which may prove to be one of the largest financial frauds in US history.' Des listened in dismay to the reporter who was covering the shocking arrest of the prominent financier he had been in awe off. He switched off the TV and put his head in his hands. He had initially invested two hundred grand with Madoff, two years previously, and the returns had been so good he'd invested half the money made from the sale of the Florida properties. Colette thought he'd invested it all in commodities. She would go freaking bananas if she knew what he'd done. And so would his bank manager.

He rubbed his hand over his jaw. He needed to take drastic measures to cover his losses. If he could pull it off they'd ride out the storm. Des picked up the phone on his desk. 'Get me Ivan Baransky in Chase, in the Plaza,' he instructed his secretary, taken aback that his palms were actually damp with perspiration and his heart was hammering in his chest.

Two hours later, his secretary glided into his office with a sealed white padded envelope. 'Mr Baransky had this couriered over for you,' she said, laying it on the desk.

'Thank you, Lauren. Just give me fifteen with no calls please,' he said crisply, opening the envelope.

'Sure.' She flashed a gleaming smile and left him to his document.

Twenty minutes later he dialled Colette's cell phone. 'Babes, any chance you could drop by? I need your signature on a document to transfer some shares to another portfolio.'

'Aww, Des, I'm going Upstate to view Clara Alton Graham's art collection. She's having to sell. You know her husband committed suicide after Lehman Brothers?' Colette protested.

'It won't take five minutes, a quick detour, and then you can take the George Washington at Exit 14. I'll send a car for you so you won't have to drive if you like,' he wheedled.

'Tsk! OK then. That sounds good, and if we get the collection I'll bring you to dinner in Boulud's. I hear that new executive chef Kaysen is pretty hot,' Colette promised, thrilled that she didn't have to drive the six-hour round trip to Saratoga Springs. Before the downturn she wouldn't have hesitated to take a Town Car and put it on expenses, but times had changed and the budget for running the New York office was a lot tighter. The financial director in Dickon and Austen's went through her expense sheet with a fine toothcomb these days.

'Deal,' Des agreed, and she knew he was smiling.

Colette dressed discreetly for her meeting with Clara. A Chanel suit, a single strand of pearls and low-heeled pumps. Clara was a small, birdlike woman; she didn't want to tower over her. The Alton Grahams were old school and old money. Highly placed on the social register. But like many of their kind, they had fallen on hard times. Dickon and Austen's would be the perfect home for Clara's very valuable collection and Colette would get an excellent commission if she secured it for the gallery.

Three quarters of an hour later she strolled into Des's twenty-eighth-floor corner office. He was on the phone and waved at her as she sank onto the soft cream Argentinian-leather sofa by the window. He cut short his call and picked a document from his desk.

'Hi, sweetie, you're a doll for coming down.' He kissed her and sat down beside her and flipped the pages over until he came to the signature page. 'There you go. I've signed already,' he said, uncapping his pen and handing it to her.

'Des, I don't have time to go through this now,' she said in dismay, glancing at her watch. 'I thought it was just a single sheet. I'll be late if I stay to go through it. I'll take it with me and give it to you tonight.' She stood up.

'There's nothing in it except legalese,' he said exasperatedly.

'Des, you know I read things before I sign them. If my name is going on a document I want to know what it is I'm signing,' Colette said firmly.

'I'm telling you, there's nothing to be concerned about. I've been through it already,' he assured her.

'I'll read it in the car. Now I have to go – the traffic is dreadful,' she said, handing his pen back.

'Ah leave it there. I'll bring it home with me,' he scowled.

'OK, wish me luck,' Colette picked up her Vuitton clutch

and blew him a kiss, trying to hide her annoyance that she had wasted time when her schedule was so tight. Still, she'd got a Town Car because of her detour.

'Good luck,' Des muttered and she knew he was annoyed but Colette ignored his displeasure. She was damned if she was going to sign papers without reading them. He was too careless and impulsive sometimes. He'd sign anything their broker put in front of them. She stepped into the elevator, anxious to be on her way. It would never do to be late for her appointment. That would not reflect well on the company she represented, or on herself. She shivered on the sidewalk as she waited for her driver to pick her up. It had turned bitterly cold and she tucked her cashmere wrap tighter around her throat, hoping that it wouldn't snow.

The black sedan purred to a halt and the driver got out and opened the car door for her. Colette sat in the back seat and stretched her legs. There was a selection of magazines in the pocket and she chose *Vogue* and began to flick through the pages, extremely thankful that she didn't have to drive. It began to sleet, and she watched people on the sidewalks unfurl their brollies. Colette settled back for her journey, glad she was in a snug cocoon as her driver headed northwest on Pine Street towards Broadway and Exit 14.

'Damn, damn, damn,' muttered Des, jaw clenched as he shoved the unsigned document back into the envelope and shoved it into his briefcase. Today was turning out to be a real bummer. He'd hoped against hope that Colette would just sign on the dotted line. He should have known better. He hadn't pushed the issue. He didn't want her to think it was anything other than a run-of-the-mill transaction. If she asked him about it later he'd just tell her that the time limit had expired for the share offer and a good opportunity had been missed.

He picked up his cell and scrolled down until he got the number he was looking for. He dialled it and groaned when it went straight to voicemail. 'I have a window between five and seven, let me know ASAP if it suits,' he said briskly and hung up. Sleeting rain battered the window, and he had a sudden memory of his boyhood bedroom and the cosy window seat overlooking a copse of bare-branched trees, dark rolling clouds shrouding the countryside, and how warm and comfy he was as the rain pelted against the panes and he read his library book – a seafaring adventure by Patrick O'Brien – and munched on a Trigger Bar and a packet of crisps. How he would love to be in that little nook right now and far, far away from the steel-and-glass building that suddenly seemed like a prison.

Colette yawned as the elevator doors slid open into her foyer. The housekeeper had switched on some lamps, but Des wasn't home yet. His keys weren't in the Lalique bowl on the fine Italian demilune console table that graced their foyer. Clara Alton Graham had some very impressive pieces too, Colette mused, dropping her keys into the bowl. That collection of Meissen bird figures was worth at least two hundred K. When the Widow Alton Graham liquidated her assets she certainly wouldn't be on the breadline or anything like it, although she might think she was pretty close to it, having lost millions in the last year.

Colette kicked off her shoes and padded into the kitchen and peered into the fridge. Encarna, their housekeeper, had left a smoked salmon mousse starter, and a casserole of Mexican chicken stew and quinoa, and a side of creamy mash for Des, who hated health foods with a passion. A chilled Sancerre would be just what the doctor ordered, Colette decided, hurrying down to the bedroom to change into a luxuriously soft, satin-trimmed towelling robe. She flicked on the TV while she took off her suit, pausing momentarily to watch the Madoff arrest, shocked at the extent of investor losses, which commentators were putting in the billions. What could those people expect? If it sounded too good to be true then it WAS too good to be true. And Madoff's returns were uncommon.

Everyone in their circle was on edge with all the financial upheaval that was going on and no wonder, Colette mused, placing her pearls in their satin-lined box. She wondered had the time come for her and Des to move back to London. Life here was becoming a grind. Des was working harder than ever but for less return. She was working two days a week in the gallery. Dickon and Austen's was, after a slow year, starting to pick up the pace again because people like Clara Alton Graham were selling off family heirlooms and investment pieces to cover debts. And investors and specu-lators were hovering like vultures. But the New York pace of life was wearing her down. London and its grace and elegance and more temperate climate seemed very appeal-ing lately. It would actually be a pleasure to spend Christmas there and not have the exhaustion of the social networking she had to do here. Jazzy would probably want to stay in New York and that was fine. She was leading her own life now, caught up in her own social whirl, and there were times Colette and Des didn't see her for a couple of weeks, and that was as it should be for a young woman of her age.

She had just finished her meal and was lounging in front of the log fire in the den when her cell rang. Des's number flashed up. 'Hi,' she said cheerily, managing to suppress a yawn. 'What time will you be home? Encarna has one of your favourites for dinner. Don't leave it too late or it will lie heavy on your stomach.'

'I'm sorry!' said a female voice with a faint Southern twang. 'I'm er . . . a friend of your husband's. He's been taken to Lennox Hill with a suspected heart attack—'

'*What*? When? Was he at work? Is he OK?' Colette shot up off the sofa, relieved that she'd only had a glass and a half of wine and still had her wits about her.

'Look, it's like this, Des was with me. He was under a lot of stress about losing a packet with Madoff. We were in bed. He told me he was going to stop paying the rent on the apartment I live in. We had words and then he got red in the face and started sweating and gasping. He said he had a pain in his arm and chest, so I called an ambulance. I'll drop his briefcase, phone, overcoat and clothes off at your building. Cheers.' The phone went dead.

Colette stared at it, dazed. Who was that woman? And what was she saying about Des losing money with Madoff, and being in bed with Des? She sat down heavily, trying to process what had just happened. Des was having an affair! That woman had just said that she'd been in bed with him!

And that he was paying rent on an apartment. She was obviously his mistress.

It was a possibility she had sometimes considered. Des was catnip for a certain type of woman. All those Wall Street hot shots were. So many people she knew, male and female, were engaged in extramarital affairs. It was a gossip staple as long as she had lived in New York.

How long had it been going on for? She'd never heard even a whisper. Tears stung her eyes. They were supposed to be a team, she and Des. They had worked very hard for all they'd achieved. They had never been overwhelmingly 'in love', but she loved him and had felt he had loved her. And they had supported and encouraged each other in all their endeavours.

At least he'd had the decency to keep it very discreet, because some well-meaning 'friend' would certainly have found an opportunity to alert her to the fact of her husband's infidelity. She had seen it happen many, many times. Des at least had played far away from home, metaphorically speaking. Some of their acquaintances weren't so considerate, she thought bitterly, feeling bile rise in her throat.

She'd better get to the hospital. At least he was on the Upper East Side – she wouldn't have to go far. East 77th just off Park. Lennox Hill's revamped and updated ER was supposed to be an improvement on what had been there before. With cardiac problems he'd be attended to promptly. Was that a consolation or not? Colette didn't know how she felt. Angry, bitter, frantic, stunned? She pulled off her robe and hurried into her bathroom to freshen up.

A heart attack! The words sent terror through her. Was he

in danger of death? Should she ring his family? His mother
was dead and his father too frail to travel. There was no
point. And what about Jazzy? Should she call her? Colette
swallowed and tried to keep calm as she sprayed on deodor-
ant. She brushed her hair, and touched up her make-up with
shaking hands, smearing her mascara. She'd go to the hospital first and see what was happening. Jazzy could meet
her there. She pulled on a pair of black trousers and a cream
V-neck jumper. Hospitals were always stuffy; she didn't
want to be baked. She grabbed a scarf before ringing down
to the concierge and asking him to call her a cab. 'Stay calm,
stay calm,' she whispered to herself as the elevator sped
silently downwards. 'Thanks, Arun.' She faked a smile at
the Indian concierge on duty as he held the door for her and
walked with her to her waiting taxi. A thought struck her.
'Someone will be dropping off some er ... items ... for me.
Will you hold them until I get back?' she asked.

'Certainly, ma'am,' Arun said politely.

'Lennox Hill ER,' she instructed the taxi driver, shivering
as she got into the cab. It was freezing and she wrapped her
black woollen coat around her and tightened the soft cream
angora scarf around her neck. As the driver drove towards
Park Avenue she gazed unseeingly at the busy sidewalks
and the blur of night-time colours that made New York as
bright as day.

There were three ambulances at the entrance to the multi-
million-dollar Anne & Isidore Falk Center. She'd attended a
fundraising dinner for this very centre, a few years back.
She hadn't thought she'd be inside its doors, ever, Colette
thought distractedly, making her way to the reception desk.

'Des Williams. Admitted by ambulance with a suspected heart attack. Can I see him, please?' she asked the woman behind the desk.

'And you are?' the woman asked politely, tapping his name on the keyboard.

'I'm his wife.'

'Fine, Mrs Williams, your husband has been triaged and has just been taken upstairs for an angioplasty. If you'd like to take a seat I'll let you know when the procedure is over and you can see him.'

'Thank you,' Colette said weakly. 'How long will it take?'

'Thirty minutes. Three hours. It depends on what has to be done. Take a seat and I'll let you know,' the woman said politely.

Wasn't the angioplasty the thing with the balloon going through an artery? That was fairly commonplace. Her dad had had one and he'd been let home the following day. Perhaps this all wasn't as serious as she'd thought. She'd hold off ringing Jazzy until she knew more. She didn't want to frighten her daughter and there was no point in both of them hanging around, and besides she needed to be on her own to think. To try and make sense of what was happening. Colette sat down on one of the dark blue sofas in a waiting area, almost in a daze. Her leather-gloved hands were shaking. She was in turmoil. Des with another woman. A woman who knew he'd taken a hit with Madoff. Colette hadn't even known he'd invested with the disgraced financier. There'd been no discussion about it because she most certainly would not have been in favour and would have made her feelings very clear about it. So Des had hidden it from her and told this other woman. What else did he tell her? What else did he keep from Colette? What did that say about their marriage? Not a lot. Another memory surfaced and she buried it deep. She wasn't going to think about that now. The past was the past: she had enough to deal with in the present.

She spent two hours alternating between rage, anxiety, grief and fear before she was finally allowed to see her husband. Des was very pale, and sedated, lying against the crisp white pillows, with an IV drip in his arm and a blood pressure and cardiac monitor attached to him.

'How did you know I was here?' he slurred when she called his name and he opened his eyes.

'Your lady friend told me,' she said coldly. 'She's leaving your phone and briefcase and clothes at our building. Arun will keep them until I get home.'

'Oh!' he said, his eyes sliding away from hers.

'I have to have surgery,' he muttered. 'I'll be here a few days.'

'I'll pack a case for you.'

'Thanks,' Des murmured and closed his eyes, the sedation taking effect as he drifted back to sleep.

Colette stared at him in the dimly lit room. This man she had shared her life with for almost twenty-five years seemed like a complete and utter stranger. She wanted to shake him, wake him up and slap his face hard and demand an explanation from him. *Why? How long? Who is she?* But his sleeping form defeated her and she stood in impotent fury and felt an irrational urge to tear his drip and his monitors from him.

'Bastard,' she swore at him. He'd even cheated her out of a scene. She wouldn't be able to rant and rave at him for fear he'd have another episode. She'd have to swallow it all down and probably give herself a stroke or a heart attack, she thought bitterly, bursting into tears of anger and frustration.

'Don't cry, Mrs Williams, your husband is stable. He'll be fine,' a nurse said reassuringly, mistaking the reason for Colette's distress when she came into the room to take a note of her patient's vital signs. 'Why don't you go home to bed?' she urged. 'Mr Williams will sleep for most of the night anyway because of his sedation. There's nothing you can do here. We'll have him ambulatory tomorrow and he'll be more with-it so you can talk to him then.'

'Right, thanks.' Colette struggled to compose herself. She picked up her coat and scarf where she'd thrown them over the side of a chair and took a tissue out of her bag and wiped her eyes. 'I'll bring his pyjamas and toiletries in tomorrow,' she managed to say.

'That's perfect.' The nurse smiled at her and held open the door for her and Colette walked out into the corridor wondering was she in some sort of surreal nightmare or could all this be really happening.

The icy blast of a needle-sharp breeze blowing off the East River hit like a slap in the face when she stepped outside, and Colette knew her life had changed completely and there was nothing dreamlike about it. The nightmare was very real indeed.

CHAPTER THIRTY-FIVE

At least Des's clothes weren't rolled up in a Macy's carrier bag, Colette thought wearily when Arun produced her husband's coat, briefcase and a Bergdorf Goodman bag from the small office behind his rosewood desk. Des's bit on the side had some cop on, Colette noted caustically. The woman had placed a layer of white tissue paper on top of the bag, concealing what lay underneath. Top marks for discretion.

'Let me get the bellboy to carry this up for you, ma'am,' the concierge offered, carrying the bags to the elevators.

'Not at all, Arun, just put them on the floor beside me, thank you,' Colette said, pressing a twenty into the young man's hand. She just wanted to be by herself to try and absorb the multiple shocks this evening had walloped her with. She let herself into the apartment and dropped the bags onto the marble floor in the hall. She'd deal with them in the morning. For now she just wanted to fall into bed with a large glass of brandy.

A thought struck her as she divested herself of her coat and scarf. She should charge Des's phone. He'd be wanting it ASAP to make calls to work. In fact she supposed she should ring his secretary first thing to let her know to cancel his appointments. Not that he deserved that she should go to such trouble, Colette thought grimly, carrying his briefcase through to the den. She flung it on the sofa and poured herself a measure of brandy and took a slug of the amber liquid, grimacing at the kick of heat at the back of her throat. She'd be taking a sleeper tonight too. If Des decided to kick the bucket that was his tough luck.

She opened the Montblanc briefcase and found the BlackBerry that he always used. Would that woman's phone number be on it? Colette wondered. She knew his password. Jazzy12. Their daughter's name and birthdate. She knew it because, when Jazzy was younger, Des would always let her play games on his phone. He had kept the same password for all his upgraded phones. She keyed it in and scrolled through his text messages. Most of them were business ones. A couple from Jazzy, and two from herself. A few from friends. But otherwise nothing untoward. She checked his call log. The last phone call was to her. The call that woman had made to tell her that Des was in hospital. She scrolled through the other calls he had made that day. Every number came up with a name. Only one, to a woman, and Colette knew by the name that she was a Wells Fargo trader. Colette had met her a couple of times. A woman in her midforties with two children, and divorced, who wouldn't have time for an affair even if she wanted one. She didn't even colour her hair any more, Colette remembered, thinking that the grey, though superbly cut, was ageing. Hardly her. Des liked stylish women who were well maintained. She switched the phone off and went over to the Victorian pedestal desk and plugged the phone into the charger. She could do with charging her own BlackBerry too; she'd charge it in her dressing room.

She flicked through the pockets in the briefcase and saw the white padded envelope that Des had taken the papers from that morning and as she lifted it out she saw an iPhone tucked in a leather case, nestled snugly in a phone pocket. She took it out, flipped it open, slid the screen across and was instructed to enter a passcode. She keyed in Jazzy12, but no luck. She tried several combinations of birthdays, names, car regs, but the phone would not give up its secrets and she knew this was the one he used to make his assignations. Were there photos of him and his mistress on it? The woman's name? Address?

'What bloody difference does it make,' she muttered, flinging the phone back into the case. The white envelope lay on the sofa and she pulled out the pages to flick through them. Her eyes widened in mounting horror as her attention was caught. She stiffened and sat up straight and studied the typescript with growing concern. He wouldn't do that to her, would he? But his signature was on the last page. The line with her name blank underneath his. No wonder he hadn't wanted her to read it, and just sign it unseen. This was unambiguous proof of how her husband had planned an even greater betrayal than the ones she had already learned about this day.

Stunned, she reread the papers just to make sure she wasn't mistaken, and what she read spelled the death knell of her marriage. She had to take action, had to take desperate measures or her future would be even more uncertain than it was now.

Colette stood up and paced the room. There was no one she could talk to or confide in. She couldn't tell her parents. They were elderly and far away and she knew they would insist on flying over to New York to be with her. She would end up having to take care of them. And besides she didn't want Frank knowing the depths Des had sunk to.

She *wouldn't* tell anyone here in New York about what had happened. How mortifying would that be? It was bad enough that her husband had got screwed by Madoff, and proved that he was not the financial hot shot he thought he was, and that he was having an affair, but this last wounding duplicity was one none of her American friends would ever know about. And she certainly couldn't and wouldn't tell their daughter. Jazzy idolized her dad. It would be bad enough that she would learn that her parents were divorcing and that their wealth was no longer secure.

Colette glanced at her watch. Ireland was five hours ahead. It was 5.30 a.m. in Dublin. There was only one person in the world she could share the horrendous details of today with, but even 5.30 was too early to ring Hilary. She'd get into bed and wait for another half an hour. She'd take a Xanax instead of a sleeper. She would need all her wits about her tomorrow without having the cotton-wool head sleeping tablets gave her. She went out to the kitchen to get a drink and a water cracker to take with her tablet. Des's side of creamy mash was still in the fridge, she remembered, having the sudden urge to eat something comforting and hot, even though she didn't feel particularly hungry. She shoved the dish of potato into the microwave and when it was heated dropped a dollop of butter into it and spooned the mash into her mouth. It was completely comforting and so very tasty and easy to swallow. There was a dish of mac and cheese covered with cling film; that would slide down easily too, Colette decided, putting that in the microwave. And toast! Hot buttered toast! How good was that?

An hour later, sickened after her binge and purge, Colette lay against her fluffy pillows, fingers trembling, as she dialled Hilary's number. It rang and rang, and then, relieved more than words could say, Colette heard her oldest friend say a groggy, 'Hello?'

'Hilary, I'm in trouble. I need to talk to you,' she managed before bursting into tears.

'What's wrong? God, I thought it was my mother. It's *very* early, Colette.' Hilary struggled to wake up, mouthing the word *Colette* to Niall who had shot up in the bed when the phone rang.

'Sorry, I just don't know who else to turn to,' Colette gulped. 'Des has had a heart attack. I found out from his mistress, with whom he was in bed when he had it. And he had it because he's lost a mint of our money with a guy called Bernie Madoff who's been arrested for running a Ponzi scheme. And I didn't know about it. And just when I didn't think things could get any worse I found out that he tried to trick me into signing a document that would put our London home, the property *my* aunt left *me*, up as collateral for a massive loan he had planned to take out without telling me. Hilary, please, please come over to me. I *really* need you.'

'Oh my God! Colette, that's *horrendous*. I don't know what to say. Will Des be OK?' Hilary ran her fingers through her tousled hair and made a face at Niall who was resting on his elbows looking at her through bleary eyes.

'I think so. He's in Lennox Hill. He had an angioplasty. I'll know more tomorrow. Could you come over?' Colette pleaded. 'Hilary, our marriage is over. I'm going to divorce him. I might have coped with the affair and losing the money but trying to trick me into signing over the flat is just devastating. I'll have to tell Jazzy some of it and I'll have to shore up whatever's left of our finances so that I won't be left penniless. Thank God I didn't sign that document without reading it or I'd have lost *everything*.' Colette's heart was doing double flips, and she thought she was going to be sick again.

'Don't do anything hasty,' Hilary cautioned, horrified at what she was hearing. She didn't particularly like Des Williams but he seemed to have played a very underhand game with Colette.

'I won't but I know exactly what has to be done and I'm going to do it. I just don't want to be here on my own when I'm doing it,' Colette wept. 'Please say you'll come.'

Hilary's heart sank. But what could she do? Her friend was in the worst trouble possible, and even though Colette could be a fair-weather friend at times, when the chips were down she had turned to Hilary, and she would feel an utter heel if she turned her back on her. 'OK, I will,' she agreed. 'Go to sleep and I'll suss out flights and I'll talk to you later.'

'Oh thanks, Hil, you really are the *best* friend ever. I'm so grateful to you,' Colette said with heartfelt gratitude.

'Go to sleep, get some rest. I'll call you later.' Hilary threw her eyes up to heaven at Niall who was earwigging.

'OK and thanks. And, Hilary ...'

'Yes?'

'Don't say a word about this to *anyone*,' she warned.

'Of course not!' Hilary exclaimed. 'Now try and get some sleep.'

'OK, bye,' Colette said tiredly and hung up. She replaced the receiver and switched off the lamp. Hilary was coming; she wouldn't have to do what she was going to do on her own.

'What's going on?' Niall turned over and put his arms around Hilary as she lay back against him. 'It sounds pretty grim.'

'It is, Niall. It's unbelievable. I don't like the chap but I never thought Des Williams would be such an underhand creep.' Hilary nuzzled in against her husband's shoulder and related the sorry saga to him.

'You do have to go, I suppose,' he said gravely when she came to the end. 'Although I'm not sure she'd do the same for you,' he added acerbically.

'Ah don't be like that, Niall,' she chided. 'I'm sure she would. Friends are friends when all's said and done. Colette's in a bad way. As if the affair wasn't enough to have to deal with.'

'He was always a very cocky guy. So superior, especially about the financial stuff. So Madoff stung him! I'm glad I didn't take any of his financial advice. We were hit bad enough with ISTEC and the bank shares, but at least we didn't borrow to speculate.'

'Yeah well that bloody bank regulator has a lot to answer for and so does that Seán Quinn and his greedy gambling that *we're* paying for,' Hilary grumbled, still smarting over the amount of money they had recently lost in the banking fiasco.

'At least we haven't gone under like some people.' Niall stretched.

'Yeah,' she sighed. 'It was horrible making the lads at work redundant; if we're able to hang onto the showrooms we'll be doing well. There's a long, hard road ahead of us. Thank God the girls are finished college.'

'And doing well for themselves.' Niall smiled at her. 'If you're going to Noo Yawk you can get them some Christmas prezzies in the sales. I'll get them some when I'm in Toronto.'

'That's what I love about you, your positivity. Even after all these years and all we've been through.' She caressed his stubbly cheek tenderly.

Niall kissed her and got out of bed. 'I'll go down and make us a mug of tea and some toast – we're hardly getting back to sleep now.' He yawned.

'Breakfast in bed will be a treat.' She snuggled down under the duvet. The heating hadn't timed on yet and there was a seasonal nip in the air.

'And we might even have conjugals after brekkie if we have time,' he grinned.

'God be with the days when we'd have conjugals first and *then* breakfast,' she teased, laughing as he went out the door.

She was *so* lucky, she thought gratefully. She and Niall had weathered a few storms to be sure, especially when she had been up to her eyes in work and feeling fraught and pulled in every direction, but they still loved each other and looked out for each other. Although the mad passion of the early years had been replaced by loving familiarity, she would say they were still in love with each other. There were couples she knew that loved each other but weren't 'in love'. She had always felt that Des and Colette were in that category. But even that wasn't certain after these revelations. Des appeared to have no feeling for his wife whatsoever. Trying to trick Colette into signing away the London flat was horrifying. He must have been extremely desperate because of the money he had lost. There couldn't be any other reason, she thought with a pang of sympathy for her friend's soon-to-be-ex-husband.

'Brekkie for my lady, and I've just had a brainwave!' Niall arrived with the breakfast tray, a broad smile creasing his stubbly face.

'A brainwave! What's rare is wonderful,' Hilary teased, taking her mug of tea from the tray. 'Tell me.'

'Nope, I'll bring someone else on a second honeymoon, for being so smart.' Niall grinned.

'What?' She spluttered her tea.

'Let's use Colette's dilemma to our advantage.' He offered her a slice of buttered toast. 'I've to go to Toronto in a couple of days. Why don't you fly to New York, and then fly up to join me? It's only a short hop, and we can stay a couple of nights and fly home together?'

'You're a *genius*, Niall!' Hilary exclaimed excitedly. 'It sounds fantastic! I'd never have thought of it. I always think Canada's much further north.' She made a face. 'It will cost an arm and a leg though and it's very close to Christmas.'

'It won't cost an arm and a leg. My flights are covered because it's work, and so is my hotel room. So we only have to pay your flights and the difference in accommodation expenses. And we can do our Christmas shopping together and have it all done and gift-wrapped. Now that's an offer you can't refuse. Come on, we deserve it. It's ages since we've been away together. Say yes before you come up with an excuse.' He eyed her expectantly over his mug of tea, brown eyes gleaming with anticipation.

'You're on! New York *and* a second honeymoon in Toronto! And you're right. We do deserve it. Christmas has come early! Lucky, lucky me.' She felt like a kid in a candy store.

'Every cloud has a silver lining. Let's get some practice in,' her husband murmured, placing his cup on his bedside table and leaning over to kiss her buttery mouth.

Unfamiliar sounds roused Des from his stupor and he lay for a few moments between waking and sleeping. He felt rough, groggy, and his mouth tasted like sandpaper. Where was he? He wasn't in his own bed. The sheets were hard and the pillows were scratchy against his cheek. He opened his eyes and blinked when he saw the monitors and felt the cannula in his hand. 'What the hell?' He sneezed. It hurt. He didn't know if he was hot or cold.

And then he remembered!

Had he dreamed that Colette had stood by his bedside? Had he dreamed that she had said his 'lady friend' had called her? He groaned. He remembered arguing with Kaylee, telling her he couldn't afford to keep paying the rent on the neat studio he'd rented for them down on West Street. And why would she want to give it up with the views of the

Harbor and Battery Park, the roof garden, and the fitness centre? He loved it himself. Skylar had dropped him without a backward glance to go off and marry an older, best-selling, much married author – who was far wealthier than Des – whom she'd met at a publishing party. He still smarted at how fast she'd dropped him to become a trophy wife to a man she didn't love. He'd decided that if he ever had another extramarital relationship he'd make sure to rent a smaller, cheaper apartment nearer to work. When he'd met Kaylee Hamilton, an administrative compliance analyst at Citigroup, at a Christmas drinks party, she had been living with a boyfriend in Brooklyn Bridge Park.

'I won't be going to see you in Brooklyn,' he'd flirted, half joking, even though he was very taken with her curvaceous, dark-haired, green-eyed, sultry looks. She'd left the boyfriend at New Year, and he'd set her up in a studio on West Street in Battery Park City. She was sparky, intelligent, very knowledgeable about the financial world, and ambitious in her job, but not socially ambitious, which was very refreshing for Des. He'd grown tired of the rounds of parties and events he and Colette had to attend. Now he loved nothing better that pulling on a baseball cap and a pair of shades and strolling hand in hand with Kaylee in South Cove on the Esplanade, exploring the winding walkways and quays, and necking a beer, watching the evening sun glittering on the Hudson and the wide vista of the Harbor. Or sitting up on the roof garden of their building, sipping a cocktail and just looking out at the panoramic views with the unmistakable, iconic Statue of Liberty, always a reminder of where he was and how far he had risen since he'd left the North East of England.

Little did he think, when he'd dreamed of moving to London, that he'd end up on Wall Street, with a mistress – his second – to boot. His parents would have been disgusted with him, Des thought ruefully. But his marriage had grown stale in the last few years. Colette was so engrossed in the demands on her time as a result of their high-powered lifestyle she didn't give a lot of time to *him!* It was so refreshing, so energizing and affirming to be with a woman who found him sexy and responded with passion to his advances. With Colette he sometimes felt she was going through the motions. And she *never* made the first move. She'd married him on the rebound from some rugby-playing medic. He'd known that and it had made her somewhat bitter towards men. Conquering that latent hostility had been challenging. It excited him and spurred him on in his wooing and he had felt he'd succeeded. The early years of their marriage in London had been good. They'd been a formidable team with a common goal, and they'd flourished, and how? But at what cost? Des thought dispiritedly. Colette would have liked another child. She'd hated being an only child and wanted a sibling for Jazzy, but after years of trying they'd gone for tests and discovered that the fault lay with him. He had a low sperm count. They had been lucky to conceive Jasmine. Once she knew the score Colette had been pragmatic and he'd felt secretly relieved on one level that she didn't have to endure pregnancy and childbirth again. It was a blow to his ego, though. He'd felt a failure and coming on top of the onset of middle age when he'd seen younger, more qualified, hotter guys powering up the scale, it had made Des begin to realize that he had more good years behind him than before him and life was for living. He had taken the opportunity to hook up with Kaylee when it came his way. His relationship with her was different from the one he'd had with Skylar, who, he wasn't proud to admit, he had used purely for sex. Kaylee reminded him in ways of a younger Colette. Vibrant, intelligent, sexy but much more laid-back and easy to be with.

He had thought Kaylee was cool with their situation, even though she had mentioned once or twice that she thought it would be nice if they could be together *all* the time. That was never going to happen. Colette and he had a lifestyle that they had slogged for, and a place on the social register that had been hard won. A divorce would cost a hell of a lot. Colette and old man O'Mahony would take him to the cleaner's. It was too high a price to pay.

What was it with women? Even the most independent of them, the most ardent feminists, the most ambitious in their careers – like Kaylee – they all wanted the ring on their finger, no matter what. Even his own daughter Jazzy wanted to be married and not 'left on the shelf', she told him once. Nothing had changed for women in that regard despite their so called liberation, he'd thought, surprised, remembering how livid Kaylee had become when he'd suggested easing back on their relationship. For him the relationship had been a respite from real life, but for Kaylee, although he hadn't realized it, it had been a means to an end. Marriage!

The financial crises that had come crashing down around him had been the catalyst for this calamity. Kaylee's studio was an expense he couldn't sustain after taking the Madoff hit. He'd hoped she'd understand, hoped she'd offer to pay the rent herself, but she had been so mad with him that he wouldn't divorce Colette and move in with her that she'd gone off on one when they were lying together after sex, and that was when the pain had hit.

He'd actually thought he was croaking it, Des remembered, shivering at the memory. Perhaps he'd have been better off if he *had* kicked the bucket. He was gutted that Kaylee had phoned Colette. She could have let the hospital phone his wife instead of doing it herself and dropping him in it. That was very low. He'd been ultra careful never to give Colette any inkling that he was seeing someone. He never socialized with Kaylee above Canal Street, never invited her to anything at work, and she'd accepted this. And because she had, Des had thought she was OK with it. *Big* mistake. Her clock was ticking and she wanted to be married, she'd shrieked at him last night. He'd never seen her so crazy and irrational. But if his mistress had flipped big time it was nothing to how Colette would react when she found out that he'd lost a mint with Madoff, as well as been having an affair. There was going to be hell to pay and more! He closed his eyes, and opened them again. What would Colette tell Jazzy? He'd have to face his daughter's wrath too.

A technician in a white coat knocked and came into the room. 'I need to take some blood, Mr Williams,' she said chirpily. She tightened the tourniquet around his arm and placed a pillow under it. 'Don't bend it, keep it straight, please, and make a fist for me,' she instructed, tapping his vein and swabbing it with disinfectant. Des broke out in a sweat when he saw the long thin needle heading in his direction. Colette, Jazzy and Kaylee faded into oblivion as he took a few shallow breaths and struggled not to faint.

Should she ring the hospital and see how Des was? Did she care how he was? 'Dumbass bastard!' Kaylee swore, jogging along the Esplanade as daylight began to streak the eastern sky with multicoloured hues. He could die for all she cared.

It was cold but she was too angry with herself to notice anything that was going on around her as she relived, yet again, the events of the night before. The worst thing of all, apart from Des being carted off in an ambulance, sirens blaring, was the way she had dropped her guard and freaked out and shown herself to be needy and desperate. She had reminded herself of Charlotte in *Sex and the City* when she shrieked at her boyfriend Harry, 'Set the date! Set the date!'

Kaylee was beyond mortified, and beyond devastated. She had given Des Williams so much more that that Barbie Doll Uptown wife. He'd more or less told her that. Des had been such a charming and cultivated man. And so much more interesting than most of the men she worked with. She liked Europeans. They had a different outlook on life that she found refreshing. She and Des had clicked, better than she'd ever clicked with any other man.

And Kaylee knew their relationship was far different from the ones he shared with his hyper wife and spoilt daughter. From what she'd heard about Jazzy, she seemed to be a rather demanding young woman who had a huge sense of entitlement. Kaylee didn't make demands on Des. That was one way of scaring off a man. She wasn't the granddaughter of a Southern Belle for nothing, she thought wryly. She had been ultra laid-back and Des had loved that about her. He'd *relaxed* with her, *and* she understood his work and the pressures he was under. He'd told her she was *wild* in bed. For all the good it had done her.

Kaylee slowed to a walk. She was thirty-five, single and childless, despite her successful career. Her high-school friends back home in Charlotte would look on her as a failure, despite all she had achieved. Her mother certainly did. 'When are you going to give your pop and me a grandchild, sugar?' Mary Beth would ask her every birthday.

Do you think I don't want to? she'd want to yell, but she'd shrug and say she hadn't met the right man yet. 'And all those millions of men in New York City!' Mary Beth would scoff. 'You need to come back home and meet your own kind.'

The lump in her throat nearly strangled Kaylee and a harsh, rasping sob escaped her. She had thought the tall, handsome Englishman with the sexy accent and the attractive blue eyes *had* been her kind.

Colette had slept a deep and dreamless sleep, thanks to the brandy and Xanax, but she felt exhausted when she awoke to find daylight seeping into her bedroom. Lying in bed remembering the events of the night before, she felt a nervous fluttering in her stomach. Life had changed. The rug had been pulled from under her and she needed to focus. She lay immobile, arms rigid by her side. She was on her own. She needed to shore up the ditches and she needed to break the news to Jazzy that her father had had a heart attack in the arms of his mistress and that Colette was going to divorce him. That was going to be one of the hardest things she had ever, or would ever, have to do. Her daughter would be *devastated*. She would not reveal the other great treachery Des had planned. Jazzy would not learn from her what a complete and utter heel her father was.

A gentle knock on the door elicited a weary, 'Come in.'

'Would you care for breakfast in bed or in the breakfast room, ma'am?' Encarna asked.

'Here, please, just juice, coffee and a fruit cup and yogurt.' Colette hauled herself up into a sitting position. 'Encarna, Mr Williams has had a heart attack. He's in Lennox Hill.'

'Oh no! Ma'am!' the middle-aged woman exclaimed as her hand flew up to her mouth, her face falling in dismay. 'I'm very sorry to hear that. Will he be all right?'

'I hope so. I'll know mòre today. Will you freshen up the guest room, please. My friend Hilary is coming over from Ireland. And would you pack a case for my husband? I'll take it in to the hospital later.'

'Of course. I'll just get your breakfast first, ma'am. Why don't you lie down and have a little rest until it's ready. You look tired,' Encarna urged kindly. 'Shall I open the drapes?'

'I think I will rest here, Encarna, and no, leave them as they are, please.' Colette slid back down under the duvet and pulled it up to her ears. She should ring the hospital and find out how Des was, and she should call his secretary, and she really had to ring Jazzy. She would make the calls after her breakfast, she decided, putting off the unpleasant tasks for just another little while. She lay motionless in the peace of her womb-like room. If only she could stay snug and warm and protected in this little cocoon forever, Colette thought sorrowfully, dreading all that lay ahead of her.

CHAPTER THIRTY-SIX

'Thank you, Lauren. I'll be bringing Des in his phone shortly. I'm sure he'll be in touch himself as soon as his doctors allow it.' Colette closed the conversation, hugely irritated at having to pretend to her husband's PA that she was the devoted and concerned wife. She sat at the desk in the den and Googled Lennox Hill, dialled the number and asked to be put through to the nurses' station on Des's floor. 'I'm Mrs Williams, I'm enquiring about my husband's condition,' she said politely, studying her manicure. Her nails needed attention, she thought distractedly while she waited to speak to Des's nurse.

'Hello, Mrs Williams. Your husband had a comfortable night. Unfortunately he has developed a fever and may have a respiratory infection. We're running tests to confirm, and then we will treat him with antibiotics. That will delay any procedures that may have to be done,' the nurse informed her.

'Oh! OK! Please tell him I will be in with his pyjamas and things shortly.'

'I can put you through to him if you wish,' the nurse said helpfully.

'Thanks very much.' She tried to inject a modicum of enthusiasm into her tone. The last thing she wanted to do was talk to her dickhead husband.

'Hello?' Des said groggily.

'Hello,' she said curtly.

'Oh! Hi, Colette.' He sounded wary.

'I've phoned Lauren and told her where you are,' she said coldly.

'Thanks ... Can you bring my cell in?'

'I have your phone packed.'

'Umm ... right. Eh ... have you told Jazzy I'm in hospital?'

'I'm going to call her now.'

'And eh ... are you going to say anything about ... er ... last night?'

'I will be telling her at some stage over the next few days that we will be divorcing,' Colette said grimly.

'Aw, Colette, can we not talk about it?' Des urged. 'I'm really sorry.'

'Really sorry you got caught, you mean. How much of our money did you lose with Madoff?' She wouldn't give him the satisfaction of referring to his bit on the side. Let him wait for that. And she wasn't going to bring up the subject of his loan application either. She wanted to see if he would bring up that matter himself and how he would weasel out of it. If he didn't refer to it, she would lull her husband into a false sense of security and wait for him in the long grass. Plans were already forming in her head for her response to *that* treachery.

Des sneezed. 'Colette, I'm not well enough to talk about that now,' he whined. 'I feel absolutely beat.'

'Fine,' she snapped. 'I've to meet Helena Dupree for lunch in the Morgan and then I'll be in. Bye.' She hung up without giving him the chance to answer. Had things been different she would have cancelled the lunch meeting in her favourite museum, and been at Des's side first thing, but she was in no rush now to go to his bedside. He was the last person she wanted to see, she thought bitterly.

Men, they were all the same. She should have known. Had it just been the other-woman stuff she would have got over it. Sex was sex. It didn't mean a lot. Des worked on Wall Street, he was a man of means. And attractive with it. She hardly knew of a marriage in their set where one half of the couple wasn't playing away. It wouldn't have been a divorcing issue for her, not that Colette would admit that to anyone. Sexual fidelity was not what had held their marriage together all these years; it was the financial perfidy that gutted her. There was no going back from that. She could never trust her husband again. She almost broke into a cold sweat thinking how close she'd come to losing their London home. *Her* London home. Des had wanted her to rent it out all the years they lived in New York, but Colette hadn't wanted strangers in it. She'd always enjoyed flying back a couple of times a year and staying for a week or two, relaxing after the hectic pace of her life in Manhattan. Some things were worth more than money.

She would not, in the future, live a life of anxiety wondering what other kind of stunts Des would pull with whatever was left of their money. From now on she would be in control of her own destiny. And she was lucky enough to have something at her back. The flat was a valuable piece of real estate. A thought struck her. Des's wallet! He'd probably be looking for that. Was it in his suit jacket? She got up and went to the carrier bag where Des's belongings were neatly packed. His car keys and wallet were in his suit pocket. She went back over to the desk, put them beside the charged BlackBerry and took a sheet of notepaper from the drawer and began to write. When she was finished, she picked up her cell and dialled Jazzy's number. It went into message minder. Colette threw her eyes up to heaven. It was impossible to get her daughter on her phone and she wasn't the type to ring her parents every day.

'Jazzy, please ring me as soon as you get this message,' she said crisply before going to dress for her business meeting at the Morgan.

Helena Dupree, an editor-at-large for a glossy fine arts magazine, was surprised but not shocked when Colette told her about Des's heart attack when they sat at one of the round tables in the glitzy lobby café where they had arranged to meet.

'Bankers and brokers and financial-industry workers are dropping like flies with all this economic uncertainty, I believe,' she remarked, scanning the menu. 'I mean can you credit what's going on with Madoff? Mamie Winston is supposed to have lost millions with him, and Lehman. She didn't host a table for the Friends of Autism and Asperger's, or the Wilcox-Morgan Wing of St Mary Magdalene's. Rumour has it she's going to be asked to resign from the boards,' Helena confided. 'I'll have the devilled eggs, please.'

Colette's blood ran cold at the news. Mamie Winston, an heiress from one of the city's oldest families, had contributed

a fortune to charities over the years, and was an indefatigable fundraiser. And now, because she was financially
embarrassed, she was going to be frozen out. Manhattan's
social register was no place for you if your star was on the
wane. Old money or no. And if there was no loyalty to the
likes of Mamie – a snooty, stick-thin matron who loved to
know everyone's business, and who only entertained Colette
because of her reputation in the world of fine art – there
would certainly be no loyalty to her and Des. The invita-
tions would dwindle. They would be quietly dropped if they
could no longer afford their lifestyle, as though they had
never been part of that privileged world. The humiliation
would be excruciating. And *that* she would not endure,
Colette decided there and then, as Helena continued to
gossip about the amount of family heirlooms that were discreetly coming on the market because of the downturn.

Colette had just said goodbye to her lunch companion and
was about to walk with her through the glass-enclosed central court to the entrance when her phone vibrated and she
saw Jazzy's name flash up. 'Helena, it's Jazzy. I have to tell
her about her dad being in hospital. You go right ahead and
I'll be in touch,' she said, giving the other woman an air kiss
and turning back to reclaim her seat.

'Give him my best,' Helena threw over her shoulder, her
Manolos click-clacking across the floor of the court.

'Sweetie, thanks for getting back to me. Where are you?'
Colette placed her bag on the table and sat down.

'I'm on East 34th and Lex. I was setting up a Facebook and
Twitter account for a client. Where are you?'

'The Morgan.'

'I could be with you in under ten,' Jazzy said breezily.

'Perfect. Would you like me to order you some lunch? I've already eaten but I'll have another coffee.'

'Mom, you're the best! I'm starving! What's on that I would like?'

'Let's see, how about the smoked salmon club? The Pierpont salad? White shrimp and creamy polenta?'

'I'll have the Pierpont. See you soooooon,' Jazzy said cheerily.

Thank God her daughter was not living at home and had her own life to lead. The marriage break-up would not be as traumatic for her as it would have been had she still been a child, Colette thought sadly, hating the thought of piercing her daughter's youthful *joie de vivre*. Jazzy loved what she was working at; she had a caring, intelligent boyfriend with a very good family pedigree. Scion of an old Bostonian family, he would eventually take over his father's law firm. An excellent match, Colette had thought with satisfaction when she'd been introduced to Jackson. She had made every effort to let him see that he would be marrying well. And for the first time in her life, Jazzy seemed to be happy and con-fident. Her teen years had been filled with insecurity about her looks, her weight, her place among her peers, but that phase had thankfully passed. Their daughter was in a good place and now Des had seriously compromised *all* their futures. She'd let Jazzy enjoy her lunch and then tell her about Des's heart attack. She would leave out the details of the affair and the Madoff fiasco for the time being. One blow at a time was sufficient.

Colette couldn't help but be proud when she saw her

daughter striding towards her, long blonde hair twisted up loosely on the back of her head, with tendrils falling around her face, emphasizing her high cheekbones and wide blue eyes. She was wearing flared Prada jeans – very bang on trend – Colette noted, remembering the bell-bottom flares of her youth that were now back in fashion, albeit more cutting edge. A preppy navy-plaid D&G jacket, a red woollen scarf wound around her neck and a red Prada bag gave her a fresh, trendy, youthful look that Colette would never be able to carry off any more. Flared jeans would be very mutton dressed as lamb on her, she thought regretfully as she stood up to embrace her daughter. 'This *is* a treat, what brings you here?' Jazzy exclaimed, shrugging out of her jacket and dropping it onto one of the polymer seats.

'I had a meeting with Helena Dupree about a charity event in the gallery.' Colette smiled at her and wondered how was it possible that she had a daughter in her twenties.

'Oh Mom, trust me, this is a lifesaver. I didn't have time for breakfast this morning – Jackson and I slept it out. We were at this really hot new club that's just opened downtown, called Greenhouse. It's all about being environmentally aware. It was completely *awesome*! Hilary would love the lighting. It's all LED, and so much more ecologically friendly, and the couches, the coasters, *everything* is made from recycled material. Really cool,' she exclaimed as the waiter laid her salad before her. She tucked into it enthusiastically, spearing smoked bacon and chicken and Vermont Cheddar onto her fork, and rolling her eyes dramatically as she ate. '*Yummmmmeeee.*'

'I ordered you a glass of the Pinot Blanc – here it comes.' Colette laughed at her daughter's antics.

'Thanks, Mom, wait until I tell you where Jackson took me at the weekend,' she prattled on, and it was only when she had placed her knife and fork on the plate and sat back in her chair, replete, that Colette leaned across the table and took her hand.

'Darling, I wanted you to enjoy your lunch before I told you, but Daddy's in Lennox Hill. He had a heart attack last night. There was no point in worrying you. I was with him for several hours but he was out of it after having a procedure, so they told me to go home.'

'Oh *Mom*!' Jazzy paled and held Colette's hand in a vice-grip. 'Is he going to die?'

'Of course not! We wouldn't be sitting here if he was. He'll be fine,' Colette said reassuringly. 'Lennox Hill has a good name for cardiology. He'll just have to start living a healthier lifestyle and cut down on his work, I expect.'

'Can I go and see him?' Jazzy jumped up from the table.

'I'm just heading over myself with a case for him. I used a Town Car today. I told the driver to give us until two, so relax and finish your wine.'

'Mom, you should have told me. I would have come to the hospital,' Jazzy remonstrated, sitting down again.

'You were in a *nightclub*,' Colette pointed out. 'You wouldn't even have heard your phone, and besides there was no point in the two of us hanging around waiting. If your dad had been critical of course I would have left a message, but he wasn't.'

'Oh poor, poor Dad!' Jazzy started to cry.

Colette handed her a tissue. 'Shush, sweetie, he'll be fine. Come on, it's almost two anyway. Put your jacket on and let's go and see him.'

The black sedan was waiting when they emerged onto the pavement and they settled back in the luxurious interior for the fifteen-minute drive uptown along Madison.

'Daddy, Daddy!' Jasmine flew into her father's arms when they entered Des's room.

'Hey, baby!' Des broke into a smile when he saw her and hugged her as best he could with the IV drip taped into his hand, and his heart monitors on his chest.

'Dad, what happened? Is it painful?' Jazzy asked, concern etched across her features.

'It was a bit when it happened, but not now. I have a respiratory infection though so that's going to delay things a bit. I've to have a triple bypass,' he said, glancing at his wife over his daughter's shoulder.

'*Omigod!*' Jazzy was horrified.

'That's very routine surgery these days, Jazzy, a dime a dozen. It sounds worse than it is,' Colette said matter-of-factly. 'I'll just unpack your case, Des.' She didn't even look at him, engrossing herself with hanging up his dressing gown and pyjamas in the closet.

'Did you bring my phone and charger?' He lay back against his pillows.

'Yes. I just brought the BlackBerry. If you want the iPhone, that's in your briefcase. I can bring that too,' she said pointedly. 'Although there's no need for you to have two in here now.' Des flushed under his pallor but was saved from responding by the arrival of a nurse to do his TPR check.

'By the way, Hilary's coming over to stay with me for a few days, to support me,' Colette remarked casually when the nurse had filled in the chart and left.

'That's brilliant, Mom. I won't have to worry about you, or come and stay with you, then. I would have if you'd needed me,' Jazzy declared, relieved that she wouldn't have to leave the comfort of her boyfriend's arms to nursemaid her mother at night.

'You don't have to worry about me at all, sweetie,' Colette said drily. Jazzy could be decidedly self-centred and did not like to be put out. They had raised a spoilt child, she admitted.

'So where were you when you had the heart attack? Were you at home? Did you pass out? Did you think you were going to die and see your life passing in front of you?' Jazzy wanted the gory details.

'Eh . . . not exactly,' Des fudged, looking at Colette.

Colette stared back at him coldly.

'Hey, you two! What's up? There's definitely an atmosphere.' Jazzy stared from one to the other. 'You didn't even kiss Dad, Mum. What's going on here?'

An awkward silence descended on the room. Des looked to Colette for support. But she couldn't give it. It was too difficult to play happy families. She just couldn't carry it off. Seeing Des in his hospital bed had not elicited sympathy, just fury and more fury, which she was finding hard to suppress. Helena Dupree's revelations about Mamie Winston had put the iron in her soul. Colette wanted out, now, before the cat was out of the bag. She wanted to go on *her* terms and not have people talking about them and their altered circumstances behind her back. 'I suppose you might as well tell Jazzy where you were when you had your attack. She's going to find out soon enough anyway,' she said flatly.

'Daddy ... Mommy, what's going on?' Jazzy asked agitatedly as the realization hit that something was seriously amiss. Colette remained mute. She was damned if she was telling Jazzy. Des could break the news of his betrayal himself.

'Daddy?' Jazzy persisted anxiously.

'I was with another woman,' Des muttered. Jazzy paled and stared at him, speechless.

'Where, who?' she eventually demanded.

'Battery Park City. She's ... ah ... someone I know through work.'

'Did you *know* Dad was having an affair? How long has this being going on?' Jasmine jumped to her feet, glaring at Colette.

'What do *you* think? The answer is no, and I have no idea,' Colette retorted angrily, picking up her bag. 'I'm going now,' she said tightly, afraid she would lose control and erupt into a furious rant. 'I have to call in to the gallery.'

'Mom, are you OK?' Jazzy's face betrayed her shock and she dissolved into tears.

Colette's fury melted when she saw her distressed daughter. 'Darling, I'm fine. Don't worry about me. Stay here with your dad for a while and we'll talk later.' She hugged her daughter and patted her on the back until Jazzy composed herself, then kissed her on the cheek, and walked out without a backwards look at her husband.

It was a cruel way for Jasmine to find out about her father's infidelity but at least she knew now. There would be no need for pretences. Weary to her bones, Colette texted her driver to meet her out front and walked to the bank of elevators. She had a lot of phone calls to make and a lot of business to attend to. As the car swung on to East 77th Colette tapped in a phone number and when a receptionist with a plummy English accent answered, she gave her name and asked to be transferred to her property maintenance manager. 'Hello, Ms O'Mahony. Good to hear from you. How can I help?' came the reassuring voice from the other side of the Atlantic.

'I'll be returning to London within the next few weeks. Please open up the flat and have it cleaned thoroughly and prepared for residency. I'd like the interior doors, ceilings, windows and skirtings given a fresh coat of cream paint. I'll be in touch nearer the date,' she said briskly as the driver turned left onto Park Avenue towards the rental apartment she now no longer considered to be home.

'Why?' demanded Jazzy, tearfully staring at her father in horror.

'These things happen, you know that,' Des said wearily. 'Lots of your friends have parents who've done the same. This is Manhattan. It goes on. You've seen it often enough. I didn't *murder* anyone,' he said defensively.

'But you never seemed unhappy. You did things together all the time. You get on well. Mom *always* supports you,' his daughter remonstrated indignantly.

'Jazzy, this isn't the time or the place to go into it,' Des protested. He started to cough, and she looked scared.

'Do you want a nurse?' she demanded. He shook his head.

'Don't panic, it's just a cough,' he said reassuringly when he caught his breath.

'Do you think Mom will divorce you?' she asked miserably.

'Right now it's on the cards, I'd say,' he answered truthfully. 'But perhaps when things have calmed down and she has time to think, and not act emotionally, we might be able to salvage our marriage. The most important thing for you to know is that we both love you very much, and that will never change.'

'Yeah well right this minute I think you are the biggest asshole going,' Jazzy said furiously. 'Just when I was like, totally happy with my life, you ruin it for me. What a bummer, Dad. What a bummer!'

'I surely can't argue with that,' Des grimaced. 'I can't argue with that at all.'

'What are Jackson's parents going to think?' Jazzy raged. 'They're very conservative.'

Frankly, I couldn't care less, he wanted to say, irritated that, as usual with Jazzy, it was me, me, me.

'It will blow over,' he muttered.

'Yeah well not in time for Christmas. They are supposed to be coming to New York and I was going to ask Mom to invite them over for dinner. That's so not going to happen now.' Jazzy burst into fresh tears.

'Look, we were thinking of going to London for Christmas anyway. I don't want to worry you but I've lost money with Bernie Madoff. We're going to have to cut back and tighten our belts considerably.' Des reached out and grasped her hand.

'Are we *poor*?' she exclaimed, horrified. 'Are we going skiing in Aspen even?'

'No, Aspen's out this year.' He closed his eyes, exhausted.

'Omigod! We *are* poor!' Jazzy felt sick to her stomach. This was the worst day of her *entire* life. Thank God she had rich grandparents to fall back on if the worst came to the worst. That at least was something.

'If you would please transfer this amount from our joint account into this other account. Our wealth manager has advised us to do so for tax reasons.' Colette slid the teller her account number and a signed withdrawal docket.

'Certainly, Mrs Williams.' The teller keyed in the account numbers and moments later handed her the stamped stub.

'I also wish to pay off the balance of my card from the joint account.' Colette put her Platinum card under the glass partition.

'No problem.' He tapped away on his computer and returned the card. 'Anything else, ma'am?'

'No, that's it. Thank you.' Colette slipped her card back into her Gucci leather wallet.

'Have a nice day,' he said before turning his attention to his next customer.

'Indeed I will,' muttered Colette, hurrying out to the car. 'Next stop Mercedes Benz.'

'My folks might be divorcing.' Jazzy cuddled against her boyfriend while they sat on the sofa having a pre-dinner beer. She had ordered Indian takeout because it was his favourite.

'That's the pits. Why?' Jackson said, surprised. He'd

thought Jazzy's parents were a cool couple and he was impressed especially with Jazzy's mother, who was a very cultured lady. The gallery she ran was ultra exclusive. His parents had checked it out online and were very happy with what they saw.

'My dad's having an affair. He was with the other woman when he had his heart attack down in Battery Park City. She works in finance too.'

Jackson gave a long low whistle. 'Badass!'

She longed to tell him the even worse news about her father's financial losses but that was a step too far. She didn't want to scare Jackson off completely. He was the nicest boyfriend she had ever had. He didn't do drugs; he was generous and thoughtful, unlike some of her exes who were tight with money, letting her pay when they were on dates. If Jackson left her she would be devastated.

'Would you ever cheat on me?' She raised tearstained eyes to him.

'Nevah, *evah*,' he said in the soft Bostonian twang she loved.

'Are you *sure*?' she probed, wishing she could believe him.

'I aam! *Absolutely*,' Jackson assured her with all the fervour of youthful principle as he held her in his arms.

'So I'll see you tomorrow then,' Hilary said comfortingly. She had just emailed Colette her flight details and had got an instant phone call back.

'There'll be a car and a driver waiting at JFK. I can't wait to see you. It's been so horrendously awful.' Colette burst into tears.

'I can't imagine,' Hilary said sympathetically. 'Try your best to rest and sleep tonight.'

'OK,' sobbed her friend, hanging up.

'I'm glad I said I'd go. I've never heard Colette in such a state.' Hilary plonked down on the sofa beside Niall.

'Just one thing, Hil!' her husband said warningly.

'What's that?' She looked at him warily.

'Don't get involved and don't give advice. It's not your drama. They have to sort it out between them. Knowing Colette of old, I'd imagine Des will pay dearly for his transgressions,' he added cynically.

'Well he deserves to, the skunk,' Hilary protested.

'Whether he deserve to or not, that's not your call to make. Support Colette by all means but stay out of their business is my advice to you, for what it's worth.' Niall looked down at her and smiled his familiar smile that always lifted her no matter what.

'Sound advice, hubby dearest,' she sighed. 'Do you want a ride before I go?'

'No I'm saving myself for that young blonde Swedish au pair down in No. 184, when you're gone,' he teased, sliding his hand up under her jumper.

'If you think Colette would be a tough cookie, she'd be nothing compared to me if I caught you with another woman.' Hilary began to open the buttons of his shirt.

'Why, what would you do?' Niall grinned.

'I'd slash your bodhráns and break your banjo into smithereens. Over your head probably,' she teased.

'My *bodhráns*! You sure know how to scare a musician. I'll *never* stray,' he murmured, kissing her with soft, lingering kisses until she moaned underneath him, tugging his belt open as he raised her jumper over her head and unhooked her bra.

'I love you, Niall,' she whispered against his mouth. 'Just shove a cushion under my back or I'll be creased on the plane in the morning. The sofa's too soft for us to be carrying on like this at our age,' she said ruefully.

'Speak for yourself, I'm in my prime, and now I'm going to prove it, if I can straighten my knee out, that is.' He smiled down at her, placing a cushion under the small of her back and tightening his arms around her as the firelight flickered in the stove and the rain lashed down on the Velux window above them.

CHAPTER THIRTY-SEVEN

'I feel like getting hammered!' Colette confessed, topping up Hilary's wine glass.

'That's understandable. Go for it, I say.' Hilary ate some of Encarna's feather-light pastry and chicken.

'I hope you don't mind us not going out for dinner. I'm completely wiped.' Colette took a slug of chilled Chardonnay.

'I'm tired myself. I was up early and the flight was very bumpy. This is perfect. And besides we can talk and get tiddly and not have to worry about getting home. We can just tumble into bed,' Hilary said reassuringly. 'And you can rant and rave in peace. Get it off your chest, Colette, because it must be hard not being able to have a go at Des. That's what would drive me mad, if I were in your shoes,' Hilary said sympathetically.

'*Exactly*, Hilary. It's doing my head in,' Colette fumed. 'I want to scream at him, curse at him, pummel him, and I can't. It would be good enough for him if he had another heart attack and died. At least I'd get the insurance.'

'Aren't you going to eat anything?' Hilary pointed her fork at Colette's plate. She had hardly touched the chicken pot pie.

'I can't! I feel sick. My stomach is tied up in knots.' Colette pushed the plate away.

'What are you going to do? Have you made any plans?' Hilary asked gently.

'I'm going back to London.'

'For a while?'

'No, for good!' Colette said grimly.

'Surely you couldn't leave Manhattan and the gallery and your friends? And what about Jazzy?' Hilary rested her elbows on the table, dropped her chin into her hands and studied her friend intently. Colette was drawn and tired and unusually pale. And utterly subdued.

'Jazzy can make up her own mind about what she wants to do. Thank God I have a home to go to in London. If I'd signed those papers without reading them, God knows what he would have done.'

'It was probably panic. I'm sure he wasn't thinking straight. It must have been awful for Des to discover he'd been ripped off.' Hilary tried to ease Colette's distress.

'As awful as it was for me to discover he was trying to pull a fast one on me,' she retorted. 'I'll never be able to trust him again. *Ever!*' she said vehemently.

'Do you know how much money is gone?'

'Nope! I'm afraid to find out. I'll hardly even get a decent divorce settlement,' she said bitterly. 'What's the point of taking him to the cleaner's if there's nothing to clean out?'

'But haven't you got properties?'

'We sold them after the Lehman Brothers fiasco. I'd say that's the money that he invested with Madoff. I'm sure we're not penniless but we can't sustain *this* lifestyle any more.' She waved around at the large L-shaped kitchen diner, and the more formal dining room behind the panelled double doors.

'Get a less expensive apartment.' Hilary nibbled on a carrot baton coated in creamy chicken sauce.

'I couldn't *bear* that, Hilary,' Colette exclaimed. 'That fucking idiot has ruined everything we've worked for. Our social standing, our lifestyle, our pensions, Jazzy's marriage prospects. You think there's snobbery at home? Trust me, it's trifling compared to what goes on here. Once you're on the slope down they don't want to know you. You become invisible. I won't stand for that. I won't let them edge me out. I won't become a nobody because my fool of a husband lost our money. I will never, ever let anyone except myself direct my life again. I have the apartment in London. I can work to support myself. And no one over there need ever know the details of what's happened here. I'll just reinvent myself and do it solo.'

'Why don't you go to London for a while and see how it goes without being too final about it?' Hilary suggested diplomatically.

'I don't *want* to live in some crappy egg box, midtown, fighting Des for maintenance money he won't have. I don't want to be dumped off my charity boards because I can't afford the whopping donation fees that are the price for being on them. I don't want to pass restaurants I didn't think twice about dining in because I can't afford to eat in them. I don't want to give up my Platinum card for an ordinary one. I don't want to slum it on public transport. I don't want to fly coach,' Colette retorted. 'Call me a snob if you like, but I worked hard for the lifestyle that I've had until now. It would just make me utterly, utterly depressed to give it up. We were supposed to be going to St Barts for a week in February. Where's he going to bring me now? New Jersey? Let him bring his mistress there and see how long she stays with him.' Colette took another slug of her wine, her eyes glittering with anger and unshed tears.

Hilary stayed silent. She certainly understood Colette's reasons for leaving New York but she didn't know what to say to soothe her, but at least Colette was expressing her anger and not keeping it bottled up.

'Should I go to visit Des?' she ventured.

'I don't care. It's up to you,' Colette said sullenly, going to the fridge to get another bottle. 'Come on, let's go into the den, I'll switch on the fire. You're doing a lot of wriggling on the chair. What's wrong with your back?'

'It's a bit dodgy at the minute,' Hilary explained, following Colette into the elegant cream-and-claret-toned room. She stretched out on a recliner chair. 'Oh! That's better,' she sighed as the niggle in her back eased. 'I suppose it didn't help having a ride on the settee last night and then having a six-hour flight today.' She sipped her wine.

'Why didn't you do it in bed?' Colette looked at Hilary over the rim of her glass as she lay curled up on the sofa.

'We got carried away,' Hilary laughed. 'We're having a revival now that the girls don't live at home any more.'

'After all these years! Are you for real? I can't remember the last time I got carried away,' Colette said morosely. 'You're a lucky wagon.'

'Yeah, I suppose I am,' Hilary conceded, hoping Colette wouldn't become a surly drunk.

'Do you think St Niall would cheat on you?' The question was fuelled with anger and drunken resentment.

'That's not nice, Colette,' rebuked Hilary. 'And the answer is I don't know. Does anyone?'

'But you have the *perfect* marriage, don't you?' Colette said sarcastically. Drink always gave her a hard edge.

'Don't be ridiculous, of course I don't!' Hilary scoffed. 'There's no such thing as the perfect marriage. Niall and I drive each other mad sometimes and we've had our ups and downs, especially when business was booming and I was flat out at work and feeling a lot of resentment towards him because I felt he wasn't backing me up, and he felt I was putting work before him. No way is my marriage perfect but we work through our stuff and we still love each other, and that's all that matters, isn't it?'

'I suppose so,' Colette muttered.

'Do you still love, Des?' Hilary demanded.

'Oh! I ... I don't know. We complement each other. We have the same interests and goals. We're a good team. *Were* a good team!' she corrected herself.

'And do you still fancy him?' Hilary asked bluntly.

'We've been married nearly twenty-five years, for God's sake. That wears off!' Colette exclaimed exasperatedly.

'Well actually it doesn't, Colette. I still fancy Niall big time. He turns me on and I turn him on and that's as important as anything else in our marriage. Perhaps you should go to counselling.'

'That would be hard if I'm living in London and he's living here,' jeered Colette.

Patricia Scanlan

'Not if you get on your broomstick,' Hilary retorted, glaring at her.

'Bitch!' Colette snapped.

'Good though, wasn't it?' Hilary grinned.

'You always were a sarky cow!'

'*Moi?*' Hilary teased. 'I was only trotting after you.' She fanned herself with her hand as a hot flush engulfed her.

'Are you having flashes?' Colette eyed her in surprise.

'If you mean flushes, yes.' Hilary blew some air up onto her face. 'Have you started yet?'

'Are you crazy? I'm not putting up with that carry-on. I'm on HRT. You should be on it too. No wonder your skin has lost its tone and you're creaking.'

'Thanks,' Hilary said caustically.

'Well you know what I mean. What are you letting yourself go for, when you can do something about it? HRT's fantastic.'

'Listen, when you come off it you'll have the flashes as you call them, so you're just putting it off. I just want to get it over and done with.'

'Well at least I'm keeping my looks and my flexibility, and I'm not a cranky dried-up old crab. The menopause is the last thing I need on top of this.'

'True,' conceded Hilary. 'That could send you over the top completely. You wouldn't even need a broomstick.' Colette laughed and the tense atmosphere evaporated.

'Are you going to tell your parents?' Hilary tried not to yawn. She was longing to go to bed but she had flown over the Atlantic to support her friend; it would be rude to plead jet lag.

'Are you *mad*? And have Dad lording it over Des?' Colette derided.

'So! You still feel loyalty towards him. That's something to hold on to.'

'No, Hil!' Colette shook her head. 'That was an automatic response, and I don't want Dad thinking my judgement was seriously flawed, which it obviously was. Des will not get one scintilla of loyalty from me ever again. He showed me none. *None!*' Her voice rose. 'He tried to get me to sign away my apartment. As long as I live I will never forgive him for that. I could have coped with the other woman. But not that! And don't tell me you could forgive if Niall did that to you, and lost the girls' inheritance because he was a stupid dumb-ass.'

'I know. I couldn't.' Hilary got up from the chair and went over to Colette and put her arm around her. 'Just tell me what you want me to do and how I can help. You know I'm here for you. And I can come over to London and help you to settle back in if you want,' she offered generously.

'Thanks, Hil.' Colette laid her head on her shoulder. 'I know I can always depend on you.'

'Jazzy, it's so good to see you, you look amazing,' Hilary said warmly the following morning when Jasmine arrived at the apartment to join them for brunch.

'Thanks, Hilary. I was only talking to Mom about you at lunch yesterday. Little did I think I'd actually be seeing you.' Jazzy kissed her and then hugged Colette. 'Hi, Mom. You look a train wreck.'

'Thanks,' Colette drawled.

'I'm sorry it's under difficult circumstances,' Hilary said kindly.

'Thanks for coming over for Mom. That was a kind thing to do. How's Sophie and Millie?' Jazzy perched on a high stool at the kitchen counter, casually elegant in jeans and a black-cashmere polo. Big silver hoop earrings her only jewellery. She had inherited her mother's sense of style, Hilary observed.

'They're good. Both working, as you know. Which is great because the job situation at home is getting pretty bad. Lots of people being made redundant.'

'Sophie and I Skype every so often. It's a great way of keeping in touch.'

'I'll be able to Skype you when I'm in London,' Colette interjected, handing her daughter a Kir royale.

'Thanks. Mom, Dad said you were going to London for Christmas, and that we won't be going skiing in Aspen because he's lost money with Bernie Madoff. Is he just doing a Dad on it and exaggerating?' she said plaintively.

'I'm going to London. I don't know what your dad plans to do. And I don't think he's exaggerating. I don't know exactly how much of our money he's lost in his investments. But it's a lot. I don't even know if he'll be able to keep up the rent here. I would imagine not,' Colette said grimly.

'Jeez, is it that bad? What about my allowance?' Jazzy's blue eyes widened in dismay.

'Look, until your dad has had his op and gets to meet our wealth manager, I don't know what the situation is. I'm going to divorce him, that's a given. It's over between us. But I don't know how much of a settlement I can expect.

Once I'm settled in London and see how I'm fixed financially I can sort out an allowance for you. Until then, if I were you, I would cut down on my spending,' advised her mother.

'What do you mean, *settled* in London?' Jazzy asked, perplexed.

'I'm leaving New York. I can't stay here. I'd love it if you wanted to come too but you have to make up your own mind and do what's best for you,' Colette said firmly.

'Leaving? For good? And what about Dad?' she demanded, appalled.

'Look, should I give you both some privacy?' Hilary said awkwardly, getting up off her stool.

'No, you're fine,' Jasmine said miserably and Hilary's heart went out to her.

'Dad might want to be with that woman. Did you ever think of that?' Colette carried a platter of antipasti to the table. 'Sweetie, bring the hummus and pitta bread to the table with you.'

'Don't you *mind*, Mom?' Jasmine couldn't hide her shock as she brought the food to the table.

'Whether I do or not, what's done is done. Your dad didn't think about us when he did what he did. I have to look to the future and start afresh. That's the only way I can deal with it, Jazzy. If I stay here I'll go to pieces and I won't allow myself to do that. So please, I beg you, don't make this any harder for me than what it is already. Now sit and eat with us and then, if Hilary wants to, she can go with you to see your dad.'

'OK,' her daughter muttered, struggling not to cry.

'Jazzy, it's not the end of the world. This too will pass and good times, different times will come again. Enjoy your life with Jackson—'

'He might leave me now that we're not rich any more,' she blurted tearfully.

'Well if he does he's not the man I think he is and he's not worthy of you, isn't that right, Hilary?' Colette reached across the table and squeezed her daughter's hand.

'Indeed it is. Look at you, Jazzy, a gorgeous young woman making a life for yourself in this fantastic city. As they say at home, "What's for you won't pass you by." If your boyfriend *is* the right one for you, terrific. If he's not, the right one will come.'

And pigs will fly, thought Colette cynically at the notion of a 'right one'. She said nothing. There was no point in making her daughter feel any more distressed than she already was.

'Sorry to see you under the weather, Des,' Hilary said awkwardly, deciding against kissing him and handing him the box of chocolates and the latest John Connolly thriller she had brought for him.

'Hey! That's kind of you. I didn't expect to see you, Hilary,' he said, abashed, hardly able to look her in the eye. He clicked off the TV and smiled at his daughter. 'Hi, Jazzy. Thanks for coming in and bringing Hilary with you.'

'Hi, Dad,' Jazzy said glumly.

'Just wanted to wish you well with your op,' Hilary said, feeling sorry for him in spite of herself. He looked red-eyed, red-nosed, pale and stressed lying back against his pillows, a far cry from the brash, supremely confident know-all she was used to seeing. He looked somehow diminished in his maroon pyjamas, with his drip and monitors attached to him.

'So how are all the folks at home? How's business?' He made an effort.

'Everyone's good at the minute, touch wood,' she said lightly. 'The downturn is hitting us badly. I had to make some of my employees redundant. Hard times universally. You're getting your share this side of the Pond.'

'Tell me about it. I suppose you know I got stuffed by Madoff.'

'I heard. We all got stuffed by the banks,' she sighed.

'That Anglo Irish carry-on is something else. Your regulator was really asleep on the job. How could he have missed that?' Des shook his head.

'How indeed, but he did, and the rating agencies were way off the mark, and we're paying for it. But hey, he got a great salary and a big fat pension. Gas, isn't it?'

'Practically everyone I knew and played golf with in Dublin had shares in Anglo,' Des observed. 'I remember an Anglo banker trying to persuade me to get into some hotel gig here in the States. Went belly up, I believe. Glad I stayed out of that one. He was a pushy little bloke, you know, smooth talker, slithery, a wide boy. I bet he didn't get caught.'

'Probably not,' murmured Hilary, thinking Des could have been describing himself and he didn't even realize it.

'Where's your mom, what's she doing today?' He turned to Jazzy who was staring out the window at the Manhattan skyline etched against a leaden sky.

'She's gone for a jog around the reservoir. We're meeting her in the Met for afternoon tea in the Patrons Lounge. She said we'd better make the most of it cos it looks like we won't be renewing our membership. She's going to move back to London! Did you know that?' She gazed at him dolefully.

'No I didn't.' He looked stricken.

'Look, why don't I leave you and Jazzy to chat for a while. I'll wait outside in the waiting area,' Hilary suggested. 'Get well soon and take care, Des.' She stood up and patted his hand and walked out the door, glad to have the excuse to leave. She didn't know if she would ever see her friend's soon-to-be-ex-husband ever again.

'That woman has a kind heart. She's a good friend to your mother. A better friend than Colette is to her,' Des remarked when the door closed and they were alone. 'When did your mom say she was going to London?'

'Today. She said I could come if I want. It's up to me.'

'And what are you going to do?' He looked at her despondent expression and felt a surge of guilt. He'd brought them to this, no one else. The responsibility was his and his alone.

'I don't want to leave Jackson, I don't want to leave you, but I don't want Mom to be on her own in London either. Do you think you could persuade her to stay?' she pleaded.

'I'll try but you know what your mom is like when she has her mind made up about something,' he said tiredly.

'Just try, Dad, try hard,' Jazzy urged.

'I will, Pippin,' he said, using his pet name for her. But privately Des felt he didn't stand a snowball's chance in hell.

*

'Jazzy tells me you're going to move back to London. Please let's talk about it, Colette, you owe me that much,' Des begged, holding fast to his promise to his daughter to try and persuade his wife to stay in New York. He had decided to call Colette on her cell as soon as Jazzy had left.

'There's nothing to talk about, Des. I'll stay until after you've had your surgery. After that you're on your own. You can get Miss Battery Park to nurse you back to full health. And just for the record I owe you *nothing!*' Colette said icily before hanging up.

Des stared at the dead screen on his phone. He knew Colette of old. When she made up her mind to follow a course of action that was it. There was no changing it. He should cut his losses and try and salvage something from his current situation.

He tapped a number he knew off by heart onto his phone.

'Hello?' came a familiar voice.

'Kaylee, it's me,' he said hopefully. There was silence.

'Hello? Kaylee?'

'Yes, Des, I hear you. How are you?' Kaylee said coolly.

'Not the best. I've to have a bypass.' He played the sympathy card but didn't say it was a triple. He didn't want to make out he was a complete crock.

'Sorry to hear that,' she said as though she was speaking to a stranger, and not someone she used to wrap her long shapely legs around and beg to make love to her.

'Look, can we talk? I want to be with you. I miss you very much,' Des said softly.

'What's wrong? Did your wife kick you out?' Kaylee sneered. 'Well it's like this, Des, you had your chance with me and you didn't take it. I'm never going to be a second choice for *anyone* and especially not for you. Don't call me again.' For the second time that day his phone went dead as an angry woman hung up on him.

If he was lucky he might die under the knife, Des thought dejectedly. Because he didn't want to have to deal with what was facing him when he left the unlikely haven that his room in Lennox Hill had become.

Kaylee lay curled up on her bed and cried her heart out. Great gulping, heaving sobs that wracked her body. She could have had the man of her dreams. He'd practically thrown himself at her just now, and for one moment when she'd heard Des say that he missed her she'd almost weakened. But in her heart she knew that if she'd taken Des back he would only have been with her because his wife had given him the boot. The knowledge would have been a malignancy in their relationship that would have eventually destroyed it. She would have despised him even more than she did right this minute.

She'd just have to endure the heartache and get through it and never, ever have an affair with an unavailable man again. She wiped her eyes and got off her bed and went to the fridge. There was cold mac and cheese. That and a glass of red might help. She took the repast and sat in front of the TV and channel-hopped until she came across an old fifties weepie with Lana Turner. Perfect, Kaylee thought miserably, curling up on the sofa for a weep fest as the skies darkened out over the Harbor.

CHAPTER THIRTY-EIGHT

'So you've made up your mind, you're definitely going back to London,' Hilary said to Colette on their last night together before she flew to meet Niall in Toronto the following day.

'Yup! There's nothing for me here. I'm done.' Colette knelt on Hilary's case for her while she struggled to close the zip. Hilary had spent the day in Macy's buying bargains in the pre-Christmas sales.

'And will you stay there for Christmas or will you come to Dublin?' Hilary sat back on her heels.

'I thought I might invite the parents over for Christmas. They always hold a big New Year bash so they'll want to be home for that.' Colette stood up.

'And will you come over for it?' Hilary wiped her brow as the familiar and unwelcome prickles of heat made her scalp so hot she felt she could fry an egg on it.

'God, I couldn't think of anything worse. The soon-to-be-divorced daughter. On her own. I don't think so.' Colette grimaced.

'Come over, and stay with *us* on New Year's Eve then. We always have a trad night. It's great fun,' Hilary invited.

'I haven't been to a trad night in *years*!' Colette declared with a hint of a smile.

'That's cos you got too posh and sophisticated,' teased Hilary. 'Come on, we'll have a laugh!'

'I suppose Queenie Harpur will be there.' Colette sniffed.

'Ah stop! Jonathan's the best. I don't know why you never took to him.' Hilary stood up and rubbed her back.

'He thinks he owns you. He's always telling you what to do.' Colette scowled.

'He organizes me. Someone has to. He's a great friend. ' Hilary had forgotten how childish Colette could be sometimes.

'Well I'm your oldest friend,' Colette declared. 'Let's open a bottle of Pétrus to celebrate friendship.'

'Maybe not, Colette,' demurred Hilary. 'It might give Des another heart attack when he comes home to find his wine cellar has been raided and the most expensive ones are gone.'

'That's not all that will have been raided,' Colette said with a gleam in her eye, going in search of the corkscrew.

Niall was waiting for her in arrivals when Hilary landed at Toronto Pearson International Airport the following morning and she abandoned her trolley and flew into his arms, kissing him soundly.

He laughed when he drew away. 'Did you miss me then?' he teased.

'Oh I did,' she said fervently. 'We are *so* lucky, Niall. I know we have our ups and downs but nothing like what's going on with the Williamses. I just feel sorry for every single one of that family.'

'Even Des?' he asked, surprised, as she linked his arm while he pushed the trolley through the terminal.

'Even Des, the prat! I really think he panicked when he tried to get Colette to sign that document. That's my reading of it, but Colette doesn't want to know. She just wants out. She couldn't bear to "slum it" around New York without her Town Cars and charity committees and the like. I hope you've booked a Town Car for us to bring us to the hotel,' she joked.

'Sorry, it's your common or garden taxi,' Niall grinned. 'But we *have* got a lovely room in the Ritz-Carlton with stunning views over Lake Ontario, and a massive bed!'

'*Excellent!*' Hilary exclaimed happily. 'What are we waiting for?'

'What indeed?' agreed her husband. 'Little did we think we'd be having a second honeymoon in Toronto this December.'

'Here's us having a second honeymoon and Colette and Des are on the skids,' Hilary said sombrely.

'You were there for them. You did your best for Colette – no friend could ask for more,' Niall approved.

'They're going to divorce. Colette's adamant about that.'

'That's tough and I wouldn't wish it on anyone. Poor Jazzy.' Niall manoeuvred the trolley through the doors and they emerged into a crisp, cold, blue-skied morning to queue for a taxi.

'Oh it's freezing,' Hilary gasped. 'Much colder than New York.'

'Never fear, I'll warm you up soon enough,' Niall promised as a cab drew to a halt and minutes later they were cuddled up together holding hands in the back seat, heading for downtown Toronto.

A week later, the day before Des was due home from hospital, Colette Sellotaped a bubble-wrapped parcel tightly, and laid it carefully into the inlaid drawer in the pedestal desk. She turned the key, locked it, and then put the key in her pocket. She walked into the formal dining room and studied the paintings and antiques she had stuck coloured labels on. She glanced at her watch. The shipping company was due at nine. To transport the items she was taking with her to London she was using a specialist company that the gallery employed to ship fine art and antiques around the world. Before they arrived she had ten minutes to herself to sip her green tea and walk around the apartment that had been her home for so long.

'Do not get sad,' she warned herself aloud as her lower lip trembled when she saw her Vuitton cases in the foyer. 'Remember what he did to you!' She had given Encarna the morning off. Colette couldn't bear to say goodbye to her housekeeper. It had been bad enough saying goodbye to Jazzy a few days previously. Jackson had invited her to Boston for a long weekend before Christmas because Jazzy wanted to be in New York when her father got home from hospital.

'So what day *are* you leaving?' she'd sobbed.

'I'm not exactly sure yet. I want to wait and see when your father is being discharged,' Colette said gently. 'But I *will* be gone before you get back. There's less that ten days to Christmas and your grandparents are coming over to

London. I need to have the house prepared. I'll tell you what, depending on what's happening, I'll come back in February and stay with you, how's that?'

'Oh please promise me you will,' Jazzy implored as they walked through the foyer of Le Parker Meridien.

'I promise,' Colette said, hugging her tightly. If there was one good thing to come out of this fiasco it was the strengthening of their mother–daughter relationship, Colette reflected, waving her daughter off in a taxi to meet Jackson, after their farewell brunch in Norma's, one of their favourite restaurants. Colette had cried, walking home along Fifth Avenue, and never felt more miserable in her life.

'Don't think about it now,' Colette told herself, standing in what was once her marital bedroom. She had stripped the bed and it looked bare and unwelcoming. Encarna could change it later, for when Des arrived home the following day. Colette would be spending her last night in New York in the Plaza, courtesy of her husband's credit card. She had booked her room online with it. She would be travelling first-class to London on the same card and had ordered, and paid for, a car to meet her at Heathrow.

She gazed out at the corner view of Central Park in the distance. She loved that park; she'd miss her daily jogs around the reservoir. She would get into a routine in London, she comforted herself. The Serpentine would be just as beautiful to run around.

The trees were grey and skeletal, their long, bony branches bare and forbidding. She was very glad she wasn't leaving in the spring when the buds were bursting into bloom and the warmth of the sun hinting at summer. Would she ever summer in Nantucket again? she wondered sadly, remembering blissful days when she was alone and not entertaining, lying on the deck listening to the roar of the ocean, sipping Pimm's and reading Elin Hilderbrand novels under the shade of the canopy.

Those days were gone. The past was the past. She had to move on, Colette told herself sternly, her heart giving a leap when the concierge rang to tell her that the removal men were on the way up.

Colette took a deep breath and straightened her shoulders and walked out to the door and stood waiting for them in her lobby. 'Good morning,' she greeted the team of men. 'Everything I've labelled is to be packed. They are antiques for the most part. And you know to be particularly careful of the paintings. I want my walk-in closet cleared of everything. And I have some linens to go also and some books. You can start now and if you've any queries ask me.'

'You heard what the lady said. Let's do it room by room.' The man in charge gave the thumbs-up and the packing began.

Two hours later, with the paperwork all in order, Colette watched the container carrying all their antiques, paintings, costly linens and most of her clothes, shoes and personal items disappear down the city street below on the first leg of its journey to the UK. She had deliberately undervalued the contents hoping that UK Customs and Excise would not see them as more than normal removal items for a relocation. It was a risk she had to take.

She stared around at the bare walls and the space in the den where the desk used to be. Des would miss that desk more than anything else she had taken. The thought, strangely, gave her no pleasure. She walked through the hallway to Jazzy's old room. It was the only room in the apartment that had nothing removed from it. It was exactly as it had always been, even to the line of cuddly toys on the bed. Her daughter would be able to close the door and pretend everything was the way it used to be.

The phone rang. 'Mrs Williams, your Town Car is outside,' the concierge informed her.

'Thank you, Davy, can you have my luggage collected, please?'

'Yes, ma'am.'

'You go down and send the lift back up to me. I just have one little chore to do,' Colette instructed the young bellboy who loaded her luggage into the lift. She walked into the kitchen and placed two envelopes on the counter, side by side. One addressed to Encarna with a letter of thanks and a hefty gift voucher for Saks, purchased on her husband's card. The second envelope, addressed to Des, was bulkier. She was sorry she wouldn't see his face when he read her note.

She closed the kitchen door behind her and stood in the hall surprised at how bare it was now that the console table and the paintings were gone. She wondered how long Des would stay in the apartment. How long could he afford to? That wasn't her worry. It was time to go. Colette lifted her chin, draped her Chanel faux-fur coat over her shoulders and picked up her bag. Without a backward glance she strode out of the door, locked it, and stepped into the elevator. She took a fifty from her wallet. Davy was her favourite concierge. She was glad he was on today. 'Thank you for all your help, Davy. Take care.' She discreetly pressed the note into his hand, as he was on the desk phone, and an elderly man was waiting to speak to him.

'Thanks to you, Mrs Williams.' He raised his hand in farewell and she was glad he was busy, it made it easier to leave. She tipped the bellboy who held the door open for her and walked out of her building for the last time. She would never come back to this place.

Her driver was waiting with the car engine running and soft snowflakes drifted down from the sullen sky. 'Lennox Hill Hospital,' she instructed, keeping her gaze averted from her building. She was surprised at how calm she was. No doubt she would fall to pieces at some stage but for now Colette was relieved that she felt quite numb.

'I'll only be in here ten minutes, max,' she said when the car pulled up outside the entrance to the hospital. Des was dressed, sitting in his chair by the window reading the *Wall Street Journal* when she knocked and walked into his room. He looked surprisingly well. The colour had returned to his cheeks and he appeared rested. He had made a good recovery from his bypass.

'This is unexpected.' He stood up to greet her, a watchful expression in his eyes. Not sure if her visit was an indication that full-blown hostilities were on the wane. 'Let me take your coat.'

'It's just a flying visit, actually. I'm not staying.' Colette felt an almighty and bewildering wave of sadness and it shocked her. She hadn't expected it. Now that her departure was imminent, the reality that her marriage was over was like a cold shower. She had shared half her life with this man and now they were like polite acquaintances. When she left this hospital room she would be on her own. Was that what she wanted? Her emotions roiled like a raging sea. Stay or go? Stay or go? All the actions she had taken could be reversed. And then she remembered Mamie Winston's fate: social oblivion. Failure!

'Are you off to lunch somewhere? You look very glam,' Des complimented her.

Colette took a deep breath. 'No, Des. I just wanted to tell you that I'm going to London, for good. I don't want to be in the apartment when you get home tomorrow. Encarna will have the bed changed for you and a meal cooked. I hope you recover well.'

'Don't go,' Des pleaded. 'I need you. *Please*, Colette. I've made some terrible mistakes. But let's at least *talk* about it. Don't throw it all away.' He gazed at her imploringly.

'You have made some terrible mistakes,' she agreed tiredly. 'I won't argue with that. But *you* threw it all away! And you might need me, but I don't need *you*, Des. My divorce lawyers will be in touch.' The devastating memory of her mind-numbing shock at seeing the loan application he'd already signed helped keep the steel in her heart. 'Goodbye, Des,' Colette said tonelessly and walked out the door.

CHAPTER THIRTY-NINE

'Let me carry that, Mr Williams.' Davy took Des's case from him and wheeled it across the lobby.

'No need to come up, Davy. I can manage fine,' Des told the concierge, slipping him a note.

He felt strange being back out in the world. Vulnerable, nervous even. He'd got used to the nurses coming in and out, doing their checks, settling him for the night. It was a comfort to know someone was there if his ticker went funny again. Tonight he would be on his own. His fleeting dance with his own mortality had dented his confidence. He was a mere mortal like everyone else, Des sighed. Anything could get him – the heart, cancer, brain tumour – he'd been getting a lot of headaches lately ... The knock on his door had served to remind him that he was no different from anyone else, and he didn't like it.

A wave of self-pity overtook him as the elevator rode silently upwards. The man he had been the last time he had stood in it was a far different man from the one standing here now. The sands had shifted. His circumstances had changed radically. His financial safety net tattered and torn. He let himself into the apartment and went to drop his keys in the bowl. Something wasn't right about the place, he thought distractedly. The keys fell on the floor. Des did a double take. The bowl was gone, as was the console table, and the three large paintings that Colette had insisted they buy as an investment. 'Another egg in another basket,' she'd said when he'd moaned about the price of them.

Had they had a robbery? How could that happen? The thought flitted through his mind. Through the half-open door of the den he saw that more paintings had gone and there was an empty space where his desk used to be. Realization began to dawn. No wonder Colette had wanted to be gone before he came home. The little thief had stolen everything of value. He went further into the room and stared around. It felt alien to him. No longer a haven.

'Welcome home, Mr Williams.' Encarna stood at the door, eyes downcast.

'Not much of a welcome, Encarna. I see a lot of bare walls and empty spaces,' he said bleakly. 'Were you here when this happened?'

'No, sir. Mrs Williams gave me the morning off yesterday. When I came in at 2 p.m. she was gone and so was the furniture. She had left me a note to say she was getting a divorce and would not be back, and to make up your bed and prepare a meal for you today.'

'What else is gone?' He dropped his case and flopped down on the sofa.

'The dining table and chairs and the sideboard. Some of the bedlinen and glassware and flatware. A TV—'

'The Bang & Olufsen?' He was stunned.

'Yes, sir. And some of the ornaments and rugs.'

'Everything of value.' He spoke almost to himself.

'Shall I serve you lunch? On a tray in here, perhaps?' Encarna tried to hide her embarrassment.

'I don't think I'm very hungry, Encarna. Go home – I can get something later. I'd just like to be alone,' he said heavily.

'Are you sure you'll be OK?' His housekeeper looked concerned. 'Miss Jazzy will be back from Boston tonight. I have her room all ready for her. Mrs Williams told me that she's staying with you for a couple of nights,' Encarna said comfortingly.

'That's nice. Great news. She did tell me that she'd see me. Thanks, Encarna. I'll be fine. You head home.' He unbuttoned his coat and unwound the scarf from around his neck and sat in the empty silence. He heard the housekeeper gathering her things, call a subdued goodbye, and then the door closed and Des felt more alone and unnerved than he had ever felt in his entire life. Weariness enveloped him. He should try and catch up on his work, he supposed, but he couldn't face it.

Colette was a tough cookie; he'd always known that. But he'd certainly underestimated her. There was a cold, hard side to her that he'd seen her use to good effect throughout their marriage. He'd seen her cut people who had offended her out of her life. The guillotine effect, he'd called it. He had never believed he would be suffering the same fate. A thought struck him and he stood up and hurried into his walk-in dressing room and switched on the light. He parted his suits hanging on the rail, and slid back the false panel to reveal a safe. He twisted the dial. Even before the door swung open he knew the gold was gone. Colette had taken her pound of flesh and then some.

His mouth felt dry and he made his way to the kitchen fridge to get a can of cold tonic. He cracked it and took a slug and noticed an envelope propped up on the counter with his name on it, written in his wife's flamboyant script.

'What new hell?' he muttered, opening the envelope warily, sliding out a torn document. 'Aw crap!' he swore. No wonder Colette had cleaned him out. He'd forgotten about the damn loan application. She must have found it in his briefcase. A small yellow Post-it fluttered to the ground. He picked it up.

The Deal Breaker was written on it in Colette's usual flourish. He knew what she was saying. Not Kaylee, and not even Madoff, would have split them up. She would have dealt with those. But trying to lure her into signing over the apartment was a step too far. No wonder she wanted a divorce. How could he blame her? But she hadn't gone quietly into the night. Not Colette. She had been as ruthless and calculating as he had ever been. The guillotine had fallen and how.

'Nice one, honey.' Des raised his drink to his absent wife.

He wondered if she would get the gold unchecked through Customs. All might not yet be lost. If she were caught bringing out more than the allowance, she'd have to leave it Stateside and pay a fine as well. He wondered what flight she was on. Had she left? Was there any point in ringing Customs in JFK and alerting them? His thoughts darted here and there.

'Ah hell, she's probably long gone,' he said aloud. She'd left the apartment the previous day and probably caught a red-eye to London. Colette didn't like hanging around when she had somewhere to go. And it seemed that she couldn't shake the dust of NYC off her feet quick enough. She was probably in the UK right this minute fighting jet lag.

Exhausted, he took off his coat and scarf and left them draped over the bar counter and walked back into the den. He lay down on the sofa wishing he was back in Lennox Hill with nothing to worry him, only what meal to select from the menu and what TV channel to watch. Had Colette told Jasmine about the 'Deal Breaker'? Would he look into his daughter's eyes when she came back from Boston later and see disgust and derision? His daughter had taken the news of the affair reasonably calmly. Affairs were commonplace in their circle. She had grown up hearing about this marriage or that one breaking up. But attempted deliberate fraud perpetrated against your mother was another matter entirely, and as she had made clear, Colette would never forgive him for that. And if Jasmine knew about it, he was sure to get plenty of flack from her. A prospect he did not relish.

His eyelids drooped. He was drained after all the unsettling trauma and being back out in the real world again. Des drifted off to sleep and only awoke when faded dusk had settled on the city and the room was dark and still. He had never felt more alone.

'Thank you, that's lovely, very chic!' Colette approved, loving the subtle tones of her new golden-honey shade. 'Wonderful cut.'

'It's a very good colour on you, Mrs Williams,' the stylist complimented, holding the mirror this way and that so that she could view her new style from every angle. Colette stared at the reflection of her immaculately made-up face, framed by her newly cut and coloured hair, and had to admit no one would guess that she was going through a life-changing trauma that had knocked her for six. She looked like a woman in her late thirties, she approved signing her name and room number and making sure she gave a generous tip, seeing as Des was paying.

'Thank you so much. I do hope we see you again,' came the gracious response.

'I hope so too,' Colette said brightly, thinking it might be a very long time before she could afford to stay in the Plaza and indulge herself in their luxurious salon. And indulge herself she had, she reflected, taking the elevator to her suite with the view of the Park. She'd been in the salon for hours. Colour, conditioning and cut for her hair, waxing, manicure and pedicure, tinting of eyebrows and lashes, *and* a make-up. The previous evening she'd had a full body massage and an hour's facial. Colette looked at her diamond-studded watch. She'd want to be getting a move on. It would be time to leave for JFK in another hour or so. She wanted to eat something light. It was a shame to waste her makeover eating alone in her room but there was every likelihood she might meet some society matron she knew in the intimate setting of the Champagne Bar and even though she loved the over-the-top decadence of the Palm Court, it would make her too sad to eat alone there and the last thing she wanted was snotty tears ruining her make-up. It was too cold to take a last stroll up to the Tavern on the Green, one of her favourite New York eateries. And that would make her feel sad too. She, Des and Jazzy had often eaten brunch there on Sundays, after a walk through the Park. She had always felt the restaurant was the very essence of New York. No, she couldn't go there. It would be way too melancholy. Best to eat in her room, Colette decided.

Dusk was falling over Central Park and she stared out greedily at the city she loved, trying to imprint it all on her mind. Two lovers kissed at the Pulitzer Fountain, a teenager munched on a hot dog, swaying to the music coming out of his headphones. A child pointed to an enormous Santa in a shop window. The gay, giddy garishness of the Christmas lights and decorations made her feel lonely and bereft. She and Des had brought Jazzy to FAO Schwarz, across on Fifth, every year. Then they would come here to the Plaza for dinner and Jazzy would demand to be told the story of the delightfully precocious Eloise, who was such an intrinsic part of the fabric of the iconic hotel.

Colette was happy then, and she hadn't known it. Those early years in New York had been the best of her life. She and Des had been united in their goals. They'd looked out for each other, delighting in each other's success. He had introduced her to people who had become her clients in the gallery and she had introduced people from her circle to him, and they had become his clients. There had been a lot of good times in their marriage, she thought, surprised. But now that life was over and she was leaving the city that had given her so much.

'Stop it! Buck up!' she told herself, flicking thorough the room service menu. She settled on the lobster salad. That would be filling enough but not too stodgy and she would just graze on the flight. She wondered was Des home yet and how had he felt when he'd seen that she'd looted the apartment. Sauce for the goose! Not a wonderful homecoming for someone who was only a few days after surgery but at least Encarna would have been there to greet him. Would he be able to continue to employ their housekeeper? How long would he stay in the apartment? How much *exactly* of their savings had he lost? So many questions for which she had no answers. Colette had never seen her husband so shaken. Part of her felt concern for him. She wasn't a total Borg. But her overwhelming feeling towards Des was *rage*. Anger with him that he had brought them to this was even stronger than the deep hurt that he would deceive her in so many ways.

She stared out of the window into the darkening night as the lights became brighter and the skyscrapers looked even more imposing than in daylight. Thank God Jazzy had finished university, Colette thought gratefully. Their daughter had received a fine, Ivy League education and she would be a wealthy young woman eventually. Jacqueline had told Colette that she and Frank had left a trust fund for their only grandchild. Jazzy would be well provided for. What would happen to Des and how he would fare she did not know, or, right now, care. For herself, she had ensured that she had sufficient funds to keep her in a reasonable lifestyle for a couple of years. The paintings, antiques and furniture acquired over the almost two decades they had lived in Manhattan – and the recently acquired gold – would liquidate into at least a quarter of a million sterling. Enough to keep her going for a while, but not enough to fund the type of lifestyle she'd been used to. From now on she'd have to rein in her spending. Something she'd never before had to do.

Colette ate her salad without tasting it, so consumed was she by the thoughts racing through her mind. She did not welcome this new aloneness. She'd always liked the feeling that she had someone at her back. Now she was dependent on herself. Returning to London to live would be a real cutting of the ties but it had to be done. She went to the desk at the window overlooking Fifth Avenue, and picked up a pile of neatly addressed envelopes. They were handwritten notes of farewell, and several of resignation from her various committees and boards. She had spent an hour after she'd arrived at the hotel the previous day going through her Rolodex and Filofax to make sure she didn't leave anyone out. She had merely said that she was relocating to London for family reasons. Let them speculate as to the whys and wherefores; she wouldn't be seeing most of them again. To meet any of her American friends and acquaintances face to face, now that her circumstances had changed so radically, would be a humiliation too far.

Pride stiffened her resolve. It was time to go. There was no point in procrastinating. A chapter of her life had ended and a new one was beginning. If the absolute worst came to the worst she could sell the flat in London and return home to Dublin. But that would only be if she was in *dire* straits. Her parents were getting old and they were beginning to show their age. A nursemaid she would not be. Frank and Jacqueline had salted away enough to have a very affluent old age. They could pay for a carer if they needed one. Colette felt another sudden surge of anger towards Des. It was unthinkable that she would even *consider* returning to Ireland to live, if she couldn't hack it in London. No! She would not run home to Mummy and Daddy like some little wimp. She had more pride than that. She *would* make a go of life on her own.

She checked her travel bag for her passport and travel documents. The neat Tiffany's box in which she had placed the dinky, one-ounce bars of gold nestled at the bottom of her bag. Would she be stopped at security or Customs and Excise? Not that it mattered. She was legally entitled to take the amount she carried in her bag. It was the stash hidden in the drawer of the pedestal desk, which was now in the container heading for London, that could cause problems if it was discovered. Or it could be stolen! But she wouldn't think about that now. She had enough to contend with for the moment. She rang down to order her car and asked for a bellboy to be sent up, before wrapping her fur around her and pulling on her kid leather gloves. 'Goodbye, New York,' she murmured when the bellboy knocked on the door. 'I'll see you in the spring.'

'Omigod, Dad! The place is so *weird!*' Jazzy exclaimed, standing in the foyer, gazing around her in dismay.

'Your mother's revenge.' Des gave a wry smile.

'Oh! I suppose. It's a very Mom thing to do,' Jazzy sighed, dropping her overnight bag and giving him a hug.

'It's good to see you, Pippin!' He hugged her back, feeling a deep gratitude that Colette had obviously not told their daughter about the 'Deal Breaker' episode. He was delighted to see her, glad that she would bring some life back into the place that had once been their home.

'How are you feeling?' She followed him into the kitchen.

'Tired! Worried! Sad! Take your pick,' Des grimaced. 'Encarna left a fish chowder, and lamb tagine and couscous for us. Are you hungry?'

'For Encarna's cooking, *always*!' Jazzy said with fake enthusiasm. She was afraid to go into the other rooms to see what Colette had absconded with. She had hoped that, when her mother had calmed down after spending Christmas in London, she would miss her life in New York and come back. Colette's actions made it clear no such return was on the cards and Jazzy realized with a deep sense of foreboding that her parents' marriage was well and truly over, and the lifestyle she had taken so much for granted was a thing of the past. Unable to hide her dismay and distress, she burst into tears.

'Jazzy, don't cry,' Des pleaded, putting his arms around her.

'Lots of women get over their husband having an affair,' she sobbed. 'It happens all the time. Why did she have to leave?'

'Mom is the kind of woman who takes no prisoners, you know that,' he said gently. 'Perhaps there'll come a time when she'll forgive me. And if you want to go to London to be with her for Christmas I'll understand perfectly and I'll pay for your flight,' he offered generously.

'Thanks, Dad, but I think I'll stay here. Jackson and I have been invited to a lot of parties and it will be my first Christmas with him, even if it has been spoilt,' she sniffed. 'Why, Dad? Why did you reach out to another woman?'

'Look, these things happen in a marriage. You get bored.

You feel you're being neglected. Your mother was always very busy with the gallery—'

'And with entertaining your colleagues too,' Jazzy cut in sharply.

'Yes, that too,' Des sighed. 'The opportunity was there and I took it and I shouldn't have.'

'No, you shouldn't have. Poor Mom going to England alone. What a horrible Christmas she's going to have,' Jazzy bit her lip.

'I know that. If you change your mind about going, let me know,' her father said dispiritedly, wondering where were the bowls Encarna usually served their chowder in. He'd better start finding his way around his own kitchen. He would be putting Encarna on a three-day week, mornings only. After New Year he would have to take a serious look at his finances and discreetly begin the search for a smaller apartment, in a less exclusive district of the city. If this year had turned out a bummer next year looked as though it was going to be even worse. Listening to his daughter's stifled sobs, Des felt like bursting into tears himself.

The comfort of walking into a warm, freshly painted, spotlessly clean apartment almost made up for the incredibly bumpy flight and the scary descent into Heathrow, when crosswinds buffeted the plane. Colette gazed around the familiar lounge with the big window looking out onto the elegant square and burst into tears. She flung herself down on the sofa and sobbed like a baby as all the exhaustion and shock of the past two weeks overcame her, and she cried until she was limp and drained and could cry no more. She had planned not to go to bed, hoping to have slept on the overnight flight, but even in the comfort of first-class it had been too bumpy to be relaxing and she had felt quite tense. Now though she was exhausted, too tired even to make herself a cup of tea.

She went down to the master bedroom and burst into fresh tears realizing that Des would never sleep on his side of the outsize bed again, and that she was now a woman alone. She switched on the electric blanket, got undressed, and wrapped a robe around her while she cleansed, toned and moisturized. Not even the greatest crisis of her life would disrupt her bedtime beauty routine.

It was raining outside, drumming against the window, and the skies were dreary with ominous clouds. It was a relief to slip into the warmth of her luxurious soft sheets, and to pull the duvet up to her chin, knowing that she had a day and a night to recover before she had to face the realities of her situation and set about arranging meetings with lawyers and her bosses in Dickon and Austen's.

Colette had thought that she would toss and turn but she fell asleep almost instantly and slept through the day, not waking until 4.30 that afternoon. Hunger gnawed at her and she pulled on a robe and padded out to the kitchen. It was dark already, and the view was so different from the one from her apartment in New York. It would take time to adjust to this life-changing move. Had she been too hasty? she wondered apprehensively, staring at the changed skyline. It was still raining and she closed the blinds to shut out the wintry night.

She had emailed a list of groceries and requirements to her

maintenance firm, and the fridge was well stocked. She heated some soup, and ate it with granary bread and Cheddar. A rare treat for someone who stayed away from carbs and dairy. She left the dishes in the sink and went back to bed and flicked on Sky News. A reporter was commenting on plans for Obama's forthcoming inauguration, flashing up images of Washington and Capitol Hill and for a surreal moment Colette felt she was back in the States. She switched the TV off and burst into tears.

She and Des had been invited to celebrate and view the historic occasion at a soirée to be thrown by the McLean-Butlers, at their Park Ave residence. They had got to know the affluent power couple in Nantucket over the years and had become friendly. Michelle McLean-Butler had bought several pieces from the gallery and Colette had made sure to give her a discount each time, knowing that she would bring other clients through word of mouth. Colette liked Michelle, who didn't give a hoot about what people thought, which was quite refreshing in the society circles they moved in. Michelle was one of the few she would miss.

Now that she was truly on her own, she felt unnerved, apprehensive even. Had she done the right thing, leaving New York? Leaving Jazzy? She was right to leave Des, of that she had no doubts. It was so long since she'd lived in London – everyone she'd known would have moved on, forgotten her even. It was daunting to think that she'd practically have to start all over again. Did she have the energy for it? The nerve to do it solo? It was so much easier making changes when you were young and fearless ... or even foolish, Colette thought with a brief spark of black humour. She was middle-aged now, used to being part of a couple for so long, it was strange being alone. But here she was, by her own choice and decision; she would have to get on with it.

Colette wiped her eyes and picked up the latest *Vanity Fair* she had flicked through on the plane. There was an article she wanted to read about Veronica de Gruyter Beracasa de Uribe, who had swept publishing mogul Randolph Hearst off his feet – and to the top of New York and Palm Beach society, and how after his death she had ended up forty-five million dollars in the red.

She and Des had never penetrated that rarefied strata of High Society, nor had she aspired to, but she had seen the Hearsts in the Met occasionally, and was aware that the hapless Veronica had hosted an intimate lunch for the late Princess of Wales, in the mid-nineties, which had truly cemented her social standing. For all the good it had done her, Colette mused, studying the glossy pictures intently. The high-flying Widow Hearst's circumstances appeared far more dire than her own, which was a vague comfort. She read the gossipy article with interest and flipped over the pages to read about Kate Winslet, before her eyelids began to droop and she fell into another jet-lagged sleep.

She was sipping Earl Grey and nibbling on a piece of toast around midnight when the landline rang. Her New York apartment number flashed up on the screen. She stared at it. It had to be Des. Colette frowned. She could ignore it, or take the call. She was going to have to speak to her husband eventually; she might as well get it over with.

'Hello,' she said in a clipped, cool voice.

'Nice one, Colette. I didn't see that coming, for sure! Or

you maxing out my Platinum card, or talking half of what was in our joint account, or selling the car. Or helping yourself to the gold. How did you get it through Customs and Excise, just as a matter of interest?' Des was admirably calm, she thought.

'That's for me to know and you to find out, Des,' she retorted. If her husband knew that it was sitting in a container being shipped across the Atlantic he'd freak. She was trying not to freak about it herself.

'Well I guess I can't do anything about what you've done, but just to let you know that when I liquidate the rest of our assets I'll be deducting what you've taken from your share,' he said grimly.

'I did what I had to do, Des. You would have mortgaged my apartment—'

'I was going to borrow that money to buy gold and flip it. Gold will go sky high – look how high it's gone since we bought in the spring. I'd have made a profit that would have negated much of our losses,' he said furiously. 'You over-reacted!'

'You'd have gambled my apartment, like you gambled our money with Madoff, you mean,' Colette snapped. 'You treated me appallingly, Des. You should have had the decency to at least ask me to *consider* the loan option, instead of trying to sneak it through behind my back. I only took what I was entitled to, and I'm entitled to a lot more, so don't think this is the end of it. And guess what? That woman, whoever she is, is welcome to you because I don't want to have anything to do with you ever again.' She slammed down the phone, incandescent. How *dare* he claim she had overreacted? Had he no conception of how badly *he* had behaved?

By the time she was finished with him, he'd understand ... and more. You did not mess with Colette O'Mahony and get away with it, as Des would eventually find, to his cost.

CHAPTER FORTY

The Bon Secours was an attractive hospital, Jonathan thought, admiring the red-brick façade and long sash windows of the three-storey building atop Washerwoman's Hill in Glasnevin. He drove past the long, sweeping, verdant lawn edged with conifers, and swung into the car park. He rooted in his coin tray for two euros. Jonathan resented paying parking fees in hospital car parks, on principle, feeling that life was hard enough for people who had sick relatives in hospital. He'd been caught for fifteen euros in Beaumont the previous week, visiting his old friend and ex-flatmate Orla who was having her gall bladder removed. An elderly woman he'd shared a lift with had told him she was spending more than fifty euros a week in parking fees, visiting a seriously ill relative who had been in hospital for many months. She'd even had to pay on Christmas Day, she'd said, disgusted. It was scandalous: greed, pure greed, and bad scran to Euro Car Parks, she'd declared crossly and Jonathan had laughed, remembering how his mother would say *bad scran* about someone when she was annoyed with them. It was a real country saying.

Night was drawing in already, he noticed, crossing the

car park and seeing the fading smudges of pink-gold sky behind the serrated rims of the trees in the Botanic Gardens. The Christmas tree lights in the houses on Griffith Avenue had twinkled brighter in the gloaming and he'd felt a fierce swell of loneliness to think that another year was almost over and he was *still* alone. He had given up on his hopes of ever finding a partner. The hurt he'd experienced at Leon's callous rejection of him, even though it was eight years ago, had brought his barriers up and he had never let himself get close to anyone since. Mostly he lived a reasonably happy life, but Christmas and New Year always accentuated his loneliness, bringing him to a dark place he would struggle not to linger in. Although he was surrounded by family and dear friends he still felt lonely at Christmas, especially when he would come home to his cottage and open the door and walk in to silence.

Stop feeling sorry for yourself. You're very lucky to have what you have, he chastised himself irritably, hurrying up the steps to the entrance to the hospital. A large, illuminated crib graced the foyer and he stood for a moment admiring it with his decorator's eye. So simple yet evocative. The scene stirred up long dormant childhood memories. Jonathan grinned, remembering a school Nativity play he'd had a starring role in: King Herod. The play had taken place in the school hall and when he had looked down from the stage and seen the audience looking at him as he waved his whip – made out of a tin-foil roll and strips of coloured paper – he had burst into tears and howled, 'I'm only *pretending* to be bad, I really *do* love Baby Jesus,' much to the consternation of his mother and teacher, but to the delight of the audience who had collectively gone, 'Awwww!' That seemed like a lifetime ago, he thought ruefully, sprinting two floors up the wide staircase to St Mary's.

He knocked on room 222 and heard an invite to come in. 'Ah Jonathan!' exclaimed Father McDaid, who was resting against the pristine white pillows, chatting to another man who was sitting in the armchair beside the bed. 'How very kind of you to visit.'

'How are you feeling?' Jonathan asked kindly, handing the elderly man a carrier bag containing After Eight Mints and an anthology of Irish poetry.

'Not too bad, not too bad at all. Well ... well this is *most* kind,' Father McDaid said in flustered pleasure at the gifts. 'Er, Jonathan, I'd like you to meet Murray Corry, a friend of mine.' He introduced the tall, lean, fair-haired man at the other side of his bed. 'Murray, this is Jonathan Harpur. I spoke to you about him. He very kindly gave me Mrs Harrison's number. You remember, the counsellor I spoke to you about?' He glanced at his friend.

'Indeed I do, Father D. Nice to meet you, Jonathan.' Murray stood up and gave Jonathan a firm handshake across the bed.

'I won't impose, I just wanted to drop in and see how you were doing,' Jonathan said.

'Arrah you're not imposing at all. T'was very kind of you to bother coming in to see me. And it's been very kind of you to even be in touch with me, considering that I upset you so terribly,' he added remorsefully. 'I told Murray about our encounter, I hope you don't mind.'

'Er ... no ...' said Jonathan, taken aback.

Patricia Scanlan

'I was Father Derek's curate for about five years before I was laicized,' the other man explained, seeing Jonathan's surprise.

'And a very good curate he was,' the priest smiled. 'Everyone loved him in St John's. I was sorry when he left the parish and sorrier still when he told me he was leaving the priesthood. We lost a good one.'

'Oh, did you leave to get married?' Jonathan asked politely.

'No, that wasn't my reason for leaving, and, even if I did want to get married, our church and our state don't allow gay marriage, unfortunately,' the other man said humorously.

'Oh ... right!' Jonathan, whose gay radar was usually pretty spot on, hadn't picked up on that.

'Your Hannah is some woman to argue the toss with,' Father McDaid said mischievously. 'Now she has me thinking: What's all the fuss about? Love is love and that's all that matters.'

Jonathan laughed, delighted. 'She certainly makes you look at things differently, I'll grant you that.'

'You can say that again. I'm reading all sorts of books I would never have picked up if it hadn't been for her.' He pointed to a book on his locker. '*The Nine Faces of Christ* is a fascinating book about the Essenes and their initiations. And, having read it, I'm beginning to think that it's very feasible *indeed* that Jesus and Mary Magdalene *could* have been married. Very thought-provoking reading. There's so much out there that has been kept hidden and now it's all being revealed. It's actually quite invigorating,' Father McDaid enthused.

556

'I must read that one,' Jonathan said.

'So must I,' Murray smiled.

'And of course Hannah would say that I had my fall and landed up here getting a new hip for a reason. I'm sure she says things like that to you,' Father McDaid twinkled.

'Indeed she does,' Jonathan grimaced.

'Yes, well, I'm being given time to "rest, think, read and be minded, as well as be renewed in body", she told me. She rings me every few days to see how I'm getting on. Could you credit that?'

'I could,' said Jonathan. 'Hannah is a very special person.'

'And if I hadn't met you in the graveyard in Rosslara, I'd never have known about her, or never have come to have peace of mind. Thank you, Jonathan.' The old man held out his hand and Jonathan grasped it and was surprised to feel a lump in his throat.

'I'm glad we met. It was meant to be,' he said. 'I'm glad you took that huge step of going to see Hannah. As she would say, it's all about moving on, and I can see it in you that you've changed and are more at peace than the man I met a few months ago.'

'Indeed I am, my son, indeed I am. I feel I've been given a new lease of life. And when I get out of here on Christmas Eve, I'm going to enjoy what's left of my life now that my burdens have been lifted from me, all thanks to you.'

'That's wonderful news, Father McDaid. I couldn't be happier for you,' Jonathan said warmly. It was true that the priest was in a far different space from the one the tormented person had been in at their first encounter. Jonathan could see for himself how the elderly man's eyes were bright, his energy

Patricia Scanlan

was invigorated and he was rested and at peace. Hannah had worked her magic for sure. Sometimes it only needed someone to point out a very obvious truth, which you'd been blind to, to set you free from a mindset that had imprisoned you, Jonathan reflected, very glad indeed that he hadn't had to wait until he was an elderly man like Father McDaid to be gifted with someone of Hannah's calibre and wisdom.

'We should send your counsellor to the Vatican,' Murray joked. 'She might sort them out.'

'She'd certainly set the cat among the pigeons. And the thing is, none of the theological arguments about being "the One True Church" would stand up to her basic premise that love is all there is, and we are all One! So simple when you think about it.' Father McDaid opened the After Eights and passed them round.

'I love these,' Murray approved and Jonathan was struck by how kind he was to his former parish priest, unobtrusively straightening up his pillow, and filling his glass with water for him to take the tablet that was in a little container on his meal trolley.

'You've a terrific view, haven't you?' Jonathan remarked as the last rays of the sunset faded and Daniel O'Connell's iconic Round Tower, fringed by dark feathery foliage, was silhouetted starkly against the indigo sky.

'Superb,' agreed the priest. 'It's a grand hospital. Wonderful care, lovely staff and spotlessly clean. But then of course the nuns still have an input and it shows.'

'It's a pity we couldn't put a few nuns in government, and in the banks, and we wouldn't be in the state we're in,' Murray observed as a knock came to the door.

'Ah it's the torment herself,' Father McDaid teased when he saw the physiotherapist appear. 'She has me wearing stockings, you know.' He threw his eyes up to heaven.

'For that now I'll make you do two laps of the corridor,' the physio riposted, handing him his dressing gown.

'Keep well.' Jonathan shook hands with him, glad he'd made the effort to visit.

'I will and keep in touch. And Happy Christmas.' Their eyes met and they smiled at each other. And Jonathan *knew* that their encounter in the graveyard had been divinely ordained.

'Nice to meet you,' he said to Murray who was pulling on his overcoat.

'And you,' said the older man. Lovely eyes, thought Jonathan, noting how green, and flecked with hazel, they were. 'Take care, Father D. I'll be in touch,' Murray said, patting him on the shoulder.

'Thank you, Murray, you're a good friend,' the priest said gratefully as the physio helped him out of the bed.

'He looks marvellous. I've never actually seen him look as good. He's a changed man,' Murray remarked as they walked along the corridor to the stairs.

'I honestly didn't think he'd go to Hannah. You could have knocked me down with a feather when she told me he'd been to see her, and then when he rang me out of the blue. What a shame it took this long for him to get some sort of closure on his past.' Jonathan shook his head.

'Dreadful! I suppose I fared somewhat better, I was in my late forties.' Murray clattered down the stairs beside him.

'Were you abused too?' Jonathan asked.

'Yeah, at school by a teacher.'

'That's terrible. Mine was a neighbour!'

'Imagine that's the common denominator in our three lives. Dreadful, isn't it? And there are so many more out there. At least we've been helped.' Murray shook his head. 'It's so good to see Derek embracing all these fresh philosophies and new ideas, compliments of your counsellor who seems to be a very unusual person.'

'Indeed she is and more. If it wasn't for Hannah I think I would have topped myself long ago,' Jonathan confided.

'That bad. Sorry to hear that,' Murray said sympathetically as they walked down the steps into the chilly night air. 'It was the Church's inexcusable and atrocious attitude and response to clerical child abuse that made me leave the priesthood,' the other man explained. 'I just couldn't hack it any more. I was in turmoil, full of anger and frustration. And I also found it hard to accept the way women were treated. I firmly believe there were women apostles. I believe priests should be allowed to get married. I was very out of step with Church teachings.' He laughed, showing even white teeth. '*Very*,' he said with added emphasis, jiggling his car keys. 'This is mine.' He stopped at a dark blue Passat. 'So, Jonathan, it was a pleasure to meet you.' He held out his hand.

'Likewise,' said Jonathan, shaking hands. 'I hope you're happy in your life now.'

'Happy enough now that I'm true to myself, but lonely sometimes. Especially around this time of the year.' He shrugged.

'Me too! I always find it ... difficult ... especially New Year's Eve.'

'Are you with someone?' Murray looked surprised.

'No! Long story! Are you?'

'No! No story,' laughed Murray. 'I think you need to be a young man to play the dating game.'

'Fancy a coffee?' Jonathan heard himself say spontaneously.

'Ahh! Yeah! Why not? You can tell me your long story and a bit more about this amazing Hannah,' Murray agreed.

'Will we go across the road to the Tolka?'

'Perfect. And there's a car park behind it. I'm damned if I'm giving this lot another red cent today.' Murray indicated the parking hut.

'Something else in common,' Jonathan remarked lightly, hardly able to believe he had been so proactive. But there was a kindness and maturity about Murray Corry that he knew would not lead to callous, calculating behaviour. It might just be a one-off coffee. It might end up as a friendship, which would be a wonderful bonus. Who knew? But all in all today had been a very good day, Jonathan decided, and the irony was, if he had not stopped at Gus Higgins's grave none of it would have happened. A divine synchronicity, Hannah would call it, and who was he to argue with that?

'You look tired, dear.' Jacqueline O'Mahony kissed her daughter and studied her under the light of the crystal chandelier that hung in the hall of the Holland Park flat.

'And skinny,' her father said, frowning. 'Scrawny even, I'd go so far as to say.'

'*Frank!*' hissed his wife.

'Well it's true! What's wrong with you, girl? And why aren't Jazzy and Des here for Christmas? And why haven't you decorated yet?' Frank was leaning on a cane, his face showing the pain of his arthritis.

'Come in and sit down and I'll get us some tea,' Colette said, pretending not to have heard his questions.

'Where's your housekeeper?' Jacqueline asked, removing her elegant black-woollen coat and burgundy-silk scarf.

'I have to get a new one. It's been so long since I've been here and the agency didn't have anyone to send so near to Christmas,' she fibbed. Housekeepers were a luxury of the past. She would employ a cleaner twice a week, in the new year, who would do housekeeping duties for three hours, but for the last week Colette had been cooking for herself and she hadn't bothered eating much. She had ordered a prepared dinner for Christmas Day from Fine Dining caterers, and she had stocked up her freezer with ready-made meals for the duration of her parents' visit.

'Forget about the tea. I'll have a brandy if there's one going,' Frank announced, handing her his coat and hat and stomping into the lounge.

'Mum, would you prefer a drink?' Colette asked, following her mother in.

'No thank you, dear. I'd love a cup of tea.' Jacqueline sank down into an armchair. Dublin Airport and Heathrow had been exhausting, packed to the gills with Christmas travellers. They had travelled first-class, of course, and had been fast-tracked through security before reaching the sanctuary of the lounge, but nevertheless the crowds embarking and disembarking and the long wait at the luggage belt after that endless walk through Terminal 1 were wearing and it shocked her to realize how elderly she was becoming.

'That's a nice tree. See, Frank, Colette *has* decorated.' She glared at her husband who was studying the red-and-gold-themed tree that Colette had paid a company to dress for her.

'I'll just switch on the lights.' Colette bent and clicked the plug. The last thing she had wanted to do was put up Christmas decorations, and a tree, but she felt she should make some nod towards the season seeing as she had invited her parents to spend it with her. The tree and some floral and candle arrangements were as far as she had gone.

'So where are Jazzy and Des?' Frank asked again, when Colette had served her mother Earl Grey and handed him a brandy snifter with a good measure of cognac. Colette took a deep breath.

'It's like this, actually, Mum and Dad. I found out that Des was having an affair and I've left him. We will be divorcing. He had a triple bypass so Jazzy is staying in New York for Christmas to be with him, and also because she doesn't want to leave her boyfriend. I've moved back to London,' she said dully.

'Oh my love!' Jacqueline exclaimed. 'I'm *so* sorry to hear that. That's dreadful news. No wonder you look exhausted.'

Frank frowned. 'Are you sure you want to divorce? Messy business, you know. And expensive.'

'I know that.' She shot a dour glance at him, irritated that he immediately honed in on the financial side of things without a word of condemnation of Des.

'Hmm ... well think long and hard. At least you have this place.' Frank took an appreciative drink of the brandy.

'Yes,' Colette murmured. *No thanks to Des*, she thought grimly. 'We took a hit with Lehman Brothers as well. We've lost a lot of money,' she added. Losing because of Lehman wasn't as shameful as being swindled by Madoff. Frank would never know that, or the fact that Des had tried to speculate with Frank's late sister's flat.

'Good God, those bloody banks! All the years your mother and I worked like Trojans and we thought we were saving our pensions in the safest place possible. Damn bank shares! Damn crooks that were running them,' Frank seethed. 'Don't get me started.'

'Did you lose much?' Colette asked in alarm. Her parents had been her standby if she ended up in straightened circumstances. She hadn't thought that they would be hit financially, she'd been so concerned with her own situation.

'Your father lost more than I did. I preferred to invest in Post Office bonds and certificates. I didn't care much for those Anglo lot, from my dealings with them. Sharks!' Jacqueline said a little smugly.

'Don't rub it in, Jacqueline,' snapped her husband, glaring at her. 'How much did you lose?' He turned to Colette.

'I'm not sure yet, but certainly enough to have a huge impact on our lifestyle. The Florida properties are gone, Aspen is for rental. Nantucket's the same, and Des won't be able to afford to rent a new apartment Uptown. I'm glad Jazzy is educated and living her own life; that makes my decision to come back to London easier.' Colette took a sip of her G&T. She'd told her parents all she was going to tell them. They were staying for Christmas week, and then she was going back to Dublin with them for New Year. It was the longest time Colette would have spent alone with her parents. She wasn't looking forward to it, but it was better than spending Christmas and New Year alone, and she knew she had the safety net of spending New Year's Eve with Hilary.

It was almost like the closing of a circle. She had always spent New Year with Hilary and her family when she was very young. But it was not how she had envisaged spending this New Year, she thought bitterly, having to struggle not to break down and bawl. Hopefully her parents would be so tired from travelling they would have an early night because all she wanted to do was crawl under her duvet and hide from the world.

'We got on like a house on fire, Hilary. I really like Murray. And don't panic, he's *nothing* like Leon,' Jonathan assured his best friend as they sat in Ten Fourteen in Clontarf, tucked in to the window table, enjoying their annual Christmas lunch date. The midday sun dazzled on the glistening sea and they watched a huge cargo ship glide up the river, nudged gently along by two tugs.

'He sounds lovely. Well done, Harpur, for being so plucky and inviting him for coffee.' Hilary raised her wine glass to him.

'I know! I heard it coming out of my mouth and couldn't believe it. But we stayed talking for ages and then we had a bite to eat and we didn't leave until after eight. We were there for nearly four hours.'

'Excellent! You need someone new in your life.'

'It's just a friendship,' Jonathan demurred.

'Of course,' agreed Hilary, eyes glinting in amusement. 'It *is!*'

'I know. And besides, I've got to meet him to give him the once-over. Are you seeing him again?'

'Yep, we're going to a carol service at St Patrick's.'

'Perfect date for the ex-altar boy and the ex-priest,' Hilary teased and Jonathan guffawed.

'Why don't you bring him to our New Year hooley?' she suggested, devouring a slice of crispy pork belly.

'Really? Would you mind?'

'Don't be ridiculous. The more the merrier. Do you think he'd come?'

'I don't know if he's got plans made but all I can do is ask,' Jonathan said, eating a piece of pan-fried salmon. 'Do you know if Colette's going to come?'

Hilary shook her head. 'Don't know! One day she says she is, the next day she says she isn't. She's in a real state.'

'It's tough. Even I wouldn't wish what she's going through on her. Who would have thought that high-powered lifestyle would come crashing down around her ears. Des was a piece of work, wasn't he?'

'You know I'm not his greatest fan but I still can't believe he acted out of malice. I think he panicked when he lost the money with Madoff. And he *was* having an affair. I wouldn't have stayed. Would you?'

'Damn right I wouldn't,' Jonathan exclaimed.

'So if she comes, be nice to her,' Hilary warned. 'No smart remarks.'

'*Moi*, make a smart remark? Hilary, you wound me.' He pointed a fork laden with creamy mash at her.

'Ha! Ha!'

'It's been a hell of a year all round though, hasn't it? You can see the business ebbing away.' She sighed.

'I know. It's been our worst year ever,' Jonathan agreed. 'And it's only going to get worse.'

'Tell me about it. That bloody apartment that we bought for the girls has lost half its value, and we're in negative equity, and the rent has gone down, so that's not even covering the mortgage. We would have been hit but not as bad otherwise. Niall's so browned off about it. It was his idea to buy it. And he's not playing half the gigs he used to because there's no one in the pubs. Did we ever think it would come to this?'

'It had to end sometime, it was mad stuff. I heard a pair whinging on *Liveline* about apartments they'd bought in Dubai and not being able to afford to pay the mortgages on them. Talk about losing the run of yourself. It was far from apartments in Dubai we were reared.' He shook his head. 'And what did you think of the Grants? I wonder what's going to happen to the fancy spa we created for them.'

'I know, scarpering off to America after declaring himself bankrupt, and transferring his assets and property to Gina. That will give her a headache and a half,' Jonathan observed.

'I felt a bit sorry for her. Her life seemed so ruled by all the socializing and entertaining she had to do. I can't see Gina becoming a "developer" in her own right with all her husband's transferred assets, like that other hard-faced blonde who's never out of the papers,' Hilary said sarcastically.

'*Dyed* blonde, dearie. She's so sharp she'd give scissors a

run for their money! I saw her in action at a party once ...
not for the faint-hearted.' Jonathan grinned.

'Are you looking forward to your party?' He changed the
subject, fed up with all the gloom and doom.

'I really am this year. It's been a tough one, sure, and I'm
glad it's almost over. But Niall and I are doing OK in spite of
the downturn. And the girls have jobs, so as a family we're
doing a lot better than most. I've missed them terribly at
home, Jonathan. I can't wait to see them and I think a good
old night of music and craic will do us all the world of good,
even Colette.'

'Can't imagine her dancing "The Walls Of Limerick" in
her Louboutins.' Jonathan rolled his eyes.

'Stop!' Hilary laughed.

'Sorry. You do know, don't you, that if it wasn't for you
and Niall and your New Year's Eve party every year I'd be
curled up in bed.' Jonathan smiled at her.

'No you wouldn't! Russell and Kenny wouldn't allow it,
nor would Orla,' Hilary retorted.

'True perhaps but I *do* hate it. I always feel such a failure.
Another year on my own. Greta Garbo has nothing on me!'

'Well perhaps you won't be on your own this year. Maybe
Murray won't have made plans and he might like to come.'
Hilary reached across the table and squeezed his hands.

'I'm afraid to even think about it. I'm afraid to even hope
something could come of it. I've lost my nerve.'

'No you haven't. You invited him for coffee. You took the
brave step and made your leap of faith. Isn't that what
Hannah would say? Now let the doors open.'

'OK, I will. Thanks for being the best friend anyone could

have and here's to the best New Year's Eve party *ever*!'
Jonathan raised his glass in toast.

'Amen to that!' said Hilary, clinking her glass with his. 'I
just have a feeling it's going to be a cracker.'

CHAPTER FORTY-ONE

She shouldn't have come to the Hammonds' party, Colette thought dourly, taking another swig from her G&T. And she shouldn't have continued to drink gin. It depressed her, soured her. Yes, that was a good word, sour. It described how she felt exactly. Sour and sad and lonely. If Des and Jazzy had been here she would have actually enjoyed the night. There was a great buzz. People were enjoying themselves in that carefree, uninhibited way she had rarely seen at the parties she had attended in Manhattan. But her family weren't with her. She was here as a single woman, her first social occasion since her split with Des, and it felt soul-destroying. Even Jonathan Harpur was with someone, she thought irritably. He was sitting on the edge of an armchair, smiling at a tall, tawny-haired, self-assured man who fitted in seamlessly and seemed very at ease, although it was the first time he'd met Jonathan's friends. Jonathan still acted as though he owned the house, just as he had the first time she'd met him all those years ago when she had arrived unexpectedly and he had ended up cooking her meal.

Tonight he had been pouring drinks and handing round

canapés with Sophie and Millie. It annoyed Colette that *she* felt like a guest and he was treated like one of the family. The girls obviously adored him and there was a lot of affectionate banter between them. She didn't know most of the guests, apart from Hilary's mum and sister, but she didn't particularly want to spend the night chatting to them knowing that they were feeling sorry for her. She should have booked into a hotel and not let on to her parents. They were so busy throwing their own soirée they wouldn't have thought to question her.

A new song began and she recognized it as 'The Coolin', a famous Irish air with haunting music. When Niall had sung the first verse in his deep baritone:

> *'Have you seen my fair-haired girl walking the roads*
> *A bright dewy morning without a smudge on her shoes?*
> *Many a young man is envious and longing to marry her*
> *But they won't get my treasure*
> *. . . no matter what they think'*

he turned and looked at his wife, his eyes crinkling in a loving smile. Hilary smiled back, seemingly unaware of anyone else in the crowded room. It was an intimate, tender moment between them that ignited a surge of envy in Cecil B. DemilleColette when she compared her own circumstances to her friend's.

Every time she looked at Hilary and Niall together she felt deep and resentful jealousy. How could they still look at each other the way they did after all these years? It wasn't for show; it was quite natural and unaffected. It didn't help that Niall looked particularly dishy in an open-necked black shirt and a pair of grey chinos. He had aged very well. The grey at his temples was sexy; the lines around his eyes and mouth added character, rather than age, to his appearance. Surely somewhere on his travels he had indulged in a liaison with some other woman. He had hardly remained faithful to Hilary all this time, Colette thought, as her friend's husband strummed his mandolin, playing the evocative air to a hushed room. The pure, sweet notes and the vibrato caught at her emotions and she felt like breaking down in tears.

'Beautiful, isn't it?' Jonathan whispered, sitting down on the sofa beside her. 'Are you OK?' She nodded, unable to speak, annoyed that he had noticed her distress. 'Can I freshen your drink?' he offered kindly.

'No I'm fine, thank you.' She swallowed as Niall and his group began the second stirring verse.

'Is that your boyfriend?' She nodded in Murray's direction. He was singing along, playing the spoons expertly.

'Well we're friends, let's say,' Jonathan murmured, delighted that Murray had been instantly accepted into his precious unit.

'A trad fan, clearly,' Colette said drily.

'Might end up in Niall's band yet. I just wanted to make sure you were OK. Tonight must be difficult for you,' Jonathan said, standing up.

'Very kind,' she said in a tight, clipped voice and he wondered why he had bothered.

'I don't know why she came. She's sitting there with a face on her. She's certainly not enjoying the evening,'

Hilary moaned to Jonathan an hour later while they removed cling film from the platters of food she was serving for the buffet.

'I know. I got short shrift when I asked her was she OK.' Jonathan handed Millie a dish of chicken *boscaiola* and a bowl of tabbouleh to carry over to the table.

'It must be very hard for her,' Hilary sighed, wishing Colette had stayed with her parents. She was in a prickly humour and the copious amounts of gin she was drinking weren't helping.

'Is she staying the night?' Jonathan murmured as a gale of laughter heralded an array of revellers come to offer help with the buffet.

'Yes, as far as I know.' Hilary gave the huge pot of curry a stir while Jonathan sprinkled freshly cut dill on the salmon.

'We're hungry,' Hilary's sister Dee announced tipsily.

'Well tell everyone to come and tuck in and help themselves,' Hilary said gaily, determined that Colette wouldn't ruin her evening. 'And, Jonathan,' she murmured.

'Yeah?'

'Murray is lovely, very easy to talk to. *Perfect* for you.'

'Don't jinx it,' he grimaced, twirling around the kitchen with a plate of sizzling cocktail sausages, tutting when Dee helped herself to three of them. The kitchen teemed with hungry guests, and the buzz of chat and laughter filled the air. Hilary was swallowed up in the middle of them, urging friends and family to partake in the banquet laid out on the table.

'Come on, Colette, chow's up,' Niall said heartily, noticing her sitting on the sofa on her own.

'I guess I'm not that hungry, Niall,' she sighed, tucking her legs up under and slanting him a glance.

'Will I get you a plate of food and bring it in to you?' he offered, hating to see her miserable.

'Ah I suppose I should make the effort and mingle, and have something to nibble on.' She took a deep breath and stood up.

'Good woman,' Niall said encouragingly, dropping an arm around her shoulder as he escorted her into the kitchen. 'Grab a plate there and fill it up – you could do with putting on a few pounds,' he grinned, and she laughed.

'You were always direct, Niall,' she said, amused, her mood lightening.

'More like putting my two feet in it, my darling wife would say.' Niall began to fill his own plate.

'She's not worried about putting on a few pounds, obviously,' Colette giggled, getting in a catty dig.

'She's a grand hoult of a woman,' Niall said appreciatively, not quite the response Colette was expecting. Didn't he mind that Hilary was at *least* a stone overweight?

'Well I'm trying hard to keep the middle-age spread at bay. I won't let myself go.' Colette took a small spoonful of tabbouleh and a portion of salmon.

'Have some cheesy potatoes, they're scrumptious,' Niall urged before turning to check that his mother-in-law had enough food.

'Colette O'Mahony, you look amazing!' Vivienne O'Hara, a mutual friend from way back, declared. 'My God, you don't look a day over thirty-five. Have you had a facelift?'

'Of course not,' fibbed Colette. 'I wouldn't go under the knife.'

'I would, if I could afford it,' declared Vivienne emphatically.

You could do with it, Colette thought, thinking how florid the other woman looked, and how even the heavy foundation she wore couldn't hide her broken veins.

'So come and sit beside me and tell me what you've been doing all these years,' Vivienne demanded. 'I believe you live the life of Reilly in New York.' She cocked an eye at Colette. 'Why does that surprise me, you were always a go-getter. Just like your parents. There was a time they were never out of the papers with all the tribunals. I believe they made a fortune and us poor taxpayers are paying for it,' Vivienne said tipsily. 'Where's your OH?' Isn't that the jargon they use these days?'

I should be getting ready to party in Park Avenue, not listening to mindless wittering, Colette thought glumly, pasting a faux smile on her face and wishing she was a million miles away.

An hour later she whispered to Hilary, 'I'm going to go to bed. I don't think I could cope with "Auld Lang Syne" and all that stuff and I want to call Jazzy. See you tomorrow.'

'Ok, I hope the noise won't disturb you. It won't be an all-nighter. People will start drifting off after midnight.' Hilary walked with her to the stairs. 'I know this is a hideously difficult night for you, but this year is almost over and a new one is starting and hopefully it will be a much better one for you,' Hilary said warmly.

'Always the optimist, you are.' Colette sighed. 'Night, Hilary. I'm off. Here's Viv and she's plastered.' She hurried upstairs, desperate to avoid another ear bashing from her former friend.

'She's got very stuck up. Mind she was always a snooty little wagon,' Vivienne declared crossly as Colette disappeared up the stairs.

'She's not feeling great,' Hilary lied. 'Come on, the lads are going to play a Dubliners set to bring us up to midnight.'

'*And the auld triangle went jingle jangle*,' sang Vivienne, forgetting all about Colette and her moods.

'So where are you, sweetie?' Colette kicked off her shoes, positioned her cell under her ear while she unzipped her Chanel LBD and shimmied out of it.

'Jackson and I are taking Dad to dinner in the Palm Court, and afterwards when we've dropped him home we're going on to a party in the Village.' Jazzy's clear tones floated down the line.

'Sounds fun. Is Des going to the McLean-Butlers to ring in the New Year?'

'No, he's not in the form for it. He's having an early night. Are you having fun? I can hear a party going on.'

'I miss you. I'm lonely. I'm going to bed now. It would be too sad to see in the New Year without you.' Colette sank onto the bed, weary.

'You should have stayed with Gran and Gramps,' Jazzy said.

'That would have been even worse. It will be over soon and I'll be back in London in a few days. You have fun tonight. You're young and in love, the best way to be on New Year's Eve. Enjoy it and don't forget I love you.'

'I love you too, Mom, goodnight. Talk soon.'

'Bye, sweetie.' Colette tried to keep her tone light, not wishing her daughter to worry about her. And as for Des, she wouldn't put it past him to have that woman sleeping in their bed with him tonight. Early night indeed, she thought furiously as she slipped her phone back into her bag. She undressed and slipped her silk nightie over her shoulders and climbed into bed. It was cold. She should have thought to put on the blanket for ten minutes before she got in.

Downstairs the party was in full swing, the group giving Dicey Reilly welly, the guests joining in enthusiastically. Colette lay under her duvet, tense and deeply unhappy. Would this night never end? Next year, even if she had to spend New Year's Eve on her own, she would stay in London and pretend it was just an ordinary night. Solitude would be far preferable to this purgatory. Outside she could hear fireworks going off randomly and dogs barking. In desperation she sat up and rooted in her handbag and found a blister of Zimovane she had filched from Jacqueline's medicine cabinet. She was tempted to take two so she could sink into oblivion but she decided against it. She wanted to be able to drive home under her own steam. The sleeping tablet took effect surprisingly quickly and by the time the clock struck midnight and the assembled guests stood at the front door singing 'Auld Lang Syne' to an accompaniment of fireworks, ships' horns and howling dogs, Colette was dead to the world.

*

'Happy New Year, Jonathan.' Murray enveloped him in a bear hug that seemed the most natural thing in the world.

'The same to you, Murray.' Jonathan returned the hug, having spent the happiest New Year's Eve in a long time. With Murray's arms around him he had the surest sense of knowing that he had found his way home.

'Happy New Year, Hilary.' Niall drew his wife to him and kissed her tenderly. 'It's a terrific party, thanks for everything. I love ya!'

'I love you too, and thanks for providing the music for my party,' she grinned, wrapping her arms around him and kissing him passionately.

'Get a room, you two,' Millie teased, embracing her parents when they stepped away from each other.

'Happy New Year, Mam, Dad, Millie.' Sophie put her arms around them all and gave a tipsy giggle, making room for her grandmother who had joined them.

'Your Dad and Margaret, I'd say, are very happy looking down on us all here tonight. It was a great party and so nice for us all to be here together. Thanks for having such a lovely family night,' Sally declared, embracing her Hilary. 'Aren't we lucky all the same when you think of poor Colette, far away from her child and husband, miserable on her own.'

'We are *very* lucky,' Hilary agreed fervently, grateful to be surrounded by family and friends, as Jonathan blew her a kiss and the ships' sirens sounded their message of celebration, and church bells pealed their song of welcome for the New Year.

Times might have turned very hard, but one good thing

austerity was doing was bringing an awareness that what really mattered was not material wealth and status, but family and friends and simple pleasures, Hilary reflected, closing the front door on the blustery night as Niall and the lads began a rousing rendition of 'Crackling Rosie'.

CHAPTER FORTY-TWO

'Oooohh!' Hilary grimaced. 'What time is it?'

'Half nine,' yawned Niall, rubbing a hand over his stubbly jaw.

'That's not too bad. I don't hear anyone else stirring.'

'Do you want a cup of tea?'

'In a minute. Put your arms around me and let's have a snooze,' Hilary said sleepily, snuggling in against her husband.

'I have a genius for a wife,' he said drowsily and moments later he was fast asleep, his breath ruffling her hair. Hilary lay dozing in his arms until a vaguely familiar sound brought her awake. It was coming from downstairs, a Bond theme. 'Goldfinger'. Jonathan's phone. The eejit, he must have forgotten it. She slid out from under Niall's arm, grabbed her dressing gown and hurried downstairs.

The phone had stopped ringing, so she dialled the number on her landline and when it started to ring she saw it halfway down the side of an armchair. She checked out the missed call and saw that it was Jonathan's landline. Hilary dialled it, smothering a yawn.

'Hello?' Jonathan sounded agitated.

'You idiot,' she said affectionately.

'Oh thank God – I thought I'd left it in the taxi!' She could hear the relief in her friend's voice. 'I'll drive over for it once I've got the pork tenderloin stuffed.'

'Stay where you are, I'll drop it over. I know you're cooking for the family lunch.'

'You are a lifesaver, Hil! Thanks!' he exclaimed.

'Just have some fresh coffee brewed,' she ordered. 'See ya!'

She opened the fridge, poured herself a glass of orange juice and drank it thirstily. She'd grab something to eat at Jonathan's.

Niall, who was snoring evenly, didn't hear her shower or dress, so she scribbled a note and left it propped up against the lamp on his bedside locker. She walked quietly down the landing and placed her ear against Colette's bedroom door and listened. She could hear little ladylike snores and she smiled, glad that her friend was having a restful sleep. At least the ordeal of New Year's Eve was over for her.

There was very little traffic. It was a beautiful, crisp, cold morning and the sun, a pale lemon drop, threw sparkles on the sea, and bathed Howth in an ethereal, opaque light as she sped along the Dublin Road to Baldoyle. Jonathan had chosen a very picturesque area to live, she approved, emerging onto the Strand Road and seeing the panorama of blue sea and sky and the emerald sward of Portmarnock golf course across the water. It was such a different vista to the one he'd enjoyed when he'd lived in his eagle's nest overlooking Dublin's quays. But one that she preferred.

She drove onto the yellow-brick drive outside his stone

cottage, and parked behind his car. It was an old railway cottage with sash windows, on whose sills Jonathan had pots of pink and red cyclamen in a glorious profusion of colour. A seasonal holly-and-red-ribboned wreath enlivened the crimson door with the gleaming brass knocker and letterbox. It was all chocolate-box pretty and Hilary wouldn't have expected anything less of him.

He had the door open before she even knocked. 'I heard the car. It really is such a tank,' he grinned, hugging her.

'Don't denigrate my trusty old Saab,' she remonstrated, inhaling the aroma of freshly brewed coffee. 'I need some of that coffee. I was lucky I didn't fall asleep at the wheel!'

'Thanks a million for coming over with the phone. I'm way behind schedule as it is,' he groaned, leading her into the kitchen where he had been preparing the main course for the New Year's Day lunch he would be cooking in Rosslara. 'The girls are doing starters and desserts and Mama will be overseeing the entire proceedings from her armchair,' he laughed. 'Thank God she's still with us for another New Year. I couldn't imagine her not being at home.' Jonathan poured the dark brown liquid into two elegant coffee cups, milked them and handed the cup and saucer to Hilary. Can I tempt you to a sausage roll?' He arched an eyebrow at her.

'Indeed you can,' she smirked.

'Guess what I had when I woke up?'

'Tell me.'

'Half a box of liqueurs.'

'Oh cripes! I thought I was bad eating two chocolate Brazils.'

'We'll start next week,' he promised. 'I'm definitely going

to walk at least a mile a day every morning, out on the seafront.'

'You do that,' she smiled, having heard about the 'mile on the seafront' ever since he had moved from the city a couple of years ago.

'I am, deffo,' he assured her, placing his stuffed tenderloins on a greased cooking dish and wrapping it carefully in tin foil.

'So, what happened last night after you left?' Hilary demanded, sipping the delicious coffee while she waited for her sausage roll to heat in the microwave.

'Nothing really, because Murray is going home to cook lunch for his family today, and I'm doing the same for my gang. Both of us had to be up early. He lives in North County Dublin, near Ashbourne, so we didn't even share a taxi because our routes were miles away from each other but we're going to meet up next Sunday. I'm going to cook lunch for him here.'

'I really like him,' Hilary said. 'And he fitted in so well. Niall was chuffed that he likes trad and can play the tin whistle and spoons.'

'He's very easy to be with. I like that about him. And he's very interested in culture and art and so much of what I like. *And* he's a photographer! He's going to show me how to take photos.'

'Nude ones, I hope.' Hilary grinned at him. Jonathan laughed.

'You durty gurl! You're a bad influence on me. Was that your phone ringing?' He cocked his ear to the hall where she had left her bag on the ornate wrought-iron coat stand. She slid off the stool wondering who would be calling her on New Year's Day morning. Her immediate thought was that it must be her mother, as it always was when she got an unexpected phone call late or early. She remembered the times Margaret would ring her to say she wasn't well and invariably an ambulance would have to be called and they'd end up in A&E.

'I missed a call from Colette.' She made a face and sat back down and took another sip of coffee and a bite of her sausage roll. 'She was sound asleep when I left.'

Her phone rang again and she saw it was from her messaging service. 'What's up with her, I wonder,' she remarked, dialling 171.

'A lot, if you ask me,' retorted Jonathan. 'You'd think I'd offered her cyanide when I asked her if she'd like me to freshen her drink last night. I was merely being kind.'

'As you always are.' Hilary patted his arm as she listened to the voice telling her the time and date of her message. 'Oh get on with it!' She could hear sounds, like someone moving around, and then she heard Niall say, 'Oh you're up, did you sleep well?'

'On and off,' she heard Colette say. 'I just feel so sad.'

'Ah you poor thing,' Niall said, and there was more movement.

'I think Colette rang my number by accident and it's gone straight into message but she's not turned off her phone,' Hilary said. 'I do that all the time with these friggin' touch phones. Remember the day I recorded us talking and I didn't even know I was doing it? Oh yikes, she's bawling now and poor Niall's trying to comfort her.'

'Better him than me!' Jonathan made a face.

'Oh my God! Oh my God! Jesus, Mary and Joseph!' Hilary exclaimed at what she was hearing.

'What's wrong?' Jonathan came round the island and stood beside her, concerned, as she switched on the phone to speaker and Colette's voice echoed tinnily around the kitchen.

'You're one of the sexiest men I've ever met, Niall. You know that, don't you? You've always known I fancied you. I just adore men with hairy chests. Des's was smooth, not like yours. Just between you and me, on all your travels, have you ever been a bad boy on Hilary? Because I don't think there's a man alive who could ever be faithful.'

'The evil little hoor!' Jonathan exclaimed, eyes wide with dismay as he saw the look of total pained shock on Hilary's face. He held her hand tight as they listened in mounting horror to the events unfolding in Hilary's kitchen.

Colette stared at her reflection in the cheval mirror of Hilary's guest bedroom. Her cheeks were flushed, her hair tousled, her black silk négligée was open to reveal a lacy wisp of black translucent chiffon nightdress that revealed the curve of her rounded breasts and deep décolletage. So sexy still, she thought admiringly. She had worn it deliberately knowing that Niall would see her in it. She had just gone down the road of no return, Colette acknowledged. Her relationship with Niall was irrevocably changed, as was her relationship with Hilary, unless Niall kept his mouth shut and didn't go blurting things out. She hoped he would for all their sakes. If Hilary ever found out that she had set out to seduce her husband, there'd be hell to pay. She picked up her overnight bag and began to pack. She wanted to be gone before Hilary got back.

Niall gunned the engine and drove out of his drive leaving tyre marks. He needed to think. Colette's full-on invitation to have sex with her was still astonishing to him. Women came on to him ... a lot ... especially when he was playing a gig, but Colette was something else. The way she used her body, the slanting seductive glances. And when she'd told him she hadn't had sex in months and she *ached* for him.

Niall groaned, thinking of what had gone on between them. What was he to do? What was he to say when Hilary came home, full of anticipation for the family dinner they were going to at her sister's this evening? She would be so hurt. So desperately hurt if she knew. She gave everything in a relationship. She was the kindest, most giving, most caring person he knew, and none of that had meant diddly-squat. Should he tell her? What was the kindest thing to do? Tell her or say nothing and let her go on in blissful ignorance of the complete and heinous betrayal that had gone on behind her back?

Niall parked the car on the seafront, and head down, hands jammed in his pockets, he strode along the promenade, his jaw tense, his eyes bleak, as he replayed the scenario with Colette over and over in his head.

'What are you going to do?' Jonathan asked hesitantly when Hilary's sobs had subsided.

'Can you believe that, Jonathan? I was her best friend, her

oldest friend. After all my kindness to her over the years. Can you believe that she would stab me in the back like that, without a thought?' Hilary hiccuped.

'Even *I* didn't think she'd sink that low,' Jonathan said solemnly. 'And I've never liked her.'

'And the irony of it is that Niall was always telling me she wasn't a real friend,' Hilary said bitterly, picking up her bag. 'Well very soon she's going to rue the day she did the dirty on me. I'm going to deal with her first,' Hilary said grimly, wiping her eyes.

'Do you want me to come with you?' Jonathan offered.

'Ah thanks, but you need to get going to Rosslara—'

'I need to be with a friend who needs me,' interjected Jonathan. 'An extra hour won't make too much of a difference.'

'No. I'll deal with this myself. I should have cut her out of my life years ago and then all this wouldn't have happened.'

'Let me know how things go, won't you?' he urged.

'Of course. I'll probably be bawling on the phone to you.'

'Bawl away, and if you want me to come back tonight to be with you, I will.'

'You're a great pal, Jonathan,' she said brokenly, tears overflowing again. He held her tight, patted her back and stroked her hair until she was calm again.

'Now I wouldn't be much of a pal if I let you out looking like a panda bear on crack!' he said firmly, rooting in her bag for her hairbrush, lipstick, dusting powder and brush. 'Sit still while I minister to you,' he ordered, rinsing a tissue under the tap to wipe her tears and mascara-run, before deftly sweeping the powder brush over her cheekbones and forehead, then tracing lipstick over her mouth. He brushed her hair, feathering her fringe, and stood back to look at her. 'That's better. Now if you feel you need reinforcements ring me and I'll be up the road after you, quicker than a crooked politician palming a brown envelope.'

In spite of herself, Hilary laughed. 'You're incorrigible, Harpur.'

'And you're amazing, Hammond. Go and do what you have to do and ring me immediately!'

'I will,' she said heavily. 'I love ya! Bye!'

Heavy-hearted, Jonathan watched her reverse out of the drive. Hilary deserved *so* much better, he thought angrily closing the door. What a horrible start to the new year for his best friend.

CHAPTER FORTY-THREE

'Just concentrate on your driving,' Hilary muttered, having swerved very close to the edge of the narrow coastal road. She could not absorb what she'd heard on the phone. Couldn't take in what had actually happened. It was like a dream but, as she slowed down to let a dog walker cross the road and heard the rhythmic whoosh of the sea against the shore, she knew it was no dream.

Would Colette be back at her parents' house yet? It was on Hilary's route home anyway; she would wait until her erstwhile friend arrived if she wasn't there. Colette had been driving Jacqueline's Merc for the few days she'd been in Ireland, and she'd arrived at the party in it.

The navy Merc was gleaming in the mid-morning sun when Hilary roared up the drive. Frank's silver Merc was parked in front of it. Hilary didn't care who was there. Colette O'Mahony had pushed her too far this time. She wasn't getting away with it.

She rang the doorbell, tempted to keep her finger on it, but she didn't want to alert Colette to anything untoward.

'Ah Hilary. Happy New Year! I didn't know you were

with Colette. She's just gone down to make herself a coffee in the kitchen,' Frank greeted her kindly, opening the door wide.

'Thanks, Happy New Year to you too,' she said, returning the greeting before marching past him along the marble-tiled hall and down to the kitchen. Colette had her back to her as she stared out of the kitchen window.

'Niall warned me about you all along and I wouldn't listen to him,' Hilary said tightly, keeping a lid on her temper with difficulty.

Colette spun round. 'Whatever he said, he's telling lies. *He* wanted to seduce *me*! *He* made the first move.'

'What is your *problem*, Colette?' Hilary roared. 'Why are you so horribly mean-spirited and jealous that you could even consider making a move on my husband? *You* made the first move! Don't lie.' She glared at the other woman and walked up to her and thrust her face close to hers. 'I dropped everything, and I mean e*verything*, in that week coming up to Christmas to fly to New York and be with you in your hour of need. I've *always* been there for you, even when you do your hot potato act, and this is the way you repay me. You're no friend, Colette, you never have been. It's all about you! You! You! You! And it always has been. Ever since we were little girls. Why, Colette? Why?'

'*Why, Colette? Why?*' mimicked Colette. 'Why don't *you* just shut up and stop whinging? You're so smug, Hilary. You call yourself a friend. How do you think I felt knowing that you only played with me out of pity, because your mother *made* you?' Colette snarled.

'What?' exclaimed Hilary, gobsmacked.

'Don't you remember? Begging your mother not to ask me to your birthday party?'

'I don't remember that,' retorted Hilary, mystified. What had childhood birthday parties got to do with how Colette had behaved today?

'Of course you don't remember. Why should you? You weren't the one standing behind the door listening to your mother telling you that you *had* to invite "poor" Colette. How would you have felt if it were you? You with your happy clichéd Walton family,' she sneered. 'The mother who was always at home with the dinner cooked, ready to help with homework, ready to bake cakes with you. And then you married your oh so perfect husband – you never had your heart broken like I did when I was young. No, because your life is oh so *perfect!* And then you had your oh so perfect daughters who never put a foot wrong, so stop bleating why, why, why,' Colette ranted as years of suppressed resentment erupted.

'Is *that* why you did what you did today?' demanded Hilary, astonished. 'Because you're *jealous* of me? Is that why you went after Niall?'

'Niall is lying, it was *him!*' yelled Colette. 'He couldn't wait to get my clothes off, and why wouldn't he want a sexy, toned woman in his arms. I haven't let myself go like you have. Look at you, you're flabby and middle-aged and—'

'I *know* what happened, you lying cow!' Hilary shouted, producing her phone and dialling the message minder and putting it on speaker. Niall's deep voice echoed through the kitchen.

'Oh you're up, did you sleep well?'

'On and off. I just feel so sad.'

'Ah you poor thing,' Niall said and there was the sound of more movement ...

Colette paled. 'Turn it off right now. I won't listen to this!' she screeched.

'You will listen to it, you lying, devious bitch, the way I had to.' The air was thick with hostility as they eyeballed each other and the recording played out its sorry tale.

'*Colette!*'

Hilary turned round. Frank stood at the door, horrified.

'Colette, how could you do that to Hilary? How could you betray a friend so *grievously*?' he demanded. 'Answer me. I'm speaking to you.'

'Are you for REAL?' his daughter shouted at him. 'Don't you *dare* judge or chastise me. Do you think I've *ever* forgotten finding *you* riding the arse off Mrs Boyle, the nanny I loved, when I was a child? With her chunky thighs, and her legs waving in the air, and your skinny, white, hairy ass and your trousers around your ankles. Do you think I've ever forgotten how you took me to the Shelbourne as a "treat" that day and fed me such rich confectionery I was sick all the way home. Do you think I've ever forgotten that it was "*our* little secret that Mummy must never know about, because it would make her very sad and she might leave us"? I haven't forgotten any of it, Dad, *any* of it.' Colette was red-faced with fury. 'I've never forgotten how I used to cry myself to sleep when I was a kid because of you. Men are shits; I learned that from a very early age. I learned it from you, first, *Daddy* dearest!'

Frank gasped, stricken, before sitting down heavily at the table. 'Colette, I ... I ... I don't know what to say,' he said lamely, head bowed, unable to look at either of them.

'Well then, just butt out,' she snapped as they heard the front door open.

Frank and Colette turned to look at Hilary. 'Please, Hilary, my wife doesn't need to know any of this,' Frank pleaded. 'Please say nothing.'

'Hilary, Mummy's done nothing to you,' Colette said in rising panic. '*Please* don't play that back to her.'

'Hello, Hilary, Happy New Year,' Jacqueline offered, leaning over to kiss her on the cheek, oblivious to the tension, as the dog she had been walking bounded around them boisterously, tail wagging furiously.

Colette looked at Hilary imploringly. Hilary gave her a cold stare over Jacqueline's shoulder. Why should she make life easy for her former friend? Wasn't that what she had always done, given her the soft option, never making a stand? And look how Colette had repaid her.

Frank sat rigid on his chair ... waiting. Hilary took a deep breath. 'Hi, Mrs O'Mahony, Happy New Year to you too,' she said in as normal a voice as she could manage. 'I'm afraid I have to rush, we're going to Dee's for lunch and I've to collect Mam and I'm late. I'll see myself out.'

'Give my regards to Sally,' Jacqueline said cheerfully, shrugging out of her Barbour. 'Colette, I'd murder for a cup of coffee,' Hilary heard her say as she walked out of the kitchen, down the hall to the front door, without looking back.

*

'Are the girls up?' Hilary walked into the kitchen. Niall was putting clean dishes away and had another pile of plates stacked ready to go in the dishwasher.

'No, not a budge out of them.' He had his back to her.

'You were right about one thing,' she said flatly.

'What's that?' He turned to look at her.

'Colette O'Mahony was never any friend of mine. And today I learned what a husband I have.'

'*Hilary*! What did she say to you?' he asked, alarmed. 'It's not what you think. *Honestly*.'

'She's always maintained that men are hot-wired to cheat, and today I found out why. According to her there's no such thing as a faithful man because—'

'Hilary—'

'Just listen, Niall. I know *everything*!' Hilary replayed the message for the second time that day.

'God almighty! She must have had her phone on without knowing it!' he exclaimed, horrified.

'Would I ever have found out if she hadn't?'

'I don't know,' he said miserably.

'Well I'm *glad* I know! I'm *glad* I heard it. I'm *glad* I know I have the most wonderful husband in the world,' she said, throwing her arms around him and kissing him ardently.

'I love you, Hilary. I couldn't believe it when she started running her hands up under my shirt and trying to kiss me.' Niall shook his head at the memory. 'And the things she was saying.'

'I know . . . like she hadn't had sex for months and she'd always fancied you and she was *aching* for you. Jonathan and I nearly fell off our stools.' She flinched at the memory, snuggling in to him as he enfolded her in his arms.

'Did you feel better when I told her that she was a disgrace and didn't know the meaning of the word friendship?' He smiled down at her.

'I preferred it when you said you loved me more now than when you married me, and that false boobs and a plastic smile would never turn you on like the real thing. And I *particularly* liked it when you said I was the sexiest woman you had ever known and there was nothing that she could offer you that would ever tempt you to betray me. I *really* did like that bit.'

'Did you?' He gave her such a tender smile she buried her face in his neck and started to cry.

'Aw don't cry, Hilary, she's not worth it. Truly she isn't.' Niall tightened his arms around her.

'I'm not crying because of her. Jealousy has blighted her life like a malignancy that's eating her up. She's such a sad, bitter, twisted woman. I almost feel sorry for her, so don't worry I'm not going to waste any more energy on Colette O'Mahony. I'm crying because I love you so much, and you love me, and that makes me very happy,' she sniffled.

'You women are such complicated critters, crying because you're happy,' he teased. 'I'll never understand you.'

'You understand me very, very well,' Hilary said, raising her lips to her husband's and kissing him for all she was worth.

Colette lay on her bed in a darkened room having pleaded a migraine. She buried her head under the pillows so the sound of her sobs wouldn't be heard. How dare Niall Hammond turn her down and speak so disrespectfully about her. How dare he imply that she was a plastic Barbie, even if she had been somewhat refreshed? How dare he order her out of his house and tell her to never darken his door again, as if she was some sort of criminal.

He needn't worry: it would be a cold day in hell when she would ever have anything to do with either him or Hilary again. They had humiliated her. They could both get lost.

Niall was an arrogant big-head, for all his 'I love my wife' crap. He was no better than her father or Des or bloody Rod Killeen who had dumped her all those years ago. She had given her heart to Rod and he had trampled all over it and she'd never got over it. Niall might have turned her down, but she was damn sure he wasn't squeaky clean. None of them were. She was finished with men, finished with the fuckers, she vowed. All they'd ever brought her was misery.

It had been so deeply satisfying to tell Hilary what she thought of her and her precious family, and to finally spew that vile secret out of the depths of her. Her father had been knocked sideways. Francis O'Mahony, lauded and esteemed senior counsel, who loved to preen and pontificate, hadn't enjoyed hearing about his white-arsed rumpy-pumpy with lardy-legs Boyle.

No wonder she was bulimic, Colette raged. Her father had used food as a treat and reward for keeping quiet about 'their' secret. She had been taken to every plush hotel in the city for afternoon tea in the months that had followed her discovery. She would never forget that day, coming back early from playing with the girl next door because they had argued, and letting herself in through the back door. She could still remember as clear as if it was yesterday the sun shining through the window on the landing. Rays of diffused light streaming onto the red-gold-patterned carpet that covered the stairs. And the sounds. The groaning and grunting. The terror she experienced, feeling that something was wrong. That her mummy or daddy was ill.

And then, the shock of discovery. The sickening tableau that was revealed when the bedroom door was pushed open. The knowledge that a secret would have to be kept. A burden was added to the hurt and sadness already borne.

Colette wept at the memory, swamped by childhood grief that had never been acknowledged properly until today.

Hilary had never had to deal with the likes of what she'd had to contend with, Colette thought sorrowfully when the weeping had subsided. Little Miss Perfect would be back sometime, knocking on her door, wanting to let bygones be bygones because 'life's too short to fight'. Hilary never held on to a fight in all the years they'd known each other. She'd always caved in. But she could knock as hard as she liked, because Colette wanted nothing to do with her *ever* again. Why would she want to stay friends with a woman who had everything she craved? Hilary's happiness only emphasized her own failure. She didn't need to have her nose rubbed in it for a minute longer.

And as for her father! Frank would pay dearly for her years of misery. If Des could no longer fund a lifestyle she had grown accustomed to, Frank would. Now *he* was the keeper of the secret, and *she* was the one in charge. A week in a villa in St Barts was just what Colette needed to get over this unspeakable period in her life. *And* she'd be travelling first-class!

Recovery

Chapter Forty-Four

'You're a better woman than I am, Hilary, because I wouldn't be going to that man's funeral,' Jonathan exclaimed.

'If it wasn't for Mam I'm not sure if I'd go. I couldn't give a hoot about Frank O'Mahony to be honest. But Mam and Jacqueline were, and I use the term lightly, "friends" a long time ago, and Jacqueline did come to Dad's funeral. I'd say it was that meltdown that Colette had last year that brought on the stroke that finished Frank off eventually,' Hilary reflected.

'And are you going to talk to Jezebel O'Mahony?' he asked bitchily.

'*Jonathan*!' Hilary giggled.

'Well are you?'

'I suppose I'll have to offer my condolences. We're only going to the Mass, not the graveyard. We'll be on our way to Leanne's wedding when old Frank is being lowered into his loamy grave. A funeral and a wedding in one day! From one extreme to the other.'

'Is Sophie looking forward to being a bridesmaid? Can't believe Leanne is getting married. It only seems like yesterday that they were giddy teenagers.' Jonathan poured boiling water into the teapot and shook come chocolate biscuits onto a plate. They were in Hilary's office reviewing their diaries.

'She's a bit nervous, but the bridesmaid dress is fabulous on her. It made me cry when I saw her. She'll be next, I'd say.'

'Well I don't know about that,' grinned Jonathan, rooting in the mini fridge for a carton of milk.

'*Really*? What are you saying?' Hilary demanded, pushing her diary away. Compared to the hectic days of the boom, there were a lot of gaps in it.

'Well you know Murray's been commissioned to do the photography for a book on Irish heritage and learning in Europe?' He cocked an eye at her.

'Yeah, I heard you talking about it.'

'I'm going to travel with him for a couple of months in the autumn and see where it goes from there.' Jonathan's face split in a melon-sliced grin.

'Oh bliss! That sounds fantastic. Jonathan, I'm delighted it's all going so well for you. Murray is all I'd want for you and more. But I'll miss you!' She made a face.

'You and Niall can fly out and join us on weekend breaks every so often,' he suggested, pouring them two mugs of tea.

Hilary laughed. 'Those days are gone. Remember when money was no object? Remember how I booked flights for myself and the girls to fly to London that time, and it cost hundreds, and it didn't cost me a thought? Can't do that any more, I'm afraid. But maybe we might manage *one* weekend!'

'We'd have great fun. How about when he's photograph-ing the Irish college in Rome?' Jonathan urged.

'I'm getting excited,' Hilary grinned.

'Oh and by the way . . . *if* Murray and I go down the aisle, you're my bridesmaid!'

'I should think so, buster. I should very much think so,' Hilary declared. 'I'd better go on a diet!'

'I think you're mad to go to that funeral. I wouldn't give that two-faced bitch the satisfaction,' Niall growled when Hilary told him she was accompanying her mother to Frank O'Mahony's funeral. 'Let Dee bring your mother.'

'Mam and Dee don't know what happened with Colette, so they'd be wondering why I didn't go, and besides, my mother is an inspiration to me. Jacqueline dropped her like a hot potato when she hit the big time and began mixing with the la-di-das and she didn't need Colette minded any more, but when Mam heard Frank was dead, do you know what she said?'

'What?' Niall asked.

'She said, "Poor Jacqueline, my heart goes out to her. I know what it feels like to lose a husband and she might need a shoulder to cry on."'

'Your mother's a saint,' Niall retorted. 'Like mother, like daughter!'

'Far from it, and you and I know that. But she's a very good, decent person and the least I can do is support her.'

'You're a very good and decent person too, and a big softie with it. Just don't let that Colette one take advantage of that softness again,' he warned.

'Don't worry, I won't,' she assured him. 'Colette has wiped her shoes on me for the last time.'

'Well that's good to know. Give her my regards, ha ha!' He grinned at her. 'Tell her I'm *aching* for her.'

'Smarty!' She flicked him with the tea towel before going off to make an appointment to have her hair and make-up done, rather pleased that she'd be looking her best the next time she saw Colette.

Des looked older, thinner, Colette noted, as he, Jazzy and Jackson emerged though the opaque doors of arrivals at Dublin Airport. She was so glad her daughter's boyfriend had accompanied Jazzy. Things were serious between them and Colette was most relieved that her precious child seemed to be having more luck with men than she'd ever had.

'Sorry about your father, Colette.' Des leaned over to give her an awkward peck on the cheek.

'Thanks,' she said coolly before turning to gather her daughter into an embrace, and then kiss Jackson.

'My condolences, Mrs Williams,' the young man said politely.

'Please, Jackson, it's *Colette*. I'm too young to be Mrs anybody,' she smiled at him.

'It was kind of you to meet us, we could have taken a cab,' Des said, falling into step beside her as they walked through Arrivals towards the exit.

'Mum insisted. And she wants you to stay in the house. It's entirely up to you, Des. You can have Jazzy's old room, and they can have the guest room, but if you want to stay in a hotel that's equally fine. Your call.'

'If it's OK, I'll stay with you. It would be nice for Jazzy to have some family time.'

'Whatever that is,' Colette said sarcastically.

'Please don't let's fight. Not at this time,' Des said quietly, to her surprise. His difficulties had certainly diminished his brashness somewhat.

'OK,' she agreed, too weary after the stress of the past few days to argue.

'If you want to, we can finalize the divorce too. I took the opportunity to have Dwayne Fuller make out a spreadsheet of our ... er ... remaining assets.'

'You mean we have some?' she said drily.

'A few, actually. It's not as bad as we thought, and we will get something back, in time, from the Madoff fiasco,' Des informed her crisply. 'Colette, will you tell me one thing?'

'What's that?' She glanced at him cagily.

'How did you get the gold out?'

Colette laughed. 'It wasn't difficult. I packed it in the drawer of the desk and had it shipped.'

'Good God! That was risky, in many ways,' he exclaimed, appalled.

'I know. I was peppering for three long months,' she admitted. 'But it wasn't spotted going through Customs, and it wasn't stolen, it got through and arrived intact!'

'You're something else, you know! I was a fool to mess you around,' Des said admiringly.

'Indeed you were,' Colette agreed matter-of-factly, slowing down to let their daughter and Jackson, who was pushing their luggage, catch up with them.

*

Colette kept her eyes on her father's coffin reposing at the foot of the altar, while walking up the aisle, her mother positioned between her and Des. All through the course of the previous evening's removal ceremony, when the multitudes from the Law Courts, their friends and neighbours and many more came to offer their condolences, Colette had been on tenterhooks wondering would Hilary make an appearance. Sally and Jacqueline had been friends once. She would have expected Sally, at least, to be there. Because Sally was elderly, she was sure Hilary would have accompanied her. She couldn't believe that they had been no-shows.

Perhaps they'd attend the funeral Mass, she thought agitatedly. She'd be exceedingly gracious if they came and *insist* that they come to the meal in the Royal Marine afterwards. Hilary *would* come. Colette was sure of it. After all it was Frank's funeral. Who could keep up bad feeling at a funeral? Colette could use the opportunity to explain that the incident that had sundered their friendship had been due to Colette's being on the verge of a nervous breakdown.

And it was true, she *had* fallen to pieces in the following months, she acknowledged, edging into the pew after her mother. She had become a recluse when she'd returned to London, and had cancelled her holiday in St Barts. She couldn't face going alone and having to think about the nightmare her life had become. She was plagued by flashbacks of the afternoon she had discovered her father's betrayal of her mother. And, although Colette wouldn't admit it to a living soul, she was mortally ashamed of how low she'd sunk, and how disloyal she'd been to Hilary, and equally horrified at her behaviour with Niall. She was no better than her father, she'd tormented herself.

The trip in February to spend time with Jazzy in New York had tipped her over the edge. She hadn't met up with Des, but when Jazzy told her he was now living near North Cove in Battery Park, she'd been gutted. 'Is he with that woman?' she'd asked, subdued.

'No, that ended when he had the heart attack. He's just had a complete lifestyle change,' Jazzy assured her. 'He jogs on the seafront, walks to work, relaxes at the Harbor, that kind of stuff. I like his new apartment. Are you sure you don't want to come and visit him?' she'd asked hopefully.

'No!' Colette said emphatically. She couldn't wait to fly out of JFK. Revisiting New York had left her feeling shaky and deeply depressed. When she got back to London she'd stayed in bed for a week drinking, and tempted to take an overdose of pills to put her out of her misery. A dose of the flu meant a visit to her old doctor and out of the blue she'd found herself howling in his office when he'd told her she looked very peaky and under the weather. She'd ended up on antidepressants and with a letter to see a therapist, which she'd stuffed in her dressing-table drawer.

It had taken the guts of a year before she'd felt more like herself. Des wasn't the only one who'd had the stuffing knocked out of him, she'd told him during one of their fraught phone calls. Thoughts of Hilary were instantly dismissed. She simply did not allow herself to think of the other woman and she had managed to blank out the mortifying episode that had ruined their friendship.

Gradually she had resumed working in Dickon and

Austen's Knightsbridge gallery and her social life had picked up again, and while she would never reach the dizzy heights she had in New York, she had begun to enjoy her life in London. Her father's death was an inconvenience she could have done without. Ireland was the last place she wanted to go to. She dreaded being reminded of the past.

Colette was surrounded by mourners paying their respects, outside the church after the funeral Mass, when out of the corner of her eye she saw Sally embrace Jacqueline. The two elderly ladies clung to each other as Sally murmured words of comfort in Jacqueline's ear, and then Hilary was there, behind her mother, looking very smart in a tailored black suit. Her make-up was subtle but classy, her hair was beautifully cut *and* she'd dropped weight.

So she'd come, Colette thought triumphantly, just as she knew Hilary would. She turned away to speak to an elderly colleague of her father's, and was shaking hands with a second cousin when Hilary appeared at the edge of the group. Colette pretended not to see her until her former friend was almost beside her.

'Hilary!' she said with feigned surprise. 'I didn't expect to see you.'

'I brought Mam. She was anxious to offer her condolences to your mother,' Hilary said calmly. 'I wouldn't go from here without offering you mine.'

'That was kind. You *will* come to the meal afterwards so they can have time to chat,' Colette said casually.

'I'm sorry, we can't go on to the grave. We're going to a wedding this afternoon, so we need to go home and change.'

'Anyone I know?' Colette raised an eyebrow.

'Leanne, Sophie's friend. Jazzy knows her. They keep in touch on Skype. I must have a word with Jazzy – I saw her earlier,' Hilary said as politely as though she were talking to a stranger.

'I see. And how are you?' Colette asked, trying not to betray her disappointment that Sally and Hilary were not coming to the meal and there would be no chance to explain things.

'I'm fine, thanks. I *am* sorry for your loss,' Hilary said quietly.

'Thanks.' Colette knew Hilary meant what she said and she felt comforted by it. 'As you now know, Dad and I had a rocky relationship. I'm very conflicted about him. That day we had our ... er ... falling out, I said things I didn't mean. I've regretted it, you know. I just lost the plot. I had a nervous breakdown subsequently – everything got too much for me. The marriage break-up, our falling out,' she said, the words tumbling out. 'I'm really, *really* sorry for what happened. I wasn't myself,' she said lamely.

'That's not surprising. I'm sure it was very difficult for you, getting your head round seeing something like that as a child. I was sorry to hear how troubled you'd been throughout your life. You never said anything.' Hilary's gaze and tone was sympathetic.

'I couldn't. I buried it deep.' Colette's lip trembled at her former friend's compassionate response.

'That was hard for you.'

'Oh Hilary, maybe we could meet for coffee before I go back to London. I really need to talk about it,' Colette exclaimed, all affectation aside. Hilary knew her better than anyone. Who else could she tell all her woes to without losing face? 'Why don't I ring you in a few days' time, and we'll arrange to meet before I go back?' she suggested eagerly.

Hilary looked at her searchingly. 'I don't think so, Colette,' she said slowly. 'What's the point? We're not really friends. We're just a habit, and a bad one at that. I could never trust you again. I've nothing to say to you actually. If it wasn't for Mam I wouldn't be here,' she added bluntly. 'I'm glad Jazzy and Sophie became friends and keep in touch. I hope their friendship works better than ours has. A long time ago, after we had the falling out when you moved to America, I remember saying to Niall that either you and I would drift apart, or you would do something that there was no turning back from. I think trying to seduce my husband would come into that category. Some things there's no getting over and for me, Colette, believe it or not, that's one of them.' She gave a shrug. 'I wish you well, always. Don't doubt that. But coffee? A chat? No, I think not. I *would* suggest that you *do* talk to a counsellor or psychotherapist to resolve all your issues, though, if you haven't already done so. I think it would be very good for you. But, if it's all the same to you, let's you and I call it a day. Take care of yourself.' Hilary gave Colette's gloved hand a squeeze and walked away, leaving the other woman standing with her mouth open, stunned.

Was that it? After all these years? Hilary had finally had enough. 'To have a friend you have to be a friend,' she'd once said to Colette during a row, implying that Colette wasn't a good friend to her. She *had* been a good friend, she assured herself, as tears filled her eyes and she was left standing alone. Apart from that episode with Niall when she wasn't herself, she'd been as good a friend as she knew how. A sob escaped her and then another and she fished in her bag for a tissue.

'Are you OK?' Des appeared at her side.

'No . . . No, I'm not, Des. I want to get out of here,' Colette wept.

'All right, let's tell Jacqueline to wrap it up and move on to the graveyard.'

'Thanks,' she managed weakly, trying to compose herself, relieved to have someone be concerned about her, even if it was her lying, cheating husband.

Des took her hand and led her towards the hearse. Her fingers curled around his. 'Chin up, Lettie,' he murmured encouragingly, using a pet name he used to call her, as Jazzy broke away from some of her Irish cousins and walked towards them.

'Are you all right, Mom? You look a bit pale,' she said, secretly delighted to see her parents holding hands. She slid her own hand into her mother's free one.

Colette lifted her shoulders and smiled at her. 'I'll be fine, sweetie,' she said, as the three of them walked hand in hand towards her mother, like a real family again, while Hilary, her arm tucked into Sally's, walked in the opposite direction, out through the church gates, disappearing from view.

EPILOGUE

'Let's get this wedding started,' Hilary declared giddily, settling the small red rose in Jonathan's lapel.

'It's a civil service,' corrected her friend.

'If I'm a bridesmaid, it's a wedding,' Hilary said firmly. 'And you will be the most perfect blushing groom.'

'Oh Hil, I never thought there was someone out there for me. I'm so excited,' Jonathan bubbled. 'I'm so happy I could burst.'

'I'm so happy for you I could burst too,' Hilary declared, raising her champagne glass to him and taking a last sip before they joined Nancy and his sisters to enter the function room where the service was taking place. Nancy was so proud to be walking her son up the aisle. And ecstatically happy that her prayers had *finally* been answered.

Murray had proposed on Valentine's Day, fourteen months after Father McDaid had introduced them, and they were holding their ceremony on Midsummer's Day in a country house hotel, just outside Rosslara. Nancy was giving Jonathan away and Hilary was his bridesmaid. Father Derek was going to perform a blessing after the legalities were complete and Murray and Jonathan couldn't be happier.

The excitement of the couple was palpable as they stood side by side in their morning suits, and heard the Registrar finally say, 'Jonathan, Murray, you are now joined together in civil partnership.' Tears slid down Hilary's cheeks as she watched the loving couple embrace. At last, her best friend had what he had always wished for. Someone he loved, and someone who loved him.

Ten minutes later, when the Registrar had left, because he was not allowed to stay for the spiritual ceremony, Father McDaid took his place at the lectern. An anticipatory hush descended on the guests.

'Dearly beloved,' the elderly priest said, smiling. 'As Jesus said, *Where two or three are gathered in my name I am with them.* It is my privilege to bestow a blessing on Murray and Jonathan – particularly as it was *I* who introduced them,' he added, to much laughter. 'In this room today are two people who love each other. *You must love one another as you love me*, our dear Lord taught. How wonderful for all of us to share in Jonathan and Murray's love. For love is all that matters and love is why we are here. I bless this union, gifted to Jonathan and Murray by God, and pray that the love that is here today will multiply and fill the world with love and grace. Amen.'

'This is the weepiest wedding I was ever at,' Niall murmured to Hilary as tears and cheers followed Father McDaid as he resumed his seat.

'Isn't that marvellous, to know that you've been instrumental in making two wonderful people very, very happy. And not only the boys, but myself included, and all my family.

We're in your debt, Father,' Nancy declared, overwhelmed with gratitude.

'And I'm in Jonathan's. He's a wonderful man. He introduced me to Hannah over there. He pointed to his therapist, who was laughing heartily at something Orla, Jonathan's old friend from his bedsit days, was saying to her. 'She's an angel in disguise,' he said enthusiastically. 'All my years as a priest and I'd been blindsided by theological arguments and this canon law or that one, and you know it's all nonsense,' he exclaimed.

'Nonsense,' agreed Nancy. 'You know that song that used to be popular once. What was it now? Oh yes, the Beatles. "Love Is All You Need" or was it "All You Need Is Love"? I can't quite remember.'

'Whatever it was, it was absolutely spot on. Love *is* all you need. And if there isn't love in this room I don't know where it is,' the priest chuckled, taking a rather large sip of his brandy. The party was in full swing and he was enjoying himself immensely. His words of blessing had been heartfelt, as he'd called on the Creator to bless the two men before him joined in civil partnership. There had been many tears when he had spoken those words, but they were tears of happiness, and the elderly priest had felt his own heart lift in joy to be part of such a blessed, happy occasion.

'Look at Mum and Father D. They're getting on like a house on fire. I *knew* they'd click,' Jonathan said to Hilary as they sat together after the toasts.

'It's a great day. I've never been to such a joyful wedding,' she assured him.

'Some day, hopefully, we will be able to marry properly in Ireland, and please God the referendum will be passed, but today will keep us going until then,' Jonathan said happily.

'You mean I'm going to get another chance to be your bridesmaid?' Hilary teased.

'You bet your ass, Hammond. There comes a time when a gal's got to do what a gal's got to do! Today was just a trial run. And a brilliant one at that.'

'I'll be there, never you fear,' she assured him.

'I know you will,' said Jonathan confidently. 'Of that, I have no fear. You know what they say, "People come into your life for a reason, a season or a lifetime." We're in it for the long haul, Hil. I love Murray, but you're my best friend.'

'And you're mine,' Hilary responded warmly, hugging him. 'And how lucky are we?'

ACKNOWLEDGEMENTS

'A friend loves at all times, and a brother is born for adversity'
Proverbs 17:17

I never write a book alone and so, as always, it is with deep gratitude I thank 'my gang' for guiding this latest book. Jesus, Our Lady, Mother Meera, St Joseph, St Michael, St Anthony, White Eagle, all my Angels, Saints and Guides and my Beloved Mother who has brought me to Simon & Schuster where the great adventure continues.

Huge thanks to: My dear and wonderful dad whose courage and humour inspire me.

To my sister Mary and all my family. To my nieces, who keep me up to date with fashion, make-up, trends, and text speak!

To Keith Farrell, nephew-in-law who is always on call for IT dramas!

This book is about friendship, and to all my dear and loving friends, who are so precious to me, there aren't enough thanks for all your love and support.

To Hannah! You are the best! A real angel.

A huge thanks to Darren Keogh, Lighting INDENT Designer, for sharing his expertise.

To my exceptional editor, Jo Dickinson, all of the fantastic UK team, and to all my dear Schusters worldwide: it has been an amazing, invigorating time, and I'm enjoying it so much. Thank you all for your great enthusiasm, kindness, and professionalism. It is a joy to be published by you. (And Matt: thank you for the gorgeous covers.)

To all my terrific agents and friends at Lutyens & Rubinstein who work so hard on my behalf. Dear Sarah: you have been with me through thick and thin over the years, and are a true friend.

To Helen (my boss, who minds me so well), Gill, Simon, Dec, Fergus, Sharon, Eamonn and Nigel at Gill Hess & Co. How lucky am I to have the best team in Ireland.

To booksellers everywhere, who despite very difficult times keep going and supporting us authors. Your backing and good-will has been constant down the years.

To the memory of a brave and special boy, Haydn Harrison, and his mother Jeanette, and family. He will never be forgotten.

To all the staff in the Bon Secours, Mater, and Royal Hospital Donnybrook who have looked after my family and me at various times in the past two years, and have made hard times easier. Thank you all.

To Dr. Fiona Dennehy, and all in the Cremore Clinic, Dr. Joe Duggan, Sadie Furlong, Assistant Matron, Bon Secours Hospital, Geraldine Tynan, Marian Lawlor and Michelle Connor, AIB Finglas, all very special people. Thank you so much for all your kindness.

To my Facebook followers who offer such support and encouragement. It is great to be able to engage with my readers during the whole process of writing the book. Thank you all, Dear Ones.

And a big thanks, finally, to all my loyal readers who have supported me and bought my books all these years. YOU are what it's all about. You keep me going and your loyalty and steadfastness mean so much. I hope you enjoy this new novel.